I0768425

KENDRELL
PUBLISHING

THE BLANCHARD WITCHES

BECOMING OLYMPIA

MICAH HOUSE

The Blanchard Witches: Becoming Olympia

First published 2024

Copyright © 2024 by Micah House

Published by Kendrell Publishing, Birmingham, Alabama

Edited by Crystal Castle

Cover design by Paul Palmer-Edwards

ISBN: 979-8-9887296-7-9

Library of Congress Control Number: 2024917826

Books in THE BLANCHARD WITCHES series

The Blanchard Witches of Daihmler County

Prodigal Daughters

Stitches in Time

The House of Duquesne

Half Sick of Shadows

CONTENTS

CHAPTER ONE

The Sisters Blanchard

Many people can identify their first full memory in life; the one where everything which comes after generates. Before that starting point in consciousness all else is simply a series of flashes. Fragments here and there. Olympia Blanchard's first real memory in life was the day her sister was born. Nothing before existed in her mind past the fleeting glimpse of something intangible. She was playing with a baby doll in the freshly painted living room of their new house. Perhaps, partially painted was a more accurate term. Fresh ochre boards still covered part of the room, not yet painted the crisp white it was slowly becoming. Her father had finished painting the kitchen and the foyer but was only just starting in the living room when he heard Olympia's mother cry out upstairs. Perhaps it was because her mother was not the type to cry out—to break her composure—which caused this to officially become Olympia's first full memory. To hear a person who never shows emotion scream can be startling.

Constantinople Blanchard set aside his loaded paint brush and dashed up the foyer stairs like quicksilver. Olympia continued playing with her doll. She could hear her father's heavy feet tromp across the floor above. He'd built the house himself, alongside some men he'd hired from town. She held no memory of ever living in any other house, but they could not have lived there long because the wood smelled so new. The house was built on the ancestral land where her father's family had always lived. It was a fine big house in some ways. A large living room with a fireplace. A study off the foyer. And a kitchen with a great big black wood burning stove. Upstairs were many other rooms—more than they needed in fact—but Olympia's father often joked that he could look into her eyes and see the many descendants he would have. Maybe he wasn't joking. Constantinople Blanchard was a very gifted witch. He was also Olympia's hero.

Olympia finished brushing her doll's hair and made a second attempt to reattach its shoe even though the shoe strap was broken so that whenever she held the doll up the shoe fell off again. Every so often, Olympia's father would poke his head over the upstairs railing to check on his five-year-old daughter below. Each time he promised that her mother was all right and the baby would be born soon. Olympia wasn't in the least bit concerned with her mother. It was the baby she wanted to see. She hoped it would be a girl. She hoped this for many reasons. The foremost reason being that if her father were to be awarded a son, he may not love Olympia the way he did now. Olympia was his whole world, and the little girl knew it. Would a boy take some of those special feelings away? She also wanted a sister because she was lonely for a female friend. Her mother didn't count. Mothers were supposed to be warm and gentle. Her mother was as cold and disinterested as any man she'd ever encountered, except her father.

Patiently awaiting the baby's arrival, Olympia pretended her doll was her new little sister or brother. She practiced holding it correctly. She practiced dressing it. But she was growing tired of this old doll and eager for the real thing to be born. Footsteps crossed over the ceiling above. Olympia turned to see her father coming down the stairs holding something in a quilt. His face looked pleased. As he knelt to show her, Olympia swallowed hard, fearing the worst, that he was about to show her a brother.

"Olympia, my dear girl," her father announced proudly, bringing the baby into her line of sight. "I present to you your new little sister. Her name is Pastoria."

Olympia's piercing blue eyes met her new sister's. They were just as blue. She felt a smile stretch across her face as she looked down at baby Pastoria. "I have a sister."

Her father patted his eldest daughter's head. "You do, my dear. And as her big sister it is now your job to always look out for her. To always guide her. To be her lifelong friend and protector. Can you do that for me?"

"Yes, Father," Olympia answered. "I promise. I'll take care of Pastoria."

And she did.

For the next several weeks, Olympia Blanchard was more like a baby nurse than a child. She heated the bottles of milk whenever her parents needed help. She fed the baby more meals than she didn't. And she would lay for hours on the bed staring at her napping sister in the crib beside her. Though this sisterly devotion pleased her father, Olympia's mother found fault with it at every turn.

"You are holding the baby much too much, Olympia," her mother scolded. "If you hold a baby too often it never learns to fend for itself."

"She won't have to fend for herself," Olympia shot back. "Pastoria has me."

This garnered a loving smile of approval from her father, but he wiped it quickly from his face when his wife looked back sternly from the sink. "I do not approve of smothering children with over-affection," her mother continued. "Children are here to grow up and be of service. There is much to be done and each must play his or her part. We do not have time for raising needy humans."

The severity in Angharad Blanchard's personality was never waning. She appeared displeased with every detail of Olympia's behavior and demeanor. Trying to gain any sort of approval from her mother was like wandering a maze with the exit long boarded up. This had become more the case in the weeks after Pastoria's birth. Her mother seemed to dislike having a baby in the house and equally resented the time its survival required of her. Olympia thought herself helpful when she took over watching the baby, yet this raised her mother's irritability to an even higher level.

"Was Mother mean to me too, when I was a baby?" Olympia asked her father when her mother took the washing upstairs, leaving them alone in the room.

Constantinople's face frowned at the edges. He disliked hearing such an observation come from his daughter's lips, however accurate it might be. "Your mother is a complicated woman, Olympia. She has lived through things you have not. Her childhood was no childhood at all. She does not understand the beauty in the small things. The tender moments life offers us here and there amid our travails are sentiments she cannot understand. Your mother does not intend to be unkind. Pity her in that way. She is incapable of feeling things the way you and I do."

Olympia tilted Pastoria towards her father and smiled. "You and I will teach Pastoria how to love. Because I love you. You love me. And we shall both love her."

Constantinople grinned, scratching his sideburns. "I love you Olympia Blanchard, more than I have ever loved anything. And yes, you and I will provide all the tenderness Pastoria will require."

Her Mother's Sister

Raised voices swelled from the lower floor reverberating off the bare walls of the upstairs hallway reaching Olympia's room. She had been asleep in her bed with her baby sister's crib a few feet away. A thin stream of light pierced through the parted curtain providing Olympia the ability to see Pastoria through the rails of her bed. The noise had not awakened the baby. Olympia slid out from under her quilt and tiptoed from the room. She could hear the voices a little more clearly from the hall although still too muffled to discern exactly what was being said. Worming carefully across the plank floorboards, avoiding the two spots she knew to creak, Olympia made her way to the edge of the stairs. The voices could be heard more plainly now. Her parents, and the voice of a woman she had never heard before. The woman began shouting.

"Angharad you must come back to our village! The evil there has almost decimated all we knew and loved." The woman's voice sounded foreign; much the way Olympia's mother spoke.

"Loved?" Olympia's mother repeated in a cynical tone Olympia knew all too well.

For a brief second nothing further was said, as if Angharad's words silenced the room. Then the strange woman spoke again, "Yes, loved."

"I do not recall having particularly loved anyone from our village."

"Angharad," Constantinople cautioned. "Let's not be unkind."

"Our parents have been wiped out, sister," the woman scoffed. "If I am to be next, would that not trouble you in the least?"

Sister? Olympia thought to herself. *My mother has a sister?* Olympia could no longer control her curiosity. She wanted to see this woman—this sister of her mother. Olympia clung to the rail of the stairs as she edged down. The treads did not make noise when stepped closer to the posts. As her feet touched the foyer floor, she summoned her daring spirit to embolden her enough to walk into the living room to get a glimpse of this woman—her aunt.

Her presence brought the eyes of her parents' and their guest upon her. Olympia knew she was not supposed to be out of bed, and she would probably be spanked for it, but she didn't care. She wanted to see her. Taking in the tall, slender woman standing with her parents, Olympia knew right away it was true. She looked almost exactly like her mother. Long midnight black hair. Pinched face with a sickly pale pallor. Her eyes were almost lavender, with a fear buried beneath them which made Olympia pity her.

"You have a child?" the woman asked, turning to Angharad.

"Children." Angharad corrected. "There is another sleeping upstairs." She walked over to Olympia and grabbed her by the wrist. "And upstairs is where you should be Olympia."

The stranger came forward, wrenching Olympia's arm free from her mother's grasp. Gently she caressed the back of Olympia's small hand with her own. The woman's long boney fingers chilled her a little. The woman ran her hand through the child's white, blonde hair. Olympia felt a kind of peace from the gesture. Perhaps affection. She'd never felt a woman's affection before, so she couldn't be sure.

"Your name is Olympia?"

"Uh-huh," Olympia nodded.

The woman lowered herself to her knees and placed her gentle hands on either side of Olympia's hips. "I am your Aunt Dagmara. I am so pleased to meet you."

Olympia looked up to her father as if asking him what she should do.

"It is all right," he smiled.

Suddenly Olympia hugged the woman. She had not expected to do this, but it felt right at the time. Dagmara's reaction was one of surprise, but she returned the embrace. For a moment Olympia felt a closeness she had never felt from a grown woman. Angharad's icy hand reached to Olympia's shoulder and gave it a warning squeeze. "Return to your room, Olympia. My sister and I have much to discuss."

Olympia ignored her mother's order just as she ignored the charged atmosphere in the room. She wanted to know something, so she asked. "What happened to your parents?"

Dagmara, undeterred by the child's age or appropriateness of the answer, looked directly into her niece's eyes and spoke her unsettling tale. "Their names were uttered by the Angelystor, who stands beneath the ancient yew tree." Her words were loaded with an ancient mysticism Olympia did not understand. "When the Angelystor calls your name, you are next to die. The tree is thousands of years old. It is kept alive with the moisture of the living. It is the birthplace of The Rain People. And they have returned to our village after centuries to decimate our people."

Constantinople intervened now. "Please do not come into my home and frighten my daughter."

Dagmara appeared puzzled. "Frighten her? I am equipping her. Does she not know what evils lurk beyond the confines of this haven you've shuttered her within? Many people are dying, Constantinople! Slaughtered by the monsters you in the new world laugh off as legends and myths. Does this child not know her purpose? Has she not been told why witches exist? It is your duty to The Natural Order to educate your progeny on how to protect the unprotected."

Rarely had Olympia seen her father in anger, but she knew enough to know when his chest raised upward and his shoulders tilted back, he was not happy. "Do not lecture me on my parenting!" Constantinople roared. "Nor question me about The Order. I have devoted most of my adult life to protecting this earth and those who live upon it. And you dare to cross the world to come to my house where you accuse me of failing The Natural Order."

Shrinking back in remorse, Dagmara bowed to Olympia's father and said, "I did not wish to offend, Brother." She waited for him to signal something, perhaps a forgiveness for the insult. His shoulders returned to their normal position as he let out a short breath. Dagmara continued then. "I am only afraid. Afraid the Rain People will drain Beddgelert dry and continue across Great Britain until nothing is left. And if they are there, you can mark my words, they are here as well."

"What do you want from us, Dagmara?" Angharad asked, losing patience. "My husband and I fight the good fight in America whenever called upon. Would you have us abandon our children and follow you to Europe?"

"It is the Angelystor, my sister!" Dagmara exclaimed. "The Recording Angel. The Evangelist. It has recorded our deaths on its breath. Our mother. Our father. And mine."

Olympia was not privy to the remainder of the conversation. Her father escorted her back upstairs, reminding her that her job was to look out for Pastoria, and she could not do that if she were eavesdropping on adult topics. He kissed her goodnight before returning downstairs. Olympia rolled over and looked at her sleeping sister, now several months old. *I will never treat you the way our mother treats her sister. If you need me, I will be there for you.*

The following morning there was no mention of the late-night visitor. Things went as they always did. Olympia's mother made breakfast while Olympia fed little Pastoria in her highchair. Constantinople tended to the chickens in the coop out back and no one said a word about the events during the night. There was only one moment when Olympia considered asking. Her father, sensing the birth of her question, sent her a look which stopped it before she opened her mouth. It was a topic to be forgotten. And so, it was.

CHAPTER THREE

The Little School Witch

It was the first time any member of her family had ever attended school. Before her, all Blanchard's were educated at home. Farmers, most of them, had little need to know the dates of important battles, or the path Magellan took. Anything they needed to know about the world could be read in a newspaper or The Farmer's Almanac. School provided nothing useful to the olden day Blanchards and might even have proven dangerous for them. Any time spent around regular people could have risked exposure for their kind. However, Constantinople Blanchard carried deep regret for having never been formally educated. This shortcoming compelled him later in life to enlighten himself in every way he could. His youth had been spent in service much like a young man might enlist in the military. But Constantinople conscribed himself to the budding group of witches determined to make the world safer by stamping out the evil creatures of the earth. His time spent in Europe showed him not only the unspeakable things lurking in the shadows who prey upon mankind, but it also showed him the value of knowledge. He spent his time back then with his nose in books of every subject whenever his fists were not otherwise occupied in battle. Because of this, he was now a man self-educated beyond his social sphere in rural Alabama. He'd decided upon returning home with his new bride that his future children would break the cycle of rural ignorance and would be enrolled in proper schooling. Olympia would be the first in her family to receive an official education, and she was terrified now that the first day of school was here. She was not normally the kind of girl to be nervous and unsure. But then again, she had never strayed too far away from Blanchard House either.

Getting out of the car, Olympia's eyes stared nervously at the schoolhouse ahead. The red brick building was a little weathered from time. The pitched roof had light gray shingles sprinkled here and there with darker, where repairs had been made over time. The windows were framed in white wood, freshly painted, making them stand out against the crimson walls. Olympia gripped her father's hand while they walked up the steps to the open door. Her free hand was swinging a lunch pail housing sandwiches and a cookie. When her shoes hit the minty colored linoleum floor tiles, her feet shuffled nervously along while the bottoms of her father's leather shoes clicked as he walked. Other children her age filed into the building with their parents, each looking as intimidated as she. Older children entered all on their own, as if they knew what to do and where to go. Several of them looked upon Olympia and her father as if they were foreign. Some whisperings hit the air around them as they walked the corridor to find Olympia's first grade classroom. Her father either didn't hear the whispers or chose to ignore them, but Olympia wasn't as adept as he. She heard some of what was being said.

That's weird Mr. Blanchard and his daughter. I hear they sacrifice cows on the full moon.

That's the Blanchard man. You know his entire family were witches.

Olympia knew her family had been in Daihmler since before it was even named Daihmler. Why these people should look upon her as if she did not belong was confusing to her young mind. She wished Pastoria was old enough to join her at school, but that'd be a few more years.

Her classroom was decorated with colorful cutouts on every wall. One grouping depicted weather such as a bright cheery sun wearing a smile, a gray fluffy rain cloud wearing a frown, wavy lines flowing from the mouth of a cloud with puckered lips (obviously, wind). Olympia wondered, why the rain cloud had to frown? She liked rain. It made the vegetables in the garden grow. On the opposite wall were a series of numbers 1-10, each a different color but all with eyes and smiling mouths. Olympia never thought of the number four as being orange, but she had always suspected 6 would be blue.

Her teacher, Miss Coley, was a pretty lady with freckles and reddish hair pulled into a bun. She greeted the new students warmly as they entered. Several parents, including Olympia's father, seemed reluctant to leave, but Miss Coley assured them everything would be all right. Before leaving Constantinople knelt to his daughter, reassuringly taking her by the hands. "Make friends, Olympia. I want you to know other children. I want you to learn all you can here. Not only from books and teachers, but from human interaction. You've lived a solitary life until now. Use this opportunity."

"I will father."

"And...", he said looking around to make certain no one was overhearing. "Do not use your powers. These people are not like us."

"I know father, I know. You've already told me."

"I'm serious Olympia," he cautioned. "The world is not yet ready to learn about our kind. We tried once centuries ago, and they did their all to wipe us out. Regular people do not understand we are here to help them, not harm them. Tell no one your secret. And never use your powers at school."

Miss Coley did not turn out to be as warm and friendly as she'd pretended to be while the parents were dropping off their children. Her softness hardened fast and the ruler in which she struck desktops seemed like an extension of her arm. The worst part, when a child openly made a remark about Olympia's family being spooky, Miss Coley acted as if she heard nothing—signaling to a full class on the first day of school, that targeting the odd girl was not something they'd be punished for. Olympia hunched her shoulders down, trying to shrink herself and be less noticeable.

The sidelong stares and covert whispers followed her every move. It only took Olympia until lunchtime to realize she would make no friends at this school. Other children laughed together and shared stories about themselves with each other leaving Olympia feeling like an outsider looking in on a world she did not quite belong to. Her first lesson in school was learning a person can feel even more lonely in a room full of people.

CHAPTER FOUR

One Real Friend

During the two years Olympia Blanchard had been in school, she'd made not a single friend. She rarely even had a moment when she was not the target of other children's insults or pranks. No matter how kind she tried to be Olympia was systematically perceived as different from everyone else, and that was always interpreted as bad. Her school life was horrendous to trudge through, but she put on her brave face every morning and with much relief dropped it every afternoon. The irony of the situation was that she could have put an end to her bullying anytime she wanted, if she would only use her powers. But a promise to her father was too sacred a thing to betray. Besides, her father was doing good in the world, using his powers to help people...even save lives sometimes. Lives like the ones of these awful children she went to school alongside. And she could never tell any of them that her very father was probably responsible for the ignorant bliss they were living in.

It was when Olympia reached fourth grade that her sister Pastoria entered kindergarten. At first Olympia delighted in the idea, thinking she would have one ally around, but she'd overlooked the fact they would be in different grades and different classrooms. Therefore, Pastoria's experience with her own classmates mirrored what Olympia had been going through for two years. It pained her to see her little sister teased and shoved and ridiculed in the hallway or see her sitting alone at lunch. Olympia did not understand why each grade had to be separated in the cafeteria. Why could she and her sister not sit together? It was only at recess when the two of them could come together and find refuge in each other. Both of their classrooms had recess at the same time, of course it was unheard of for a third grader and a first grader to mingle, but the Blanchard girls did not care about such traditions. They found one another at every recess and hid themselves off alone together in a small cluster of trees at the edge of the playground. They did not play. They did nothing more than attempt to remain unnoticed as the other children took over the swings and slides and monkey bars. It was a lonely existence, but they had each other for at least half an hour each day.

Then a day came about two weeks into the new school year which changed everything for the Blanchard sisters. They had seen the new girl in the hallway once or twice, a transfer from Oneonta, Alabama. The girl was in Olympia's grade but was placed in a different classroom. Still, Olympia heard that the girl's name was Zelda Cooper. Possessing the name Zelda did the new girl no favors. Some of the teasing reserved for Olympia was dispersed to Zelda for having a funny name. Of course, there was still plenty to go around for Olympia. But one day, while the two 3rd grade classes were standing on opposite sides of the hall waiting to go into the lunchroom, Olympia found herself standing directly across from the new girl.

"Can you hear me?"

The voice rang out clear as a bell, but no one else seemed to hear it. Olympia knew she had not imagined it. She glanced around but saw no one's lips moving. Whenever classes stood in the hallway silence was strictly enforced by the teachers. Had anyone else heard the voice one of the teachers would have immediately reprimanded whoever spoke. Then Olympia heard it again. *"You do hear me, don't you?"* She stared across from her and saw the new girl looking back at her, half smiling. *"You do hear me, don't ya?"* The new girl was speaking to her, only her lips were not moving. Still, Olympia, and only Olympia, had heard her plain as day.

Olympia almost said something out loud to her but stopped herself the moment she saw Zelda Cooper shake her head.

"Naw," Zelda's voice said inside her mind again. *"Talk to me the other way."*

What other way? Olympia thought to herself.

"That's it!" Zelda said again without moving her lips, although they were smiling Olympia's direction.

Flabbergasted, Olympia thought again without verbalizing the words, *"Are you speaking to me in my brain?"*

The child across from her smiled a great big smile, missing a couple of side teeth where her permanents hadn't grown in yet. *"I sure am! Name's Zelda! I figured you was one of us. Just felt it."*

As the classes filed into the lunchroom, the other children exhibited surprise as Olympia Blanchard and Zelda Cooper took seats together. Barty Simmons approached, making an argument that Zelda had taken his chair.

"I don't see no name on this thing," Zelda said waving him off. "Get on outta here 'fore I tell the class you peed your bed last night."

Barty's face flushed red with anger or humiliation, but he didn't argue anymore. He took a different seat further down.

Olympia giggled demurely into her hand, afraid to rouse Barty's anger if he saw. "Why would you ever say something like that to someone?"

Zelda laughed loudly; a trait Olympia would grow accustomed to in time. "Cause that boy did pee his bed last night. Saw it in my head the second he walked over here."

Olympia was shocked. Not only did Zelda have powers but she talked openly about them. "You saw it?"

"Oh yeah, I see stuff all the time. Keep it to myself mostly. But I can tell you and me are the same. Don't care if I tell you." Zelda gulped down a pint carton of cafeteria milk and wiped her mouth on the sleeve of her faded dress. "What can you do?"

Olympia did not know what to answer. "Do?"

Zelda smacked herself on the forehead in an exaggerated way. Leaning over closer to Olympia's ear, she said, "You know what I mean. What are your powers? You a witch too ain't ya?"

Never in Olympia's short life had she truly known what the feeling of relief felt like until the moment her new friend made it all right to share the truth about herself. Neither ate much during that first lunch period together, far too busy whispering and chatting together openly about their lives. It was the first time Olympia felt safe at school. She had a friend now. A real friend. One exactly like her.

The other children did not let up on the torment of Olympia, Pastoria, or Zelda, but it didn't seem to sting so much now. As the weeks passed, Olympia found she could withstand anything as long as she had Zelda as a respite during lunchtime. And at recess, both she and Pastoria shared the comfort of having such a wonderful new friend.

They learned a lot about one another in those first weeks. Olympia and Pastoria found out Zelda had a little brother at home. Her parents had taken over the lease on an abandoned store front downtown and started a little market. According to Zelda, most of her life was spent sweeping and mopping up the store or looking after her kid brother Zeb.

On one pleasant Saturday morning in early October, Olympia and Pastoria accompanied their father into town for household supplies. Normally the girls disliked going into town because it was always uncomfortable. Passing other citizens of Daihmler on the sidewalks was an exercise in forgiveness for the girls. Men and women, upon seeing the Blanchard family approaching, stepped off into the street or ducked into stores they had no intention of visiting, simply to avoid any close contact with the strange family everyone whispered about. Their father walked with his head held high as if he did not notice or was not affected by the slur. Try as they might to summon his inner strength, it did bother the girls when they noticed the slights. They heard the whispers. They saw the astonished faces look upon them only to quickly turn away, pretending they hadn't noticed the Blanchards. Olympia could not understand how people could treat someone they did not know, and had not taken the time to know, with such blatant prejudice. She wanted to question her father about it, yet somehow, she thought she shouldn't. If he were strong enough to not allow the hatred to seep into his spirit, perhaps she shouldn't either.

Pastoria took a different stance in her young mind. The way she saw it, the people of Daihmler disliked her family for being different, not because of the rumors of witchcraft, but because they were indeed different. Although most everyone in Daihmler was on equal ground financially–except maybe the rich family the town was named for–just about everyone else in Daihmler made a meager living. Whether you were a merchant, a schoolteacher, a farmer, or worked in one of the factories in Tuscaloosa, Daihmlerians were all in the same class. Yet when the Blanchard family came into town, one would have thought Mr. Blanchard and his wife were descended from European royalty. They carried themselves differently than the drab men and women around them. Their speech was lightly accented. And there was a sleekness in the way they moved, a regal air which was not one of arrogance, but of knowing things no one else knew. Pastoria viewed the rudeness of passersby as a jealousy. As if they could sense her father's power and importance, even if no one knew its origin.

As they walked along the narrow sidewalk of Main Street, Pastoria watched the hustle and bustle go by. People carrying brown paper bags full of their groceries, storekeepers sweeping their doorways, and the little woman writing in colored chalk on a board in front of her store. BACON 59 cents a pound. EGGS 64 cents a dozen. CAMPBELL'S SOUP 3 for 25 cents. Pastoria wondered how much money her family could make off eggs. The Blanchard coops had lots of chickens.

Constantinople stopped in front of Dawson Feed and Grain. The doors were always open to allow the cool breeze in. Olympia disliked the way it smelled inside. She tugged at her father's sleeve, gesturing across the street to Wilson's Market. He knew what she wanted. Old man Wilson, now unable to handle the daily grind of running his store, had turned his business over to a couple from out of town. That couple was their friend Zelda's parents. He'd heard her name bandied around Blanchard House for weeks. Zelda had become quite an important staple in his young daughters' lives. Their only friend. Constantinople immediately understood the value of this budding friendship when his daughters asked permission to go visit her. Mr. Dawson at the feed and grain was one of the few townspeople who was ever kind to the Blanchards. He always insisted the girls reach into the giant jar of wrapped candy on the counter and take a handful each with them before they left. If the girls were willing to sacrifice sugary goodness to drop in on their new friend, he would not deny them.

"Watch as you cross the street," he cautioned his daughters. "After I get the chicken feed from Dawson, I'll come over to get you. Maybe we will buy some of our groceries there and give your friend's family a little business."

Walking into Wilson's Market, Olympia and Pastoria were taken by surprise when they saw their friend on her knees with a pale of water and can goods stacked around her while she washed the shelves. Sitting beside her sat a small boy, already trained as free labor, wiping dust from the cans before handing them back to his sister to replace on the newly scrubbed white metal shelves.

"Hi, Zelda," Pastoria said softly, unsure if their presence would embarrass her or not.

Zelda, never one to be embarrassed by anything, popped up from her work with a great smile on her chubby face. "Lympy! Pastoria! What brings ya'll into town?"

"Father is buying food for the chickens and some groceries we need."

"Your momma with him?"

"No," Olympia answered. "She dislikes coming into town unless necessary."

"Can't blame her," Zelda quipped. "I only been here a little while and these people 'round here are snooty as all get out. Won't nobody hardly talk to us, 'cept when they gotta come in here for vegetables."

A stubby balding little man wearing a grimy apron stepped onto the aisle, clearing his throat. Olympia looked up with a smile, expecting the same from his fat cheeks, but he offered nothing in return to suggest friendliness.

"These gals are the friends I told you about, Pop." Zelda informed her father.

It was obvious the man did not care. "Friends ain't for workin days, Zelda. You got lots to do."

Olympia felt bad that she might have gotten her friend in trouble by dropping in. "We just wanted to say hello," she said. "Our father is meeting us here to buy some things."

The little boy, now really taking notice of Olympia, reached out his hand to her as if to shake. "Zeb's me." Perhaps it was his chubby cheeks, or his outgoing personality, but Zeb seemed more like a tiny little man than a little brother.

Olympia laughed and shook the little gentlemen's hand. "Hi, Zeb. My name is Olympia." The boy giggled and went back to wiping the cans.

Breaking the awkward moment, Constantinople entered the store, spotting his daughters on the aisle opposite the door. "Well, you must be the illustrious Madam Zelda I have heard so much about from my daughters."

Never in her life had Zelda Cooper ever seen a man as grand and impressing as the one smiling down at her, and never in her life had she ever felt as important as she did now when this man addressed her so fancily. *Madam Zelda*. She liked that.

"Hey, Mr. Blanchard. Nice to meet ya."

"It is indeed my pleasure completely," Constantinople replied. "Your friendship has meant the world to my children. I am very grateful to fate for having brought you girls together."

Zelda's father, not quite sure what to make of the man before him, simply grunted, "Girls say you want some stuff. Watcha need and I'll fetch it for ya."

Constantinople addressed Mr. Cooper, "I am in your debt, sir. I have a list my wife made for me."

As Mr. Cooper took the list and began filling the order, Constantinople followed, attempting to make polite small talk. Zelda's father seemed very uninterested, which did nothing to dissuade Mr. Blanchard. "It is nice to have another family in the vicinity like my own," he began. "I hope that you and Mrs. Cooper will consider the Blanchards your new friends. I am sure we will be seeing one another from time to time, especially with the girls so close. And of course, there are the Consort meetings."

Mr. Cooper looked around nervously. Even though there was no one else in the market with them, he was clearly annoyed at having anything regarding the witching world mentioned aloud. "We don't talk about such stuff. Don't practice. Don't attend."

Constantinople was astonished to hear this. "My dear Sir, surely you do not deny your heritage. We do great things for this world we share with so many others."

"Ain't nothing but trouble if folks find out." Mr. Cooper said flatly as he handed his customer the crate full of provisions from the list. "Me and the missus do our work and stay out of the crosshairs. Don't expect we'll see much of your family, 'cept in town."

It was not terribly uncommon to occasionally run across witches who were too afraid to become a part of the witch community. Though it was always disappointing to discover witches still in hiding even from their own kind, it was understandable. Persecution was still a risk, although it was now more of a public ostracization than any mortal danger. Still, it was a shame to hear that the Cooper family not only avoided fellow witches, but they also did not even practice themselves. To a man like Constantinople Blanchard, this was the equivalent of squandering God's gifts when they could have been used for such good.

Accepting Cooper's stance against the magical world, Constantinople wanted to ensure his daughters' friendship was not part of that bargain. "You do not mind however, that our daughters have found one another in friendship? And perhaps Zelda might come to our home sometimes for a visit?"

Mr. Cooper wiped his sweaty brow and said, "I don't care. Long as my girl gets her work done 'round here, don't much care what she does after. Keeps her outta our hair."

Mr. Cooper's statement and the lack of affection it implied, was pretty much all Constantinople Blanchard needed to know about young Zelda's home life.

CHAPTER FIVE

Madam Zelda

Constantinople Blanchard picked his daughters up from school every afternoon at 3:00 and almost every afternoon he observed little Zelda exit the building with them, only she marched to the school bus while Pastoria and Olympia walked to the parking lot. Much like his daughters' disappointing connections at school, he watched young Zelda board the school bus as if completely invisible to the other children, even worse, an onslaught of snickers. Despite the treatment, her indomitable spirit never broke. He found himself liking this child very much.

It was a Friday afternoon at school pickup, when Constantinople surprised all three of the girls. As his daughters said their goodbyes to their friend for the weekend, he stepped out of the car to stop the trio before they parted. Zelda was turning to make her way to the school bus, when she heard Mr. Blanchard call out to her.

"Zelda!" he cried, cupping his hand to amplify his voice. "You can get on the bus if you prefer, however I have a bag in my car with some of your clothes in it if you would rather spend the weekend with us."

Turning around to look back, Zelda's face was frozen in complete surprise, as were the Blanchard sisters. With mild trepidation, young Zelda came closer. "You got my stuff in your car?"

"I sure do," Mr. Blanchard answered. "I went by Wilson's Market earlier and asked if you could spend the weekend with us."

"What did they say Father!" Pastoria exclaimed excitedly.

Not even waiting for his reply, Zelda started marching towards Mr. Blanchard's red DeSoto. "They don't care," Zelda said over her shoulder. "Won't notice if I'm there or not anyways."

Olympia and Pastoria ran after their friend, overwhelmed with joy to have company for the weekend. Constantinople followed behind, head low, disturbed by

Zelda's words. And she was not wrong. Her parents didn't care one way or another. When he'd driven into town to the little food market, he'd hoped perhaps his one exchange with Mr. Cooper a couple of weeks ago might have simply been a bad first impression. Unfortunately, his second impression of Mr. Cooper was just as sterile. Constantinople fully understood the Coopers possessed none of their daughter's exuberance or amiability. Mr. Cooper, the dingy little man in a dirty apron, did little more than grunt, "I don't care. Can probably get more done round this store without her pesterin' me. Gotta ask the wife though. Zelda helps her with the cleaning. This store gets dirty but quick with folks traspin' in and out all day."

Mr. Cooper disappeared up a tight set of stairs at the back of the store. When he returned, he had his wife in tow behind him. Mrs. Cooper was equally as grim as her husband. She was a pudgy woman with beady little eyes disappearing inside an overly round face. Her hair was ashy colored with strings falling out of the bun tied in the back.

"You say you wanna take Zelda home for the weekend to play wit' your kids?" Mrs. Cooper said wiping brow sweat on her wrist.

"Yes, ma'am." Constantinople answered. "It seems she and my two daughters have become fast friends. I thought the girls might enjoy a weekend—"

"Here," Mrs. Cooper said thrusting a sack of some of Zelda's clothes forward. "She and me done washed the fruit bins and cleaned out the expired meats this week. Just got the upstairs where we live to clean up, but I reckon she can do that Monday night."

Constantinople did his best not to allow his face to reveal his disdain for the Cooper's. More eager than ever to bring young Zelda home with him, he was aghast at what the child's homelife must be like.

The drive from town to Blanchard House took twenty minutes, but with the car radio turned up and the girls singing along to the music as they went, gave Constantinople a great deal of pleasure. They were so happy. Of course, as the DeSoto turned onto the dirt road to Blanchard House, the singing stopped as Zelda hung her head out of the window, mouth open, staring ahead.

"This is your house?" she exclaimed.

Constantinople had never seen his daughters view their home through another person's eyes before. Everything they took for daily granted was presented now in a whole new way. To Zelda Cooper, they lived in a palace. Even Constantinople looked ahead at his home with a fresh perspective. He admitted to himself it was rather a nice house. Tall, at three stories, with a four-story tower centered at the roofline, and painted crisp white, it had to seem especially lovely to Zelda compared to her set of rooms over the market.

Angharad met them at the door, wringing her hands into her apron, she had undoubtedly started making dinner. Olympia and Pastoria dragged their friend to the porch steps, excited to make introductions. "Mother, this is Zelda!"

"I gathered it would be," Angharad replied stiffly. "Seeing as how I recognize the two of you."

The girls ran past her into the house as Constantinople approached his wife. "I have never seen the children so excited."

His wife gave a slight nod, "I suppose it could be a positive thing for the girls to know another witch. There is safety in numbers, and one does need allies in battle."

Constantinople grinned and rubbed the sides of his short cropped black beard. "I doubt the children will find too many battles in our backyard, my dear. Although I appreciate your acquiescing to allow their friend to visit."

"And her people?"

Angharad watched her husband's grim face, "They are terrible I am afraid. I get the feeling she is little more to them than free labor. I do not foresee you and I becoming friends with the Coopers. But it is Olympia and Pastoria who matter, and I have a feeling they have acquired a lifelong friend."

Zelda found that Mrs. Blanchard was not terribly unlike her own parents in demeanor. The only thing separating them was that she was beautiful, and they were not. Zelda could not help but stare at Mrs. Blanchard across the dinner table. Her long raven hair and high cheek bones. *She looks like a cat*, Zelda thought to herself. With an awkward silence hanging in the air as everyone ate their meal, Zelda could feel in her senses that her friends shrank back into their shells when in the presence of their mother. Zelda wanted to break the ice and attempt to get Mrs. Blanchard talking at least a little, to break the boredom.

"So, you come from overseas someplace?"

"Are you addressing me?" Angharad asked the inquisitive little girl across the table.

Zelda gulped nervously, wondering if she perhaps shouldn't have spoken. "I just was wonderin'," Zelda stuttered. "I can see you walkin' through some mountains. Got black stuff all up the sides. Looks like black dirt."

Angharad glanced at her husband, then back to the odd chubby child. "Coal dust. Do you see coal dust marring the hillside of my village?"

"I don't know. Just see you walkin'. Got another girl by you. Looks like you a little. Her name is weird. Dogmud or something."

"Dagmara," Angharad replied. "My sister."

"Ya'll got rushed by some kinda coyotes. You flung em' back into a pit. Then covered it up with those black rocks."

Angharad leaned across the table, interested. Olympia was in complete astonishment. She had never witnessed her mother take interest in much of anything before. "Child...Zelda, isn't it? You have the gift of second sight."

"Yeah," Zelda said as she chomped down on a bite of hamburger steak. "I see stuff a lot about people. My parents make me shut up about it, say I don't never need to say out loud things I see."

"Your parents are fools." Angharad responded tersely. "In this house Zelda, you are free to speak anything you envision and at any time you wish to speak it. Never deny what you are. It is your strength. Your power might mean the difference between life and death one day to any number of people."

Constantinople did not know which person he felt the proudest of in that moment; the young stranger who felt brave enough to speak her mind, or his wife who never showed such passion to anyone, especially a child. He sent his wife a grateful wink simultaneously reaching over to tousle the hair of their guest. "Why Madam Zelda...I do believe you are a psychic."

CHAPTER SIX

The Magic of Summer

By the time the last homework assignment was turned in, the drudgery of school was over. As the dismissal bell rang for the final time, a wave of happy children were released to the lazy days of summer. Zelda had become a regular fixture at Blanchard House. She'd learned to get her chores around the store done quickly in the early part of the week so that her weekends were clear to be with her friends. Tasks which might have normally taken her an entire day to complete were done in a couple of hours now that she had a reason to finish.

The Blanchard girls and their friend spent their summer days roaming the two hundred acres of Blanchard land like explorers cutting through wilderness. It wasn't long before smooth grass worn paths were forged leading to all their favorite spots. They didn't know it at the time, but these fresh trails they were creating would become the regular routes future generations would use when they traversed the land. The humidity came early that summer, reducing most Alabamians to sweat laden, pitiful, heavy breathing drones. The stillness of the air pressed the heat down into the soul, making most afternoons unbearable for anyone who lacked the resources to cool off. For the Blanchards, things were not as oppressive. The three large oak trees in the front yard helped to shield the front porch and the living room from the intensity of the sun. The acres of forest also provided relief with their thick canopies of limbs and leaves, making late afternoon walks a necessary routine to combat the midday swelter. Olympia, Pastoria, and Zelda had their own private place to fight the summer heat. The stream that ran through the woods behind the back meadow could always be counted on to cool them off. Sometimes they would wade their feet through the crisp, clear spring water. But on especially miserable days, they would lay down in it, allowing the refreshing water to swirl over their necks and backs like nature's air conditioning.

Constantinople was often away a few days at a time, working on something secret with the Consort. When he was, Zelda did not visit, making the time go by even more slowly. On these days, the girls stayed as far away from the house as possible to avoid their mother assigning a meaningless task to them just for the sake of it. Of course, some chores were fun. Olympia and Pastoria rather enjoyed picking peas and butterbeans from the garden. The buckets could be a little heavy for their small arms and legs to carry, but surprisingly, their mother taught them a trick to it.

"Daughters," their mother called out from the back yard as she observed her daughters dragging a single bucket brimming over with pea pods. "Is it the best use of your time to both be dragging a single bucket home from the garden?"

"It's heavy, Mother." Olympia explained. "We can't manage it alone."

Angharad walked closer to the girls and removed the bucket handle from their little hands. "Pastoria Blanchard. What is your power?"

As if someone turned on a light in her brain, the young girl realized the obvious she had not yet considered. "I can move things with my mind."

"Such as a bucket." Angharad replied. "Move the bucket to the house."

Pastoria stood for a moment, focusing her mind on lifting the bucket of peas into the air. It wiggled at first, not exactly moving, but trying to. "I think it is too heavy."

"This is precisely why I consistently urge your father to force you girls to practice. Nothing should be too heavy, certainly not a bucket of purple hull peas."

Pastoria's mother advised her to concentrate harder. She told her not to focus on the bucket itself, but the miniscule pockets of air between it and the grass. "You are not moving a bucket, Pastoria. You are directing the currents of air around you, directing it into the grass beneath the bucket. Use the air to push the bucket upward."

The child imagined she could see the air. She chose to imagine it as silver in color. As if understanding how her power worked for the first time, Pastoria envisioned silver strings coming towards her from all around, merging into one large thread weaving through the blades of grass to press into the bottom of the bucket. When the bucket began to rise into the air a few feet, Pastoria had a look of amazement on her face. "I'm doing it!"

Angharad gave her further instructions. "Now with the air holding the bucket in place, direct another wave to push into side of the bucket, moving it forward in the direction you would like it to fly. Set the peas by the house."

The three witches watched as the peas floated slowly towards the house. Angharad cautioned Pastoria to decrease the flow of air the nearer it came to where she planned to set it. The bucket of peas slowed its pace. Angharad then directed her to reduce the current underneath until the bucket settled safely onto the ground. Olympia cheered her sister as the challenge was completed!

"Excellent, daughter!" Angharad praised, perhaps even smiling, though it was hard to tell. Pastoria felt immensely proud. Her mother was never pleased with her. This might be the first time. "Now, girls. Go pick the rest of the peas and Pastoria will fly the buckets home."

Olympia and Pastoria filled nearly nine bushels of peas that day with Pastoria successfully sailing them all home, with very little spillage. That evening the girls sat on the porch shelling the peas into a ceramic bowl and discarding the shells into a paper sack. Olympia liked the slick sensation on her thumb as it ran down the inside of the pod, freeing the peas. Drifting through the open window from the living room came the voices of Hollywood movie stars acting out radio plays in back-to-back episodes of *Suspense*. The Blanchards loved that radio show. Not only was it fun to hear the voices of their favorite actors, but the shows were often quite thrilling. This one starred Judy Garland from *The Wizard of Oz*. She was playing a drive-in waitress who mistakenly hitches a ride with a murderer. If it hadn't been for the almost forgotten saltshaker in her apron pocket, she would never have escaped becoming his next victim.

Every now and then, Angharad came outside to collect the shelled peas to take back to the kitchen where she dropped them in bowling water for two minutes, long enough to blanche them, stabilizing their freshness so they could be frozen for future meals.

There would be more to preserve in the coming days. The butter beans would have to be picked, shelled, blanched, and frozen. The corn would be ready to shuck, boil, and freeze. The snap beans would need to be picked and, well…snapped. Surviving on the things your own land grows required a great deal of work during harvest months, but none of it seemed like work to the Blanchard sisters. Of course, they were not allowed to participate in the harsher things. Such as killing one of the pigs, or a chicken when it stopped laying eggs. Their father handled the pigs, their mother handled the chickens. However, once the pork was cut into sections, the girls did get to salt the meat down and hang onto hooks in the smokehouse in the back yard. The little fire in the center of the small wooden structure was covered by a metal cone with many slits and holes in it to allow the fire to breathe and the smoke to spill out into the shed. Over time the salted meats cooked to a delicious flavor, but it took a long time.

Constantinople returned home after several days. Just as with all the other times he was away, he was met at the car by his daughters, eager for his hugs and kisses. Sweeping his girls into his arms, he supplied any shortage of love they might have missed since his departure. Angharad stepped out onto the porch. His gaze caught hers where he immediately saw her concerned expression. He knew she could tell right away. As the girls removed themselves from his embrace their attention turned to the little trailer hitched to the back of the car. They inspected the crates their father brought back with him.

Pastoria squealed in excitement, "A new baby pig! And five new chickens!"

"Yes," their father called to them as he approached his wife. "The people I helped wanted to give a token of their appreciation. You girls take the chickens to the chicken house. I'll take the pig to the pen later. He's a heavy one."

"Not for me, Father!" Pastoria bragged as she used her powers to levitate the pig crate and sail it across the yard towards the pen out back.

Constantinople winked at his wife. "I see you've made good use of the time alone with the girls. Pastoria's power has grown."

Angharad ignored his comment as the distraction it was. Once the children were out of their line of sight, she unbuttoned her husband's shirt and lowered it to his elbows. "Stanton!" He grimaced as she traced the long scar across his shoulder—dried blood still crusted to it between the sloppily applied stitches.

"I knew when I saw you embrace the children," she remarked. "This arm moved differently. Are you alright?"

"I am."

"I will properly restitch the wound," she told him, pulling his shirt back and rebuttoning it so the children would not worry.

"It was a nasty little monster," he chuckled as they walked up the steps to the house. "I have never seen anything like it before. I am still flummoxed as to what it was. Almost as if a Leprechaun had a baby with that Tasmanian Devil character in the cartoons at the movies. He sliced me deep with one talon."

"I will make a potion cream to heal the muscle. It will take time however to heal. You must not lift anything for at least a week."

"I will be your obedient patient my dear."

She surprised him with her next statement. "Since you insist we shield the children from the dangers we face, it is probably a good idea to have their friend stay a few days. She is always a good distraction and will lessen the chance of the girls playing with you and noticing the injury."

He grinned at the suggestion. It was a clever one, which would indeed curtail his opportunities to keep the girls entertained. Still, he wondered how much her suggestion was for his benefit or if perhaps quirky young Zelda was growing on her. He had little time to consider the matter as Angharad switched subjects, outstretching her hand for the one thing he had forgotten. Constantinople reached into his front pocket, withdrawing a small roll of cash, his payment from The Witches Association for his service. Handing it over to his wife, Angharad placed it with the rest of their household money, under a loose floorboard beneath the potted rubber tree plant. Once the girls came back to the house, no more was said about Constantinople's mission or his secret wound. The family had dinner and made plans to pick Zelda up the next morning.

CHAPTER SEVEN

The Princess, The Gypsy, and The Cowgirl

A coolness wormed its way in to penetrate the sticky air summer left behind. It was a welcome shift from the months of humidity which crushes Alabamians. The doors and windows to Blanchard House stood open all day now allowing breezes to drift through cooling rooms which had felt like an oven a month ago. Things didn't stick now, Olympia noticed. Throughout August and September, she'd found herself making a habit of walking through rooms slightly shifting objects which sat around on side tables, shelves, or mantlepieces. She liked the way things felt in her hands when she ever-so-lightly tried to move them from their sticky places. Candlesticks and vases were the best to achieve the sensation. Placing her little hands on each side of the object and giving a slight twist, made them emit a tiny little clicky sound as they let go of their humid hold on painted shelves. Now that the summer air had floated away, no sound came when she took a vase or ceramic statue and gave them her daily twist in place. It was definitely Autumn.

The leaves among the many trees on the Blanchard property were starting their colorful change now. Oranges, golds, deep beet reds made the outdoors seem newly painted somehow. Her sister Pastoria was already starting her annual collection of the prettiest leaves she could find and pasting them into her collection book. Pastoria made a book every year since she was 6 years old. She was now eight. Oddly enough she never looked at the collections of past years. If she had she might have noticed those leaves were no longer colorful and long dried out.

A car door shut outside, ringing the attention of the two little girls in the house. Olympia and Pastoria came running from different rooms out to the large porch to see their father trapsing forward holding two large bags in each hand. Behind the girls, standing in the doorway behind the screen stood their mother presenting a disapproving face as she wiped her hands on her apron.

"Are those our costumes?" Pastoria cried sprinting forward, snatching one of the bags. A quick look inside told her it wasn't hers. "Cinderella!" she snarled, thrusting the bag towards her older sister. "Of course, you have to be a princess."

Olympia took the bag in hand and gingerly lifted out the sky-blue dress as if it were made of glass. Her eyes bulged at the embroidery and delicate details of each cuff and collar. "Father, this didn't come from Woolworth. This isn't the same dress they are selling in their costume department."

Constantinople Blanchard stroked his twelve-year-old daughter's soft blonde hair and answered, "No. I had these costumes specially made by Mrs. Browning in town."

"You didn't," his wife scolded, coming out to the top step. "Stanton, we cannot afford to spoil these children the way you insist upon spoiling them."

Pastoria had already withdrawn her cowgirl outfit and was marveling at the hand stitched rhinestones on the vest and hat. She paid no attention to her mother's annoyance. Her mother was always irritated about something.

"My dear Angharad," Constantinople smiled. "They are only children once. Allow me to indulge them a little before life forces them into adulthood."

Angharad Blanchard did not release the severity in her face as her husband encroached onto the steps. "And how do you presume we are to pay for the automobile repairs or Olympia's dental work when you waste our hard-earned funds on such nonsense."

He reached the top step, now on equal footing with his wife, which made him six inches taller. She was less foreboding when they stood face to face. He leaned towards her to give her a gentle kiss. As she always did when the children were around, she turned, allowing the kiss to only hit her cheek. "Let me worry about our finances, my dear. You are much too lovely a creature to develop worry lines."

For a fleeting second, a twinkle registered in her eye before it disappeared back behind the blackness. He knew she liked it when he complimented her appearance although she never would indicate such vanity. Constantinople moved past his family into the house where he laid another bag on the entry table. She said nothing about this bag because she knew it was pointless to do so. She knew he had also brought home costumes for them as well. She returned to her kitchen to finish preparing the evening meal.

"I'm sorry she is angry with you over our costumes," Olympia murmured to her father. "You should have just gone to Woolworth."

Her father raised a playful brow. "You mean you do not like your Cinderella dress?"

She gasped and shook her head. "Oh, Father, I just love it! I do! But she..."

He wrapped his arms around his sensitive daughter and smiled. "Your mother is not as fierce as she presents herself to be." He paused, grinned, and winked. "Well... she is actually. But I have ways of soothing her. You just enjoy being Cinderella tomorrow night. I bet you will get lots of wonderful treats when we go to town."

He went upstairs to shower before dinner. Olympia watched as he disappeared down the second-floor hallway. Pastoria joined her, still marveling at her elaborately stitched cowgirl costume. "Why is she so mean?" she asked her sister. "She's never happy about anything. And she always picks on Father. I wish he'd tell her off."

"I think he loves her." Olympia explained. "I don't know why, but I think he does."

The next day was a school day, despite it also being Halloween, but being a holiday meant teachers would be a little more lax with lessons. In Pastoria's class, instead of the grind of afternoon lessons, the final two hours of class were spent coloring fun Halloween pictures of pumpkins, ghosts, graveyard cats, and witches. Of course, the latter handout sheet sent a shiver of apprehension through Pastoria as virtually every classmate turned her general direction, flashing the picture of the witch at her accompanied by a disapproving face or cutting remark. "Hey, is this one of your relatives?" Dodie Meyer called out after he'd scribbled green crayon across the witch's face. Pastoria simply ignored the comment as the rest of the class snickered. In Olympia's class, things were practically the same, only her classmates were too old for Crayola's. Olympia's teacher spent the final hour regaling the class with spooky seasonal stories. She began with a factually incorrect lesson about the witch trials in Europe and Massachusetts. Like in Pastoria's classroom, this talk of witches brought undesired attention Olympia's way. "How many of your ancestors got burned alive?" Lisa Hawkins exclaimed from two rows back. Of course, the teacher ignored the insult as if she hadn't heard it, but everyone had. Olympia simply smiled and replied, "Those poor people were all innocent. A real witch would never have been burned alive. No one would have been able to catch her." She knew she was exacerbating the rumors about her family with her flippant remark, but she'd been through enough of this treatment over the years. She frankly didn't care anymore.

She had no need for their friendship. She had Pastoria and Zelda. Olympia had no need for anyone else.

Once the bell rang, Olympia gathered her books and exited the classroom to wait by the water fountain for her sister and Zelda. Zelda bounded up to the water fountain, taking a big gulp, dripping most of it onto her bright purple dress. "Am I glad class is done!"

Olympia smiled at her friend and asked, "Did they give you a hard time too when any talk about witches came up?"

Zelda let out a howl, "Foot no! I gave them the hard time! That dumb teacher was a talkin' about that face in the courthouse window in Carrollton. Miss Smith says he was wrongly convicted of stealin' and they was gonna hang him. Then lightening flashed and froze his reflection in the window. I let her know right off that ain't what happened. He ticked off the sheriff's wife who was a powerful witch and she cursed his soul into that glass. We all know that story. I guess these regular folks hear a different one."

Olympia couldn't help but laugh. Zelda feared no one and cared very little if anyone thought she was different or crazy. Olympia wished she could muster the same kind of gumption, but the truth was Olympia cared very much about other people's opinion of her. Try as she might to convince herself everyone's vitriol didn't matter, it did. And it hurt.

Pastoria soon joined them at the water fountain ready to make plans for the evening. "Did your parents say you could come home with us to trick or treat?" she asked Zelda.

"My Pop said he don't care as long as your daddy don't mind bringing me home after. Got my costume in my backpack."

Constantinople Blanchard picked up the three girls in his red DeSoto and drove them out to Blanchard House. He enjoyed the ride home with his girls even more whenever Zelda joined them. The addition made the ride all the more animated. Until young Zelda's family moved to town, he'd never witnessed his girls engage with a friend. Gossip about the Blanchards from the mouths of parents spilled over into the children, causing his daughters to be shunned from their junior society. It caused Constantinople deep sadness for his children to pay the price for the legends floating around about his family. It wasn't their fault, or anyone's really.

The Blanchards had lived in this region longer than most and the stories about them had always been woven into the fabric of Daihmler history. Constantinople's resentment of the ostracization of his girls diminished a bit once he could see they were growing up to be strong independent young women. But now that they had a friend, he felt truly happy for them. True, little Zelda was an unconventional friend—odder than any child he'd ever seen. But her nonconformity amused him. How she had sprung from such unremarkable parents was a mystery. The Coopers were poor, uneducated, and frightened of the world around them. But even their dullard personalities could not squelch Zelda's zest and vitality. Once, early into the friendship, when Angharad voiced protest of how the new girl was not up to the standard of people their girls should associate with, Constantinople simply pointed out that Zelda's strength of self—especially for someone so young—was exactly what the daughters of Constantinople Blanchard needed as an example in their lives. From that moment on, his wife offered no more criticisms and young Zelda became a regular fixture at Blanchard House.

The children were anxious to hit the road and begin trick or treating, but Angharad insisted everyone have dinner first to prevent becoming sick later after too much candy. Olympia and Pastoria moaned over the decision, but Zelda cheered Mrs. Blanchard on once she smelled the pork chops frying.

Once the table was cleared and the dishes washed, everyone journeyed upstairs to dress in costume. Constantinople was the first to come downstairs to wait for the others. He was dressed in a black suit, complete with matching waistcoat, and a tall black top hat. It was his intention to be Abraham Lincoln, and if told beforehand, people probably would have made the connection. However, with his trimmed brown beard and mustache, he more resembled a magician. All he needed was a small red cape and wand. His costume was not new. In fact, it wasn't a costume. The suit already belonged to him; he'd only purchased the hat for the final effect. Pastoria and Zelda bounded down the stairs with the excitement of a couple of charging bulls. Pastoria looked precious in her pink and white cowgirl costume. She placed one hand on her holster where a plastic gun was fastened at the hip balanced on the other side of her waist by a braided tan rope wound through one of her beltloops.

"Are you my little girl, or has Dale Evans come to pay a call?" Constantinople teased as she spun around to show him the full view.

Zelda was dressed as a gypsy fortune teller. It was a costume she'd obviously cobbled together herself. It wasn't so much a costume as it was a navy blue tablecloth she had glued yellow and white construction paper cutouts to in the shapes of moons and stars. Rather crudely she had cut a hole in the center of the tablecloth for her head and two slots on the sides for her arms to poke through. For homemade, it really wasn't that bad. He admired her ingenuity.

"You know Zelda, you are missing something."

"Really Mr. Blanchard?"

Constantinople moved into the little study off the foyer where he withdrew something from a drawer. Returning to the child he presented a long, beautiful, multi-colored silk scarf. It was a swirl pattern of orange, lime green, pink, and magenta. "This belonged to my mother. She believed it to be the most beautiful thing she owned because the colors were so vivid. I think it is the perfect adornment for your costume tonight."

He tied it sideways around the crown of her head, draping the two long ends across her right shoulder. Directing Zelda to the hall mirror, he watched the grateful child admire the thing of beauty on her head.

"Oh, I can't wear this Mr. Blanchard. I wouldn't want it to get dirty."

"Then if you don't stick your head into any puddles tonight, I'm sure it'll be just fine, Zelda." His grin pulled a smile out of her. He knew she was never fussed over in her own home. He didn't believe his long-departed mother would have minded if her prized heirloom went out trick or treating tonight. "Madam Zelda, I do believe these colors suit you."

Olympia, always the longest of the children to dress, now came down the stairs in her elaborate Cinderella gown. The plastic rhinestone crown on her head glimmered under the lights. "How do I look, Father?"

"Exquisite, my pet. Walt Disney himself would be proud."

A dark figure emerged from the upstairs hallway to descend the stairs behind Olympia. Angharad was dressed in shimmery black chiffon which hugged her hourglass curves. A long veil cape trailed behind her. Atop her head she wore a tall conical hat with her cascading raven hair pulled over her shoulder.

"Really, Mother?" Pastoria scoffed. "You are going as a witch?"

"I am a witch. Why conceal it."

"Don't we get enough flak from people already?" her youngest daughter whined.

Angharad Blanchard did something she almost never did. She bent her legs to lower herself to eye level with her two daughters and their friend. For a single moment the iciness which always frosted her tone and the severity which always peered from her eyes, vanished. Gently she drew the girls' hands into her own. "People will always target those they fear or those they admire. The strong remain true to themselves. They do not fold in intimidation. Hate is only cleverly disguised admiration. We are Blanchards. We are witches. Why should we fear anything?"

No one ever drove all the way out to the Blanchard property for trick or treating. It was far too remote an area of town. For this reason, the Blanchards never had to worry about remaining home for trick or treaters. And truth be told, the children of Daihmler were probably far too afraid to venture out to the house where witches were rumored to live. Constantinople drove the family into town, parking at the Piggly Wiggly which was on the corner of two very large neighborhoods. He and his wife escorted the three girls along the dimly lit sidewalks where herds of children meandered from house to house. Ghosts, spacemen, Frankensteins, Draculas, Lone Rangers, and more than one Davy Crockett dodged and darted around people, hedges, and fence lines to gather their sugary sweets.

Olympia, Zelda, and Pastoria recognized a few faces from school. The other children noticed them as well, but none dared to even say as much as a friendly hello. It mattered little to the trio as the excitement of the holiday swept them up completely. Besides, they had each other. As they approached one festively decorated house with jack-o'-lanterns rising up the porch steps and swaying ghosts running the perimeter of the trees, Olympia felt a sudden shove upon her back. She stumbled, caught before hitting the ground by Zelda's quick reflex. Billy Zato turned back to give a menacing laugh as he beat her to the front door.

"He shoved you!" Pastoria cried out indignantly.

"He's a pest." Olympia said, waving it off. "It doesn't matter."

It stung her father's heart to see other children so brazenly cruel to his daughter. He had to remind himself to take the high road and not publicly admonish other people's children. That would not make things easier for his daughters. Yet as Billy Zato rushed back past them toward the next house, Constantinople heard a loud bang ring out behind him. Whirling around to see the commotion, he observed the rude young boy standing shell shocked on the sidewalk staring incredulously at what had been his plastic jack-o'-lantern pale full of candy. All around his feet lay broken bits of the orange plastic bin, and the surrounding candy lay melted to the ground. Billy looked at his hand where he still clutched the handle of the now incinerated pail. Constantinople's eyes moved towards his wife. Angharad stood triumphantly presenting a devious smile. He looked at his daughters, now thanking the woman at the door for the Milky Way bars she dropped into their sacks. They never even noticed their mother's act of retribution on their enemy. Of course, sometimes bad people do not suffer their comeuppance as they should. Instead of mourning the loss of his loot, hoodlum Billy Zato simply tossed down his broken handle and grabbed the first bag of candy he saw from a nearby child, sprinting off down the road. The girl, similar in age to Pastoria, began to cry.

Constantinople was just about to abandon his rule of disciplining other children when he saw his daughter Olympia dart off down the sidewalk after the thief. Pastoria and Zelda walked over to the heartbroken candy victim to console her. It became clear from the interaction; Pastoria knew the girl. They were classmates. Constantinople moved quickly down the street to follow his daughter in her pursuit of the wicked boy. As he rounded the corner of the block, he stopped in his tracks to witness the scene. Olympia stood with her hands outreached towards Billy. Billy was not moving. Completely frozen in place by the young witch's power.

Seeing her father now, Olympia gave him a sorrowful look. "Oh, Father, I am sorry. I know I am not supposed to use my powers in front of people." She lifted the bag of candy from the stone-still boy's hand.

Constantinople approached the child lovingly. Placing his gentle, but firm hand upon her shoulder, he simply replied, "Our purpose on this earth is to protect The Natural Order. Thievery is wrong. You were righting a wrong. I will overlook your actions this one time." She smiled up at him and took hold of his hand to lead him back to the other street. "Olympia, my dear," he said. "Haven't you forgotten something?"

"Oh, right!"

Olympia turned back towards Billy and cast her spell again, freeing him from his suspended state. The boy stared at her with a mixture of fright and indignance. Olympia simply gave a little wave as she and her father returned to the scene of the crime. Pastoria's classmate was still crying as Zelda and Pastoria tried to soothe her feelings. Then they saw Olympia coming back—bag of candy in hand.

"Here you go," Olympia told the younger girl, returning her stolen property. The girl was extremely grateful. So much so she almost hugged Olympia...that is until she spotted other children approaching who she knew from school. She took her bag and ran off unceremoniously.

Olympia, Pastoria, and Zelda stood together for a moment watching her flee. They understood. Though grateful and possibly comprehending she may have been wrong in her preconceived notions of the three outcasts, the little girl was still not brave enough to befriend them in front of the rest of their little society. And that was okay. Olympia, Pastoria, and Zelda had each other. And that was all they really needed.

CHAPTER EIGHT

Olympia's First Consort

Over the last century it had become clear to the many witches scattered across America that an association was needed to unite them all together. Originally this unification served as a way to assure safety and secrecy among their kind. It quickly evolved to become an organization which also provided a network of assistance to any fellow witch in a time of need. Annual gatherings, called Consorts, began to bring witches together in fellowship. As membership increased, so did Consorts. Soon it became necessary to hold quarterly meetings to address all the needs of members. Disputes between witches, punishments for crimes committed by magical means, and the cremation of the dead all fell under The Association's scope. Within a few years it became necessary for The Association to branch off into four divisions to ensure proper representation as well as make attendance easier. By separating into four quadrants, witches had less of a journey to attend a Consort. Once membership grew into the thousands, each Association added a new agency to their government, one of protection and defense. The world had long been plagued by dark creatures rarely seen but prominently at large. These beings had free reign in a world which shrouded them in legend. Civilized mankind did not believe any longer in the monsters their forefathers wisely feared. Because of this false enlightenment, human beings and witches alike met brutal and mysterious deaths at the hands of evil. The Witches Association forged this new branch of protection to hunt down and eradicate those monsters no one thought to be real anymore. This arm of the Association is what employed Constantinople and Angharad Blanchard.

The Autumn Consort fell two weeks after Halloween this year. Each season a new site was chosen to house the quarterly meetings of the Southeast Witches Association. This ritual was a holdover from the days when The Consort was kept moving, making it impossible for frightened non-witches or the monsters of the world to target their headquarters. Often a Consort member of wealth and means volunteered their home to host the meetings. However, if this was not possible, a site would be rented for the occasion.

The location for the Autumn Consort this year was to be in Eufaula, Alabama. The site chosen was The Cowan-Ramser House. Built in 1840 in the Greek Revival style by physician William Cowan, it wasn't an ostentatiously large structure. It was a simple square, wood planked, two story house with four bedrooms upstairs and four rooms downstairs. It began life as a tragic place almost from the start. Dr. Cowan and his wife lost three of their young children while living in the house. Misfortune did not stop there. Later in 1862, one of the family fell from the porch balcony while sleepwalking in the night. After the Civil War, the property was sold to a furniture craftsman named Jacob Ramser, who later became Eufaula's mayor. In 1948 the house was sold to another family who turned it into a funeral home—which it still remained.

Though a Consort had never before been held in a funeral parlor, this was not a terrible choice of setting this season due to the fact that three Association members had died since the summer meeting–two having lost their ongoing battles with Polio, and one from a terrible automobile accident. The three bodies had been sent to Colonel White's Funeral Home after the Consort setting had been decided, making this an ideal location for the Autumn meeting place.

This was Olympia Blanchard's first Consort. Deemed too young in the past, her parents decided the Autumn Consort was the perfect introduction to society. Olympia was maturing now and could be counted on to behave properly. It also helped having the meeting place so close to home. Eufaula was not terribly far from Daihmler. Pastoria was still decidedly too young to attend, which posed a babysitting problem. With a little coaxing, the Blanchards were able to get Zelda's parents to permit Pastoria to stay the night with them. After having hosted their daughter so many times at Blanchard House, the Coopers could hardly refuse. And Zelda was pleased as punch to have Pastoria stay with her.

Constantinople drove his wife and eldest daughter to the town of Eufaula, easily finding the historic home turned funeral parlor. "Grisly locale, I must say," he noted to his wife as they parked across the street. "However, I do see the beneficial aspect. The poor Dreshers. Polio is a dastardly disease."

"Father?" Olympia spoke up from the back seat as he switched the car into park.

"Aren't there witches who could have healed them?"

Her mother answered the question as she stepped from the car to open the back door for her daughter. "The power to heal is a very rare gift, Olympia. It is not typically a witch's power. It comes from something greater. Only the most deserving souls are bequeathed such an ability."

For a moment, Constantinople thought his wife might be about to share a secret he never thought she would divulge. Something from long ago in her life. But he was mistaken. She left her sentence where it was and never revealed the secret. It was for the best. Some things need not be mentioned, especially something most witches have forgotten even existed. The God Strain was something of legend, never spoken about anymore. In fact, Constantinople himself had never known of its existence until his wife told him her story. Through an act of extreme courage, she had been bestowed with the mythical gift. Deeming herself unworthy of its magnificence, Angharad denied the honor, decreeing it should pass through her blood to the sixth daughter of her lineage. Having born no other children, The God Strain and all its responsibility, would fall to a daughter or granddaughter of either Olympia or Pastoria. She prayed they would better portray its worthiness.

As the Blanchard family entered the parlor, it was quite clear this was a funeral home. Round back chairs padded in mauve with brown varnished trim sat side by side against the walls with a matching settee placed between every third chair. The center of the room housed similarly upholstered low back sofas with coffee tables. Most of the seating was occupied by older Association members not interested in standing on their feet for long, while clustered around them stood younger witches engaged in conversation with them. There was an air of power and mystic charging the room. It occurred to Olympia she had never been in a room with so many witches before. She imagined what kinds of powers were gathered there and what all had their worldly eyes seen.

Olympia noticed the subtle shift in attention as many faces turned to stare at her family. It was very different from the way people looked at them when they walked through their hometown. These eyes upon them here were not suspicious or afraid, they seemed to hold a sense of admiration. She had always revered her father, thinking him the most important person in the world. But now she saw for the first time the extent of his influence reached further than her own family; it radiated throughout this society of witches. Men came forward to shake his hand affably while women cut their eyes towards him, eyeing him with delight in ways they shielded from their own husbands. Angharad, on the other hand, garnered her own unique reverence. Olympia's mother was greeted cordially by members, yet with a wall of formality they did not reserve for her father. Olympia knew right away this distinction was something her mother preferred and most likely implemented years ago. A deliberate boundary she kept between herself and everyone else in the world, even her children. Women largely steered clear of Angharad after greeting her. Olympia wondered if they feared her, envied her, or just disliked her as much as she did. Of course, the men eyed her mother with the same covert admiration as their wives gave her father. Olympia understood quite clearly now the Blanchards were a team not to be reckoned with and people knew it.

Making their way through the crowd, Olympia observed people bow their heads respectfully or nod a silent hello to their little family. She could not understand what made her parents so important to these men and women. Yet this air of authority bestowed to them became clearer by a few of the comments overheard as they passed. *Did you hear about Constantinople taking down that Wendigo in Boston? Remember when the Blanchards hunted down the Hidebehind creature killing all those people in Orson Falls?* Striding across the parlor, Consort members stepped back, giving the Blanchards pathway across the room. The experience of the night so far revealed a new dimension to her parents as pillars of this secret world. Olympia felt proud to be a Blanchard yet now somehow weighted by a responsibility to be part of a legacy that went beyond her own understanding.

Her parents came to a stop on the other side of the room where a man pushed forward, tugging a boy around Olympia's age with him. The man was stalwartly with a bushy mustache and graying sideburns. His son, though only a child, had all the makings of growing into just as much a bastion of staunchness as his father. Still, he presented young Olympia with a cheery smile.

"Blanchard!" the elder gentleman bellowed. "I see you have finally graced us with the introduction of your lovely daughter." He turned to address Olympia directly. "My name is Bristow Uding, my dear young lady. This is my son Brimford."

"Pleased to meet you." Brimford said, bowing. Olympia in return curtseyed although she was not sure why. She'd never curtseyed in her life.

"My dear Angharad," Bristow charmed. "Ever as radiant as always." Olympia's mother mildly nodded but said nothing in return. The older man went on, unaffected by—or perhaps accustomed to—her cold countenance. "We have a peculiar case in our files I must speak with the two of you about at some point in our near future. I believe only the Blanchards are equipped to handle such a matter."

Constantinople glanced down at Olympia, as if reminding his fellow witch of her presence and his desire to keep her shielded from certain things. "We will speak soon, Bristow."

Another man, rather somber, cunning perhaps, approached quite suddenly, taking them by surprise. Olympia wondered if he'd been eavesdropping. Judging from her father's face, he did not hold a high opinion of the man. Even Olympia immediately disliked him. Something about him made her shudder.

"A new member to our Association I presume?" the interloper said, eyeing Olympia. "It is always refreshing when the youth join our society."

Constantinople turned to his daughter to make the polite overture. "Olympia, this is Mr. D'Angelo."

Perhaps a little of her mother's disinterest in others had rubbed off on her because Olympia found herself unresponsive to the introduction. She simply stared at the dastardly looking man with the dark beard and mesmerizing eyes. She neither greeted him nor smiled.

"How are things in Charleston, Gerald?" Constantinople asked without much interest in the answer.

"Nothing changes much in South Carolina," Gerald D'Angelo replied. "Business is booming. The shipping industry is growing. My son Hugh is almost of age to leave school and join me in my endeavors. And my daughters are making their debut into society next Spring."

"Will there be a ball at The House of Duquesne?" Bristow asked.

Mr. D'Angelo bristled. "Doubtful," he said. "It is regretful, but Wadmalaw is a bit remote for most Charlestonians to travel for parties. My daughters Abigail and Esmeralda will make their debuts in the city."

The D'Angelo man dismissed himself under the pretense of needing to speak to someone else across the room. After his departure Olympia listened closely to the things the adults were saying.

"As if distance is the reason polite society avoids his place," Bristow whispered. "You've never seen his family home, have you Blanchard?"

"I have not."

"It is a monstrosity." Bristow divulged. "The entire structure is a colossal disfigurement upon the land. It is said it was an architect's revenge on one of D'Angelo's unfaithful ancestors. The architect was the ancestor's brother-in-law. It is an old story, but still interesting when retold. Because of it, the D'Angelo's are stuck with an eyesore they can never sell. They still seem to love it though. I never understood why."

"How many children do the D'Angelo's have?" Angharad asked with uncharacteristic curiosity.

"Three," Bristow answered. "They always have three. Gerald's father had a boy and two girls. I believe his father did as well. Curious really because Gerald has the same. I presume one day young Hugh will also have a son and two daughters. Family lines can be strange things, can't they?"

The conversation was interrupted by the strong hand of an extremely tall man griping the shoulder of Olympia's father. Seeing the man standing beside her dad was an amazing sight to behold. Constantinople was a tall man himself, but this guy was almost a foot taller. She found him mesmerizing. He was dressed in a very dapper dark blue suit with a golden tie with dark green swirls on it. His hair was maple colored, groomed with men's hair oil and parted to the side. He was as handsome a man as Olympia had ever seen. She watched as her father turned to greet the fellow with a warm embrace. The gesture startled her a little. She'd never witnessed her father hug another man.

"Bedwyr!" Constantinople exclaimed. "You are looking well my friend! Ready to begin your reign?"

The man nodded proudly as he pinched the lapels of his jacket between his forefingers and thumbs. "Ready to do what I can for the Association, Con. If everyone has trusted me with their vote, I vow to do my utmost."

Olympia jutted her chin back a bit, taken by surprise. She had never heard anyone shorten her father's name to "Con" before. Of course, her mother always referred to her father as "Stanton", also a shortening, but somehow *Con* seemed brash.

"Angharad, my lovely." Bedwyr bowed, kissing her mother's hand. If she had been shocked by this man's informality with her father, Olympia was left dumbfounded by her mother's reaction to his forwardness. Angharad did not bristle, nor did she harden at his touch. In fact, a layer of her iciness melted, and Olympia watched in awe as Angharad Blanchard met his remark with a smile and a kiss to the cheek.

"Bedwyr," she beamed. "I have never been prouder to know you. You were the proper choice for our leader, and it was a well-deserved victory."

Olympia continued to watch, flabbergasted, as this man stood with his arm perched around her mother's waist. Even her father did not do that. Her eyes moved from his shoulder to her waist several times, disbelieving what her eyes claimed to see. No one touched her mother. How was this happening? Olympia's attention to the arm clasping her mother was broken when her father addressed her directly. "Olympia, I would like to introduce you to a great friend of your mother and mine. Your King. King Bedwyr Kraven."

Again, Olympia curtseyed. She'd never known a real-life King before. "Are you King of England?" she asked timidly.

The man laughed raucously as he removed his arm from Angharad's waist to place both hands atop the child's shoulders. "No, my dear child. I am merely the King of The Consort." Realizing her confusion had not waned, he clarified. "I am King of the witches."

She sighed in understanding and told him it was nice to meet him. Before she could barely get the words out, a woman rushed forward, sweeping Angharad up into her arms, embracing her emotionally. Again, her mother did not seem ambivalent to the affection. Never had the young girl witnessed her mother respond to anyone so effectually. Releasing Angharad from the embrace the woman spied Olympia standing to the side. "Angharad! Is this your daughter?" Without awaiting an answer, the woman lifted Olympia into her arms, smothering her cheek with kisses.

"This is my wife, Beryl." King Bedwyr smiled down to Olympia.

"Nice to meet you, your majesty." Olympia greeted the woman, resisting the urge to wipe the wet kisses from her cheek.

The men laughed out loud. Constantinople kneeled, placing a confidential hand on his daughter's back as if conveying important inside information. "Spouses of Kings and Queens of the Consort are not Kings and Queens themselves. Mrs. Kraven is suitable enough."

"Oh."

Beryl Kraven leaned down to the child and gave her another kiss, this time on the head. "Sweet little girl. Did you know that your mother was my own personal hero, child?"

Olympia looked at her questioningly.

Angharad blushed, something else Olympia had never witnessed before. "It is not necessary to explain things to the child, Beryl."

"Oh, I disagree." Beryl Kraven replied. "I would sky write it if I could. Miss Olympia, your mother saved the life of my only child, Brustius. Just a year or so before you were born, the four of us were back in our homeland of Wales for a festival. Your mother, myself, and my husband grew up together. I was presenting my son to my family for the first time since his birth. However, during the festival, while all the children were at play in the meadow, Brustius, only four at the time, wandered down to the lake following a few older children." Beryl's eyes lit up wildly as she continued the tale. Olympia was glued to her every word as she went on. "We heard the screams all the way to the village. It was the Cyhyraeth."

Olympia wanted to ask what she had said, unable to pronounce the thickly accented Welsh, but Beryl Kraven answered the question for her as she went on. "The Cyhyraeth is the specter of death. She cries three times for each death she sees, alerting man that Death has come. We heard twelve cries before we made it to the lake. Your mother glides upon the wind like she has always been part of it. She reached the lake before any of us. Three children were drowned, taken by the dreaded Llamhigyn Y Dwr—the Water Leaper."

"Water Leaper?" Olympia gulped from her swelling, frightened throat.

As Beryl continued, she knew she had the child's attention, and whether she embellished the tale for effect to entertain the curious child or whether every breath she spoke was true, Olympia would never know for sure. "The Water Leaper has no hindlegs but a long tail with a stinger on its end, like a scorpion. It has wings like a bat, and it lives to punish the innocent. It stung the children as it dragged them into the waters, leaving them for dead. Only one child remained. The smallest and the most vulnerable...my son. But your mother, Olympia! Your mother got to him first, welding her powerful magic she ripped branches from the nearest tree and shot them into the ground encasing my Brustius, protecting him on all sides. And as the Water Leaper took his attempt on her, she swept him backwards into the broken stump of the tree branch, impaling him to his death."

"Wow." Olympia gasped.

Placing her arm back around the child's shoulders, she looked up at Angharad with Olympia. "Your mother is a fierce warrior, unafraid of anything. And because of her, my only child is alive to this day."

Many wondrous things happened that night for young Olympia Blanchard. She took part in her very first Consort meeting, witnessing the Council of Witches talk over the business matters of the season. She saw her first cremation of fallen witches, burned to ash on a pyre of wood–their brittle bones then crushed and presented to their surviving family members. Many of the things she would see over and over throughout her life, were seen for the first time that early November night. But nothing stuck with her more than the story she was told by the King's wife. All the way home while she pretended to be asleep in the back seat, her little girl's mind ran through the story again. She could almost see it perfectly. Though she disliked her mother most of the time, it was quite rewarding to learn her mother had made a difference in someone's life. She saved a little boy. Olympia knew she would never forget meeting Beryl Kraven. Her name would stick in her mind for years. She might even name one of her children after her one day.

CHAPTER NINE

Attack of The Rain People

Things were beginning to prosper in the Blanchard household somewhat lately. Olympia and Pastoria were not quite sure as to why although they had suspicions. There had been a five-week period when their father had not been around. Angharad told them frightfully little on the matter except that he was working for the Consort. Olympia recalled the Consort meeting when Mr. Uding mentioned a certain case needing her father's assistance. She knew these weeks he was absent from Daihmler, he was working on that case, whatever it was.

The weeks without their father were dismal ones for the young Blanchard sisters with only their cold unfeeling mother for company. A few times Olympia attempted to get her mother to share stories from her life or her adventures with the Consort. Her mother always refused, replying, "The past is where dead moments are buried. Dwelling there offers nothing worth reviving." The resistance to share her life dashed Olympia's hopes of better understanding, or even liking, her mother. Had she been successful in getting Angharad to reflect on the old days, Olympia might have been able to show Pastoria a glimpse of the zest their mother momentarily displayed at the Consort when her friends had spoken with her. Abandoning the effort, Olympia refocused her attention to trying to get her mother to permit Zelda to stay over. Angharad denied each request, stating how Zelda's company was better suited to when their father was home.

Meals were spent in silence at the table, illustrating just how much vitality their father produced when home and how lifeless it was without him. Weekends were spent upstairs in the fourth-floor tower room with their mother. It was known as The Magic Room—the place where the girls were pushed to hone their powers. Insisting the girls master their abilities as witches for the future day when such skills might be needed, Angharad did not let up on them. Hours and hours passed as Olympia practiced freezing time and Pastoria tried to intensify her telekinesis. No matter how often the children argued how they could already perform the feats asked of them, their mother demanded they continue to focus harder.

"It is true, Olympia, you can halt time in this room." Angharad pointed out. "But what of the time outside this window. I still see a bird winging by. Why have you not stilled it as well? I can tell you why. Because you are contented with mediocrity. You refuse to expel the effort to do more. But enemies travel far distances. If you were in danger from someone no further than our front yard, you'd have no time to escape. Your reach must grow in range!"

Every day was the same, until Constantinople Blanchard returned home from his mission—and with him came a valise full of money. Where it came from the children were never told, only it had been payment for something quite extraordinary he'd done to help a township. They rewarded him greatly for it.

It was not long after when Charles Caldwell came into their lives. Caldwell worked at the bank and was undoubtedly now managing Blanchard's newfound gains for them. As time went on, Mr. Caldwell came out to the house often with his wife Clara and their son Nate. On those visits while the men disappeared into the study off the foyer, it was up to Angharad to entertain Mrs. Caldwell and the girls to entertain Nate. Nate was a year older than Olympia and a grade higher than she was in school. Though he'd never been one of the students who harassed her at school, he was aware of the situation. But the more often Nate visited Blanchard House, he found himself beginning to like the Blanchard sisters, especially Olympia. He even put a stop to the harassment at school—when it happened in his presence.

Of course, there came a day when, for a brief moment, Nate Caldwell became afraid of his new friends, even considering the kids at school might have been right in their assessment of the Blanchard girls. His father had brought him to Blanchard House to play with the girls while he met with Mr. Blanchard. The children decided to take a walk down to the creek in the woods to wade their feet in the crisp cool water.

Along the way, they took the path through the apple orchard, grabbing a ripe apple to munch on as they continued toward the trail in the woods. It was a short trek from the start of the tree line to where the creek flowed through the heavy canopy of trees. Nate and the girls laid their shoes on top of the old broken log at the creekbank before tiptoeing into the water. As the creek deepened, Nate rolled his pants legs up while the girls tied their skirt hems around their knees. The water trickled over their ankles providing a nice respite from the noon day heat.

"I wish I had a creek in my yard," Nate noted. "You guys have everything here. You can even go pick your own apples or grab grapes to eat off the vine whenever you want."

"Apples and grapes," Pastoria smirked. "Big deal. You live in town. You can walk to the picture show or have a scoop of ice cream at the drug store, or even get a Coca-Cola at the filling station anytime you want."

"I guess." Nate replied.

"Well, I love it here." Olympia declared. "I plan to live here all of my life."

Nate grunted in opposition, wading further into the stream where the water rushed over his calves. "What happens when you get married? You must go live with your husband."

Olympia took a ribbon from her wrist and tied her long blonde hair into a ponytail. "I'm never getting married."

"Never?" Nate gasped.

"I don't see why I should," Olympia explained. "I certainly do not want to be a wife. My mother is not anyone I care to be like. But mostly, I just never want to leave here."

"Can't blame you for that." Nate agreed.

A gust of wind happened by, increasing intensity through the trees until it rocked one of Nate's shoes off the log, sending it floating downstream.

"Oh no!" Nate cried. "Those are new! My dad will kill me!"

"I've got it," Olympia announced. Without thinking first, she lifted her hands and with a gentle flick of the wrist, stopped the shoe. In fact, she stopped the flow of the water.

Nate stared ahead at the now completely still stream. His shoe had stopped its sail downstream and was now halted in place four feet away atop the stationary water. "What did you do!"

Pastoria exclaimed hysterically, "Olympia! You're never supposed to do that in front of a regular person!"

Olympia placed her hands to her cheeks, the realization dawning that she'd just exposed herself in front of the banker's son. "I wasn't thinking."

Nate could do nothing but stare at her, his mouth open, his heart racing. "What is going on here?"

In the sardonic way, which was becoming a part of her budding personality, Pastoria broke the moment by simply saying, "Well...are you gonna grab that shoe or what? She can't hold the current in place forever."

Nate walked forward. The water displaced against his movement but never splashed or rippled. It was as if he were pushing through heavy clear syrup. He reached the stray shoe, grabbing it in his hand. Olympia flicked her hands once more, returning the stream to its natural flow. Nate rushed to the shore as if the very water might contaminate him. His rapid movement caused the splashing water to soak his pants. Once the children were back on shore, he demanded answers.

Olympia did not try to make any excuses, she replied quite honestly, "I am a witch. So is Pastoria. And my parents. We are all witches."

Nate slanted his eyes as the edges of his mouth turned upward. "Come on, Olympia. Seriously, what just happened?"

"I told you. I am a witch. I can stop things in place."

Another eye roll from Nate began to exhaust her patience. A bird was swooping by a few feet away. Olympia reached her hands outward and stopped it mid flutter. Nate stared unblinking at the motionless creature. He plopped to the ground in bewilderment. "Is this for real?"

"Yes," Pastoria answered. "But you cannot tell anyone. It's too dangerous."

"Yeah!" Nate cried. "Cause you are witches! They used to hang witches!"

Olympia scoffed at the remark, taking a seat beside him. "Yeah, there is that. But mainly you cannot tell anyone because if people found out they would be afraid. They'd try to harm us, and we do good things."

Nate shook his head, "You ever seen the Wizard of Oz? Witches are evil."

"First of all, "Olympia began. "That was a movie. Second of all, Glinda was also a witch."

Pastoria jumped into the argument now. "Look Nate, our father helps people. There are bad things out there in the world. Things you regular people don't know about."

"And the reason you don't know about them," Olympia chimed in. "Is because of witches who stop them from doing the bad things. We protect your kind. Its why we are here. We ensure that The Natural Order of things continues."

Nate was unsure what to think, but after a little more coaxing from the sisters, he promised to keep their secret for the time being. As much as the idea frightened him, he knew in his heart his friends were kind people. He'd spent a great deal of time with them over the last few months. There was no way he believed Olympia could be evil.

Though the Blanchard sisters were nervous having someone else know their secret, Nate proved to be as good as his word. He never told a soul—not his father, not the children at school. Olympia came to appreciate having a friend among normal people who she could confide in. She felt less alone. But then that special gift was taken away from her.

It was a Saturday afternoon, Olympia's 13th birthday. Her father insisted upon a party for her. Of course, there were no guests other than him, Angharad, Olympia, Pastoria, Zelda, and Nate. His daughter had no other friends. Still, Constantinople went to the bakery in town and bought the biggest and most delicious chocolate cake they had. The picnic table in the side yard was dressed in a beautiful tablecloth with three vases of wildflowers picked from the meadow. The weather threatened rain, but so far none had fallen. Angharad prepared hamburgers in the kitchen and served them to the children outside. It was adding up to being a very enjoyable day, until that forewarned but evasive rain began to fall.

The storm came suddenly and without warning, still nothing about it seemed odd enough to arouse suspicion. Grabbing their plates and making a dash to the front porch, they resumed the party under the covered roofline. Olympia and her friends continued their idle conversations. However, Zelda suddenly removed herself from the banter. She stood from her chair and said the strangest thing. "For the wicked are like the troubled sea, whose waters cast mire and dirt. There is no rest, saith my God, for the wicked."

Constantinople turned to look her way, then back out to the storm growing in intensity. His wife joined him at the porch rail and asked, "What disturbs you, Stanton?"

"The rain," he whispered. "It falls too fast and too thickly. Look at the ruts on the road out there and here in the yard where we pull the car up. The ruts are full. Look out into the yard. The whole yard is filling with water."

"You don't believe it could be—"

"I'm not sure, Angharad. Just ready yourself."

"How could they know where you live?" she asked. "You destroyed them all, didn't you?"

"I thought so," he answered grimly, his eyes transfixed on the odd composition of the rainfall. "Perhaps not. Perhaps even Zelda can feel it."

As if his confidential words to his wife had been drawn to Zelda's own mind like a magnet drawing a paperclip, the child rose again. This time her eyes were glazed, as if in a trance. Constantinople was about to go to her when his wife touched his arm, signaling to allow Zelda to feel whatever she was sensing. Zelda opened her mouth and said, "And the Lord sent the rains to flood the earth and rid the world of evil. So the Devil put the evil in the rain."

Without warning, the children on the porch were startled from their innocence as three figures seemingly dropped from the sky, landing sure-footed on the lawn a hundred yards away. Nate jumped from his chair, overturning his paper plate. Olympia, Pastoria, and Zelda rushed to the railing to get a closer look. Angharad pushed them back against the house.

The three figures were male and unlike anything the children had ever witnessed. Though rain was falling in torrential waves, the three men were not at all wet. To the contrary, from all appearances the rain coming down looked to be merging into them. No matter which part of their bodies the rain drops hit, they absorbed into the creatures leaving their skin, hair, and clothing entirely dry. The men began to stalk forward, their evil twisted faces so menacing it was undeniable they meant to kill everyone on the porch. One of the men landed his foot onto the water-filled rut in the road. Instantly his form vanished, liquifying into the very water beneath his feet. In the flash of an eye, he reappeared on the other end of the rut, all the closer to the house. It had been as if the trench of liquid acted as a conduit, moving him lightning fast without effort. He had been one with the water. They all were. Any place water collected in reasonable quantity; these men could traverse instantaneously to the other side.

Angharad sprang into action, leaping over the porch railing like an ancient warrior. Extending her hand, she sent a powerful blast forth landing into the torso of the closest man. The creature toppled backwards, but the fall did not deter him. Using another puddle on the lawn, he traveled its path with no effort, retaking his original position. At the corner of the porch, Constantinople was blasting his own magnificent energy at the second man charging forward. The impact of the witch's force struck the creature mid-center but did not kill him. The blow did manage to jolt his body with enough force that it looked like water burst out of him much like a gunshot might cast blood outward. He appeared dazed for a second, but the falling rain acted as fuel when it fell upon and merged into him. These creatures were charged by water and most likely were comprised of it.

Something then happened which changed Olympia and her sister forever. Whenever the girls would look back upon this moment in their lives it would be regarded as the day they stepped into their destiny. It was also the first time their mother required their assistance.

"Pastoria!" Angharad shouted over the roar of rainfall. "Use your powers! Move the water away!"

The child was paralyzed with fear for a second, but only for a second. A supportive nod from Olympia emboldened Pastoria to trust herself and believe she was up to the task. With her eyes intently focused on the pools of water spreading across the lawn, Pastoria Blanchard swiped her arm to the right. To not only her own surprise, but everyone else's, the groundwater rolled away as if an unseen wind tossed it. The water did not move very far, only a few yards, but it was enough to prevent these weird water creatures from accessing it. Still more rain was falling from the sky. It wouldn't be long before other pools formed. It was then when Olympia was called upon.

"Stop them in place, Olympia!"

Olympia obeyed her mother, pushing forth her great immobilizing power toward the three monsters. Hit by her spell, the attackers were rendered motionless. But it wasn't going to last. Every fresh drop of rainwater from the sky absorbed into them, making them more resistant to Olympia's hold. It was not important, her spell held them long enough for her father to forge his massive power between his hands. Nate watched in sheer terror as Mr. Blanchard materialized a large sphere of fire between his rotating palms. The fireball grew in size with each rotation until it was the size of a basketball. As powerfully hot as it was, the flames never scorched his hands. Constantinople tossed the flaming cannonball at the creatures whereupon it exploded into them with expanding volume, engulfing all three. A horrifying cry rang out as the three fiends were incinerated, evaporating into the air. The rain stopped.

Angharad sighed, releasing a breath she'd been holding too long. Her husband smiled her way, then addressed his children. "Why look at you two!" He was profoundly amazed by his daughters. "You helped stop a trio of Rain People! Not an easy accomplishment even for adults."

Angharad approached her daughters ceremoniously, placing a hand of approval on both their shoulders. "You have done well, girls. Never have I been so proud of you both as I am now."

And with that, Constantinople Blanchard turned his attention to his daughters' young friend. "Nate, my boy. I am afraid you have seen too much this afternoon. I am going to have to wipe your memory of all the magic you have seen."

Olympia and Pastoria exchanged concerned glances but said nothing to their father. It wasn't necessary to erase Nate's memory. He already knew the Blanchards were witches, but they were not going to reveal this fact to their parents. They watched downtrodden as their father performed a simple spell, removing every memory of witchcraft from Nate Caldwell's mind. When it was over, he no longer remembered Olympia and Pastoria's secret.

CHAPTER TEN

Another Year, Another No

The days were growing shorter, and a distinct crispness was in the air. The trees which had cloaked the house in shadow at the start of Autumn, now stretched long dark arms across the yard cast by the retracting Winter sun. Once the shadows began to take their new December path, the grass faded from its green, withering to a dismal gray. The leaves had long rejected summer's conformity to identical green, demonstrating their arrogance of scarlet, amber, and gold. Their hubris was fading now, browning to dry brittle paper, loosening their hold onto cold branches, falling to the crunchy ground. It was that time of year again, and with the beginning of Winter came an old argument which was never won.

"Please, Father, please!" Pastoria begged. "Everyone else gets to have a Christmas tree. Why can't we?"

Angharad, usually the stern one, simply shrugged her shoulders towards her husband, acquiescing to his decision. But Constantinople was adamant in his point of view. "I believe it is a sin to destroy the life of a living thing, just to use as decoration for a few paltry days."

Pastoria wasn't letting it go that easily. She'd been practicing her response well before she engaged in the fight. "But we cut flowers and put them in vases. You don't mind that. In fact, you say it is lovely."

"The cutting of blossoms does not kill the plant itself. Quite the contrary, removing blooms propels the plant to grow larger. Chopping down a tree only kills the tree forever."

Olympia, grateful to her sister for taking up the mantle this year, knew from her past experiences the argument was futile. Still, she couldn't allow Pastoria to stand alone. Olympia joined in to try to sway him, "But Christmas trees are so beautiful. Just think of it, Father! We could stand it in the window with pretty colored lights and tinsel. We could string popcorn to wrap around it and hang some of the apples we have in the barn that we picked at harvest. It would be so festive."

Constantinople made an unapproving face and replied, "Remember when our cow Millie died? Would you have thought her pretty had we covered her with lights and strands of aluminum string? Would the dead cow have been festive had we wrapped her with strings of popcorn and apples?"

Olympia furrowed her eyes, "Well that would have been disgusting."

"Precisely, daughter. And it is the same thing with a tree. The trees on Blanchard land are just as alive as the cow was."

"We ate the cow," Pastoria murmured under her breath.

For a split second, Olympia thought she saw a smile she could not suppress come to her mother's mouth, but Angharad stopped it before she could be certain.

"Mother," Olympia asked. "What do you think?"

Angharad stood from her chair and glided to her husband, placing her long thin hand upon his foreman. "I believe your father has spoken. We do not question his wisdom in this house."

The children stomped angrily up the stairs to their rooms, murmuring comments their parents could not hear but were certain were disrespectful. Angharad was about to follow them to discipline them for their insolence, but her husband pulled her back gently. "Let them enjoy their disappointment."

"I will not have them denigrate your authority," she said haughtily. "I should take switches to their legs for it."

"Let them be," Constantinople grinned, pulling her onto his lap. She tried to rise, but he held her down playfully. "They are upstairs. You are free to show a little affection, my love."

"I do not like them dissenting from your word."

He laughed at her. "Like you?"

Angharad eyed him indignantly, "I always defer to your decisions. You are my husband. I never defy you."

"No," he agreed. "You don't. But you do believe I am wrong." She made an attempt at acting offended, but he didn't allow her the chance. "I saw your face. You were disappointed for them. You see nothing wrong with the children having a tree."

"No," she admitted. "I do not. I have killed many a tree in the line of duty. It was necessary to save lives. I believe the earth forgives me for the slight. I too have great respect for nature. But Stanton, a Christmas tree is only once a year. We had trees in my village when I was a girl."

It grieved him how none of his family quite understood his point. If he could only make his wife understand. "A great many trees are led to the slaughter for the celebration of December 25th."

"I suppose you are correct, husband. It does seem a frivolous fancy and I am not prone to frivolous fancies. However, a few trees..."

It was that very reasoning which bothered Constantinople the most. "There are far more trees living upon this earth than there are people. Still, I have seen you risk imminent death to save humans from danger. Could I not simply say, there are plenty of people. Why bother?"

She lowered her head in defeat. "And we all spring to existence from the same ground," she noted. "All life is precious."

Deciding to chastise her no more, he gave her a pat on the leg and admitted, "With total certainty I know I am being inflexible. However, my beliefs are mine to honor or dishonor. And I do not feel like dishonoring them this year. We will still have a Merry Christmas, with or without a tree. The girls will have presents from St. Nikolas, and it will be a fine holiday."

Angharad nodded in agreement, resting her head uncharacteristically against his chest. "Perhaps the girls can string popcorn along the stair banister and hang apples from the rail?"

Lifting her head into his hands, he kissed his wife passionately. "I wish they knew how much you *do* care. You are such a cold little thing to everyone but me."

"I only have capacity for one great love, Stanton. It is not my fault you claimed the position long ago."

CHAPTER ELEVEN

A Walled Heart

If there was one thing Olympia Blanchard despised about school, besides the cruel taunting children she was forced to spend her day with, it was taking a math test. In most all other subjects she excelled, but not math. Ironically, Zelda was a whiz at mathematics, yet terrible with Geography—Olympia's best subject. It stood to reason the two of them should help the other study for the two upcoming exams.

The girls sprawled themselves leisurely upon the living room floor, books open and pencils clinched between their teeth as they scanned the chapters to be included in tomorrow's test. Olympia did her best to learn on her own but as she stared at the complicated fraction problem before her, anything she'd learned in class rushed out of her head.

"I don't think anyone could figure this one out!" she exclaimed, slapping the pencil down.

Zelda titled her head to scan her friend's work and answered, "It's 2 and 6/8ths. Reduce it down to 1 and 3/4ths."

Olympia sighed in frustration. "How do you know that? You didn't even write it down or work it out?"

"I dunno," Zelda remarked. "I jus' know numbers pretty good. One day I'll make a fortune running odds at the racetrack."

Realizing she hadn't reciprocated the help in a while, Olympia leaned over to glance at Zelda's map of the United States. The entire paper was smudged from erase marks and rewritten names of states. "How is yours going?"

Zelda scoffed at the sheet and said, "Terrible. We got 48 states. But I done listed 56."

Not meaning to laugh, Olympia couldn't help it. "How did you arrive at 56 states?"

"Beats me," Zelda said thrusting her worksheet into Olympia's hand.

Olympia's parents had always stressed the importance of Geography. Perhaps it was because their work with The Consort took them all over the nation and even sometimes into Europe. The Blanchard children could locate almost any country, state, town, or territory known to civilized man. A quick scan of the sheet alerted Olympia to the issue.

"So right here, Zel, you've messed two up. Hawaii and Alaska are not states. They are about to be, but it hasn't passed yet." Olympia bit the metal part of her pencil, tasting the eraser on her tongue. "And Boston isn't a state. Neither is Chicago."

"They ain't?" Zelda asked. "We learned a lot about that massacre and those tea people in the state of Boston."

"The city of Boston," Olympia corrected. "It is in Massachusetts."

"Well, I didn't forget Massachusetts! Its writ down right there by Pennsylvania."

Olympia nudged her shoulder into Zelda's as she chuckled again. "Yes, but Massachusetts is not by Pennsylvania. Since you have Massachusetts listed, you can erase Boston. Also, Chicago is a city in Illinois. Those corrections along with Alaska and Hawaii, will eliminate four of your eight extra states."

Zelda reached over to retrieve her paper only to have Olympia pull it back as her eyes looked more closely. "Zelda, this is still all *really* wrong. And you completely forgot about West Virginia."

"That ain't a place." Zelda sneered.

"Yes, it is!" Olympia exclaimed in amused frustration. "It is to the left of Virginia."

Zelda took another look at her map and squinted her eyes, "Then where's East Virginia?"

"There is no East Virginia. It's just called Virginia."

Zelda was thoroughly confused. "Why ain't it called East Virginia?"

"Because it is just called Virginia."

"Well, that's stupid," Zelda cried. "Why name two states the same name anyway? Why not jus' call it Adams?"

Olympia looked at her friend inquisitively, "Why Adams?"

As if it were the most obvious explanation in the world, Zelda slapped her forehead and answered, "He was the second President. We already gotta state called Washington, but we ain't gotta state named Adams."

Ignoring her ridiculous argument, Olympia stated, "Because they called it West Virginia. There is no place called Adams."

"Well, that ain't my fault."

The study session was interrupted when Olympia's parents came home from town, Pastoria with them. Immediately, they knew something was wrong. Pastoria looked as if she'd been crying. Angharad passed through the room, silently stepping over the girls on the floor to carry her two sacks of groceries to the kitchen, Constantinople stood towering over them.

"Zelda," he asked softly. "May I speak to you privately in my study?"

Swallowing a big lump in her throat, the nervous child stood from the floor to follow. Olympia clasping Zelda's hand, walking with her to the study where she gave it a quick squeeze in friendship before Zelda disappeared behind the door with Mr. Blanchard.

Returning to the living room where her sister still stood, Olympia asked, "What's going on?"

Holding back tears, Pastoria told her, "Zelda's little brother died."

"What?" Olympia shrieked, covering her mouth quickly. "How?"

Pastoria sat on the edge of the coffee table. "We were at the store—not the one Zelda's parents run, but the good one, you know. Then an ambulance came screeching down the road and stopped in front of their market. Father walked over to see what was happening. He came back and told us. Little Zeb was all by himself in the stock room when a wall mounted shelf collapsed on him."

Olympia began to cry, "That poor little boy! This is terrible! Oh my God, poor Zelda."

The study door opened. Zelda, red eyed and puffy cheeks, was completely distraught. Somehow Constantinople's hand on her shoulder was helping her hold it together. Olympia ran to her friend, flinging her arms around her. Zelda cried on her shoulder for a minute until she forced herself to stop.

"Zelda will be staying with us for several days," Constantinople told his daughters. "Let's give her parents time to process what has happened."

What he did not tell them, especially Zelda, was that her parents had shown little emotion after the accident. They had appeared more concerned with how the accident happened rather than the accident itself. Their comments to the sheriff sounded as if they blamed the boy for climbing the shelves instead of grieving the loss. Constantinople held hope that perhaps they were the stoic sort and by providing them time alone they might begin to process their grief. The last thing he wanted to expose young Zelda to was the apathetic indifference of her parents.

Angharad returned from the kitchen. Without saying a word, she drifted into the room and took Zelda gently by the hand, withdrawing her back to the small Blanchard kitchen just off the living room. Sitting her at the small Formica table in front of the stove, Angharad grasped the child's hands across the table.

"You have suffered a loss. Your very first in life. It is an important moment."

Zelda found herself almost mesmerized by Mrs. Blanchard as she spoke. She knew her to never be a very caring woman and these words she spoke to Zelda carried a coldness which should have been off putting, yet it wasn't. Zelda understood she was being given a piece of wisdom from someone who knew a great deal about life and the world.

"Death is always coming, Zelda." Angharad continued. "It will eventually catch each of us. It has captured your young brother this day, and for that you have my deepest sympathy."

"Thank you." Zelda muttered, not really knowing how to reply.

"Steel yourself Zelda." Angharad's eyes flared with an urgency—or perhaps a caution. Whatever she was conveying, it was clear to Zelda that Mrs. Blanchard meant to be helpful. In her own severe way, she was imparting her wisdom so that the child may never suffer the same pain again. She continued her thought, "Steel yourself against the agony too much love can bring. You cannot be hurt if you do not care."

Zelda's eyes rose to meet Angharad's as she now understood the meaning.

"You love greatly child. You love my daughters. You have become their sister. That is fine. It is too late to prevent. But let that be your only love. Love no more if you can. Love is power. And we must always shield our power from anything designated to take it. A walled heart is a difficult thing to break."

CHAPTER TWELVE

The Metamorphosis

Time was passing quickly for the Blanchard sisters. Weeks became months, months became years. It was Autumn once again and the trees surrounding Blanchard House began to shed their green apparel for warmer shades of red, orange, and gold. Olympia and Pastoria were getting older. Gone were the puffy round cheeks and scraped knees of childhood. In their place were slender figures, unblemished skin, and the delicate features of young ladies.

The Blanchard girls, despite their growing up, were still being shielded by their father from whatever evil things were happening in the world. They remained in the dark on the various missions assigned to their father or mother when such events occurred. Constantinople clung to his adamancy his daughters should be shielded from the knowledge of what existed out there beyond the sanctuary of Blanchard House. "I want our girls to feel safe. Time will come soon enough when they must know what lurks in the shadows."

"They are not girls any longer, Stanton," his wife argued. "They are young women now. If properly trained, they could be warriors. Think of the assistance they might provide in the field. Take for example their help when The Rain People attacked two years ago. They are ready."

Rarely had Constantinople ever raised his voice to his wife as he did now. "I will never allow them to accompany us on our missions, Angharad! There will be no further mention of it. I have allowed you to train them. That must be enough."

Had he been any man other than her husband, Angharad would have struck him for his tone with her. However, warrior she might be, she was still conventionally a woman of her time and when she chose to marry him, she elevated him to a standing which her convictions would not challenge. "I withdraw my opinion."

He suddenly felt ashamed for having spoken harshly to her. Whereas her convictions kept her from contradicting her husband's authority, his principles dictated he upheld his wife with honor. "I barked unnecessarily, my dear." He took her hand. She was not eager for him to but did not retract it. "Perhaps they will never have to fight. The Association missions have all been rather successful as of late. Perhaps, just perhaps, by the time they are adults the evils will have been eradicated."

Those evils of which he spoke were not eradicated yet, and when the call came from the King of The Consort, requesting that both Constantinople and Angharad depart on a particularly dangerous mission, there was no other choice than to leave the girls at home alone. Constantinople was not in favor of this but understood there were no alternatives. The assignment required the skillsets of both he and his wife, leaving no room for refusal. Angharad held no qualms about leaving the girls for a few days. Olympia was 14 years old now, more than capable of managing things around the house, Angharad asserted.

Olympia felt emboldened by the turn of events. She and her sister had never been allowed to stay alone. Typically, on the rare occasion where both their parents were away, the Council sent an elder woman to stay with the girls. To now be of age where that would not be necessary, made Olympia feel an independence she'd known. With much reluctance, Constantinople said goodbye to his daughters, kissing them each on the cheek as he made his way to the car. Angharad delivered no tender partings, she merely said goodbye and reminded the girls to tend to the animals and the gardens. As the car disappeared out of sight down the long dusty road, the Blanchard sisters were exhilarated to have the house to themselves.

"We gotta throw a party!" Zelda exclaimed the moment the sisters called her to say they were home without supervision.

"Can we, Olympia?" Pastoria squealed.

As if summoning a portion of her mother's severity, Olympia shook her head. "No parties. Father trusts us. Besides, who would come anyway? Nate? Lorna Daihmler? Maybe Cheston Burke. Who else even talks to us at school?"

No, the Blanchard girls threw no parties as other autonomous teenagers might have done. Olympia ruled the house as though her parents were still there. Vegetables to pick in the garden. Grapes to gather from the vineyard. Clothes on the line to be taken in and ironed. And a large house to keep spic and span. Not to mention they still had school to attend and homework to complete. Luckily, Nate Caldwell was more than willing to pick them up every morning and drive them home every afternoon.

It was quite a change to have the house to themselves, but after a day or two it came to feel quite natural. Olympia was pleased with how well they were managing things. It was only on the fourth night of her parents being away, when she began to feel an anxiousness, she could not quell. She found herself unable to fall asleep that night. The chirping sounds of cicadas which normally went unnoticed by her, kept her mind alert and on edge. Something felt *off*. Had she tried to describe it to someone, all she could have said was that it felt like a shuddering within her blood. She crept out of bed and stepped into the darkened hallway. A sliver of moonlight cast through the window at the hall's end, lighting a triangular pattern along the wall. She saw a doorknob turn as it caught the light. Pastoria stepped out from her bedroom into the moonbeam.

"What's happening?"

"I don't know," Olympia replied softly. "I feel strange."

"Me too," Pastoria replied. "Like something drained out of me."

Olympia nodded silently, afraid to speak her thoughts to the air as if it might give them power. But it was exactly as Pastoria described. She'd felt the same only had not been able to put it into such adequate words. Something from inside her essence emptied out. She'd never felt anything like it before. The sensation frightened her. Refusing to voice the fear, Olympia was nonetheless plagued by the thought. *Did Father die?* Pastoria accompanied her sister back to bed, deciding to sleep the remainder of the night together but unable to explain why they felt they should. Pastoria returned to sleep after half an hour, snoring lightly into the soft down pillow. Olympia did not sleep. Her mind racing with worries. She wondered if perhaps there might be someone she could call in the morning. Perhaps that Mr. Uding she knew from the Consort meetings. She had gotten to know his son Brimford rather well. They always hung out together at the Consort meetings. Perhaps she could rely on his friendship to coerce his father into providing answers.

When morning came, Olympia phoned Nate to tell him she and her sister were feeling unwell and would not be going to school that day. Pastoria came down the stairs as Olympia wrapped up the call and asked, "We are staying home?"

Olympia gave her a concerned look as she set the receiver back down on the telephone. "I believe we should."

Both girls jumped suddenly as the phone rang on the table with the receiver still clutched in Olympia's hand. She snatched it back up to her ear, "Hello?"

"Lympy!"

"Zelda? Is that you?"

"Yeah," her friend shouted through the telephone. "Girl, I got a bad feelin'. Woke up from it last night."

Olympia locked eyes with her sister, still standing on the stairs. She could hear Zelda clearly even though the phone was pressed to Olympia's ear. Zelda had one of those voices. "We felt something last night too, Zelda." Olympia replied.

"Zelda too?" Pastoria whispered. "Weird."

Olympia continued, "Zelda, did it feel like something inside you just emptied out?"

"Naw," Zelda replied. "Nuttin' like that. It was like when I get one of my premonitions. I just could tell something bad just happened. But weirdly I knew you and Pastoria was safe."

"I think something might have happened to my father." The moment Olympia spoke the words she felt she'd set something terrible into motion by speaking it aloud. Pastoria's eyes betrayed the same fear.

"I'm comin' over." Zelda announced.

"How?" Olympia asked. "You do not have a car. You don't know how to drive anyway. And no bus runs all the way out here. We are alright. If we hear anything we will tell you. Go to school and get our assignments for us. Tell the teachers we are sick."

"Okay," Zelda said. "But I wish I was there with ya'll. Keep me in the loop."

Throughout her 10 years of life, Pastoria Blanchard had always known her sister to be her friend, her partner, her confidante...her equal. She now began to observe a different side of Olympia growing through this uncertainty they were feeling. Whereas Pastoria found herself nervously ungrounded by the possibility something might be wrong, Olympia was presenting a quiet collectedness. Pastoria tried to distract herself with television or listening to record albums. Anything to cut through the noise in her head. But Olympia situated herself in a comfortable chair in the fourth-floor tower room looking out in quiet contemplation. From her vantage point she could see all four corners of the Blanchard land. Sipping from a glass of sweet tea she only refilled when needed from the pitcher on the table beside her, Olympia waited. She spent hours watching for any sign of her parents returning down the long country dirt road. Pastoria brought up a tray of sandwiches for lunch and then later a tray for dinner. Sometimes Pastoria sat with her, neither girl saying much, until the younger Blanchard's nerves could no longer take the idleness. Her patience was not as steely as Olympia's. The quiet driving her back downstairs again to watch television.

As darkness fell and bedtime loomed, Pastoria once again climbed the three flights of stairs to where Olympia still sat watch. "We should go to bed." Pastoria advised. "No word has come. Brimford said he could not reach his father. There may not even be anything to worry about. We just had a strange feeling, that's all."

"It was more than a feeling."

"Still. You can't just sit here until they come home, Olympia. Let's go to bed."

Olympia turned away from the window just long enough to give her sister a small smile. "You go. It's all right. I'll come down later. I just want to sit here a while longer."

"How can I go to bed and leave you sitting up?"

Olympia gave a short laugh, "Because I am the big sister. It comes with the territory."

Pastoria bid her goodnight and went downstairs to her room. Olympia continued her watch into the night. She never wavered from her vigil. She never drifted off in accidental sleep. It was as if she could feel something approaching out there in the recesses of the night. Whatever had happened, she would know very soon.

It was just a little before midnight when she saw the faint headlights pass behind the trees lining the road. As the car came closer into view beneath the moonlight, she recognized the red DeSoto. She stood from her chair, her legs wobbly from inactivity, and made her way down. She was at the top of the second floor landing when she heard the front door unlock, keys flung onto the foyer table. Her father was standing in the doorway.

"Father."

Without removing his eyes from the floor, he greeted her. "Hello, Olympia."

All her life, Olympia Blanchard marveled at her father's indelible spirit. He filled any room he was in with whatever gregarious and powerful aura existed within him. But now, now he seemed different. Deflated. He looked almost shrunken, and his eyes had still not looked at her. Bruises covered some of his face, and the way he held his right arm gave her the impression it might be injured.

She walked down the stairs, placing her gentle hands upon his cheeks. Lifting his face to meet hers, she asked, "Father, what has happened?"

She had never seen her father cry before. Never even considered it was possible for him to do so. Now with his face resting in her hands, Olympia saw the tears flow from his irritated red eyes. Her hands were wet from it. He looked pitiful as she looked up at him. Broken.

"Mother did not survive?"

He collapsed into his eldest daughters' arms, sobbing uncontrollably for many minutes. It was a strange new arrangement for her. Always it had been him to provide comfort. He who knew how to soothe her anguish. And now as she lowered them both to the floor to better cradle him in her arms, Olympia understood she was to be his rock now.

How long she held him she did not know. She kept him in her arms as long as he needed to be there. Once he was cried out, he rose to his feet, pulling her up with him, and bid her goodnight. Olympia watched him climb the stairs. His arm was injured—she could tell now by the way he didn't grasp the handrail. His leg was limping too. She would see to his injuries tomorrow.

Olympia stood in the foyer for the longest time. She felt similar to a caterpillar taking its required moments to shed its cocoon. What was being born now was something new. A new Olympia. One much would be required from. She felt no sadness other than what she felt for her father. She felt no personal grief. No tangible loss. Angharad was gone and with her the brittle energy she gave off. The four were now three and Olympia was woman of the house.

The days following Constantinople's return changed the dynamic of Blanchard House forever. Lost without his wife, Olympia's father began turning to her with questions, seeking her opinion on practically everything. Pastoria was keenly aware of the change as she watched her father lose some of his strength and Olympia appeared to be gaining her own. Pastoria tried to comfort her father as best she could, but like Olympia, it was difficult to pretend to grieve someone you never felt close to.

There was no funeral for Angharad Blanchard because there was no body. Try as she might to discover why no remains of her mother existed, Olympia's father refused to speak on the subject. In his mind, Angharad was dead, and everything must resume without her. He would not even explain her death to her daughters because it was inconsequential. Or perhaps, it had been too horrible for him to relive.

It was a few days after Constantinople's return, when Olympia answered a knock at the front door. As the visitor came into view, she thought for a split second her father had been mistaken and her mother was alive after all. But when the light from inside hit the woman's face, Olympia realized it was not her mother, although they shared many similarities. The woman stepped inside without invitation and greeted

Olympia. As if recognizing the voice from a dream long forgotten, Olympia knew at once who she was.

"You are my mother's sister. I met you once when I was little."

The austere woman forced an insincere smile. "I am Dagmara."

Constantinople had been in ear shot of the door and upon hearing Dagmara's voice came quickly, escorting her to the privacy of his study. Not much could be deciphered from behind the door as Olympia and Pastoria tried to listen. Voices were raised then lowered several times.

When the doors opened and the two came out, Dagmara stared at her nieces for a moment then approached them almost nervously. Outstretching both hands towards them, she waited an uncomfortable amount of time before they reciprocated and clasped her hand.

"It is regretful we have not been close." Dagmara began. "Your mother's demise most likely dissolves any future possibility of knowing one another. I wish you well in life girls. If you ever have need of me, your father knows how to contact me."

She turned to Constantinople. He gave her a slight nod of compliance before saying, "You will let the family know?"

Dagmara answered, "I will. I will explain she died valiantly, and the means of her death erase any possibility of a cremation. I bid you good fortune Constantinople Blanchard." With that, Angharad's sister disappeared out of the door and out of their lives forever.

Confused by the vagueness, Olympia questioned her father. "That was Mother's sister, correct?"

"You already know that it was, daughter. Ask your true question."

Olympia stepped closer to him, ensuring she could see his face when she asked, "She mentioned 'the family'. Does Mother have family besides her sister?"

Constantinople sighed and nodded his head. "She does. In Europe."

Pastoria was amazed. It had never occurred to her there might be more relatives out there. Her mother never spoke of any. "Why have we never met them, Father?"

Constantinople held firm in his response implying this to be the last time the subject was to be spoken. "Your mother's family come from dark places. They are best left to themselves. You two are Blanchards. Blanchards only. It is all you ever need to be."

CHAPTER THIRTEEN

The First Christmas Tree

Though she'd never had too much trouble wheedling what she wanted from her father throughout her life, Olympia Blanchard had never been successful in winning the Christmas tree fight. All during her formative years Constantinople Blanchard denied very little to his daughters, especially to his eldest. But no matter how many years she tried; Olympia could never convince him to allow Blanchard House to have a Christmas tree. It wasn't as if her father was against Christmas. Every December 25th his children were the recipients of presents just like other children their age. Yet when it came to the tradition of a tree, he had proven himself unyielding. While most modern Americans of the 1950's lived under the assumption the Christmas tree was as old a tradition as Christmastime itself, Olympia's father knew from the history his father taught him, that the Christmas tree was a relatively new idea—not even 100 years old. It was England's Queen Victoria's husband, Prince Albert, who began the implementation of a Christmas tree in the mid 1800's. Within a few years, everyone in Europe and America was pretending it had always been the custom.

Constantinople Blanchard cherished life. All life. And he felt it his duty as a witch to protect natural life to the fullest. In his eyes, a living tree was as sacred as a newborn baby or a freshly hatched sparrow. The now ubiquitous custom of chopping evergreens down every December to wither and die in a living room was an abominable attack on The Natural Order.

"Why if you consider all the millions of households in the world who chop down a living tree simply to string decorations and lights across it every year, imagine how many trees this earth loses." His argument was sound, and he knew it. "Trees in which we derive oxygen. Trees which house and shelter other living creatures. It is a despicable custom which holds no moral merit."

No, Olympia and Pastoria had never won the Christmas tree battle in all the years of their childhood. But things changed after their mother died. Their father lost most of his passion for things, even arguments.

Angharad's death was still shrouded in mystery for them. The most they could ever get their father to say was she died heroically in battle and the evil they'd been sent to destroy was destroyed. He would say nothing more. But more than Angharad died in that enigma of a battle. Constantinople died as well, or at least half of him. Perhaps that was why when December rolled around, and Olympia posed her yearly request to install a Christmas tree, he did not wage his annual fight. It was quite a shock to Olympia when she heard him reply, "I really don't care. As long as it is artificial. No real trees. There are fake ones now in stores. If you and your sister need a tree to make this season merry...go buy one."

He might as well have told her she'd won the Irish Sweepstakes. Never in her life had Olympia felt she'd scored such a win! Without a moment's hesitation she dragged her sister out of the house by the arm, hopped into the family car and drove immediately into town to pick up Zelda. Zelda was as shocked as they were to hear Mr. Blanchard finally caved on the subject of Christmas trees. This would be a historic event and the three of them decided to make a day of it!

Before setting out on their task, the teenage girls detoured to the Rexall drug store on Main Street to have a chocolate milkshake—sustenance for the mission of finding the perfect tree. While sitting at the counter sipping their delicious frosty treats, a boy they knew from school wandered in. He plopped down on the stool beside Olympia.

"How many times have I asked you to come here with me so I could buy you an ice cream float, Olympia Blanchard?"

Pastoria rolled her eyes at Zelda. It was going to be yet another scene where a boy was going to flirt with Olympia, and she was going to play him like a yo-yo. Olympia gifted the boy one of her trademark smiles as she flashed her azure eyes his way. "Now, Nate Caldwell. You haven't asked me for a date in over a year."

The handsome teenager frowned as he adjusted his baseball cap so the bill face behind him, allowing his face closer proximity to hers. "Guess I got tired of you saying no. Are you saying now you'd go out with me if I asked?"

Olympia twirled a few strands of her platinum hair around her slender finger as she pursed her lips to take another sip from the straw. Once she'd finished, she nudged her shoulder into Nate's and gave a playful wink. "I suppose we will never know until you ask."

Nate blushed but felt empowered by her newfound interest. "Consider yourself asked. This Friday night? Movie? Then here for a sandwich and shake?"

"We'll see," Olympia replied. Pastoria and Zelda exchanged one more exasperated look as they watched Olympia remove herself from the stool in an almost sultry manner—much slower than she would normally rise. The way she shifted and turned, the way she delicately swayed her shoulders to allow her hair to fall against the side of her cheek, looked like something a movie vixen would do to entice her latest prey. And Nate Caldwell was eating it up. Nervously he shifted the cap back again and smiled for no good reason other than he had no idea what to say.

"Call me, Nate." Olympia said as she moved to the end of the counter to pay the bill. Nate nodded a wordless yes and stumbled awkwardly towards the door.

"What the hell was that all about?" Zelda exclaimed once the boy was gone.

"It is called being a woman, girls." Olympia said with an arrogance she had acquired a few years ago when puberty gave her the extra helping of everything she now possessed.

"Since when do you like Nathan Caldwell?" Pastoria demanded to know. "He's chased after you for years and you just ignore him."

Olympia peered out of the drugstore window, watching the boy walking away. "He didn't look like that last year. He's very cute now. Really cute."

Zelda got up from her stool and downed the rest of her milkshake with one gulp. "Are we buying a Christmas tree today or are we watching Lympy practice her mating call?"

The three teenage girls left the drug store and walked down the block to Ward's Department store. Upon entering the building, the girls were mesmerized by the shimmery tinsel Christmas garlands overhead and oversized Christmas trees decorating the store for the holidays. They didn't often come to Wards. It was much too far out of Zelda's family's price range, and although Constantinople Blanchard had managed to earn a reasonably comfortable income for his family, he was a frugal man when it came to such things. Olympia was still finding it hard to believe he'd given her a blank check to buy a tree.

It took some prodding to urge Olympia out of the clothing section. She spied several garments she longed to try on. For a moment she considered using the check for new clothes. She felt certain her father wouldn't care as long as she kept the cost in line with what she was allowed to spend on the tree. And if she bought fashion rather than the thing he was normally so opposed to, she felt sure he wouldn't squawk. But upon further reflection she admitted to herself it would be a shame to forgo the tree she'd wanted all her life and only now won the battle for, just for a couple of new dresses.

The Christmas tree section was elaborate. Trees of varying heights and widths filled the space. Some were made of aluminum tinsel. Some from plastic fibers emulating pine needles. Some appeared to be made of silklike threads. After about an hour of consideration, Olympia and Pastoria agreed the faux pine tree was the right height and width for their living room. It was also much simpler to assemble. One center pole with holes painted various colors which corresponded to the painted ends of the different tree branches to be placed there. It was easy to understand, although Olympia feigned confusion long enough for the handsome store clerk to demonstrate the method twice. It also was on sale, which allowed more money to be spent on lights and decorations.

Olympia paid for the tree and decorations at the counter and arranged for the store's delivery man to bring it out to the house that very evening. Normally delivery would be the next day, but Olympia gave a repeat performance of her vixen persona and within minutes the drooling delivery boy agreed to drive the tree out personally after he got off work.

Constantinople did not come downstairs while the girls were decorating the tree. He often disappeared to his room after dinner these days. His grief for his wife reached even deeper than his daughters were aware. Perhaps this was because he shielded them from it. He never wanted them to sense he was not the picture of strength they so heavily depended upon. Or perhaps, it was simply that his daughters were teenagers now. Too wrapped up in their own self-serving machinations to notice anyone else at all. But he wasn't fooling anyone. His daughters knew he was not the same man as before. His anguish covered him like a long trench coat. The girls pretended not to notice as to not make him feel worse. It was also easier to ignore his pain in order to hide the fact they felt none of their own. It was the unspoken truth between the sisters that neither of them missed their mother.

With their father upstairs, the Blanchard sisters began their joyful decking of the halls. The living room began ringing with the sounds of a Bing Crosby Christmas album on the record player. With Bing's buttery voice dazzling the senses, she and

Pastoria began stringing the shiny new colored Christmas lights.

"Is it weird us doing this?" Pastoria asked, speaking the long unspoken thing between them. "Are we wrong to be this excited about Christmas? I mean, Mother is gone. Shouldn't we feel something? Shouldn't we be sadder, like Father?"

Olympia was on the floor reaching behind the tree, placing a strand of lights as best she could without moving the tree away from the window. She poked her head out from the bottom branches and answered. "I don't know, Pastoria. I have thought about it a lot since she died. But when it boils down to it, it isn't our fault we aren't grieving. Isn't she responsible for that?"

Pastoria gave a silent shrug, ashamed of herself for being in agreement. They said nothing for a long time. It was only once all the lights were up and they had begun streaming red and gold garland around the tree when Pastoria admitted, "I didn't love her."

Olympia paused, letting the garland she was holding fall to the floor. She grabbed her sister's hand in her own and with a grimaced face, replied, "I didn't either. I think that's okay."

The tone was turning serious now. "What do you think will happen when it is just the two of us?" Pastoria asked.

Olympia gave her hand another squeeze. "Then you and I will look after each other, sister. It has always been you and me. And we have Zelda. If we have each other, we have family."

A little while later, with the living room lights doused so only the tree illuminated the room, Constantinople came downstairs. He paused in the doorway looking at the tree in its full brilliance. Olympia and Pastoria held their breath a moment, worried he would disapprove. But something unexpected happened. A smile they had not seen in months crossed his face.

"I must admit, it is lovely."

His girls moved to him, wrapping their arms around his waist, and tucking their heads under his strong arms. "It will be a cheery Christmas Father," Olympia said. "You will see."

Their father forced a polite grin and squeezed his girls close. "And I have the two of you. I'm sure we will have a merry Christmas together. And I truly do like this tree. I admit I was wrong. I suppose there is a first time for everything.

CHAPTER FOURTEEN

Another Consort

The new year came and went with little fanfare. The Blanchard family, now reduced to three, found their new footing. Olympia took complete charge of the house, including looking after her father when he was home, which wasn't often. The death of his wife sparked a fury in him to seek out and destroy as many of the worlds demonic forces as one man could. When he returned home, he now shared his adventures with his daughters. Olympia and Pastoria began a crash course education in the hidden things roaming the earth. Vampires were real. Werewolves were real. Ghosts. Poltergeists. Demons. Genies. Rogue witches. Cat people. Winged creatures some called Mothmen, some called Thunderbirds. He even talked of something called The Jersey Devil. He spoke of such creatures as if their existence was no more shocking than the African Zebras or Komodo Dragons of Indonesia which were also creatures the girls had never seen.

Olympia and Pastoria listened intently to every breath of his stories. All of them resulted in at least one of the monsters, if not all in the pack, being destroyed by their father's powers or his sword. Their father spared no detail in his exploits and the importance of the work he and other Association members did. He recognized his daughters were no longer children. His wife's words echoed in his brain pushing him to prepare them for the fight they may be forced to enter one day. The fourth floor Magic Room became a staple of their daily life. It was bothersome at first to the sisters who would rather be doing almost anything else. Dreary weather gave them some motivation to learn as Winter hadn't yet released its frigid hold over the outside. With nothing luring them outdoors their lessons did help pass the time. Constantinople no longer accepted complacency from his daughters when it came to their powers, pressing them harder and harder to grow them. Within a few weeks Pastoria could levitate the car with her telekinesis. And twice Constantinople directed

Olympia to pause the entire block of Main Street while in town buying provisions.

"Your powers are growing exponentially daughters," he told them. "One day you will have children and it will be your duty to teach them all I have taught you. The Natural Order must always be protected, and it is the witch who is divined to be its champion."

"If this is true," Pastoria asked him once, "Why are there sometimes bad witches you have to stop?"

Her father looked down upon her grimly, shaking his head in sorrow. "With immense power occasionally comes an equally immense narcissism. Witches who decide they are meant for greater things than their path dictates. They want to rule over others. Crush those who stand in their way."

"How can they live with themselves if they are hurting people?"

Her father could still see glimpses of the innocent little girl behind his maturing daughter's eyes. "A witch is also a man, or a woman. And for eons men have sought to consume the earth for their own selfish reasons. Look at Hitler. Genghis Khan. And this Fidel Castro fellow in Cuba right now. Man can be prone to corruption. They can become insatiable with power. Witches fall prey to the same."

It seemed impossible for Olympia and Pastoria to believe a witch could be evil. Of course, movies and books always wrote them that way, but every witch they'd ever known was kind and altruistic. But the Blanchard sisters were about encounter such a witch without even knowing it at the time.

The Consort was held that Spring in Nachez, Mississippi. It would indelibly stand out in Olympia's mind for many reasons, its location chief among them. As their father drove onto the Longwood plantation property, Olympia and Pastoria marveled at the glorious structure ahead. They'd never seen a completely octagonal house. Standing three stories tall with its own tower set atop it, the red brick mansion was the most beautiful house either of them had ever seen. The crisp white balconies lining each of the six sides looked like frilly lace curtains framing the illustrious balustrades.

"Father, this place is amazing!" Pastoria squealed from the back seat.

"It is an exercise of man's folly." Constantinople laughed. "In fact, it is nicknamed Nutt's Folly."

"I don't understand." Pastoria replied.

"You will."

Constantinople parked in the field adjacent to the great house where other arriving members of the Consort were parking. Exiting their own car a few yards away, Bristow Uding and his son Brimford waited for the Blanchards. "Constantinople! Good to see you, my friend. Isn't this an interesting location this season?"

"I find it rather amusing," Constantinople answered, shaking his head. "I must admit I've been curious to see the place. I have read stories."

Bristow bellowed, "Leave it to Paula Perkins to lease this place for the evening. You know the Nutt descendants have tried in vain to sell this place for years. I believe they are now hoping to donate it—if they can find an organization befuddled enough to take it on."

The Blanchard girls still had no idea what the men were talking about as they began to stroll towards the massive house. It was only when young Brimford took Olympia by the arm and began to explain when it all made sense. "Back before the Civil War began, Dr. Haller Nutt was immensely wealthy. He began construction on this house to be a showplace. Of course, the war changed all of that. He lost his lands, his fortune, and his slaves. What is left is a crying shame, but a testament to avarice."

Olympia was confused. "I don't know what you mean. It is simply gorgeous."

Brimford laughed and squeezed her arm. "It's a shell my sweet girl. Only a shell."

Upon entering Longwood, Olympia understood the joke everyone found so amusing. There was no interior to the house. The massive octagon mansion was completely unfinished as if workmen had evacuated the job that very day. Even after 70 years the wooden worktables still housed stacks of ossifying wood. Antique tools lay dust covered, abandoned by long ago workmen walking off a job to join a war of ideals they would never win. Tucked against red brick walls sat unopened wooden crates, possibly housing ornate cornices or carven trim pieces that would never be used. Rusty metal paint buckets with long dried paint clinging to the rim sat inside fireplace hearths where half painted mantels rotted from decades of dampness. High above her head Olympia could see the octagon atrium which would have been the domed cupola had it ever been completed. Now only a decaying plank board stairway to nowhere rose up in broken sections where workers once climbed to partially built higher floors, now collapsed and hauled away. Longwood was indeed a folly.

Of course, hostess for the Consort, Paula Perkins had done her best to spruce up the place. Hundreds of candles and gas lamps spread about the large enclosure, perched upon any table, crate, jutted brick, or edge of wood large enough to hold it. There were several ornate columns, never erected into place, still laying on their side across the floor. People were using them as benches while chatting with friends, catching up before the meeting. A refreshment bar and table buffet lined the back wall. Though there was not ample room to house the entire Consort, there was plenty of room for the curious to pop into the mansion's shell while grabbing something to eat or drink. Most of the meeting was to be held outdoors. Chairs, tables, and all the necessary amenities were lain out appropriately on the back lawn under covered tents.

Once she wandered outside to see the official setup, Olympia found herself drawn back inside the skeleton house. The sadness of its unfinished condition weighed upon her. She did not understand exactly why. Yet for some reason she was struck with an overwhelming pride in her own home. Blanchard House was not magnificent by any stretch of the imagination. But she liked its shape, and she liked its lack of pretension. No red brick folly for her family. White boards and solid construction were all she needed. Longwood never got its sweeping marble staircase, and Blanchard House didn't have one either. Plain and efficient was Olympia's home and she was proud of it. Even if by chance she did somehow marry well and become very rich, she would remember Nutt's Folly. Blanchard House was good enough for her for all the rest of her life.

"I suppose my family is luckier than the family who own this travesty," a young man said to Olympia as he approached her without warning.

She turned to see him. She'd never seen him before. He was sinister in appearance although not necessarily threatening. Handsome. But dastardly somehow. She did not like him although she had no reason as to why.

"We have never officially met, although we have seen one another at past meetings," the young man said with an old-world bow.

"Have we?" Olympia replied. "I have no recollection of it."

"Well perhaps my face is not memorable to one as lovely as you. It is doubtful you have a lack of suitors. You are an exquisite creature." As he said this, he brazenly stroked her long flaxen hair, grazing her bare shoulder with his knuckle. She pulled away.

"I am Olympia Blanchard." She said it not as an introduction but more of an explanation of why he was not worthy to be so familiar with her.

"I know who you are Miss Blanchard. I am Hugh. Hugh D'Angelo."

Disregarding her dislike for him, he gently perched his hand beneath her elbow, barely touching her, yet guiding her into a circle as he analyzed the room. "My family has a similar story as Longwood. Of course, our home was completed."

"I believe I have heard the tale," Olympia replied. "The House of Duquesne. It is said to be quite the monstrosity."

Hugh grimaced at the insult but did not deny it. "True, the outer structure of my ancestral home is a bit of an unpleasing visage. However, inside is quite magnificent. If you are ever in Charleston, I would deem it an honor to show you."

"I doubt I will ever be in Charleston."

Her coldness did not dissuade his pursuit of her company. "You never know Miss Blanchard. We have fine Balls in Charleston. Even a girl as refined as you would be impressed. And I would be most agreeable to escorting you to any one of them."

"That is kind." Olympia said through gritted teeth, doing her best to not resort to her mother's style of iciness but wishing this young man would go.

"You know Miss Blanchard," Hugh continued. "The D'Angelo family is as old and esteemed as the Blanchards. Imagine what a powerful dynasty could be forged if you and I were to one day marry."

She did not mean to laugh. He was oddly serious. Yet it escaped her mouth before she could suppress it. "Marry! And marry you? I don't even know you Mr. D'Angelo."

"Sometimes the most epic marriages come from strangers pledging their family's unity in wedlock. We are of age you know."

"I am 16 years old," Olympia scoffed. "And I have no desire to marry anyone, least of all you. I find you boastful, distasteful, and you waaaayyyy overestimate your own charm."

With that, Olympia strolled away from the impudent young man and found her sister outside on the lawn. Hugh D'Angelo was not the kind of person who forgave an insult. Still, an alignment with a Blanchard could be very fortuitous one day. He would swallow the egregious behavior and make a mental note to better woo her again in another year or two.

The fundamentals of The Witches Association meeting were pretty routine. A few votes were held over mundane things such as member dues and the location of a school planning to be built to house and educate orphaned witches. For the most part, Olympia and Pastoria looked to their father for how to cast their vote. Being full-fledged members of The Association now, their votes counted as much as anyone else's, even if they were a little uninformed on the topic. However, there was one vote where Olympia parted ways with her father. It concerned the witch's asylum known as Dredmore. Only a few times in her life did Olympia or her sister ever hear its name mentioned. From what she understood of the place it was dreadful (perhaps fittingly named). The worst of the worst were sent there. Witches who broke the laws of The Consort, or of man, would be stripped of their powers and confined to the asylum as their punishment.

The item on the ballot concerning Dredmore that night was whether or not nonwitches could begin to be confined there. Arguments were posed by some Association members that there were certain benefits to imprisoning beings such as Vampires and Rain People who could be starved and tortured into revealing the whereabouts of their nests. An almost equal amount of Association members opposed this idea, believing such fiends should be put to death the moment of their capture to eliminate any risk of their escape. With the Consort split over the issue, every vote was important. As Constantinople Blanchard spoke his vote against the measure, and his youngest daughter joined him with her vote, Olympia felt a twinge of guilt casting her vote in favor. She looked over to her father sitting on the other side of Pastoria. He gave her a gentle nod. When the votes were tallied, Olympia's side won. Dredmore could now be used to imprison all supernatural beings if the need arises.

With the members of the congregation now dismissed from the official meeting to go back to their socialization, Olympia took her father's hand timidly, "I'm sorry Father. After listening to the arguments, I feel as if the information they could acquire from such monsters carries a higher chance of saving lives than endangering them. But I did not wish to oppose you."

He patted his daughter on the shoulder, "Olympia, there is never a need to apologize for having a mind of your own. You voted how you felt. No shame in that at all."

Bristow Uding interrupted the Blanchards with a gregarious smile peeking out beneath his bushy moustache. "Well, well, Olympia, you are a woman of foresight! I too hated to disagree with your father, but I think we did some future good tonight with that last measure."

"Perhaps so." Constantinople offered generously.

"You know, Con," Bristow added. "I was just thinking...Olympia could make quite a good addition to our Protection department." He now addressed Olympia personally. "Many of us in The Consort have heard how valiantly you and your sister assisted your parents a few years ago when some of those Rain People attacked your house. You could be quite an asset to us."

Constantinople did not like the suggestion. Olympia read it plainly on his face. Trying not to be rude, but not minding being abrupt, Constantinople placed his hands upon his daughters' backs, escorting them away as he replied, "I have lost enough of my women to the cause. My daughters are not interested."

CHAPTER FIFTEEN

Zelda Sees All

It was nearing midnight when the ringing telephone startled Olympia from her sleep. Though faint, the shrill echo of the sound swept up the stairs to her bedroom. Jumping from bed, she dashed down to answer before her father was awakened. She'd warned her suitors not to call late in the night but that did not mean one wouldn't. Boys her age had recently discovered how easy it was to sneak liquor from their parents' cabinets before meeting friends out somewhere during the night. After a few shots of whatever was the easiest to steal, some of the boys had enough liquid courage to phone girls they were interested in. Of course, Olympia never entertained such calls from inebriated boys. Adolescent bravado was not the way to win her attention. Still, sometimes they tried.

When Olympia reached the downstairs foyer, she discovered her father was already holding the receiver in his hand. *Please don't let that be Paul Turner on the phone,* she quietly prayed to the universe. *He is such a sloppy drunk.* Her father saw her standing on the stairs but did not look cross with her. It probably wasn't one of her beaus.

"Are you alright?" Constantinople asked the caller, furrowing his brows to Olympia and waving his hand to urge her closer. As she moved nearer to him, he held the receiver away from his ear so she could hear as well. Immediately she recognized Zelda's voice. "No, do not worry about it. I am glad you called me." Constantinople told Zelda. "I will be right down to get you, my dear. You did the correct thing."

Hanging up the phone, he looked at Olympia with concern in his eyes. "It is Zelda. Her father has been drinking heavily. He is smashing things and she is afraid."

"Let's go."

On the drive to town Olympia thought about all the horrible things her best friend had been through in the last few years. After losing her little brother, Zelda's already sorrowful life took a darker turn. Her father began drinking. Her mother became even more disinterested in Zelda than she'd been before. Zelda's daily life was predominantly spent slaving in the store when not at school. Her only sanctuary being the times she could sneak off to Blanchard House. Then a few months ago her mother, too discontented with life to stay another day, ran off leaving Zelda and her father totally alone. That was when the drinking worsened. The store began to lose much of its business as the town figured out the only reliable time to even attempt to shop was after school hours when Zelda was home.

Downtown Daihmler was silent and empty of traffic as Constantinople parked along the sidewalk in front of the store. Before leaving the car, he turned to Olympia. "Normally I would have you wait. But I cannot use my power on him if he is behaving irrationally. I do not desire to harm the man. You stay behind me. If it seems necessary, I will direct you to freeze him in place while we get Zelda out of there."

Olympia obeyed and followed quietly. Constantinople did not ring a bell or knock. He used his powers to break the door bolt and let himself in. They could hear the commotion from the little apartment above the store. Marching up the rickety stairs, Olympia watched her father kick open the door to face the drunken man.

"Get the hell outta my house Blanchard!" His slurred words did not hide his agitation. Mr. Cooper grabbed a table lamp and tossed it at Constantinople, who simply used his powers to send the lamp crashing to the opposite wall. Mr. Cooper swayed a little from his alcoholic stupor. "I got witch powers too you know, you son of a bitch!" Zelda's father attempted to use whatever magic he assumed he still possessed. However, too many years of inactivity fogged his ability to summon them. Whatever his power might once have been, all that happened now was a table leg fell off the small dining table, causing the table to tip over, spilling his bottles of whiskey.

"Damn you Blanchard! You owe me three bottles!"

"I am here to collect Zelda," Constantinople announced. Peering around the room he spotted the teenage girl's eyes peeping from behind a door across the room. "It is alright Zelda. You are coming home with us."

"That gal's my kid, not yourn!" Mr. Cooper bellowed as he stepped forward and swung his mealy fist Constantinople's direction. Olympia's father needed no magic to combat the blow. He simply took one side step out of its path and watched the drunken imbecile fall over from the effort.

"Get some clothes together Zelda," Constantinople said gently. Zelda disappeared back behind the door where she could be heard rummaging around her room.

"You ain't taking that girl," Zelda's father said, attempting to stand by grasping the fallen table. The tabletop being round, only rolled to the right, causing him to lose his footing once again and land with a thud onto his knees.

"Mr. Cooper, you are not equipped at present to provide a stable home for your daughter. Until you can get yourself together and begin to make a decent life for the two of you, Zelda will be staying with me."

"That girl's got work to do round here and you ain't her daddy. I'm her daddy!"

Never had Olympia Blanchard witnessed fury in her father. She watched in astonishment as Constantinople lurched forward, snatching the disgusting man up from the floor by his arm. Slinging him into the wall, Constantinople roared directly into Mr. Cooper's face, "Then act like her father!" He released the man's arm, allowing him to slump back to the floor. Zelda came out of the back room with a sack full of clothes. She looked scrambled and afraid. Her normally high head was pushed down firmly between her shoulder blades. Constantinople reached out to place his reassuring hand onto her shoulder, directing her towards Olympia. He addressed Mr. Cooper again. "Until you can successfully provide for this girl and learn what it means to cherish a child God has gifted you, she will be with us. If you try to come after her I will report you to the authorities for child abuse." Olympia could not believe her ears when she heard what her father said next, "Or....I just might kill you and save everyone else the trouble."

Both Olympia and Zelda's eyes grew round as dinner plates as they made their way back down the rickety storeroom steps. As Constantinople opened the car door for the girls, he let out a raucous laugh. "Well, I suppose that scared the dickens out of him." He slapped Zelda on the back lightly and added, "Come Madam Zelda. You have a home with us for as long as you wish."

Once Olympia explained to Pastoria the following morning, nothing was said over the next few days about Zelda's father or the situation she'd fled. Life at Blanchard House went on as it normally did with the exception of Zelda's being there, which wasn't too strange of a situation considering she was there fairly often anyway.

No one at school knew anything about Zelda's problems primarily because she had few friends in the first place. Olympia, Pastoria, and Zelda rather enjoyed the new circumstances because they never tired of one another's company. School days were spent in classes, followed by homework, dinner and chores. No stranger to hard work, Zelda pitched in with everything, finding the work around Blanchard House to be far less taxing than her usual pursuit at home. On weekends when the girls weren't down at the creek fishing, or strolling through the woods, they were watching old Universal Monster movies in the afternoon on television or being escorted to the movie theater by Constantinople. Occasionally, Olympia had a date call for her and when this happened her father was even gladder to have Zelda for company with Olympia away. Pastoria was of the age now where she kept to herself listening to record albums or attempting, rather badly, to teach herself guitar. Zelda was a welcome companion in the house for Constantinople.

"Foretell the future, Madam Zelda," he would tease, trying to subtly help her hone her powers without it seeming like a lesson. He soon came to discover she was very skilled at the practice. She correctly predicted, two days before, the tornado which struck the town of Fayette. She also correctly declared the film, *On the Waterfront*, would sweep the Oscars. And she insisted the City Council had been bribed by a land developer to rezone a residential area for commercial property. Three days later, he read about the decision in the paper.

One evening while Olympia was out with Nate Caldwell and Pastoria was in her room strumming, out of tune, a song no one could recognize, Constantinople handed Zelda a Celtic designed carved wooden box housing a brand-new set of beautifully drawn Tarot Cards. "I ordered these for you, Madam Zelda. I noticed when you tune in to your power, you fiddle with the things around you. These will help you retain focus...and look very professional while doing it."

She laughed and thanked him. Opening the box, she inspected the cards carefully with her hands as if they were made of glass. The artistry of design was unlike anything she'd ever seen. These had to cost quite a lot of money, she thought to herself. "They are beautiful. Just so beautiful! I will cherish them forever."

"Read my fortune, my dear."

They settled themselves at the kitchen table where she withdrew the cards from the box, spreading them upon the table. The cards provided her no clairvoyant information, her own powers did that for her, but the cards did seem to calm her nerves and give her fidgety hands something to do while connecting to her second sight. Her visions came clearly and quickly regarding Mr. Blanchard. She described seeing him as a little boy, living there on Blanchard land, although it was a different house. She saw him walking to the creek to fish. She saw him reading at night to an elderly aunt who lived with his family before she died. Constantinople smiled at the memory, "She was my aunt Blaze Blanchard," he told Zelda. "I haven't thought of her in many years. I was boy when she died." Constantinople had always known Zelda had the gift of premonition, but seeing the past was not as common a gift. The part about fishing, or his family's old house could have been small things he or the girls may have mentioned in her presence over the years. But Blaze Blanchard was something he doubted he had ever talked about. He didn't even think his daughters knew about her. As he marveled at Zelda's keen insight, she said something else which took him by complete surprise. Something he had never divulged to anyone, proving this teenage girl indeed had a magnificent psychic ability.

"Who is Nacoma?"

His face turned a shade of white as he muttered, "Pardon me?"

"Yeah. I see a gal that calls herself Nacoma. Or Nikky. Nacarna? It's fuzzy. She was here. Not here 'excatly. The old house that used to be out in the back meadow. You was little. She looks some like Lympy, or how Lympy will look older. Was she a sister or cousin a' yours?"

Constantinople was astounded. How could she see this? It was bewildering. He stared at her in amazement. Zelda was seeing a person who did not even exist yet, but who had been a very fleeting part of his past.

"Madam Zelda," he smiled. "Your gift is truly remarkable, but I fear I can no longer allow you to read my fortunes."

She looked embarrassed. "I'm sorry, Mr. Blanchard. Did I offend you?"

He laughed and patted her hand. "No, my dear. Nothing of the sort. However, you did tap into a subject I am not at liberty to ever discuss. I assure you one day, many many years from now, you will know the answer to this woman's identity. She was a relative. Extremely distant, but a relative. One day, one day you will understand this special memory I possess. Alas, I cannot divulge its meaning without risking a great deal of harm to my family."

"Gotcha," she said, perfectly happy to drop the subject as long as she knew she had not done something wrong to this man who was always so good to her.

He leaned back into his chair and placed his hands behind his head. "I must say Zelda, I believe this is your true calling. You have a deft ability to see into people's minds. You could be a great source of guidance for people in need of it. No one can hide the truth from you. This could make you the greatest advisor anyone would ever know. This ability to see into people's minds coupled with your keen sense of seeing future events might provide quite a reasonable living for you in this world."

"Like it be my job?" She was all ears now.

"Why not?" he answered. "I have seen far more witches with far less power than you possess who make a living as paid psychic advisors. Not to mention the number of powerless charlatans out there amassing fortunes from their smoke and mirror trickery. You, Madam Zelda, are the real deal. Think about it."

"I will, Sir." She paused a moment, considering whether to say what she wanted to say. Again, she did not want to offend the only adult she'd ever known to be her champion. Yet she was compelled to say it, just in case it was something he might be haunted by. "Mr. Blanchard?"

"Yes, my dear," he said rising to return his coffee cup to the sink.

"I know something else. Something I seen last time I read you."

He stopped halfway across the tiny kitchen and turned back towards her. "What did you see?"

"She heard everything you said, Sir."

He dropped the coffee mug, shattering it on the linoleum floor. He darted back to the table and retook his seat. He faced the teenage soothsayer eye to eye. "What do you mean, Zelda?"

"She wasn't dead yet."

He gasped.

"She was very still and had her eyes closed when you found her. But she wasn't dead yet." Zelda empathically reached across the table and clutched his hands. She gingerly stroked his left-hand ring finger, where he still wore his marriage band. "She opened her eyes a bit and watched you kill that water sucker. She was weak, but she had jus' enough strength to look. She saw you take his head off with your sword. She knew you killed the monster that killed her."

Tears welling in his eyes, he repeated her words, "She saw it?"

"And she heard you when you went back to her. She heard you say those lovely things you said. She moved on knowing how much you loved her. And Mr. Blanchard, it made her real happy."

Constantinople leaned over and kissed Zelda's forehead gratefully. He wiped a tear from his cheek and left the room. Young Zelda remained in the kitchen, giving him space. She was glad now she'd told him. He did need to know. She understood now he had been wondering far too long. But she would never tell anyone of that memory. It belonged to he and his wife. He'd never wanted his daughters to know about their mother's awful and grotesque death. Zelda respected him enough to make sure they never heard it from her either.

CHAPTER SIXTEEN

Educating Olympia

During his senior year of high school, and the summer after, Nate Caldwell and Olympia Blanchard were considered a regular item. With the arrival of Autumn and his beginning Freshman classes at The University of Alabama, their dates had become infrequent. It had always been his father's plan for Nate to join him in the Finance business. Between his studies and working part-time in his father's office, Nate was left with little time for a social life. Olympia, a senior in high school now, was still living a carefree life with an unlimited number of suitors. Nate Caldwell was still her favorite beau, but she did not spend her nights waiting around on him to call. Once deemed the weird girl in her early school days, puberty had long shed that moniker and Olympia Blanchard was now regarded as the town beauty. She never went dateless on Saturday nights. Of course, she had heard nothing about Nate seeing other girls, so she still considered herself his girlfriend, even if she didn't consider him her boyfriend.

It was quite evident Nate was hearing rumors about Olympia being seen out with other boys when he called her up to practically demand they go on a date that evening. It probably eased some of his worry about Olympia and other guys, that she was never seen out alone with any of them. Not even in a car ride. Constantinople had seen to that, never wanting his daughter to be at the mercy of a date she wanted to escape, he purchased a car for her to maintain her independence. It was a little unheard of for a girl to have her own automobile, but Constantinople Blanchard didn't understand the logic. Most fathers worried themselves into a frenzy when frisky teenage boys drove their daughters off into the night. Olympia's car eliminated the concern as she always drove herself to and from dates. Olympia Blanchard was often seen tooling around town in her 1953 Chevy Sun Star convertible. She was quite a sight to behold on the streets of Daihmler in her mint green, chrome laden car riding with the top down, wearing large dark sunglasses with her long blonde hair sweeping back in the wind.

She parked in front of the diner where she was to meet Nate. Exiting the car brought her the usual number of heads turning to see her. She made a striking figure in her black and white polka dot dress as she strutted into the café. Two women on the way out of the diner took immediate offense when their husbands nearly knocked them down turning back to take a second look at Olympia.

As she made her way to Nate's table, he rose gallantly. "You look radiant tonight, Olympia."

"I always look radiant," she teased, allowing him to withdraw the chair for her. "Maybe you have just forgotten."

"Sorry it's been a while," Nate apologized. "Dad has been teaching me the ropes with the accounts he handles, and school is kicking my butt."

"I understand," Olympia said in a tone which made Nate think she didn't mean it. "Of course, there is no school or office work on Sundays...but I suppose you must study sometime."

Nate eyed her sarcastically, "From what I hear you haven't been too lonely."

Olympia tossed her platinum hair over her shoulder indignantly, "Don't expect me to sit home simply because you do."

Nate shook off the topic and said no more on the subject. He understood more than she thought. Growing up the way she had, one of those *mysterious Blanchards*, could not have been easy. She'd had a miserable time in grade school. Of course, everything was different now. The once ridiculed little girl now had the boys circling her like flies to honey. And she reveled in it.

"Graduation is coming up in a few months," Nate said. "Do you plan to go to college?"

Olympia scoffed at the idea. "I have had enough school for a lifetime. I have no plans to begin again someplace else. Besides, Father needs me to take care of him at home."

"Wouldn't you like to grow your education more?" Nate asked. "Learn more about the world and all it has to offer?"

"Not at all," Olympia answered. "I know enough about the world for my tastes. Besides, college is for girls who can't be sure anyone will marry them. I doubt that will be a problem for me."

Nate laughed at her insipid vanity. "Are you saying only ugly girls need to better themselves with an education?"

Olympia shrugged, "I'm not saying anything of the sort, but I suppose it couldn't do them any harm. I myself do not think I need any bettering. My job is to look after Father. Then, when and if the time comes, I'll look after my husband and do what I can to help better him."

"You'll make some lucky man a wonderful wife one day." He gave a playful wink. "Maybe even me?"

"If that is your attempt at a proposal Nate Caldwell, you'd better go back to the drawing board. Besides, I am a long way from being ready to marry. Father relies on me a great deal. He hasn't been the same since his wife died."

His wife. Not *her mother.* Nate decided to leave that blatant distinction alone. He continued with his topic. "How is Pastoria coping?"

With a confused expression, Olympia asked, "With what?"

Nate narrowed his brows as if it was a stupid question for her to ask. "Losing your mother."

"Oh," Olympia replied. "She's fine. Like me, she worries about Father, but other than that she is just busy with school and starting to date for the first time. Of course, none of her suitors are acceptable, but she will learn."

Nate was curious as to what Olympia thought was suitable. "And what makes them so unsuitable?"

Olympia sipped her tea again and let out an amused giggle, "One of them takes her on dates on the bus. His driver's license was revoked for parking tickets."

Nate laughed. "I suppose that gives your father some peace of mind. Not much necking to be done on a public bus." The waitress took their order and once alone again, Nate picked back up where they left off. "Speaking of buses, "Did you hear about that colored woman in Montgomery who was arrested on the bus last month? There is a big boycott going on because of it."

"No, I didn't hear anything about that. What happened?"

"How did you not hear about that?" Nate scoffed, smacking his forehead. "It was all over the news last month."

"We were busy. I do have a house to run, chickens to tend, pigs to feed, and several vegetable gardens." Olympia said defending herself. "Besides, I don't watch the news. It's always the same thing every day anyway. If anything really important happens, I'll hear someone talking about it."

Nate was dumbfounded by her statement. "So, you hear about the world from the lips of other people rather than taking an interest yourself? Don't you see, Olympia, when you do that, you get a skewed view of what is happening in the world." She made a face, not understanding his point. He went on, "This is how society gets in trouble. Too many people forming their opinion based on someone else's viewpoint. More often than not, important details get omitted."

"Anyway," she said dismissively. "What happened in Montgomery?"

"Well, a colored woman named Rosa Parks, refused to give up her seat to a white person, and the police arrested her. Now there's a whole bus boycott going on because of it."

Olympia pressed her hands to the table as if in outrage. "That is reprehensible! They arrested her? What if she were elderly? Or injured? Perhaps she required a seat when the other person didn't. Why should a person have to give up their seat to someone else simply because they are a different color?"

"I agree." Nate said. "But a lot of folks don't. You know how things are. This woman's act of disobedience has hailed her as a hero to some people and painted her as a radical troublemaker to others."

"Well, I think it's a terrible practice. If we had any black people in Daihmler I would hope we wouldn't treat them the way they apparently do in Montgomery."

Nate didn't immediately reply, unable to find words after such a statement. Was she possibly being serious right now? Finally, when she did not laugh at her joke, he realized she didn't understand she'd made one. "Olympia. There are black people in Daihmler."

"Yes, I know," she replied. "Maids who come into town to work or kitchen help in restaurants. I mean there are no colored people who live here."

Again, he was flabbergasted. Trying his best to not openly laugh at her asinine remark, he said, "Olympia. Black people do live in Daihmler."

Expressing surprise in her face, she replied, "Really? Where? I've lived here all my life and I have never seen any. I come into town quite often and I don't see any colored people. I went to school here. I go to the movies here. I eat out in restaurants here. Where are they?"

"That's the segregation part, Olympia! That is what people are fighting about. They aren't allowed in the places you go. There is an entire section of Daihmler where people of color live and shop. Surely, you've heard of Daw's Crossing?"

Certainly, she'd heard of Daw's Crossing. It was a slum no one ever went near. From early childhood she heard stories of how you could be robbed or killed by even going near that section of the county. It was where low lifes, drug addicts, and shiftless no-count people lived. As she heard her own description play in her mind, she realized for the first time the truth those commonly held opinions of Daw's Crossing covered up. Never in her life had she thought it to be populated with colored people—only dangerous, scary people. Had everyone really been using that language to refer to black people this whole time?

Seeing the dawn of revelation come across his girlfriend, Nate shook his head. "Really, Olympia Blanchard, I think it is time you took your head out of the sand and looked around a little at the world you live in."

"Well, maybe I will." Leaning over the table on her elbows she presented a coy smile and added, "But don't paint me as a woman unfamiliar with the evils of the world. You do not know all my secrets Nate Caldwell. I will help shape the world in other ways. Ways you'll never hear about, but I will be shaping them."

"I'll alert President Eisenhower to be on the lookout for you and the changes you'll be making."

Constantinople was sitting in an easy chair in the living room, thumbing through the day's mail when Olympia returned from her date. She was rather animated coming in the door and confronted him with hands on her hips. "Father, did you know there are black people who live in Daihmler?"

Completely bewildered by the proclamation, her father set aside the mail and asked her to clarify her statement. He did not understand her meaning or the indignance behind it.

"I just learned that Daw's Crossing is the black part of town. All this time I just thought it was where dangerous criminals live."

A bemused grim came across his face as he scratched the side of his beard. "Olympia, are you being serious?"

"Yes," she exclaimed. "Why does everyone keep asking me that?"

Staring at her in utter disbelief, he asked, "You truly were unaware that Daw's Crossing is a colored community?"

"Father, I had no idea. People always just casually describe it as this bad place to be avoided."

"Simply talk from prejudiced minds." Constantinople said. "I agree, it is a dreary part of town, but that has less to do with who lives there than it is the condition in which they are forced to live."

Olympia sat down with a thud on to the coffee table, exasperated. "Why isn't something done? Why do they have to live there in terrible conditions?"

"Segregation, daughter," her father answered. "It is the way things are. It has been the law since the War Between the States. Why has this upset you so deeply?"

Feeling very naive for never knowing any of this, she felt an equal amount of confusion as to why her father did not seem as outraged. "Because it is wrong, Father. I didn't know people were divided up by the color of their skin. Imagine not being allowed to walk into a store simply because of something you have no control over whatsoever. It isn't fair. Why aren't we doing something about it?"

"Some activists are, Olympia. Many people are beginning to change their ideas regarding equality in the races."

"No, Father," she asserted. "I mean why are witches not doing anything? Isn't this something we should take up as a cause?"

Her father moved to the fireplace to stoke the fire. It did not require it, but he needed the distraction while he came up with a proper response. It was not something he had ever considered himself. "Daughter, civil rights are an issue of man, not witches. We do not use our powers to intervein in situations men are fully capable of deciding and solving for themselves."

"I find that absurd," declared Olympia. "All my life you have taught me witches are supposed to protect the vulnerable. Those who cannot protect themselves. Yet we draw the line at this?"

Constantinople sat back down. He propped his elbows on the arms of the chair, clasping his fingers together. Olympia knew what this position meant. He always did this, when explaining something he recognized she would not understand. "Olympia, we protect powerless people from the powerful, yet menacing, beings they have no way to defend themselves from. We are designed for such involvement. If we were to assert our beliefs or desires onto man by using our abilities to enforce them, we would be the same as the creatures we are here to save them from. Ordinary people set their rules and enforce them the best way they can until they grow and learn which rules should evolve and which shouldn't. It is not our place to bend them to our thinking."

Strangely, her father's words of wisdom did not settle her mind as they used to. He'd always been infallible in his beliefs. Perhaps it was because she was older now and did not need to have her opinions shaped by him any longer. Or maybe, and this was the hardest to consider...he was wrong. Of course, she would never win that argument, so she altered it, drawing attention to the same injustice but in a world witches had all authority to shape. "And what of the Association, Father? Why have I never seen a person of color at a Consort? Surely not all witches are white people. Where are the others? Why have I never met a black witch?"

He did not have an answer for her. It was not a question to have ever crossed his mind. He had only known witches to be Caucasian. The thought intrigued him now. He was well aware of the African blooded Voodoo sects running through Jamaica and Haiti; And there were quite a few followers of Voodoo and Hoodoo in South Carolina and Louisiana, but they were not actually considered witches. Were they? Was the distinction solely based on color? Were their families just like his, bestowed with God gifted powers? Was race the only distinction in their classification? He did not have an answer. Though it had never been something he considered lengthily in his life, he naturally assumed witches to be descended from the same regions of Europe where their powers originated. This was why every witch he had ever known was Caucasian. Or was he, like all the other white men of his time, indoctrinated into believing people like him were only *people like him*?

CHAPTER SEVENTEEN

Childhood Ended

Graduation was two days away and Olympia was glad of it. Glad to be finished with high school and glad to be entering adulthood. She had no future plans for herself beyond graduation other than maintaining Blanchard House on a daily basis just as she had since Angharad died. Still, she felt a kind of liberation now. Possibilities were endless. She could take a job if she wanted. Or marry one of her many suitors. Or join her father on his secretive Consort missions, if he would allow. She was free to do as she pleased now.

After school was over for the day, Zelda and Olympia's musings on the future were boring Pastoria. Envious of their freedom from school, Pastoria still had five more years to go. The girls were in the living room discussing the upcoming graduation party when Constantinople came in holding three elaborately wrapped boxes in his arms. They did not see him standing in the doorway, allowing him to appreciate the moment. He looked at the three teens spread out across the room. Olympia was laying on the sofa, stomach down, feet raised, chewing on a plastic straw. Pastoria was spread diagonally over an easy chair, one leg over the arm, the other draped over the back while she ate an apple. Zelda was on the floor, her legs tucked under the coffee table while she flipped through the class yearbook they'd undoubtedly received that day. The lives of his three girls flashed through his mind. He remembered holding Olympia the night she was born, understanding he had never known love so deeply. Likewise, the day Pastoria arrived when he held her down for Olympia to see. So many memories flooded back. Olympia's first day of school. Pastoria's first tooth he pulled. The day he met little Zelda and admired her spunk. These girls and their years raced through his mind as if seeing it all for the first time. They were grown now, practically. And each one becoming a remarkable woman in her own right.

Olympia's eyes looked over and caught sight of her father in the doorway. Shaking him from his thoughts, she raised up and asked, "What is in the boxes?"

He smiled, "Presents for you girls."

"Presents?" Pastoria cried, leaping up excitedly.

Constantinople made a frown as he admitted the disappointing news. "I am afraid King Horace has asked me to go to New Mexico. There is something out there he needs me to investigate. There are reports of a rogue witch reanimating the bodies of the dead to avenge a wrong she feels is waged against her."

"Zombies?" Zelda exclaimed with a hearty chuckle. "Are you talkin' about zombies, Mr. Blanchard?"

He smiled her way and answered, "I suppose I am. Hadn't thought of it like that before, but yes." He looked at Olympia. "I am afraid I will miss your graduation. But I wanted you to look especially beautiful for the party. I bought you this."

He presented her with one of the dress boxes. The other two he handed to Pastoria and Zelda.

"I'm not graduating." Pastoria reminded him.

"Yes, but you will be at the party too. You should also look lovely."

Zelda held her box as though it were treasure. "And one for me?"

Constantinople smiled at the grateful girl, "Of course my dear Zelda! You are also graduating. And you deserve to feel like the magnificent creature you are on such a special night."

"But Mr. Blanchard..."

"Hush. You are one of my daughters as well, in my heart at least." Rushing him with arms open, she hugged him around the waist and cried.

After dinner, as Zelda and Pastoria washed the dinner dishes and put everything away, Constantinople asked Olympia to join him in the study for a conversation. Closing the double doors behind them, he took a seat in the chair opposite his eldest daughter.

"What is it, Father? Have I done something?"

He smiled. "Of course not, I simply desire to chat with you."

Although he was doing his best to seem casual, there was a seriousness about him which unnerved her. "Tell me, Father."

"There is nothing exactly to tell, Olympia. Only I will be going away on a case for The Consort, and I will unfortunately miss your graduation."

She'd never noticed how loudly the grandfather clock in the foyer ticked. Possibly it only sounded exaggerated because it sat against the other side of the office wall. Still, it seemed that the pendulum was amplified. Distracted by it, her reply was delayed a few seconds. "Father, you already told me you would miss graduation."

"I know, but graduation is a milestone in a young person's life. There are things I would like to say to you now." He reached out, stroking her long soft hair. Before removing his hand, he caressed her cheek. "I am immensely proud of you, Olympia. I have always been proud of you. You are an extraordinary woman. The power you wield is enormous even by a witch's measure. I am confident you will always use it wisely. You will be an inspiring leader to your coven one day."

She laughed, not meaning to. "Coven? You, me, Pastoria, and Zelda."

"It will grow," he said without smiling. "You will be revered by many, and you will earn this reverence over your years. The Blanchard family will be a force to reckon with and you will be at its helm."

He spoke with urgency now it seemed. As if he were imparting something he may not have a chance to say later. It intensified her anxiousness, but she understood whatever emotion was compelling him to say these things, would unburden his mind on his mission.

He then told her a secret out of character for him to reveal. "I have seen our family's future once, long ago. Trust what I say to you, daughter. If anything should ever happen to me—"

She clutched him firmly by the arm. Even the idea of it was beyond her comprehension and she did not want it spoken into the air. "Nothing is going to happen to you Father, and I won't listen to talk like this."

"Olympia, none of us leave this life alive. You are a woman now. I can coddle and protect you no more. Every time I have ever departed this house on a mission there has always been the very real possibility I may not return. It is my fervent hope this case will return me safely as all the others have. But you are now old enough for me to drop the pretense of childhood and speak to you plainly. As I always spoke to your mother before I would leave."

Everything made sense now. She had never heard talk from him like this because she had been his child before. She was the woman of the house now. Her role was different. She was his equal. "I will not interrupt again, Father."

"If I do not return from this, or from some other future endeavor, I have utmost confidence in you to guide this family to its exalted future. Olympia Blanchard, you are a strong witch. An intelligent woman. You will always know the proper thing to do to hold this family together and keep the Natural Order protected, even at the most personal of costs."

"I will Father. I promise."

"You will be my successor. Hecate of the Blanchards. You will inherit this house and all that I possess. You will look out for your sister and for Zelda. And I ask only one thing of you, daughter."

"Anything, Father."

"Never let go of your name." His eyes glistened now with tears not full enough yet to shed. "I never had sons. I never needed one. I had you girls and I would have had it no other way. Yet I do not want the Blanchard line to end. I do not want our bloodline to be usurped by the surname of a man who can never measure up to your esteemed lineage. We are Blanchards. Nothing else. And we will be nothing more."

A shiver went through her. It was one of pride. Her father was not a boastful man, but his recognition of those who came before them and those who would come after was as close to arrogance as she had ever seen in him. It was well deserved. "I promise Father. I will remain Olympia Blanchard all my life. And I will accept nothing less of my children or Pastoria's."

"It will be a glorious life, you live, Olympia," he said. "I hope to be around for more of it."

The afternoon after graduation, Olympia and Zelda stood in the floor length mirror of her bedroom admiring what they saw. Constantinople had spared no expense on the formal gowns they would wear to the party that night. Olympia's gown was the most exquisite thing she'd ever worn. It was light blue with a fitted bodice adorned with intricate beadwork. The bottom draped to the floor in a delicate play of iridescent threads creating an ethereal shine. Her father had chosen it perfectly to match her eyes. Zelda, who tended to prefer a more colorful palette, gasped at herself in the mirror when she put on her dress. The lavender and chartreuse colors were symphony of avant-garde audacity in silk. The waist billowed out to help distract from Zelda's lack of curves. It had a sweeping train of matching lavender and chartreuse swirls, tinged with a hint of orange. For the first time in her life, Zelda felt beautiful. She wished Mr. Blanchard was around to thank again properly, but he'd already left on his mission to New Mexico.

The high school graduation dance was held in the ballroom of the Ramada Inn hotel in nearby Tuscaloosa. Though the ballroom was not what one would consider grand, the decoration committee added touches of shiny gold and silver streamers, balloons, and romantic candlelight. The band was playing big band music, with occasional Sinatra thrown in. Olympia, Zelda, and Pastoria entered without dates, a deliberate choice on their part, as to enjoy the night together rather than with boys they were likely to never see again.

As the trio made their entrance, gasps of admiration swept through the room. Olympia observed the other girls in her class. Although they all looked lovely, none of their dresses matched in elegance. She realized in that moment just how much her father must have paid for the gowns she, Zelda, and Pastoria were wearing. Suitors immediately began to make their way towards them, side-eyeing each other as they increased their speed to beat out the competition for the first dance. James Yerby got to Olympia before anyone else, asking her if she would care to share a dance with him. Although she never did like James very much, he was one of the more goodlooking males in her graduating class, and if she must dance with someone, it might as well be someone attractive. With a nod of acceptance, Olympia moved to the floor, twirled by her partner beneath the chandeliers. Bart Chadwicke was as surprised as everyone else when he found himself eyeing Zelda. It was as if seeing her in a whole new light. Not as dashing as Olympia's partner, Zelda wasn't so sure she felt like accepting a lower rung on the senior ladder. With his round face and doughy arms, Zelda had always thought Bart looked as though he would grow up to bake and sell butter cookies. Still...no one else was asking, so she agreed to his request for her first dance. Though Pastoria was not a senior, she was not the only younger person at the dance. However, it was not a boy her own age who won her favor. She was escorted to the dance floor by a popular senior, Kirk Lenser.

Zelda, never known for her gracefulness, struggled a bit to maneuver around the floor. Her dress, though stunning, was not the length she was used to, and she found herself stumbling occasionally when her feet got caught up in the fabric. It didn't help that she was also not accustomed to a dance partner leading her through the song. At one point during her third dance, when her partner attempted to twirl her too fast, she lost balance and collided into the dessert table, knocking plates and forks off the side where they crashed to the floor. The commotion drew laughter and applause. The band even switched into a jaunty tune to match the moment. Zelda was not the least embarrassed, crying out, "What a stupid place to put a table!" before rejoining her dance with vigor.

By the fourth dance, the three friends desired a break from socialization and excused themselves from their admirers to step outside for air. They shared stories about their various dancing partners, giggling over who stepped on their feet and who made torrid advances. They also noted to one another how many of their classmates they'd overheard bragging about the big plans they imagined for their lives. Some of their dreams would come true, and some would not. The Blanchard sisters and Zelda realized they had never applied much thought to what their own futures might be.

"Me," Zelda said, pointing to the ground beneath her feet. "I'm stayin' right here in Daihmler." Pastoria laughed, adjusting her finger to point south.

"We're in Tuscaloosa. Daihmler is that way."

"Whatever," Zelda chuckled. "I'm gone do what your daddy said. I'm gonna start me a business telling fortunes."

"Fortunes!" Olympia replied. "Well, there are a great many people who need a dose of reality." She wrapped her arms around her companions and added, "I will be staying in Daihmler, as well. You two are all the adventure I need."

"Let's make a pact," Pastoria suggested. "We stay together. No matter who gets married or what comes, the three of us always remain the best of friends, always there for the other for the rest of our lives."

Olympia smirked, squeezing their shoulders against her, "I think we already did that, years ago when we met. I knew the moment you were born Pastoria. And I knew the moment Zelda mindspoke to me in that elementary school hallway. We are sisters forever."

Blanchard House was dark when Olympia pulled her car up to the porch. The house was shrouded with the shadows of nightfall. Lightly slapping her head, Olympia remarked, "I should have put on the porch light before we left." Still giddy from the party and chattering away about it, the girls climbed the front steps without noticing someone was waiting for them. The man lit a cigarette, the strike of his match startling them, only briefly illuminating his face amid the background of darkness. "Hello?" Olympia called nervously, readying herself to freeze him in case he was a maniac.

"Didn't mean to alarm you girls," the man said rising from the rocking chair. Olympia knew him immediately by his voice.

"Mr. Uding?"

Bristow Uding took a couple of drags from his cigarette, then tossed it away over the rail. Olympia watched it as it fell to the ground. It landed on a small pile of others. Mr. Uding had been waiting there for a while. Returning her gaze to his face, he looked as he always did, like a portly nobleman or a city mayor—or as Pastoria once described him, Mr. Fezziwig from Dicken's A Christmas Carol. Yet his eyes seemed troubled, causing Olympia's fear to swell.

"Miss Blanchard," he began, addressing only Olympia before correcting himself and including Pastoria. "Girls, the Council tasked me to come out here to see you. Even had they not I would have come myself anyway. Your father being a great and longtime friend of mine."

Pastoria, as if remembering her manners or trying to stall whatever was about to depart his lips, unlocked the door of the house and asked him inside. Zelda rushed in ahead of them, clicking on the lights. Bristow Uding entered with Pastoria and Olympia trailing behind. The butterflies which were beginning to stir in the pit of Olympia's stomach took flight when Uding stepped into the light. She could see now what he carried in his right hand. Pastoria was not looking at what Mr. Uding had with him, too intently focused on the expression across the anxious man's face. It was not a face with happy news.

Olympia lifted the long silver sword from Mr. Uding's grasp. Her father's sword. The sword he always took on missions. Gripping the cold metal sheath in both hands, she asked, "When did he die?"

Bristow Uding bowed his sorrowful head. "Last night. In Roswell. I identified his remains this morning personally."

Olympia wobbled backwards against the wall, steadying herself with a hand on a side table. Zelda rushed to her, sliding under Olympia's arm, placing one of her own around her friend's waist. Pastoria sunk onto the couch, hands on her knees, her eyes staring blankly ahead.

Recovering herself from the shock, Olympia leaned the sword against the table. Mustering her indomitable strength to hold back her tears, she asked, "Was he successful?"

A little surprised this was her first question, Uding quickly reminded himself she was the daughter of Constantinople Blanchard—of course this was her first question. "Yes. He stopped the forces he was meant to stop," Bristow said. "Tragically, he'd been mortally wounded minutes before."

Pastoria began to cry. Zelda, unsure where she was most needed, took her cue from Olympia who gestured towards her sister. Zelda left Olympia, joining Pastoria on the couch to comfort her. The sound of her sister sobbing stabbed into Olympia's soul. She pressed her feet hard into the floor as if she were trying to push her toes through. It forced her legs to lock in place. She felt her body's rigidity spread through her arms and torso, then her shoulders. It was a purposeful stance, imperceivable by others, but Olympia's secret way to stop herself from shaking. Although it gave an impression of cool resilience, it was all a facade. And it was working. Olympia was as still as the sword standing against the table. She could tell Mr. Uding interpreted her countenance for strength.

Uding continued, recounting the events of their father's heroic sacrifice. "It should be with great pride for you to know Constantinople finished the fight, despite grave injuries, until the evil was destroyed. He saved hundreds of people. He fell to his death with the knowledge he had been victorious. We are all in his debt."

Olympia remained stoic, relentless in her resistance to burst into tears. A child would have. But Bristow Uding had just ended her childhood. No, perhaps it had been her father himself to end it when he'd called her into the study days ago, warning her—preparing her for what he must have foreseen coming. Olympia Blanchard was a woman now, as well as the head of her little family. Childhood was over. She would not embarrass her father by crumbling into hysteria.

Zelda continued to hold a weeping Pastoria. She channeled Olympia's fortitude, subduing her own desire to cry, for someone she greatly loved was gone. However, his daughters needed her strength now, not her anguish. Zelda swallowed down her pain, readying herself to be their rock.

Olympia outstretched her hand to their grim visitor. "I thank you Mr. Uding for coming out here to give us the news. How shall I make the arrangements to bring him home?"

"No need, my dear." Bristow informed her. "His remains have been sent to a storage facility until the Consort meeting next month."

"You have my gratitude." Olympia said, escorting, or perhaps ushering, him to the door. "We will see you at the Consort for his cremation."

"Miss Blanchard," Bristow stammered, as he was practically driven out of the house. "If you girls need someone to stay with you...if you need someone to talk to...several female Consort members have offered to come here or take you into their own homes."

Her eyes narrowed in offense at everyone's underestimation of her. Her look spoke volumes, conveying her annoyance of anyone assuming she required a guardian. "I am sure they meant to be kind," she said, softening her reaction a little. "Please do thank them for me. However, my sister and I are perfectly fine alone. We will remain at Blanchard House."

Not accustomed to a female as young as she possessing such determination, Bristow stuttered nervously, "But how will you—I mean—do you have the means to—"

Fixing her eyes to his with unwavering confidence, she answered, "All of that is my concern now. I am Olympia Blanchard, Mr. Uding. I believe you will discover I am a resilient woman. My sisters and I will be alright."

CHAPTER EIGHTEEN

Constantinople's Cremation

It worked out rather conveniently for the Blanchard sisters that the Summer Consort meeting was to be held in Tuscaloosa. It might not have been a coincidence. Many in the Association were taking pity upon the orphaned sisters and may have deliberately chosen the neighboring town to remove one less burden from them.

The Jemison Mansion was chosen as the Consort location, large enough to hold as many members as possible who might attend. And attend, they did. There were few among the Witches Association who had not been touched in some important way by the heroics of Constantinople Blanchard. Once word got out about his death, members thought of little else than paying their final respects to such a great man. Jemison House was the perfect size for the occasion.

When local politician and planter, Robert Jemison, moved into his completed mansion in 1862 it was a showplace of beauty and technology. The Jemison house boasted modern plumbing, including flushing toilets, a copper bath, and a water boiler. His home was also one of the state's first to include gas lighting and a kitchen stove that required no wood for heat. Of course, the days of elaborate plantation homes in Tuscaloosa were long over and the house passed through the hands of several descendants. It was only a few months ago it had been donated to the city of Tuscaloosa to be converted into a library. That project was scheduled to happen within the next few weeks, but for now it sat empty, and the Association had managed to rent the grand house for the evening.

Olympia and Pastoria drove to Tuscaloosa in her mint green convertible and parked on the street around the side of the block. As they made their way to Jemison House, they spied the run-down truck belonging to Zelda's father. Both girls wished Zelda had ridden with them, but since Zelda's father stopped drinking, Zelda was trying to give him another chance to be part of her life. One of her conditions being he reconnect with their witch roots.

As Olympia and Pastoria entered the mansion, a stampede of sympathetic friends swarmed them, each expressing sorrow for their loss and reiterating what a magnificent witch their father had been. They swelled with pride as person after person shared heartfelt stories about their father's impact on their lives. The Blanchard sisters had been to many Consorts in their time and seen several cremations, but never had they witnessed so many people so personally grief stricken by the same loss. Constantinople Blanchard had left an indelible mark in the world, one Olympia knew she must strive to live up to.

Amid the passing faces and kind words, one she had all but forgotten came forward. Since their first meeting at the hollow octagon house a couple years prior, she hadn't seen the repulsive Hugh D'Angelo at any Consorts till now. He attempted to convey a pretense of sympathy, but it did not fool Olympia. His callous ambition shined through that sleek, refined mask. "Tragic loss you have suffered, Miss Blanchard. You have my deepest condolences."

"Mr. D'Angelo," she replied, allowing her acknowledgment of his presence suffice as her response to his hollow words. "I haven't seen you at recent Consorts."

With an almost arrogant swell of the shoulders, he answered. "We do not attend many Consorts. My family is much too pressed by responsibility. However, once I heard the ghastly news, I felt I must be present tonight, despite the great journey from Wadmalaw Island. Afterall, my dear lady, you have lost your beloved father."

If he sought praise or gratitude for his insincere charity, Olympia offered neither. "Are you alone? Or has the rest of your family come with you?"

Pointing across the mansion's parlor to an adjoining sitting room, Hugh identified his two sisters who sat charming a couple of young men around them. "I fear my sisters may marry off soon, leaving me without anyone my age for companionship."

Searching her surroundings for practically anyone else to talk to, Olympia replied dismissively, "Yes, well, these things happen."

Placing his hand upon her arm, making Olympia's skin crawl, Hugh asked, "And what becomes of you now, Miss Blanchard? With your father's untimely passing, might you be in search of a husband? If you recall, I once made mention of how our two families could form quite the powerhouse if they were to merge."

Recoiling from his unwelcome touch, Olympia curtly remarked, "I am not interested in marriage. Nor am I charmed by your mercenary suggestion."

"Mercenary?" he laughed. "My dear Miss Blanchard, the D'Angelo's are immensely wealthy. If anyone would be suspected of self-serving intentions if a marriage between us occurred, it would not be me. I hear you are now left with little means of support. Consider my offer. It will not be made again."

She drifted back towards him, her face boldly close to his own, uncomfortably eye to eye. "Those are marvelous words to hear, Hugh. As I can think of nothing more repugnant than suffering your company another minute."

As if knowing she needed a rescue, or perhaps disliking Hugh's presence near her, two people appeared at her side, edging Hugh D'Angelo away. Olympia was thrilled to see them and would have been even if they hadn't just spared her from Hugh.

"King Bedwyr!" Olympia smiled. "Mrs. Kraven!"

The King of the Consort and his wife gave Olympia a sincere embrace. Pastoria was with them, as well as another young man, a little older than Olympia. "Please, Olympia, you are an adult now. Please call me Beryl." Olympia gave her sister a brief refresher on how Bedwyr and Beryl had grown up with their mother, as well as the story they once told her about Angharad saving their son's life.

"And this is he," the king introduced, pulling the young man forward. "Our son Brustius Kraven." Olympia greeted him warmly.

"You know, Olympia," Beryl Kraven winked with a coy smile, "I secretly hoped one day Brustius here might sweep you off your feet, making you, our daughter. Alas, his heart has found true love with another. She is a delightful girl, so I am not displeased. She will be joining our Association once they are married next Spring. Living in Denver, she belongs to the Northwest Witches Association now."

Congratulating Brustius, Olympia wished he and his fiancée the best. The official beginning to the Consort meeting was about to commence, but before having to take his place at the Council table, King Bedwyr and his wife conveyed their sincere sympathies to the Blanchard sisters over the passing of their cherished friend.

"If ever you should need anything," the king offered. "You have only to ask."

Unoffended by his authentic sincerity, Olympia genuinely thanked him but insisted she and Pastoria would be alright.

"Of course, you will," Beryl smiled. "You have your mother's fortitude and your father's heart. I would place no bets against the likes of you, Olympia Blanchard."

As she and Pastoria took their seats for the business portion of the Consort, Olympia reflected on her words. She resisted the inference that she resembled her mother in any way, yet she could not deny its truth. She did possess a steely strength within her, but she had always attributed it to her father. However, she was now at an age where she could see a broader view of herself. Despite how much her childhood-self detested her mother, Olympia could no longer deny her icy resilience was purely Angharad. Though everything else comprising her character could be credited to her father, that impenetrable armor...that was her mother.

Interrupting Olympia's unsettling epiphany, Zelda plopped down in the empty seat next to her, citing she'd instructed her father to sit in the back where he would feel more comfortable. The meeting began, and nothing all that interesting took place during it except when Olympia was installed as the new leader of the Blanchard Coven.

"Big deal," Pastoria whispered to Zelda as she watched her sister stand proudly to accept. "There are just the three of us. Some coven."

Once the meeting was over and refreshments were served, Bristow Uding approached the Blanchard sisters solemnly. "My dears, we have your father's remains prepared on the pyre in the courtyard."

With a gentle hand to her back, Bristow's son Brimford asked his friend, "Are you up to this, Olympia?" Olympia swallowed the lump in her throat, clasped her two hands thankfully over Brimford's, then released his hand to take hold of her sister's. With Pastoria's hand in her own, Olympia started towards the doors to the courtyard. Pausing a moment, she looked back to find Zelda, who gave a nod letting her know she was right behind them.

As Zelda attempted to follow, her father cut her off at the door. "That's Blanchard business. None a yours."

Zelda gently swept her father out of her way with her arm, "Those two are my best friends. They are sayin' farewell to their daddy. I'm goin' to be with them."

"You ain't one of them." Zelda's father scowled.

"I'm more one of them than I have ever been one of you," a defiant Zelda sneered. "Mr. Blanchard treated me more like a daughter than you or momma ever did. Now get outta my way while I go be with my family and pay respects to somebody I love."

Outside, on the sprawling lawn, a sacred pyre of wood had been erected four feet high. Atop this wooden altar lay the colorless body of Constantinople Blanchard. Even in death, he exuded an air of regality, dressed in a finely tailored blue suit emphasizing the commanding presence he possessed in life. Olympia and Pastoria stood before their father; their fingers tightly interlocked. The weight of the moment hung heavy over them as a mournful assembly gathered behind the sisters. It was not customary for Consort members to witness a fallen witch's cremation. This was usually something only family members observed. The congregation of unrelated witches stood as a testament to Constantinople's impact on their community. Bristow Uding came forward holding a lighted torch in his hand. She had not planned to do it. She had resigned herself to present her more courageous nature to the Consort. She had even convinced herself this event was strictly ceremonial. But as Bristow Uding was coming forward to pass her the literal and figurative torch, Olympia found herself overcome with the girlish need to share one final moment with her father before he was returned to ash. With a discreet flick of her hand, she cast everyone around her into suspended animation. Olympia was the only person with any present awareness or movement.

Looking at her father's body laid atop the bed of timber, she walked to the edge of the piling. Even dead there was no denying his handsomeness. Laying with his hands gently folded together over his chest, he appeared every bit as powerful as he had in life. They had dressed him in a navy-blue suit with a yellow and blue striped tie. She wondered if he could see himself, wherever he now was, and could he see her with him.

"I don't know why I froze everyone," she told him. "It isn't as if you and I have left anything unsaid. I have known my whole life you loved me, and I have never concealed how much I love you. I guess I just needed a second for myself." She started to walk around the pyre although she had no specific reason for doing so. It was something to do while she pondered her final words. "I will take care of Pastoria. And Zelda. I will do my best to look out for them as you always have." Her voice seemed unrecognizable as she heard it for herself. It occurred to her that she was still presenting her brave self, even though the masses were completely unaware of anything at all. She did not have to be that person for him. She could drop the façade. Her next words sounded more the way she felt inside, with a slight tremble to them. "Father, I am frightened. I don't know if I can do this." Olympia admitted. "Can I live up to who you were to us? Am I enough to be there for Pastoria and Zelda? I have never lacked for confidence and yet now I am questioning myself at every turn. My confidence came from being your daughter. But I'm not your daughter anymore. You are gone. I am just Olympia."

As she bent down to place a final kiss upon his forehead, she suddenly realized she had stepped into the pyre at some point without noticing. As her lips touched his cold skin, she righted herself and backed out of the timbers without upsetting them. A gentle wind rolled by and as it pushed into her it seemed to take her fear with it as it left. She looked back at her father. "But *I am* your daughter. Whether you are here or not changes nothing." She smiled his way then turned her back to the pyre as she retook her place beside Pastoria. "Don't worry. I've got this Daddy."

Olympia returned everyone to normal without a soul suspecting she'd halted time at all. Bristow Uding handed her the torch. Gripping it firmly, Olympia approached the pyre, signaling her acceptance of her new position as head of her family. She tossed it at her father's feet, igniting the fuel-soaked timbers. Within seconds the fire spread with ferocity across the timbers, cloaking him in flames. Returning to Pastoria's side, Olympia took hold of her sister's hand once more, seeking and sending strength between them. She felt Zelda's hand grip the back of her shoulder as the other hand did likewise to Pastoria. The Blanchard sisters leaned back into their friend. The three young women, sisters all of them, stared forward into the red-orange inferno engulfing the greatest man they'd ever known, returning him to the earth.

CHAPTER NINETEEN

The Art of Finance

Beneath a dismal summer sky of gray, as if nature was also grieving, Charles Caldwell drove out to Blanchard House on necessary, albeit unfortunate business. His heart felt heavy for everyone's loss, including his own. Constantinople Blanchard was more than a client; he had been a friend. Charles had diligently managed Mr. Blanchard's financial affairs for many years and now he would do the same for the daughters he left behind. Accompanying Charles was his son Nate and a young attorney hired to represent the girls in probate court.

As the three men stepped up onto the front porch, the door opened before they reached it. Framed by the crisp white doorway, looking like a portrait come to life, stood the new mistress of Blanchard House. The young lawyer's jaw nearly hit the top of his brown wing tip shoes when he saw her. Olympia Blanchard was the most stunning creature he'd ever laid eyes upon. Nate took notice not only of the lawyer's reaction, but how it was equally reciprocated. Olympia, never one to lose her composure, looked into the stranger's eyes and stammered to greet them.

"Olympia," Charles introduced. "This is John Windham."

Smiling girlishly, she asked, "You must be our attorney?"

Reaching to shake the other's hand, neither of them made it that far. The moment their fingers touched, they stood eyeing one another as the electrifying connection between them was born. With only their fingertips touching, almost dancing together, the attorney lost himself in her crystal blue eyes. Seeing the exchange between them, Nate understood instantly that Olympia Blanchard was not his girl anymore.

Settling in the living room, where Pastoria was waiting, Charles introduced her to John Windham. Olympia took a seat in her father's high back chair and instructed Pastoria to pour their guests some coffee from the tray she had prepared. Charles and John began their business with the Blanchard sisters. Both opened briefcases full of papers to be signed and many financial matters to discuss. Pastoria and Olympia exchanged like-minded glances at one another. Cutting to the chase, Olympia asked flatly, "How bad off are we?"

The elder Caldwell was not as accustomed to her candor as his son. "I wouldn't exactly use those terms—"

Nate cut his father off, knowing their client better than he. Olympia had little patience for inconsequential details. "You are going to be okay," Nate told her. "With some guidance." It was immediately clear Nate was well versed in the Blanchard finances. It made sense he would be. He cared very much for the sisters. "There is enough to live on for a while. We can also sell this house if—"

"Blanchard House will never be sold." Olympia declared. "This estate is to always remain in this family."

Charles cleared his throat and adjusted his tie, "My dear, this house is a bit isolated. Not to mention it is much too large for two young ladies to maintain. You must consider your future. Surely whenever you marry, your husband will prefer to live—"

"Any man who marries me, marries Blanchard House."

The was no room for questioning Olympia's declaration. The matter was off the table for further discussion and both men knew it. Charles moved to other business. He listed the two or three accounts Constantinople held in banks, all of it now falling on Olympia to manage. As she sat listening to the review of her assets, she understood she and her sister would not starve, although there would be little extra money available to pay for anything except utilities and household necessities.

"Will I be able to send Pastoria to college?"

Nate inadvertently made a grin, "Have you forgotten your view on girls who go to college?"

Pastoria made a confused face. Olympia simply smiled, stroked her sister's cheek and replied to Nate, "Everything I said still holds. But I think Pastoria might need to go to college."

Pastoria spoke up in protest, "I have no desire to go away to school and leave you here by yourself. I can get a job."

"You may both need to get a job." Charles added. "Especially if you refuse to sell this land."

Affronted by the idea and amused at Mr. Caldwell's lack of confidence in her options, Olympia laughingly replied, "I doubt I will have trouble acquiring a husband if it should come to saving Blanchard House. However, it seems we have nothing to worry about for a few years. My sister and I will get along."

The elder Mr. Caldwell bid goodbye shortly after all the legal documents were signed. He stepped outside to wait, allowing his son time to have a private goodbye. Nate clasped Olympia's hand in a gesture of reassurance. "I won't let anything happen to you. I will make sure you aren't destitute a couple of years from now. Just live frugally while I invest on your behalf."

"Thank you, Nate. For everything." Olympia said, kissing his cheek, signaling to him again, the romantic part of their relationship was over now. "You are a good friend."

"Well," Nate blushed. "I try." Ever aware the young lawyer John Windham was still standing beside them, Nate made one subtle attempt to stake his claim. "And if you don't succeed in finding a rich husband, you can always marry me. We can pinch pennies together."

Not giving the beautiful young lady the opportunity to respond, Mr. Windham took her hand in his and gave it a noble kiss. "Miss Blanchard, please call on me whenever you have questions or may need guidance on legal matters. I am at your disposal, day or night."

She did not call on him. And he did not call on her. Both were accustomed to being the one who was chased, and neither of them had the time or inclination to switch roles. Moreover, Olympia was not interested in dating in the months after her father's death. She had far too much going on at Blanchard House and helping Pastoria finish school.

The money held out over the following year in large part due to the diligent work the Blanchard girls put into their main asset. Olympia and Pastoria kept the gardens always planted so at harvest time there was plenty to can and store. The apple orchard and grapevines provided enough fruit for an entire shelf of jellies and jams. And the chicken houses supplied enough eggs and poultry to keep them from rarely needing to buy food in town. Of course, other expenses mounted up. Property taxes, inflation, utilities, home and auto repairs, and all the routine costs any household incurs began to dwindle their accounts. With no additional income streaming in, Olympia made a decision; It was time to take a small mortgage out on the house.

What to wear to the bank when asking for the loan presented the most immediate problem. Olympia pondered her choices for over an hour, eventually calling her sister in for advice. Pastoria entered the bedroom to find five different outfits laid across the bed.

"Why does this even matter?" she asked.

Olympia seemed surprised by the question. "Everything matters my dear little sister. If I dress too well, he will think I'm a spendthrift and won't trust us with a loan. On the other hand, I cannot appear too dowdy, lest he believe we are poor and a bad credit risk. I must strike the right center of both. Then, with a few flutters of my eyes, a couple impish laughs, and a toss of my hair, I should be compelling enough to charm the banker into submission."

Ridiculous as it sounded, Pastoria had to admit she made sense about the outfit. As for the charm part, she had long known her sister possessed enough allure to charm the rattle right off the rattlesnake. Olympia finally settled on a demur blue dress accentuated with a white belt, white gloves, and small white hat crowned with a pale blue ribbon. Pastoria wished her luck as Olympia departed for town.

She was only a few minutes late to her appointment at the bank, but the dashing man she was to meet with did not mind. She was worth the wait. Olympia could tell by the way his eyes danced upon first sight of her that she'd dressed perfectly. He escorted her into his small office, pulling out a chair for her before taking his own behind the desk. "My name is Martin Caswell, loan officer here at Daihmler Trust. How may I assist you today, Miss Blanchard?"

Presenting her brightest smile, she placed her folded hands in her lap and began her pitch. While she spoke, not even fully aware of what she was even saying, she could tell he was not closely listening. He was far too mesmerized. She played up her devotion to her sister and her family home. She feigned interest when Mr. Caswell shared his advice or spoke about himself. Olympia blushed, laughed, fluttered her eyes, and dazzled him completely. Within the hour, the young and beautiful Miss Blanchard left Daihmler Trust with a new admirer and an approved mortgage loan despite having no means of employment. Martin Caswell was so smitten with Olympia, he called her at home that very evening to ask her out for the following Saturday.

The Waysider restaurant in Tuscaloosa was a favorite dating spot. Once a residence, the renovated space was known for delicious food and an intimate atmosphere. Inside over a candlelit table, Martin Caswell and Olympia Blanchard began getting to know one another better.

"I cannot for the life of me fathom how it is you and I have never crossed paths in Daihmler before, Martin," she said with a winsome smile.

"I am relatively new to town," he answered. "My uncle founded Dixie Trust Bank in Nashville many years ago. Since then, he has opened several branches throughout the South. When he took over Daihmler Trust, he sent me here."

"To be Bank President?" she asked excitedly.

Martin chuckled, "Eventually. Right now, I'm head of loans. But I'll get there."

She liked his face when he laughed. Somehow it made him better looking. Although not quite as attractive as John Windham, Mr. Caswell was handsome enough in his own way. His light brown hair was prematurely graying around the temples, providing him with a distinguishment matching his business acumen.

Ever aware of the placement of overhead lighting and the light cast from the flickering table candle, Olympia utilized both to frame herself properly. She knew exactly which way to shift her shoulders for her soft blonde hair to best glisten while her azure eyes illuminated by the light reflecting into them. Once she knew she presented a most irresistible visage for him, she gently touched his hand across the table and said, "So, you are all alone in a strange town."

Martin smiled at her sweetness, marveling at the way she looked in the light. Sighing, he replied, "I am not exactly alone. My sister is with me, and I have a son from my previous marriage who comes home some weekends from boarding school."

"A son?" she said, even more intrigued now. She knew Martin was a little older than she but now he seemed all the more interesting. "You are divorced? I don't really know any divorced people."

"Widowed," he corrected. "My wife died a few years after our son was born. He is twelve years old now. I provide for he and my sister."

Olympia broke her southern belle act for a moment, lifting her wine glass to the air. "We are comrades it seems. My father died a year and a half ago. I am responsible for myself and my sister as well."

"No other family at all?"

"None." Olympia replied. "I have no idea what a large family would even be like. Doesn't look like I'll ever find out either. We keep dropping off."

Martin grinned once more, giving her a slightly flirtatious wink, "You may still have time to make a big family. Who knows?"

CHAPTER TWENTY

Working Witches

With an influx of cash coming into the household from the mortgage Olympia secured, she felt it was time for an update to the family home. Tired of seeing the same four walls and boring furnishings in the living room, she went into town to Anderson Carpets and Upholstery to borrow some sample books for wallpaper and carpeting. Now reclining back on the decades-old sofa, she was flipping through the more modern selections.

"I ain't one to dip into your business," Zelda offered up somehow with a straight face. "But shouldn't ya'll be spendin' as little as possible. Hell, you got this money to survive on so neither a you had to take jobs."

Pastoria frowned from the floor where she was finishing her homework, "Does that mean we can't get lava lamps?"

Olympia laughed, reaching down to pat her sister's shoulder. "I think we have enough to live on and still be able to spruce things up around here." Inspecting the plain walls and simple, yet functional, furnishings no one had ever described as stylish, Olympia announced, "I believe we need some color in here."

"Mother hated color." Pastoria remembered.

Beaming ear to ear as if about to do something triumphant, Olympia replied, "Exactly!"

Had the Blanchard sisters had any friends other than Zelda or Nate; they might have thrown a party to show off the new look of Blanchard House after the paper hangers, carpet layers, and furniture delivery men did their magic. The living room was almost unrecognizable now. Wheat colored shag carpeting covered the dark hardwood floors. The stark white clapboard walls were now swathed in psychedelic swirls of pink, orange, red, and yellow. Funky egg-shaped swivel chairs sat where Angharad and Constantinople's worn early American chairs once anchored the fireplace. And two oversized hot pink bean bag chairs flanked the wooden coffee table—the only remaining piece of furniture from the old days, now painted vivid orange.

Things were changing in Zelda's life as well. After her father succumbed to liver failure, Zelda was surprised to discover he had kept up a small insurance policy to which she was beneficiary. Though not much money, only $10,000, it was enough to bury him and take a lease on a small cottage two streets off the main thoroughfare of town. Olympia protested at first, citing she should continue to live with them at Blanchard House, but Zelda insisted it was time to have her own place.

"You girls gone be meetin' up with fella's soon and wantin' to get married. Ain't no room for a best friend to be lingerin' around."

"No man comes before the three of us," Pastoria argued. "We are sisters, all of us."

"Yeah, well, wait till that right man comes walking in. I ain't never seen a sister chose a sister over a well-hanging successful man!"

Zelda had other reasons for moving out as well. Reasons only she could understand. After being told all her life by her parents she was worthless, she thought it was time to prove what all she could do in life. It was Constantinople Blanchard who gave her the idea as to how to achieve it. Outside her newly rented house hung a sign, "Private Psychic Readings by Madam Zelda."

Madam Zelda. Mr. Blanchard gave her that name. And atop her head for her very first customer, she wore the scarf he'd loaned her that first Halloween. It was a slow start during those first weeks, but soon word of mouth got out about the young fortuneteller's accuracy and before she had paid the fourth month's rent, her weekly calendar was filled with appointments.

Pastoria was having drama of her own, drama Olympia largely ignored. A random boy she dated a few times was moving away from Daihmler because of some legal troubles his father lost his job over. Pastoria was distraught for days, but Olympia's only words of comfort were, "Sometimes the trash takes itself out," and suggested she start dating other boys.

As harsh and dismissive as Olympia's words were received, she was speaking from experience. After succumbing to boredom after her hiatus from dating, Olympia had become the belle of Daihmler. More than once she'd been to dinner with the young lawyer John Windham, who had finally given up on his wait for her to contact him and made the first move. Though nothing reached commitment level yet, she was in no hurry for it to do so. From time to time, if she needed her line of credit increased, she would make a date with banker Martin Caswell. Both men were quite smitten by the ravishing blonde beauty. Her hold over men was a power in and of itself, rivaling even her witchcraft—which neither suitor knew she possessed. Occasionally, there were other men who sought to woo her, but she never paid them much attention unless she was bored or desired a free but expensive dinner.

"You ain't doin' things good girls ortta not be doin' are you, Lympy?" Zelda asked over Sunday lunch one summer afternoon. "No man wants somebody else's stale leftovers."

Outraged by the implication, Olympia cried, "Of course I haven't! You know me, Zelda. No man is going to claim me unless I am his wife. And it will take a very special man to make that happen."

"Time is runnin' out. You're near twenty-two now."

Olympia made a face. "That is still young in the dating world Zelda. Besides, I have other, more important plans." She clasped her friend's hand in excitement. "You know how I told you that I wanted to take up Father's work with the Consort. Well, I have been in contact with Mr. Uding, who has suggested me to the King. King Bedwyr adores me! He has agreed to a test. I drive to Atlanta tomorrow to meet with a representative from the Council who will challenge my abilities. If I pass, I can be assigned to a case."

Zelda shot up from her chair, "I didn't think you was serious about that!"

"Of course!" Olympia replied. "The Consort pays quite handsomely for witches willing to go on missions. Calls come into a covert office every day from people all around the country seeking help from things the police would never believe. Those people pay for the service."

"This is how you plan to earn money?"

"At some point I must start paying this mortgage off. I don't think Mr. Caswell will lend me money forever. There is a limit to this land's worth."

"Lympy, I love ya too much to let you do this fool thing. Alone out there you'll get killed in a second. All you can do is stop people in place. But what if somebody sneaks up on you. How you gonna see them coming?"

Olympia smiled deviously. "Because I put your name in with mine. You will know when danger is coming because you, my love, are psychic."

"Hell no!"

Even as she heard herself refuse, Zelda knew she would eventually be worn down and agree to go. No one alive had ever been able to refuse Olympia and Zelda was no better. And if the two of them were going, Pastoria would insist as well. Despite how much Zelda and Pastoria tried to reason with Olympia, they knew the stubborn girl would do exactly as she pleased. There was really no alternative but to join her, to become a team together for the Consort because frankly, they were all they had. If something happened to one of them, it needed to happen to all of them. There was no life for one without the others.

The training, such as it was, consisted of a series of tests Pastoria deemed "lame". The Consort agent gauging their powers was assisted by two others. A man with a pistol who hid himself in an abandoned warehouse and a woman who possessed the power to shoot fire from her fingertips. Olympia, Pastoria and Zelda began their challenge by finding a way into the heavily secured warehouse.

"Really?" Pastoria remarked sarcastically, surveying the flimsy setup from outside. "A steel door and barred windows."

"Well, its locked up tight." Zelda pointed out. "Got any ideas as how we get in?"

Arrogantly, Pastoria answered, "Just one." Shoving her sister aside, she outstretched her hands towards one of the metal panels lining the warehouse walls. Within two seconds the rusty bolts affixing one panel unscrewed themselves, dropping to the ground. The section of sheet metal simply fell off the building. "I mean a man with a screwdriver could get in here."

Olympia giggled, patting her sister proudly on the back. She entered first, stepping through the slot in the outer wall carefully. The agent secretly observing their skills, probably thought she moved cautiously in case an assailant was waiting inside. Truthfully, she was merely trying to not snag her pretty dress on the metal edges. Once inside and seeing there was no immediate danger, she waved her partners in. The warehouse was stacked high with wooden crates in no specific order. It was impossible to see around corners, making everything more precarious.

"Guess they felt like a maze was scarier." Zelda noted. "I don't sense nothing around though. Keep movin' forward."

The warehouse was indeed a labyrinth of shadows and silence. Olympia moved cautiously, pausing every few steps to listen for any distant echoes which might mean approaching danger. The absence of immediate peril, coupled with the deafening silence inside the warehouse, made it even more eerie. Waiting for something to happen and wondering what it would be once it did happen, only amplified the tension. Olympia's earlier confidence in herself and her team was something she was questioning now. It was dawning on her just how perilous a mission could become. With her breath starting to catch in her throat, she was reminded of her parents, who lost their lives on missions far more treacherous than this test. Behind her, mirroring her apprehension, Pastoria shuffled hesitantly in her steps.

The corridors of crates were narrowing as a turn approached. Just about to round the tight corner, Olympia felt Zelda tap her shoulder. With a swift, silent gesture, she motioned for Olympia to crouch down before taking the turn. Olympia lowered herself to the floor. Peering around the turn near ground level, a gunshot pierced the silence, whizzing over her head.

"Gun!" Pastoria screamed. Pointing out the obvious.

Reacting on instinct, Olympia dropped to her stomach, tossing up her hands to send her immobilizing power casting out. She rose to her feet, motioning for her team to follow. They all saw the gunman a few yards away with his pistol aimed at them. His second shot, stopped by Olympia's power, hung mid-air a few feet from the end of the barrel.

Olympia walked forward, gripping the bullet between her fingers, dropping it safely to the floor. Her earlier lapse in confidence was restoring itself. Her adrenaline was surging. She felt very much in control of the situation. Wrenching the gun from the immobile man's grip, she passed it to Zelda. Pastoria was ready, poised for action, as Olympia released the man from her hold. A burst of power from Pastoria sent the gunman crashing backwards into a tower of boxes. The force of his impact collapsed the crates down over him. Zelda ran to him, pushing boxes away until she found him disoriented on the concrete. Pulling a long yellow scarf from her head, she hogtied him.

Emboldened by their success, Olympia triumphantly shouted, "Next!" as she raised her hand to the air above making circular motions with her index finger. "What else you got?"

The fire witch was still unaccounted for, likely to be their next task. The test subjects pushed ahead, continuing through the warehouse. Row by row, every twist and turn through the maze of crates shrank their confidence and reignited their anxiety. Midway through the facility, Zelda felt a tinge of a vision coming into her mind. Though the image did not reveal the enemy witch's whereabouts, it did provide an important clue. "Ya'll, wait," Zelda whispered to her friends. "That lady just got a splinter."

"What?" Pastoria asked in confusion.

"Yeah," Zelda went on. "She's walkin' somewhere behind us. Moved her hand over the side of a crate. Got a red splinter in her hand."

Olympia grinned. "Three rows back. Remember those crates with the red writing on them?"

"Exactly," Zelda nodded.

Doubling back a couple of rows, Pastoria used her telekinesis to shift the crates stacked with the red lettering into a pen. It took her a few moves to forge the enclosure around the enemy witch, but she was successful. "Let her try to burn her way out of that," Pastoria laughed. "She'll either roast herself to death or cause the boxes to fall and crush her."

"Well, this was too easy," Olympia celebrated. "Where is that test manager. I believe we just got hired."

It was then when their premature bravado switched to panic as a horrifying twist came their way. Six of the crates surrounding them exploded open, revealing a danger none had prepared for– vampires! No one had to tell the girls what the monsters were. They'd seen enough horror movies to know one when they saw one, although these blood suckers were far from the well dressed, sometimes charming Bela Lugosi types. Their faces were sunken, skin parched and creviced. Their ravenous eyes gleamed with insatiable hunger above their razor-sharp teeth. Whoever placed these creatures here had subjected them to an elevated starvation before unleashing them upon the girls. The murderous devils rampaged towards them, claws outstretched like switchblades, ready to eviscerate. Yet it was the screeching cries erupting from their blood deprived throats which shook the witches to their core.

Olympia managed to freeze one of them, but the others, sensing her melee, leapt out of blast range. She required time to concentrate in order to widen her scope if she hoped to catch them all in her power, but they came too quickly, giving her no time. Thinking quickly, Pastoria sent a wooden crate hurtling towards two of the vampires. It had little effect other than distracting them momentarily. Meanwhile, Zelda, basically useless in the situation, decided her best contribution to the fight was to act as a decoy. She sprinted back toward the front of the warehouse, hoping to lure the vampires away from her friends, buying them time to do something—anything. It worked. Three of the monsters chased hard on her heels.

As Olympia dealt with the other two by pausing them in motion, she noticed the first vampire she'd frozen earlier was shaking loose from his immobilized state. Evidently, her power had limited effectiveness on the undead. Pastoria was running after the three vampires pursuing Zelda. Using her power to will objects, she swept the broken boards from the earlier fallen crates, sending them stabbing forward. Two of the monsters were impaled through the heart, while the other was only tripped by the projectile. Pastoria ran toward Zelda, snatching one of the boards from the chest cavity of a fallen vampire as she passed. The third vampire, now caught up to Zelda, was seconds away from sinking his fangs into her arm. Pastoria found the extra push she needed to sprint faster, like a marathon runner almost to the line. Thrusting the shard of wood in her hand forward, she stabbed into the vampire's back, piercing and pushing his unbeating heart from his chest, killing him instantly. Zelda rolled clear of the board before it got her too, then jumped to her feet to thank her friend. Still holding the board, both Pastoria and Zelda gagged at the sight of the dead and shriveled heart hanging onto one splintered shard broken off and dangling from its impact. Tossing it aside, they looked back to where they had left Olympia, only to see her cornered against a wall by the remaining three vampires.

Panicked and with no other options, Olympia did what instinct told her to do. She thrust her hands forward, attempting to freeze the vampires once more. But this time, something unexpected happened. No one understood it at first. Zelda, Pastoria, and Olympia stood in shocked silence as bloody pieces of tissue dripped from their faces and hair. The vampires were gone, exploded into gruesome bits now littering the floor, crates, and walls.

"Lympy?" Zelda called out, stumbling forward, gasping for breath. "Did you just blow those...*things,* up?"

Still bewildered herself, Olympia stared wide-eyed at her friends. "I think I did."

"How?" Pastoria squealed.

Olympia leaned down, resting her hands on her knees, regulating her own breathing as her adrenaline still surged. "I have no idea. It just erupted from me. I swear I didn't know I could do that."

Stepping from the shadows as overhead lights clicked on, bathing the warehouse in fluorescent white, the Consort agent began clapping. "A powerful team you three could make. Oh, you have a great deal to learn and will probably perish on your very first case, but you have impressed me enough to give you a chance. You'll receive your first assignment from the Witches Association, very soon."

Olympia, only just realizing she was covered in disgusting bodily fluids from the exploded vampires, lifted the hem of her once-pretty dress and asked, "Do you reimburse for a clothing allowance?"

CHAPTER TWENTY-ONE

The Haunting at Colburn Farm

The order came a few days after they passed the test. They were offered their very first assignment. The timing meant she would need to cancel her upcoming date with Martin, which she did not mind because there were no other rivals for his attention. Or so she thought. She went to the bank to break the news, but upon entering his office–without knocking or even allowing the secretary to announce her–she found another young woman seated across from his desk.

"Olympia!" Martin exclaimed, rising abruptly.

Olympia sneered slightly at the back of the woman's head, which was now turning around to see her. "I did not mean to interrupt you with your companion."

The young woman stood, presenting a radiant smile Olympia's way. Olympia did not enjoy the fact this woman was rather pretty. She was sleekly built, almost frail in fact, or perhaps delicate was a nicer word. Her hair was golden, shoulder length but not quite as light in color or perfect in texture or sheen as Olympia's own. Still, she was more attractive than was comfortable for Olympia. Having never occurred to her that Martin, or anyone for that matter, might seek additional female company while also dating her, Olympia found herself feeling an emotion she'd never experienced before. *Is this what jealousy feels like?*

Rushing excitedly towards her, the girl squealed almost piercingly, "You are Olympia? You must be! I'd know you anywhere. I have longed to lay eyes on you."

"And you are?" Olympia asked impertinently.

Martin, now around the desk and grasping Olympia's hand, made the introduction. "Miss Olympia Blanchard, I would like you to meet my sister Lauralee Caswell."

"Sister!" Olympia said, replacing her indignation with a smile she hoped would be interpreted as genuine. "Miss Caswell, I have heard so many wonderful things."

"Please, call me Lauralee. And I'll call you Olympia," she said grabbing Olympia's free wrist. "I think we are going to be great friends."

"I hope so."

Martin let a grin escape, yet he appeared somewhat dislodged from his usual composure. His eyes reflected an awkwardness she had never seen in him. It appeared as if he was anxiously uncomfortable by the two women in his life coming together. Olympia wondered why, but only for a moment.

"Friends are so important; don't you think Olympia?" Lauralee beamed with an exaggerated exhilaration. Olympia gave a polite, although confused nod, as Lauralee went on. "You know it was Albert Einstein who said friends are like golden chalices of nectar. Drink from the cup and know you've had a good sip of something."

Olympia's eyes widened slightly, inadvertently making a face she hadn't meant to. She glanced at Martin, who only smiled nervously. "I do not believe I have ever heard that particular quote." Olympia replied to Lauralee.

"Oh yes, he was always talking about friendship." Lauralee answered. "Or was it math? I don't really know. He talked about a lot of stuff in his time. I read a book on him once. Did you know he discovered gravity when a pecan fell out of a tree onto his head."

"That was Newton and an apple." Martin said growing pink faced. "Excuse my sister, Olympia. She misquotes quite often."

Lauralee laughed aloud. "It's true. I am not too bright. Momma used to say my head got watery when I almost drowned in the bathtub at two years old. But I think I'm a friendly person. Isn't that the most important thing? Being kind? I hope you will like me, Olympia."

Understanding fully now the complete innocence of the soul before her, Olympia clasped her hand over Lauralee's and said, "I like you already." The words immediately filled the girl's face with a joy that made Olympia feel as if she'd just gifted the sweet soul something precious.

Taking control of the situation, Martin lifted Olympia's hand from his sister, clutching it into his own and asked, "What brings you here, my dear?"

"Oh," Olympia answered, almost forgetting the purpose herself. "I came to tell you I have to cancel our date tomorrow night. I must attend to a matter with my sister and Zelda."

Martin asked his sister to excuse them a moment so that he could walk Olympia back to her car. Lauralee shouted out her hope she might be allowed to call on

Olympia soon. Olympia said it would be her pleasure to receive her at Blanchard House anytime. As Martin steered Olympia through the bank lobby, he made a blushed apology. "I am sorry about my sister, Olympia. I did mean to prepare you before the two of you officially met."

"I knew you took care of her," Olympia replied. "I suppose I just naturally assumed you meant you provided for her financially because she was unmarried."

"No, it's a little more than that." Martin said. "She's a fine girl. Never was there a more loving heart. Yet she was correct in what she joked about. When she was little, she drowned in the tub when my mother left her for only a moment to get a fresh bath towel. Lauralee thankfully did not die, but we think the incident is the reason why her mind is so...well so..."

"So delightfully unique." Olympia offered. Martin smiled with gratitude. "Martin, I think she's wonderful. We are all a little different in one way or another."

"Thank you," he said. "Now as for our date, is everything all right?"

"Of course," she told him, only slightly lying. "I simply have a private family matter I must see to. I will phone you once I am free again."

Martin released her from their plans graciously with full understanding. He had no idea she also made two other stops on the way home to make other cancellations with other men whom she had other dates pending. One of these stops was to the law offices of handsome John Windham.

Of all three dates she was forced to renege upon, the date with John was the only one she regretted. He, and he alone, received profuse apologies and the chance for a raincheck once she was available again. Though they had only been out a few times—his heavy caseload preventing much time for socializing—Olympia kept careful track of him.

It wasn't because she worried he might meet another girl who would interest him; she knew that was next to impossible in comparison to her. However, men like John Windham often lose themselves so deeply to their work it often consumes their every thought. To keep this from happening, Olympia made a point to stroll past his offices on Second Street at least twice a week. Brinkers Martinizing Cleaners was located two doors down from the law firm. For a dry-cleaning store, it was very modern, which pleased Olympia who considered herself the same. Its dark red and green counter and equipment were quite a contrast to the Fluff and Fold three streets over. Of course, Olympia had no real need for dry cleaning, but marching her single piece of clothing back and forth did provide an opportunity for John to spot her if he happened to look down from his window. And sometimes he did.

"Are you picking your dress up, Olympia?" he asked her the very first time he came outside to greet her. "I saw you bring it in two days ago. You do know *Martinizing* means they have it ready within an hour?"

Toying flirtatiously, Olympia replied, "Now do I look to you like the sort of woman who waits around an hour for a dress to be cleaned? Of course, I suppose I could scare up a lunch companion to while away the 60 minutes and save myself that second trip into town."

While Olympia lived life believing all men in her presence were bewitched by her charm, John was not naïve. He proved a formidable opponent in her game when he did not take the bait and invite her to lunch. Watching her pretend his unchivalrous inattention wasn't a blow to her ego, amused him. Of course, even a man as resilient as John Windham was unable to dodge her allure forever. After two weeks he could stand it no more, and their weekly standing lunch dates went into effect. Now, due to work, she had to break their date.

The case file was sent by special messenger to Blanchard House, concealed in a thin brown envelope. Olympia opened it immediately and settled down at the kitchen table with Zelda and Pastoria. As she read the first page aloud, detailing the circumstances and the objective, a pesky housefly buzzed around her head. For a first mission, it was an interesting one, although Olympia was not quite sure how to handle it. Considering the level of danger involved with their test trial, she half expected a similar circumstance for the first case. Another vampire perhaps or something equally as dangerous, but what their new little team got assigned...was a ghost.

"Ain't that a little silly?" Zelda declared after Olympia finished reading. "I mean, a ghost. Hell, the south's full of 'em. Ghosts don't hurt nobody."

"Well, this one does." Olympia replied, scanning the second page of the report. "It's quite malevolent." The fly continued to buzz overhead, undeterred by hands swatting the air around it. Without looking up from the report in her hand, Olympia flicked her fingers above the table, immobilizing the fly. It fell instantly to the floor. "In fact, it has killed someone already."

"Killed someone?" Pastoria gasped. "A ghost?"

Gingerly lifting the housefly between her fingertips, Olympia walked to the open window over the sink. "Ghost. Poltergeist. Demon. I don't know which it may turn out to be, but it is real enough that the Council has asked us to investigate." She tossed the fly outside, freeing it from her spell before it hit the ground. The fly winged away into the sunlight.

Pastoria sighed in disappointment, "I was really hoping to impale some more vampires. I was pretty good at that."

"Why us?" Zelda asked. "Our test didn't include no ghost training."

Olympia withdrew a photograph of a little farmhouse from the folder. "This is close to us. The proximity probably dictated the assignment. It's in Brookwood, just a few miles away. The family is really frightened."

The ladies made the short drive to rural Brookwood, Alabama only a few miles outside of Daihmler. Turning onto Covered Bridge Road, Olympia steered carefully through the twists and turns of the gravel and dirt road. Up ahead they saw the covered bridge which the road was named for, stretching over Hurricane Creek. Olympia knew a little about this very bridge, remembering something in school about how it was the last surviving bridge of its kind in Tuscaloosa County. It was a bit of a landmark for Brookwood, an area possessing no other merit other than farms and coal mines. Long covered bridges such as this one had been rather important a generation or two ago when wagons were the main means of transportation. Towns were few and far between then. Many travelers took refuge from surprise thunderstorms beneath the shelter of its strong oak timbers and tin roof.

"This bridge ain't gone be here long," Zelda remarked, as they slowly drove along its plank ledges.

"I think it will," Pastoria said. "It is preserved by the Historical Society. They wouldn't tear it down."

"Naw, but its gonna burn down." Zelda explained. "I sense it. Not too long from now some dumb fool boys are gonna start a fire and its gone fall into the creek."

Olympia frowned as the sunlight hit her face in waves through the lattice framed sides. "That's a shame. But we aren't here to save bridges. I think the Colburn farm is up ahead."

The Colburn mailbox, painted red, alerted Olympia where to turn. The craggy rutted dirt driveway caused her car to jostle uncomfortably until she slowed her speed a bit. Passing through a patch of thick trees and brambles, the little road opened to a sunny patch of land with a gray wooded shotgun farmhouse. The dogtrot hall separated the two portions of the house, something not unfamiliar to Olympia although she had never actually been to one before. This house was constructed well before modern conveniences when only a cool breeze running through the divided house was all there was to combat a hot summer. A woman was standing on the porch, her hand to her forehead shielding the sun from her eyes as she watched the car drive up. For someone living in so ancient a home, the woman was dressed relatively modern.

"Hi," the woman called out as the trio of witches exited the car. "I am Judith Colburn. I called the office to request your help."

The office to which she was referring was a front for the Consort. The only information the magazine and newspaper ads for the office divulged was a vague statement advertising assistance for anyone experiencing paranormal or supernatural danger. The person fielding the calls in the office never revealed its association with a league of witches. The Consort insisted on keeping their existence a secret for the safety of its members. Only once a case was deemed to be valid would anyone be dispatched to help.

"I saw a little snippet in the back of Good Housekeeping," Judith explained. "You know, in the back where all the kooky ads are. Never thought I'd call one before, but after what we been through, I took the chance."

Olympia extended her hand to shake with the woman. "I am Olympia Blanchard, and these are my sisters. We are here to help if we can."

Judith led them inside the left portion of the house, where Olympia and her companions were quite surprised to see was rather cheerily decorated. If the outside of the house seemed strictly 1880 the inside was absolutely 1960. "Don't you love shag carpeting!" Olympia remarked as they sat down in the front room. "I just got some for our house."

"Our farm has been doing well lately," Judith admitted. "Wasn't the case not too long ago, but now we are making money. My husband and his brother grow cotton. Had a good many years where the land just wasn't working right. Soil went bad. But now everything is good again and every field is flourishing."

"Funny how things can change so quickly," said another woman, a little younger, coming out of the back kitchen. She was smiling in a way which made Olympia suspect she held a secret she enjoyed keeping. "I am Easty. Judith's sister-in-law."

The Colburn women starkly contrasted each other. Judith, probably only a few years Easty's senior, was weatherworn from years of field work on the farm. Her face bore marks of sun damaged along the bridge of her nose, top of her cheeks, and the edges of her forehead. Easty, on the other hand, was not yet scarred by the harshness of farm life.

"Nice to meet you," Olympia said, greeting Easty. Returning her attention to Judith, she began, "Tell us what is going on here at the farm. I heard someone died."

Judith seemed to shudder at the mention of the death. She took a moment to begin her tale, but when she did, she made no mention of the person who died. She spoke of minor things at first. Household items being moved to odd places, such as a saltshaker on the windowsill or a fork stuck into the leg of the kitchen table. The more she shared the more animated she became explaining the peculiarities they were experiencing. The more she spoke, the faster she spoke as she spilled the secrets her family had been trying their best to conceal from the neighbors. "It's like the second this farm got prosperous; a curse fell on us."

"A misplaced bottle of salt doesn't sound too threatening." Pastoria commented.

"That was just the beginning," Judith explained. "Windows broke all by themselves. The tires of the truck exploded. Then we started hearing things outside at night. Sounds I can't even put into words coming from the barn, then the chicken coops. Next day, the cow wouldn't give milk and none of the chickens had laid any eggs. Then the combine broke and those things don't come cheap. Zeke managed to fix it, but it set us back."

Pastoria weighed in again, "Those things sound like a run of bad luck, but nothing that proves a supernatural occurrence."

Easty interrupted, feeling the need to clarify her sister-in-law's statement. "Judith doesn't mean we came home to a broken window, or the truck tires went flat. She means we were all sitting around the table when every window in the house blew out as if something invisible smashed them. And when the truck tires blew, we were all out there, unloading supplies, when all four tires just popped!"

Changing her position from her earlier remark, Pastoria said, "I admit that is curious."

"There's more," Easty continued. "Furniture started smashing against the wall. The dog fell over dead, choking on something nobody could see. Then the barn…"

As Easty mentioned the barn, Judith's face went pale. "The barn," she repeated softly.

"There is definitely something here," Easty Colburn insisted. "Something evil haunting us. And you can call it up too if you try."

"What do you mean, call it up?" Olympia questioned.

Easty walked outside onto the porch where the others followed. Calling out to the air, she shouted, "You wanna put on a show you old haint! Show these women what you can do!"

"Easty, don't rile it!" Judith pleaded, but it was too late.

As Olympia and the others followed onto the porch, something was different outside than it had been before. The atmosphere felt thick with an unexplainable tension as if the fabric of reality were on the verge of flipping. The women glanced uneasily at each other. The quietude of the remote farm broken by an unsettling sight. The dust and dirt along the road began to writhe upward in sheets, swirling together forming an ominous cyclone. It spiraled more slowly than a storm born by natural means. No, this manifestation seemed created with, and directed by, malevolent intent. Inching closer and closer to the unsuspecting group, the swirling spiral moved over the yard, intercepting once dormant patches of dead grass now disconnecting from the ground, joining the vortex as if compelled by an invisible force. As it moved over the yard the storm changed form, widening into a towering wall of debris rushing towards them.

Rendered into self-preservation by the hostile force coming for them, Judith and Easty retreated into the house for cover, their faces twisted in terror. Olympia stood firmly in place, with Pastoria and Zelda standing their ground beside her. With trembling hands, Olympia released a blast of her power towards the approaching menace, stopping it in place just a few feet from the house. Pastoria took over then, sending out a shockwave which collided into the entity breaking it apart into the fragments of earth comprising it, raining it back down onto the yard.

A piercing shriek erupted from the air, as if the presence behind the attack had been wounded somehow.

Judith's eyes were bulging in disbelief as she came back out to the porch. Turning to the Blanchards, she muttered, "How did you?"

"You wanted supernatural help." Pastoria called over her shoulder to the frightened women. "You got supernatural help."

"Anybody wanna tell us what the heck jus' screamed?" Zelda exclaimed.

The men returned home from the fields shortly after the sinister manifestation. The little Colburn family sat down with the Blanchard witches to explain what little they understood about the happenings on the farm. "It's some blame spook come to haunt our land now that we are finally making money." Zeke Colburn, Judith's husband, told them. "My daddy bought this place back in 1910 and it never did do much. Spent his life workin' this land and we barely got by. One year'd be alright. Next year we'd get infested with bollworms. We'd get rid of those and get spider mites next. Soil problems too. But even then those were just the normal blights any cotton farm has. We never had problems like we got now."

"Your wife told us the farm is doing well these days." Olympia remarked.

"Yeah. Now." Zeke answered. "When Pa died and my brother and I took over runnin' things, it started getting better. Guess God figured we needed some blessin'. Rains tend to come regular when we need 'em to. Ain't had a hailstorm or drought ruin a crop in years. Bugs don't seem to fool with our cotton no more either. We got successful harvests comin' now year after year."

Zeke's brother Barney spoke up next, "Now when we finally got money comin' in, this blame spirit we can't even see, comes cursing us." Addressing Olympia, whom he assumed to be the one in charge of the odd trio of ladies there to help, Barney asked, "You figure it's the ghost of the old owner angered we made a go of it?"

Olympia considered the thought a moment. "Possibly," she said. "But ghosts do not possess the type of power your particular haunting has. Oh, yes, they can open doors and topple furniture. Perhaps make a tire go flat. But to summon a dust storm and will it towards an intended target, that's different."

"And don't forget it screams!" Zelda interjected.

Nodding in agreement, Olympia added, "Yes, clear and audible cries is not something you find with average ghosts."

"Poltergeists are stronger than ghosts, I hear." Easty remarked. "I read about all kinds of interesting stuff. Got some books on things like that. Aren't poltergeists supposed to be real powerful?" Olympia admitted she knew very little on the subject of Poltergeists, but asked if she might take a look at some of Easty's books.

Following the young woman across the dogtrot to the other side of the house where the bedrooms lay, Olympia began to contemplate a possibility she had, until now, not considered. Upon entering Easty and Barney's room, she noticed a few things out of the ordinary for a simple rural farm couple. To an unfamiliar eye, the contents of the room wouldn't have sparked suspicion, but Olympia recognized several items inconsistent with a simple farm wife. Candles were scattered around in various places, all colorful. A blue candle rose from a small pewter holder on the top of a shelving unit. A few shelves down, two green candles sat on a saucer plate. One wick burned, the other untouched. A round hand mirror lay on the shelf as well, with what looked like melted black wax marring it. Most country people use candles for necessity, not decoration. Colored candles cost a great deal more than plain white. Why would Easty have paid more? On top of the dressing table near the bed, Olympia spotted what looked to be a little patch of dust or dirt. While Easty rummaged through her books to find the one on Poltergeists, Olympia inspected the dresser. It was not dirt or dust. It was the remnants of some kind of crushed herb. She touched her fingertip to it then sniffed her finger. Sage. *Why would sage be in the bedroom?* Easty withdrew a thick book from her shelves to hand to Olympia. It was entitled Ghost Hunter by an author named Hans Holzer. Olympia was more interested in the other books she now noticed on Easty's shelves.

"You have quite a collection of material here." Olympia said. "The Lost Ways. Witches and Witchcraft. Candle Magic. Are you by chance a practicing witch?"

Easty smiled broadly, "That has to be our little secret."

Taking a seat on the edge of the bed, Olympia gently interrogated Easty Colburn. "Your husband doesn't know?" Olympia asked. "Doesn't he see your books?"

"Barney can't read. Never went to school. He grew up on this farm."

"Does Judith know?"

"It's touchy for her," Easty frowned. "See, her kid sister was the one that got killed by the ghost. Her name was Emily. Me and Emily started learning the craft together. We were tired of being poor. Thought we could use magic to make some good come about. And we were right. We did it. Place is making lots of money now."

"What exactly did the two of you do?"

The young wife seemed very proud of herself when she lowered her voice to quietly confide, "We found a few spells in a book claiming to attract money and prosperity. We did 'em. Was mostly us just having fun at first. Didn't think much about it. But then we had a run of really good weather. The crop took off. Barney and Zeke worked a better price with the buyer cause our cotton quality improved.

We were suddenly a profitable farm."

Olympia motioned for Easty to sit beside her on the quilted bedspread. "How did Emily die?"

She was hesitant to answer. Olympia sensed she wished she had not revealed her magical secret. "It is important," Olympia urged. "What happened to Emily?"

"She was in the barn when it burned down. She slept out there in the loft on warm nights." Easty's eyes glistened with emerging tears as she recounted the tragic event. "I heard her screaming. Terrible screams. Never heard sounds like that before. The pain she must have–. By the time we got outside, there was no way we could get into the barn to help her. Whole thing was blazing. Could hear Emily all the way to the end."

Olympia offered a sympathetic nod. She had only one other question for the distraught Mrs. Colburn, "How do you know the barn was burned down by the ghost and not some accident regarding Emily? Perhaps a fallen kerosene lamp or something?"

Easty looked directly into Olympia's eyes as if making a confession. "Cause the ghost told us. It writ it right in the dirt in the yard."

"What did the ghost write in the dirt?"

"The Devil is Here."

CHAPTER TWENTY-TWO

The Blanchard Witches of Daihmler County

Promising to return to the Colburn farm the following morning, Olympia drove her little trio of detectives back to Blanchard House. Over a hastily prepared dinner of cornbread and fried ham, they discussed the case.

"So Easty thinks she's a witch, does she?" Zelda chuckled. "These girls with their catalogue ordered books and magic candles make me laugh out loud. That girl ain't got a lick of power in her. She's playing parlor games."

"I know," Olympia said. "Yet, I can't help but believe this is related to the haunting."

"The Devil is here," Pastoria repeated. "Sounds satanic. Could a demon be the culprit?"

"Why would a demon be concerned with a cotton farm?" Olympia asked. "These people are not important. Why mess with them? I think the ghost's message refers to their practicing of witchcraft, rather than it is announcing Satan moved to the farm. Which would mean whoever the ghost is, is obviously upset by their use of magic."

Zelda scoffed at the theory. "Why would some ghost care if a couple of silly girls cast a dumb spell?"

Pastoria pointed out the obvious by saying, "Doesn't sound as if it was a dumb spell. It clearly worked. Those girls, naive or not, have the ability to cast a working spell."

"You sayin whatever spirit inhabits that farm got offended? Like maybe the ghost of some devout Christian?" Zelda replied. "Could something like that be offended enough to kill?"

Olympia folded her hands together on the table, puzzled herself by the case. She remembered something her father once told her; the simplest explanation is usually the accurate one. "Who knows if the Emily girl was truly murdered by the presence or if she just happened to be in the wrong place when a barn fire erupted. There are a hundred explanations for why that barn could have caught fire, and none of them of the spirit world."

"How do we know this girl doesn't have real powers," Pastoria asked. "They were pretty poor before she began casting spells."

Olympia rose from the table and began pacing the kitchen floor. The others remained silent, assuming she was evaluating the evidence before them, but Olympia's mind was weighing far more than the Colburn family troubles. She was wandering into territory she probably should have avoided, momentarily questioning if she was equipped to handle this situation. Until now, her experience with real danger was limited to the one time she aided her parents during an attack and the test run the Consort agent had given them. Her only expertise in supernatural matters was whatever she might remember her father recounting from his work. Could she truly be of help to these people? It all seemed so simple in theory when she decided to take up her father's work. It was imaginary then. She assumed her powers would be sufficient to save the lives of people unable to save themselves. Now that her know-how was being tested in actual practice, the real-life ramifications of making a mistake weighed heavily on her. But it was too late to turn back now. Olympia had to make the choice to believe she and her sisters had what it takes to handle anything that came at them. She sat back down with the others, releasing her self-doubts and returning to finding solutions.

"We all know there is immense energy in everything around us," she began. "It is a force we tap into to accelerate our power. Any person who can train their mind to dial into that energy can manifest *some* magic. I have no doubt Easty Colburn managed to do this to propel good fortune their way. If we are to presume what she did has riled up an unseen entity, we must discover who that entity is or was."

"Well, the thing we gotta do is cut to the chase," Zelda said. "Hold us a séance. I'm a gonna talk to that ghost tomorrow."

The next morning after a restful night's sleep, Olympia drove her sister and Zelda back to the Colburn farm. Easty squawked at the idea, adamant a daytime séance would not work. Zelda assured her *the other side* could be as easily reached by day as by night, and not to let the gimmicks of Hollywood fool her. With the séance beginning in the light of day, the Colburns were left a little disappointed by how ordinary it all seemed. No one was required to hold hands. No candles were needed.

The ceremony had no embellishments at all.

Zelda spoke unceremoniously as she attuned her mind to the spirit plain. "I know there's a few spirits on this farm cause I can feel ya'll. But the one I'm interested in is the one that whipped up that dust storm yesterday. So, whoever you are, come and talk to me a bit." For a little while Zelda simply sat staring at everyone, herself waiting for something to happen. After a few minutes, she perked up in her seat, straining to listen to some distant sound no one else could hear. Relaxing back in her chair, she waved her hand as if dismissing someone, "Did you not hear what I said?" Zelda scoffed. "I am addressing the one that blew up that dirt wall yesterday. These people ain't interested in the rest of you." Pausing as if being spoken to by someone unseen, Zelda answered the spirit callously, "Don't nobody know or care where your mama's Bible went. I guess one a'your kinfolk took it when you died. I ain't here to get it back to your daughter. You shoulda give it to her when you was alive if it was that important. She can buy her own in a store. Those things are everywhere."

Pastoria snickered into her wrist.

Returning to her task, Zelda reiterated, "Like I said, I only wanna talk to the one who caused that storm. The one who has been menacing these people who live here. The rest of you stay quiet."

Wind could be heard outside. It grew intensely, causing the old rickety house to shake slightly under its pressure. The uneven edges of the windowsill allowed rushing air to pass raising whistling sounds which grew higher in pitch like that of a teapot. The experience sent a few shivers up everyone's spine although it did not appear to bother Zelda in the least. "If you got a voice, use it. If not, speak to my mind. I'll hear ya."

Nothing happened for several more minutes other than the rushing wind pushing its way into the house through any crack or loose shingle it could find. No one broke the silence as Zelda sat eyes closed in deep concentration. Despite the flow of air seeping in around them, a stillness of anticipation hung overhead. An eerie chill infiltrated the atmosphere, something otherworldly. A sense of sorrow for forgotten times and unfulfilled destinies weighted the room. Everyone felt it. The sadness lifted as a harder, fiercer emotion set in. Rage.

Zelda gave off a slight shiver. "Oh. You are an angry little cuss ain't ya," she said. Placing her hands firmly on the table, Zelda declared, "Don't be getting all fussy with me. I can't help what they did to you. You were treated bad, I admit. You didn't deserve all that, but you are wrong too. I'm *proud* to be a witch. I help folks. You ain't helping anybody. You killed that poor girl. I see it all. I know 'xactly what you did. You tossed a lantern at her bed and burned that poor child to bits while she was asleep in that loft."

"Emily!" Judith gasped. "The ghost did do it!"

"Zelda," Pastoria said softly. "What does the ghost want?"

Zelda opened her eyes which she fixed upon young Easty. "For you to stop."

"What?" Easty exclaimed. "What have I done?"

"You used a rudimentary form of witchcraft to make your family lucky," Zelda told her. "But you stirred up a mess of hate when you did."

The men erupted with outrage. "You did what?" Barney exclaimed.

Zeke stared viciously at his brother's wife, "You brought the devil to this house?"

Not in the mood to entertain a swell of misinformed infuriation, nor the personal insult it implied, Zelda shouted out, "Oh, Good Lord, shut up and calm down! Men are about the dumbest critters this world ever made. This girl ain't summoned no devil. She just practiced a little magic. Nothing wrong with what she did. She just wants to help."

Outraged, Zeke yelled, "You call what she done to us *help*!"

Zelda pounded her fist on the table, "Weren't you two fools poor as a pissant before she did what she did? Miss Easty is the only reason you got a prosperous farm. She turned your old dead dirt into nutrient rich soil and saved your damn lives. You owe Easty some well deserved thanks. Girl ain't really a witch, but she figured out how to twist earth's natural power to her benefit and saved your hides."

"Thank you." Easty said to Zelda with a grateful smile. "I was only trying to help the family. I want children. I want them educated. I don't want us to remain poor and struggling all our lives. I don't want my husband broken and old before his time trying to squeeze out a living from used up land." Easty looked at her husband. "I wanted something more for us, and I went about it the only way I could."

Olympia patted her hand. "No one is faulting you for your actions, Easty. At least we three aren't. Unfortunately, it does seem to have come with some repercussions."

"You can say that again," Pastoria snorted. "You awakened someone who isn't very understanding."

Easty hung her head in shame. Zelda reached her finger to the girl's chin and lifted her head back up where it belonged. "You ain't got nothing to be ashamed over." Easty smiled once more. Zelda cradled her cheek in her hand and asked, "You know anything about your background girl? Do you even know where your name comes from?"

"I have no idea what you mean," Easty Colburn replied. "My family originally comes from Boston, but I was born here and so was my mama and daddy."

"Well girl sit back and listen," chuckled Zelda. "That pissy spirit done showed me what's got her so riled. You're about to get a history lesson."

Zelda began a tale which would prove shocking to the little Colburn family of Brookwood. It all began back in old Salem, Massachusetts. "Yes," Zelda reiterated, as their dumbfounded faces stared back at her. "That Salem."

Mary Eastey was a respected citizen of Salem, as was her sister Rebecca Nurse. Though both women were held in the highest regard prior to the infamous witch trials, their reputations and standing in the community would not be enough to protect them against the wave of hysteria overcoming the town. The tyranny of a court radicalized by baseless fear allowed the charge of witchery to mark many innocent people, resulting in most of their deaths. It all started when a group of prepubescent girls pointed the finger of accusation to a few women for being in league with the devil. Once these attention-starved girls saw the influence their testimony garnered, there was no stopping them. Day after day, these girls performed their dramatic little plays before the court, condemning scores of women and men for being a witch. No one dared step forward to challenge the claims of these brutal girls—perhaps from fear of falling accused themselves.

Finding herself now accused, Mary Eastey sat in the courtroom with folded hands proclaiming her innocence to the unyielding and gullible judges. As she tried to reason with the court pointing out the absurdity of the claims, the deceitful girls interlocked their own hands to mimic Mary's, claiming they could not separate them due to Mary inflicting her powers upon them. Accepting her fate and understanding the court was incapable of thinking for itself, Mary hung her head in disbelief at her neighbors falling for such childish gimmicks. The story of Mary Eastey stands as a tragic example of how fear and manipulation can lead to the downfall of a society. At the gallows, she gave a speech which brought tears to the onlooker's eyes. She spoke to her family of her earnest loyalty to God and beseeched the judges to stop murdering innocent Christians based on the lies of attention starved children. Mary was hanged immediately after.

"And that gal who got hanged 400 years ago, Miss Easty..." Zelda said, wrapping up her tale. "Was your direct ancestor. Your grandma in a matter of speakin'. And she's real pissed one of her kin would take up witchcraft after she, her sisters, and many of their friends died for such and weren't even guilty."

"This is crazy?" Easty Colburn exclaimed.

"Naw, it ain't so crazy." Zelda said. "You done disrespected your ancestor. She suffered horrible things for being falsely accused of bein' a witch. They didn't just kill her. She went through days bein' tortured and personally humiliated in front of folks she knew all her life while they tried to coax her into sayin' she was a witch. And now here you are tryin' to be one. Her own ancestor playin' around with the very thing she got killed over."

Easty was dumbfounded. This was a revelation she had lived her life completely unaware of. No one in her family ever mentioned any of this to her. Most likely, even they had not known.

"You want this spirit to go back to rest?" Zelda went on. "Cut your witch shit out."

"But what about this spirit?" Zeke asked. "This Mary Eastey person? Will she haunt us the rest of our lives?"

"Nope." Zelda said, rising from the table to make her way towards the front door. "I'm gonna spend some more time wandering around out here and commune with her. Think I can get her to go back to where she came from. She's still of a mind of Old Salem. She don't know any more about life now than she did back then. I just gotta educate her a bit on what's what in the 1960's."

Hoping to assuage some of Zeke's concerns, Olympia added to Zelda's pronouncement. "We can also cast a protection spell over this farm and all of you to shield against malevolent spirits." She followed Zelda to the front door.

"Ain't that just more witchcraft for her to be furious over?" Zeke shouted after them.

Following her companions to the door, Pastoria presented a little laugh before replying, "Mr. Colburn, Mary Eastey is only a specter. Easty Colburn is just a curious girl. My sisters and I are the real deal. I assure you no ghost can break one of our protections."

"What exactly are you people?" Zeke Colburn asked. "We paid good money to get ya'll out here. How can you be sure to deliver on what you promise?"

Turning back to face the Colburn family, Olympia smiled brightly and proudly, clasping both Zelda and Pastoria's hands with her own. "We, my dear fellow, are the Blanchard Witches of Daihmler County. And we are capable of almost anything."

CHAPTER TWENTY-THREE

A Walk on Water

There may have been no shortage of suitors out to win the charms of Miss Olympia Blanchard, but the clear front runner was John Windham. The young attorney was moving up in the world, already promoted to junior partner in his firm. Though there were other men of means in Daihmler, Martin Caswell to name one, John had somehow warmed his way into a part of Olympia's heart she never knew she had. If ever she seriously considered the idea of marriage before, it was only as a last resort to save she and her sister from poverty. However, now as she was beginning to make a little money here and there with The Witches Association assignments, she was able to pay some of her mortgage down, lessening the need for a husband. The irony was not lost upon her how now that she didn't require a man for support, she found herself daydreaming of becoming Mrs. John Windham. Like it or not, (which she didn't), Olympia was indeed capable of falling in love after all.

"I suppose I do," Olympia relented softly as she sat with John along the banks of The Black Warrior River. Muted music streamed from the open windows of his car parked a few yards away, the crescent moon reflecting from the hood.

With a shake of the head, John chuckled, "Well, that isn't the most ideal way of being told I am loved in return. But I suppose when it comes to you Olympia, it's the best I should hope for."

She bristled from his words, snuggling her head into his shoulder. "I did not mean it that way, John. Of course, I love you. And that's not an easy thing for me to say, but I do. I cannot see myself finding happiness with anyone other than you."

Tightening his hold around her waist as she leaned back into him, he teased, "Not even that old numbers cruncher Caswell at the bank? I know you've seen him too a few times."

Olympia gave off one of her trademark flirtatious laughs, replying, "Oh, I have seen several other men, John. After all, you don't own me...yet. Martin is a kind man. I like him. And he isn't much older than you, I'll have you know. However, I will admit he doesn't give me the bells and whistles you do."

He enjoyed hearing this as he'd often wondered if her feelings for him were genuine or was John simply another plaything for her vanity. "Shall I take that to mean you are serious about me, and only me?"

Olympia looked into his eyes, dropping all playful pretense. For possibly the first time since they'd met, he trusted she was being real with him. "I think you may be the one John. And I never envisioned a man ever being that for me. Men were there to amuse me or for me to use if I needed something from them. But I don't want to use you, John. I think I just want to love you."

Kissing her passionately, he whispered into her lips, "I believe, Olympia, that is probably the most beautiful thing you've ever said to me."

Allowing his lips to explore her mouth and neck for a few moments, she eventually pulled away to add an addendum. "But for now, let's keep our budding relationship quiet," she suggested. "My sister isn't your biggest fan since you worked on the case that sent her boyfriend away. Besides, before we go any further with this, there is something you must know."

Grinning he teased, "Now I am afraid."

"You possibly should be."

She stood up from the grassy bank, moving to the edge of the river. Staring out onto the shimmering black surface, she gestured to the yellow and red lights of a passing barge. Just behind it was a speeding motorboat out for an evening ride. "If you are the man for me, John, I must know if you can handle some things about me. Qualities which are not going to change but will absolutely affect our life together."

John joined her at the water, apprehensive as to what she might possibly have to reveal. "What are you saying to me Olympia? If there is anything I should know about you I would like to know it now."

"And you are going to." She stretched her hand out towards the water, "Watch the boats, John."

His eyes forced themselves to refocus, trying to decide if they were seeing what he thought they were seeing. The barge and the motor craft stopped suddenly. They did not slow to a stop; they simply were no longer moving across the water. Not only did the watercraft stop, so did the very water itself. He couldn't be sure in the darkness, but from all appearances the current showed no signs of movement. Only a few feet from the water's edge, he no longer heard the slapping sounds of flowing against the riverbank. His mind could not account for what he was witnessing. John strained his eyes against the backdrop of darkness around the lights of the two halted vessels. Blinking several times to refocus his vision, he accepted that his eyes were not lying. The barge and the speedboat were definitely not moving, stopped abruptly by some unseen force. But it wasn't an unseen force which stopped them. It was the hand of Olympia. His mind struggled to find any other logical explanation for what he saw.

"Those boats stopped moving."

Olympia turned to face his confounded eyes. "They did, John."

"And...and the water. Did it stop flowing too?"

"It did."

Olympia began walking towards the river–not merely towards it, but onto it. Her feet tread across the glassy top of the stationary waters as if it were only a floor of thick rippled glass. With his own eyes trying to process the impossible sight being shown to him, John accepted her outreached hand, joining her. They walked silently for a moment across the solid surface. With careful footfalls he waited for the seemingly solid surface to break, and he fall through. It didn't. Scanning the surface with his curious eyes, his feet began to trust the situation and he walked more at his normal pace further over the river.

With a girlish giggle, Olympia placed her hand upon his cheek and said, "John, you are the first man—well, perhaps the second–to walk on water."

Standing twenty feet from the shoreline, still mesmerized by the experience, he reached for Olympia's hand and twirled her across the water. He did not know why he did it, it just felt like the thing to do. When would something like this ever happen again? She returned to his arms where his spontaneity was now replaced with a stare of seriousness. "Olympia...what are you?"

"I am a witch, John. I have the power to stop time."

Looking at their feet, he added, "And walk on water?"

She laughed. "No, I'm not Jesus. But water molecules, I recently discovered quite by accident, become secure enough to stand on if I hold them in place."

John Windham, forthright, legal eagle, educated man that he was, now understood he knew very little. The law of physics and science were upended forever for him. "A witch. Witch? Like in MacBeth or Oz?"

"Fiction, darling," she smiled. "Witches are real, but you have never seen an authentic depiction. We do good for the world. We protect the world in a sense. Think of us as Earth's magical police force."

"Take me back to the shore, Olympia. I need to sit down."

She returned him to the surety of solid ground, whereupon she released the river and its occupants back to their normal pursuit as if nothing had ever paused them. John sat on the edge of his car bumper; hands planted on his knees as he bent over letting it all sink in.

Olympia touched his shoulder gently, not certain if he would recoil from it. He didn't. She permitted her hand to press him more firmly. "John, I only tell you this because I will not deny who I am. Although I keep my nature secret from society for my own protection as well as my kind, I cannot in good conscience continue my relationship with you without you being fully aware of what it would mean to be my husband."

"And what does it mean Olympia?"

In an uncharacteristic move on her part, she knelt between his knees, lowering herself before him so that he might see the sincerity in her eyes. "My children will be witches. They will have powers."

"Damn Olympia, are you just another Samantha Stephens from Bewitched?"

She laughed, appreciating he was at least calm enough to make a joke. "Not a bad analogy. But I will not marry a Darren. My husband must accept me for all I am and understand all I might have to do."

"All you have to do?" he repeated.

"From time-to-time Pastoria, Zelda, and myself must go away for a few days. There are people in the world who need our help. There are a great many things in this world you know nothing about, John. Bad things. And sometimes I am called upon to stop them. I get rid of the monsters lurking behind the shadows."

"Monsters?' John exclaimed. "Are you telling me if I marry you, I get monsters too?"

She tilted her head, narrowing her eyes in a way which almost seemed condescending. "Well, the monsters do not exactly come *with me*. They have been here all along. You've been living your entire life in their presence whether you realized it or not. Evil is on this earth whether you are married to me or someone else. At least with me, you'll know what and where they are, and I will always be around to protect you first and foremost."

"And Pastoria is a witch? And Zelda?"

"As was my father. And his father. There are hundreds of us all around the country, John. Thousands around the world. Had we not always been here, this world would be a markedly different place than you recognize today."

Looking off into the distance, as if looking into his own future, he asked, "This isn't something you can turn your back on?"

"No. It is not. To do so would be the equivalent of watching a car driving straight towards someone at a crosswalk, and not scream out to warn them. My abilities make me duty-bound to protect people. It is as much a part of me as my beautiful blonde hair and gorgeous face."

Her vanity, especially inserted into such a serious moment, made him smile. He kissed her cheek. "And children I might have with you—"

"Will have great powers. And I will train them as to how to use them."

"Do you age?"

The question caught her off guard. She didn't mean to laugh, but it was something she never considered he might ask. "Unfortunately, yes. I am still a human John. Just *enhanced*. Gifted with abilities."

"By who?"

"By God of course," she said sternly. "I realize mankind spent centuries considering my people devil-made. I was recently reminded of that, in fact. But quite the contrary. Who else but God would insert angels on earth to watch over His creation."

John stood up and walked around in circles for a moment, kicking rocks with the tip of his shoe as he went. "It's a lot, Olympia."

"It is, John. So, think about this for a while. If I do not hear from you again, I will certainly understand. It will hurt, but I will let you go and wish you well. But I had to tell you before this love consumes me beyond being able to get over it."

"I'll drive you home now."

CHAPTER TWENTY-FOUR

Lauralee

It had been a few days since Olympia revealed herself to John Windham at the river. Though she was not yet overly concerned he would bolt from her life, she was beginning to think he'd had ample time to make a decision. The day now being Sunday, when she knew John would not be working, she half expected to hear from him. This was the main reason she thrust $5 into Pastoria's hand after breakfast, insisting she go see the new Elvis Pressley movie *Jailhouse Rock* with Zelda. If John was going to drop by, or telephone, she certainly did not want her sister around.

As she finished washing the breakfast dishes and was deciding what next to do, she heard a knock at the door. She did not rush to answer, giving it at least two more good attempts before opening the door. John had made her wait these many days; he could knock a few times more. Opening the door to greet him, she saw it was not John calling on her. Much to her surprise, it was Lauralee Caswell, holding a small rose bush with the root ball wrapped in burlap.

"Hello, Olympia!" the peculiar young woman said, walking in. "I told you I would call on you."

"Yes, you did." Olympia replied, closing the door behind her before walking her unexpected guest into the living room.

"Oh, my what a colorful place you have here," Lauralee exclaimed. "I love bright colors. You know they say we don't really see color; it is just a trick of light played on our eyes. But I have tried and tried to squint long enough to make colors look different, but so far, I can't do it."

Directing her guest to sit, Olympia joined her on the sofa. "May I offer you some tea or coffee or something Lauralee?"

"Oh no thank you. I just felt like dropping in." Suddenly remembering the plant in her clutches, she thrust it forward and added, "This is for you. I just love yellow roses. Yellow is the color of friendship."

"Why thank you, Lauralee." Olympia took the rose bush, sitting it aside on the floor. "Did Martin drive you out here?"

"Oh no, I have a license. Took several tries to get it but I eventually got the instructor to pass me. Martin lets me drive our father's old car. Well, don't betray my secret. I'm only supposed to go to town for things. Never this far out. But some nice man in town told me how to get here so I just came on out."

"I promise not to tell," Olympia smiled. "I am sorry I haven't had the opportunity to see you or Martin again since I returned from handling that family issue. I have been a little preoccupied."

"Oh, you don't have to account to me for your time, although I will tell you Martin has been on eggshells waiting to hear from you. He really cares for you. But I don't get the feeling you care as much for him as he does for you." Olympia immediately felt awkward, but Lauralee graciously put her at ease over it. "Oh, don't misinterpret me. I don't care. Martin's a swell guy, but a girl has got a right to spark to who she likes best. I just didn't see much of a spark from you that day in Martin's office. But I hope that doesn't mean we can't stay friends. I don't have many friends. And I liked you right off."

Olympia patted her knee, "I liked you right off too Lauralee. No matter what develops or does not develop between your brother and I, I will consider you my friend regardless."

"Me too!" the odd young woman beamed. "Well, I wanted to call on you. And I guess I have. Martin knows how long it takes me in town so I best hurry home before he gets suspicious that I drove further than he allows. May I come see you again sometime Olympia?'

"I hope you will."

Lauralee gave Olympia a swift hug and rose spritely to her feet, hustling to the door. Olympia watched her drive away, still clueless as to what any of this meant. She was a strange creature, but for some reason Olympia did truly like Lauralee. She found herself hoping she would come back to visit again.

And she did. Lauralee began popping in at least once a week to say hello, each time she brought another rose bush in a different color. She never stayed very long. Sometimes her visit lasted only the time it required her to drink a glass of tea or lemonade. Sometimes she simply lazed on the porch swing with Olympia chatting about nothing of particular importance. Olympia humored her delicate friend and discussed whatever subject she brought up. To Olympia, these talks were frivolous, though enjoyable, ways of passing time. Yet she recognized that for Lauralee these moments were probably the most important and anticipated minutes of her week. Lauralee was like a tiny bird temporarily freed from a cage. A bird unable to fly, but content to rest in another's hand as it looked out into the world.

Only once, when she was feeling rather drained, did Lauralee Caswell mention her *illness*. It was spoken of only as an explanation as to why one of her visits would be shorter than usual. Lauralee was not a person who complained or sought attention through sympathy. Whatever sickness plagued her she did not identify or elaborate upon. Olympia did not press for clarification. It was Lauralee's malady to discuss or ignore, and Olympia followed her lead. She felt a strong sense of protectiveness over her. No matter how busy Olympia might be, when Lauralee showed up at the door, she stopped everything to spend those short spans of time with her. These visits were the highlight of her fragile friend's week and Olympia made sure her hand was always available for that beautiful bird to perch upon when out of her cage.

CHAPTER TWENTY-FIVE

A Blast from the Future

Beryl Blanchard knew instantly something was wrong. Moments ago, she'd been seated at the picnic tables in the side yard of Blanchard House with her entire family reminiscing about old times. She'd stood up to carry some of the empty dishes back to the kitchen, her sister Fable accompanying her. But now as she stood in the yard, her hands were empty of the plates and utensils she'd been holding. The picnic tables weren't there either. And none of her family were in the side yard anymore, not even Fable who was standing beside her only two seconds ago.

She was alone in the yard now. She continued moving towards the house—the only familiar thing left. Or was it? Beryl knew the house standing before her was Blanchard House, yet something about it was changed from the house she'd lived in her entire life. Moments before, when she still clutched the dishes to her chest, she had been heading towards the back door of the kitchen. But now the door was as absent as the dishes. There was no door on the back of the white wood house. In fact, there was no kitchen. Only a blank, windowless exterior wall stood where the family kitchen should have been. Beryl turned around again, just to make sure one last time that her family were not in the yard behind her. The yard remained empty. Despite this fact, she still knew she was home. This was unarguably Blanchard House.

She wandered around to the front porch since there was no longer a back door to enter. As she made her way, she noticed the pool was gone as well as the wall around it. Her grandmother's rose garden was gone. And all the flowers along the porch were missing too. With the exception being the year after her grandmother's death—when Aunt Artemis was in mourning—flowers had always bloomed in hanging baskets and pots on that porch. Flowers were as much a facet of Blanchard House as the white painted exterior or the four-story tower.

Only one possible explanation sprang to mind...*I am in the past*. Why she would have known this was a mystery to Beryl, but somehow, she knew it to be true. The oak trees, the house, the general size of the yard, the chicken houses in the distance, were all recognizable. But the differences told the story. The driveway was not graveled. The new addition of the east wing was gone. And the absence of the kitchen really cinched it. Grandfather Windham built that kitchen, she remembered. Her grandmother had told her the story a dozen times. John Windham constructed the kitchen with its hidden room beneath for Olympia to house all her magical potions and witch-related items. He wanted the remainder of the house to seem as normal as possible. *If the kitchen isn't there, then this could only mean this is Blanchard House before Grandfather came along. But how far before?*

Beryl stepped up onto the front porch. As she did, she could hear voices inside. She knocked on the front door and waited to see who was going to open it. Her great grandfather? Her great-great grandmother? She hadn't a clue. The door opened and a beautiful young woman stood before her with long canary blonde hair. She wore a peachy colored baby doll dress with a wide plum belt and long dangly plum colored hoop earrings. Beryl's initial thought upon seeing her was *I really need that outfit.*

"Hello?" Olympia said answering the knock. She did not recognize the young woman standing at her door. She certainly wasn't one of the girls she'd gone through school with. The woman appeared to be around Olympia's age. She had a smooth round face with honey brown eyes. Her hair was golden with shoulder length curly ringlets. Olympia made it a point to always know who any of the females in town were who might come near to approaching her own beauty. This woman came close, but Olympia had never seen her before.

"Hi," Beryl nervously said. "I don't really know how to say this, but I have somehow—" she paused herself. How in the world was she supposed to explain this? How could she convey to this person that she had somehow launched herself back in time? She decided to just continue talking and hope for the best. "You must be a Blanchard," Beryl smiled at the woman with the long flaxen hair. "At least I am hoping you are, so maybe you'll understand and believe me..."

Beryl Blanchard stopped talking. Upon closer inspection of the exquisite woman's face things began to become clearer. She knew that face. There were no wrinkles, no age spots, no signs of the white hair which had been teased into an old lady hairdo all of Beryl's life. But the face...the face was the same, though it had been years since she had stared into those tender blue eyes.

"Hecate!" she cried as she pulled the startled stranger into her arms.

"Who the hell is this person, Lympy?" called a familiar voice from the next room.

Beryl let go of her grandmother and turned to see a sight so familiar it almost made her laugh. Zelda. Zelda looked just as ridiculous younger as she did old. Her mousy brown hair wasn't the magenta of the old woman she knew, but it was definitely *still* Madam Zelda, dressed in the most colorfully ridiculous attire. She wore an oversized orange and purple tunic wrapped at the waist with a long-braided cord. Her flowy pants were fuchsia, which matched the scarf tied over the top of her head.

"Zelda!" Beryl cried rushing to hug her friend. Zelda pushed back with a suspicious eye, but Beryl didn't care. She was so relieved to have found people she knew, even if they did not know her. Another woman came into the room from the hallway. Her shoulder length brown hair cut into a bob was almost the exact same style as it would be sixty years later. "Aunt Pastoria!"

"Aunt?"

Bursting into a rambling spiel, Beryl probably said far too much. "Yes! My Aunt. Great Aunt actually. And Zelda! Lord Zelda, I would know you anywhere! I was just with you not 10 minutes ago outside at our family picnic!" She whirled back to face Olympia. "And you!" Beryl beamed, clutching Olympia's hands. "I am so happy to see you."

"Oh my," Olympia Blanchard sighed. "Miss, I think I am afraid to ask this question, but are you by chance from the future?"

Sighing in relief, Beryl exclaimed, "Yes! Oh, thank God you understand! Yes, Hecate. I am your granddaughter."

"Well fuck me," Zelda exclaimed, grabbing the sides of her temples with her hands. "How the hell can you be her granddaughter?" Zelda bellowed to the stranger. "She ain't even got kids!"

Taking a seat on the edge of the living room coffee table, Pastoria smirked, "Apparently she's going to."

Olympia directed her mysterious guest into the living room. Beryl's eyes widened as if in complete shock at Olympia and Pastoria's home. To them it was merely their living room. Nothing spectacular, although tastefully done. But to the stranger the living room was an explosion of vintage nostalgia. Avocado green pod chairs flanked the fireplace where, in Beryl's time, Olympia's more traditional beige wingback chairs had stood. Thick, high-pile tan shag carpet covered the entire floor and two paisley sofas in psychedelic colors flanked the rather mod coffee table. The white painted plank walls of Beryl's Blanchard House were nowhere to be seen. Swirly wallpaper with orange, pink, and yellow covered the wood.

"This is crazy," Beryl observed, turning around to see everything. "Are those actually lava lamps?"

"You don't like contemporary decor?" Pastoria snorted.

"Oh, don't be offended," Beryl apologized. "This is spectacular. You just must understand that Blanchard House does not look like this in my time."

"No?" Olympia frowned. "This is so very me. I'm shocked I'd change it."

"Very you?" Beryl laughed. "Wow. You were different when you were young."

Olympia observed how overwhelmed their unexpected guest seemed to be by the things she was taking in. It surprised Olympia to see how surprised Beryl was behaving. Of course, it was a startling situation, however, being that they were all witches it couldn't be all that outlandish in the larger scheme of things. Though Olympia had never heard of any witch with the ability to time travel, and never once heard her father mention such a thing, it clearly appeared possible now.

Oddly enough, Zelda exhibited the most fascination of all, grabbing Beryl by the arm and pulling her to the vivid sofas. "What's Lympy like old?" Zelda asked. "And me? You said you just saw me in your time, so I must still be alive too!"

Their guest seemed hesitant to respond. She looked to Olympia as if for guidance, but when none was offered, she said, "I don't think I should say very much. I might inadvertently tell you something you might change. That could undo the future as I know it."

"Oh, I doubt that would happen," Olympia scoffed. "Tell us everything!" she shouted with exhilaration. "Who will be the next president? Are there any stocks on Wall Street I should buy? Do we ever go to war with Russia? And what am I like? Please tell me I stay thin after giving birth. If I lose my figure I don't think I could take it. And my hair! Do I go gray? Please tell me I never go gray. I have such lovely hair."

"Good Lord Olympia!" Pastoria chimed in. "Let the woman breathe a second. Can't you see she is still in shock at all this?"

Beryl stared at Olympia in amazement. She was nothing like the grandmother she'd known. Olympia Blanchard was not this vain. Or this cavalier about divulging information which might topple the world from how it was supposed to be. "I think my grandmother would warn me against telling you any of that stuff. I shouldn't tell you anything about the future which isn't absolutely necessary."

Pouting, and tossing her hair exaggeratedly over her shoulder, Olympia scoffed, "Your grandmother sounds like an old fuddy duddy."

"Aren't *you* her grandmother?" Pastoria snickered. "Boy, you must change a lot, Olympia!"

"Hell Lympy," Zelda cried realizing the possibilities now implied. "Does this mean we can just go to the future if we want to? I mean if this girl can go backward, why can't we jump forward?"

As Zelda and Olympia broke off into a wholly different conversation about what opportunities time travel might provide them, Pastoria proved herself to be the only adult in the room concerned with how and why this visitor from the future had come. "How did you even get here?" Pastoria asked. "What happened to send you to us?"

"I have no idea," Beryl replied. "We were all having a family cookout and I was walking back with Fable to bring the dishes to the kitchen when suddenly I was here in your backyard."

"Fable?" Olympia asked.

"My sister."

"I have two grandchildren?" Olympia's voice raised an octave as if inwardly thrilled by the prospect. Her vow to her father before he died would come true after all.

"You have lots of grandchildren," Beryl revealed, knowing as she said it, she shouldn't, but she had the feeling the knowledge might amuse Zelda and Pastoria considering how vapid this version of Olympia Blanchard seemed to be.

"No," Olympia said, shaking her head. "You are probably right. You really shouldn't tell me."

Beryl guessed that her young grandmother had probably not been seized with a sense of propriety but was rather disheartened now at the realization she would one day be someone's aged grandma.

"Do I have children?" Pastoria asked excitedly, clutching hands with Beryl.

Scowling at her sister, Olympia remarked, "What did she just say about telling us about the future!"

"You got to know that you do," Pastoria whined. "That's not fair."

Pastoria tapped her fingers on her folded arms staring impatiently at Beryl. She wanted an answer to her question. Beryl shrugged and looked back to Olympia. "I don't know what to say. Do I tell her?"

Olympia waved her hand to the air in defeat and said, "Just tell her. Otherwise, she's never going to shut up."

"Yes, you have children and grandchildren."

"Yes!" Pastoria exclaimed. "I won't die a virgin."

"Girl, you ain't been a virgin in years," Zelda scoffed.

"Shut up, Zelda!"

"Don't start you two," Olympia warned. "Obviously, we have a problem on our hands here. This woman needs our help. She's family and we don't even know her name."

The bickering trio reminded Beryl of her own relationships with her sister and the cousins she had grown up with. Outstretching her hand to shake, she announced formally. "I am Dr. Beryl Blanchard."

The three women looked at each other as if Beryl just said she was the mayor of the moon.

"A doctor?" Pastoria cried. "Like a real bonafide doctor?"

"Yes."

"Wow," Pastoria marveled. "There aren't many lady doctors around, not around here anyway."

Beryl gave a little nod of awareness and replied, "Many things change in the future."

"I knew a lady doctor once," Zelda declared. "Dealt with babies only though. Maybe she was more of a midwife come to think of it." Zelda stared upward to the ceiling as if trying to remember. Then her eyes lit up, and she grasped Beryl's arm excitedly. "You got men patients?"

"Of course," Beryl laughed.

"You ever see em' naked?" The way Zelda said the word naked sounded more like nekkid, and she had a mischievous glint in her eye as she asked. Beryl ignored the question.

Olympia was quietly lost in her own thoughts, remembering something from her past. *Her name is Beryl.* A smile crossed Olympia's face as she recalled the evening so long ago at the very first Consort she'd ever attended. She met a woman named Beryl. A beautifully kind woman. The mother of the child Olympia's own mother had saved from death. *I suppose I suggest the name to one of my future children,* Olympia told herself.

Pastoria had taken the lead of interrogation away from Zelda and was now posing her own questions. "If you are really a Blanchard, then what is your power?"

"I heal people," Beryl replied. "I'm a pretty popular doctor obviously."

Pastoria was impressed and decided to share their abilities with their newfound relation. "I can manipulate molecules, and I have telekinesis. And Olympia can-"

"I'm very familiar with everything you guys can do," Beryl laughed.

"Enough of this idle chit chat," Olympia announced. "We need to figure out how to get this girl back home. And to do that we have to figure out how she came to be here in the first place."

CHAPTER TWENTY-SIX

The Fourth Witch

The Blanchard sisters and Zelda escorted their new guest into the kitchen for a glass of sweet tea over which they hoped to straighten out this mystery. Walking through the swinging door off the living room, Beryl gasped at the size of the kitchen. "This is so small. Nothing like our kitchen at home."

"Well, excuse us for not being the Rockefellers." Pastoria snapped.

Beryl flinched in shame, "I am sorry, I didn't mean to insult your home. It is just that in my time our family kitchen is rather large. We have wide countertops and cabinets against the far wall, double fridge and freezer. There's a big island in front of the sink where we cut vegetables and prepare the meals. And our kitchen table is pretty big. Much bigger than this four-seater. Of course, we have a lot more family members I suppose."

"Interesting," Olympia commented, although not actually interested at all. Withdrawing one of the chrome back chairs she sat down at the moss green Formica table. She observed the marred surface of the decades old relic. The prospect of one day having something new appealed to her. She gestured for Beryl and the others to join her.

Beryl was inspecting the kitchen as if trying to recognize something, then exclaimed, "Oh! This is our dining room. I can tell by the window looking out to the side yard. If you take your sink, fridge, oven and pantry out of here it's not too small of a room. Our long dining table sits in the center and the door to our kitchen is where your stove is now."

"I doubt you came all this way to give us architectural history," Olympia quipped. "Beryl, I think we need to figure out what happened to bring you here. Tell us again exactly what occurred the precise moment you left your timeline."

Beryl rehashed the scene again, still garnering no new clues as to what could have caused the incident. Olympia suggested they go upstairs to peruse her family's books on spells in hopes they may run across something to explain the situation. As they moved back to the foyer and began climbing the stairs, Pastoria and Zelda grilled Beryl more on what it was like to be a female doctor. Beryl was too busy observing the changes to her family home. There were no pictures lining the walls of the second-floor hallway. But of course, there wouldn't be. Those photographs were from Beryl's years, not these ladies. The family photos had been placed there by the hands of Old Olympia commemorating her memories of her family. This Young Olympia had not even begun to start that family.

They began climbing the stairs to the third floor and for a moment Beryl assumed they were going as far as the fourth-floor tower, but she was mistaken. Olympia stopped to open the door to the tower room on the third floor. This room was not a place Beryl often went into in her time. The tower room of the third floor was always used to store things, such as holiday decorations. Walking into it now, she realized in her grandmother's youth, it was the equivalent to the vault under the kitchen in Beryl's time. The vault was a secret hidden room where all the spell books, talisman, bone dust jars, and witches brew ingredients were stored. But here, all those things sat atop shelves lining the windows on all three sides.

Olympia went to a shelf to remove a worn leather-bound book which she began perusing at a small table. "This was my father's father's book of spells, histories, and observations. I believe once when I was a child, I read something here about time travel."

The others remained quiet while Olympia flipped through the pages. After several minutes she slammed the book cover shut and only said, "Aha!"

"What aha?" Pastoria asked.

"Time travel is possible," Olympia explained. "Our grandfather Victor Blanchard tells of it here."

"Well, flaming toads, Lympy!" Zelda scoffed. "We already know it's possible. She's here ain't she? What else does that book say?"

Olympia frowned. "My grandfather knew as little as we do. He too was once visited by a couple of relatives from the future, but he doesn't explain how they came to be there or how they left. He only mentions he met them."

"Who were they?" Beryl asked.

Olympia shook her head. "He doesn't say. Just mentions two future Blanchards paid a visit."

Pastoria folded her arms and said, "Okay. It is rather obvious we are not solving this today. I suggest we show this lady to a bedroom, and she will be our guest for the foreseeable future."

"How ya'll gonna explain her to folks?" Zelda asked. "You know how gossipy ever'body in Daihmler is. They are bound to ask questions."

Olympia laughed, "The people around here have been asking questions about this family all my life, what's one more? However, the simplest explanation is that she is our cousin from out of town. Richmond perhaps?"

"Mobile." Beryl said.

"Why Mobile?" Pastoria asked.

Extending her arm around her great aunt's shoulders, Beryl smiled and said, "Because Aunt Pastoria, that is where you live in my day."

Pastoria was aghast. "Why would I ever move to Mobile? Not that it isn't a perfectly lovely place. Father took us there once to see the Gulf, but I cannot imagine I'd ever leave Blanchard House to live there."

Beryl kissed her cheek and whispered, "Oh, Pastoria, you fell in love."

Leaving the tower room, Olympia and Pastoria invited Beryl to select any bedroom in the house she'd like to have as her own while staying with them. It was an easy choice. Beryl picked her own room on the second floor overlooking the back yard. Swinging the familiar paneled door with the flecking paint open, the squeaky hinges made her feel safe. Those hinges always did squeak. No matter how often she'd squirted a little WD-30 on them through the years, after a few silent days they would begin to squeal again. More than once those very hinges got her in trouble with her mother and Aunt Artemis when she and Salem would sneak in after curfew in high school.

Almost everything in the room was as she kept it in her own time. The headboard of the bed was the same. The antique dresser and mirror were the same—although probably not considered antique right now. Except for wall decorations, her own books and keepsakes, and a different color paint, the room was exactly the same.

CHAPTER TWENTY-SEVEN

Sister Fight

Being trapped in the past was disconcerting for poor Beryl Blanchard but it did have its merits. Having the opportunity to get behind the wheel of Olympia's light pink Ford Thunderbird convertible was one of them. Though Pastoria persisted she should be the one to drive, Olympia handed Beryl the keys instead. "You are the reason I had to trade in the Chevy! You stripped the gears until they wouldn't hold."

"I was learning how to drive, Olympia!" her sister argued back. "I know how to now. I haven't even had a chance to crank the new one."

"I think I'll trust the doctor for this drive into town." Olympia said, closing Beryl's hand over the set of keys.

The pink car was unlike anything Beryl had ever seen. She felt as if she'd stepped into an old movie as she slipped inside and closed the long heavy door.

"If you wreck this car she will kill us," Pastoria cautioned. "It's brand new and her prize possession. It's the first Thunderbird to have real leather seats."

"I will be careful," Beryl promised touching her fingertips to the pristine white leather before taking the wheel. It took her a few seconds to acclimate to the machine. Her first inclination was to search around the console for the start button. Pastoria looked at her peculiarly, but Beryl didn't bother to explain what she was looking for. *There are no key fobs and push button ignition in the past. Just put the old-fashioned key in the hole and turn.* As the engine roared to a start Beryl was a little taken aback at how loud engines used to be. At home, her car barely hummed when it cranked and moved down the road. Sometimes she wasn't even sure it had cranked until she pushed the button again and turned it off. But there would be no confusion when this car was running. It was loud.

As she switched the gear into reverse and began backing up so she could pull out of the driveway, and onto the road, she struggled at the wheel. It was sluggish, or stuck, or something. Moving her arms hand over hand over hand simply to turn the wheel wide enough to back up, and leave the driveway, nearly wore her out. *Oh….* Beryl remembered, *they don't have power steering yet.*

Once she had the car on the street, she had little difficulty maneuvering it, except around bends—again, the no power steering situation. Making her way along into town, Beryl found the landscape remarkable for what all it lacked. So much she was accustomed to passing on her way to or from home was missing in this timeframe. The Daihmler Elementary School building was not the modern design of wood, glass, and stone she knew it to be. It was a rectangular red brick plain boring thing. The traffic lights weren't there either, only a series of yield or stop signs at crossroads. Beryl knew how to get downtown, it was still where it was supposed to be, only it was not at all as large. Still, she enjoyed seeing it in its early stage. Everything was so vintage! Seeing her hometown in its first stages of growth was perhaps one of the most interesting things about this leap backwards in time.

Seeing an empty parking slot in front of the feed store, Beryl parked the car—but not without an excessive amount of stops and starts struggling to maneuver the cumbersome steering wheel. "Good Lord, girl!" Pastoria cried. "Do you not have steering wheels in cars at home?"

"Not like this!" Beryl wheezed, catching her breath from the workout. "I don't know what they do to make it easier, but in my time, you can turn the wheel with just one finger. I need the arms of Superman to move this thing!"

Getting out of the car, Beryl glanced up at the feed store sign and remarked, "I don't believe I have ever seen a feed store before. We order the chicken food online."

Sending a quizzical look her way, Pastoria repeated, "On line? Like a washing line? You do what? Hang an order note and somebody delivers it? Like the old milkmen?"

"Not quite," Beryl answered, believing it best to leave the topic alone. Walking past the feed store, they passed Burkalter's Shoe Repair. "This is a Baskin-Robbins in my day."

"I've been to one of those once!" Pastoria exclaimed. "One on the way to the beach. Good ice cream. Speaking of food, I'm hungry. Let's stop at Shackleford Drug's for a bite."

They entered the drug store to the sound of an overhead bell dinging when the door pushed open. Beryl recognized where she was although it certainly did not look the same. "This is the CVS drug store."

"No, it's Shackleford's."

"No, I mean where I come from this becomes a CVS drug store—only it's not this same building. They must have torn down this beautiful old place to construct it. Why do people do that where I come from? All these lovely old places they demolish to build something new and cheap looking."

"I couldn't say," Pastoria replied. "This is new, too. They tore down the old Five and Dime to build this. Now that was a lovely place back when it was the old post office—before they built the new one and put the dime store there."

Beryl mused for a moment, the irony dawning on her, "I guess nothing is really all that historic after all. Every generation paves over the last."

Having never experienced eating at one of the old drug store lunch counters she had so often heard her grandmother reminisce about, Beryl found herself excited. She and Pastoria found two empty spots along the counter where they sat down on shiny chrome plated stools with turquoise vinyl seats. The counter was the same turquoise Formica with matching chrome edges. Beryl was in retro heaven!

"Would you please stop rubbing the counter?" Pastoria whispered. "You look weird."

"Sorry," Beryl said. "It's just that people pay a fortune to recreate this style."

"The future sounds like it is full of stupid rich people," Pastoria remarked as she perused the menu board on the wall. "The burgers here are really good."

"I'm craving a tuna melt," Beryl replied. "I wonder if they have one here?"

"I have no idea what that even is," Pastoria answered. "But it sounds disgusting."

Settling on burgers and fries, Beryl felt safe in the choice because what could you do to mess up a hamburger? At the first bite she was delirious. As juice dripped from her lips she exclaimed, "This is the best hamburger I have ever eaten!" Eating more of her burger with gusto she elaborated on her delight. "That was real meat!" Beryl exclaimed. "Like someone in the back made the patty by hand with real ground beef."

"Of course, they did," Pastoria replied. "What the hell are burgers made out of where you come from?"

"And these fries!" Beryl cried, shoving several into her mouth at one time. "I haven't tasted fries like this in years and years."

"Are fries of the future made from carrots or something?"

"No, it's the oil. In my time they stopped using oils with saturated fats and other additives because they are grossly unhealthy. But all that gunk sure does make fries taste delicious!"

A man approached the end of counter next to Pastoria and patted her on the shoulder. Beryl caught sight of him in the mirror. He was very handsome. His hair was dark brown, she thought. It was a little difficult to tell with the greasy oil it appeared to be combed with. She remembered from movies, this was the style back then—*or back now*—or whatever it was. Men didn't have the same assortment of hair products as the future. Despite the hair oil, Beryl thought him handsome, and his blue suit accentuated his eyes and dimples. All the while she was admiring his appearance, he must have been doing the same to her because when she met his eyes in the mirror, they were staring back at her.

"Pastoria Blanchard, I thought I knew everybody you know. Who is your lovely friend?"

Pastoria turned to the man and replied, "This is Beryl. She is a distant relation who has come to visit. Beryl, this is Nate, a good friend of ours and sometimes Olympia's boyfriend. Are y'all on again or off again these days Nate?"

"Mostly off," Nate chuckled. "I think we learned we are better as friends. Besides, I've seen her head turning more toward John Windham lately."

"John Windham!" Pastoria scoffed. "That jerk? She hasn't said anything to me about it."

Beryl was a little affronted by Pastoria's outrage. John Windham was a name not unfamiliar to Beryl Blanchard...John Windham was her grandfather.

"I've seen them out a couple of times," Nate said, never removing his eyes from the mirror where he watched Pastoria's lovely companion. "Maybe it is supposed to be a secret."

Pastoria was not happy. Not one bit. "She would keep that quiet," she huffed. "She knows I can't stand John Windham."

Ignoring Pastoria's fury, Nate moved his attention to his friend's visiting relative. "Beryl, is it?" he said, finally addressing her personally. "Where are you visiting from?"

"Mobile."

"I love Mobile. It's the oldest city in Alabama." Nate smiled.

"I suppose it is." Beryl answered timidly.

Nate edged closer, practically leaning across Pastoria's lap. "I am coming out to Blanchard House tomorrow afternoon to see Olympia. On business." It was not lost on Beryl the way he stressed, *on business*. "Would it be agreeable to you if I were to call on you as well while I am there? Perhaps we might have dinner together?"

Not expecting an offer of a date from her excursion into town, Beryl was unsure how to answer. "Well...I. I'm not sure if that would be all right," Beryl looked to her aunt for guidance.

"Go on and go out with him," encouraged Pastoria. "It's clear to see he's mooning all over you."

Nate blushed but did not deny the accusation. Beryl knew she should refuse the invitation. Her grandmother would have vehemently advised against it, warning how any interaction with a person in the past might alter the future. But Beryl's wise old Olympia wasn't with her here in the past and there was something about Nate she really liked. Hesitantly, she gave Nate an agreeable nod as Pastoria moved to the cash register to pay the check.

The errands they'd come to town for did not seem as important to Pastoria now. She was rather eager to return home to confront her sister over the John Windham matter. The entire drive home she driveled on to Beryl in outrage. "And here I thought she was all set to get engaged to that banker, Martin Caswell, and the whole time she's been running around with John Windham behind my back."

Beryl was not a stranger to the name Martin Caswell either. Oh, how she wished Salem or Fable were here to share this surreal step back into nostalgia. Martin Caswell was the man Olympia married after John Windham died. Of course, Beryl never had known either man, both passing on well before any of the grandchildren were born. But the names were names engraved into her memory. In fact, their graves were in the backyard of Beryl's Blanchard House.

Upon returning home, Pastoria had swirled herself into such a fit of anger she couldn't even say anything at first, allowing Beryl the opportunity to seek Olympia's counsel when she found her in the living room watching a daytime soap opera. Besides the risk of interacting with another person in the past, Beryl was feeling a tinge of guilt for having agreed to go out with Olympia's ex-boyfriend. She asked if it would make her uncomfortable.

Answering gregariously, as if this somehow absolved her of any guilt from jilting him, "Oh, you should totally go out with him! Nate's the best. And he is a gentleman. You'll have a great time."

Beryl still felt some qualms about it, "Are you sure? Maybe going out with him is a bad idea. What if I inadvertently do or say something that changes the future?"

"My goodness, girl, what do you think will happen?" Olympia scoffed. "It is only dinner. Do you think saying your chicken tastes delicious could alter the course of the universe? I think you'll be okay. Just go out, have a few laughs, and enjoy his company."

I wish Fable was here to see this version of our grandmother.

Pastoria cut off the conversation to address the other tidbit which had come out over lunch. "So, were you ever going to tell me you are dating John Windham?"

Olympia's face fell. She looked almost ashamed. Beryl had never seen her grandmother look ashamed in her life. "I am not dating John. We have been out a few times is all."

"That's called dating, Olympia!" Pastoria yelled. "I cannot believe this. You know I can't stand that man."

This was just about the last conversation Olympia felt like having at this time. John Windham still had not contacted Olympia since that night at the river when she revealed herself to him; and it had been well over two weeks now. John quite possibly had moved on. It certainly felt as if he had. Olympia was managing to distract herself enough to where she only thought of him twenty times a day instead of a hundred. Arguing with her sister over him might be a moot point anyway.

Beryl knew she should allow the sisters privacy to have their squabble, but she stayed downstairs anyway. After all, it sort of concerned her too, even if they were not aware. They were fighting about her biological grandfather after all. She wanted to see how it ended.

"Why don't you like John Windham?" Beryl asked Pastoria.

"Oh, she's just being ridiculous!" Olympia exclaimed. "She hates John because he was the lawyer who sued her friend's father."

"Because of John Windham, Perry had to move away from Daihmler! And he was not only my friend—we were practically engaged to be married!"

"You went out with him for one month!" Olympia sneered. She turned to Beryl and elaborated. "Perry was a guy she went out with a few times when he was in college. It was not serious."

"It was serious!"

Olympia shook her head at Beryl, "It was not serious. Pastoria had it bad for him is all, but he was going out with several girls. His father defaulted on a loan and was evicted from the house. John is a lawyer who represented the Daihmler Trust Bank.

Perry's family had to move to Memphis to live with his grandparents. Pastoria just likes to hold grudges."

"I don't care what you say, Olympia! I blame John for Perry having to leave, and I cannot believe you have the audacity to go out with him!"

The argument went on for a lengthy duration. The sisters could be quite vicious with one another—a fact which shook Beryl. All her life she'd never known Olympia and Pastoria to be anything but the most supportive of sisters. But here they were fighting like...like...*like me and Fable.* The comparison eased her mind somewhat as the Blanchard sisters continued their rant to one another. Beryl understood, this is what sisters do until they reach the age where things just aren't so dramatic. She and Fable were famous for their arguments, but always they loved each other and would do anything for the other one.

"It is my job to make sure you marry someone worthy of you," Olympia announced, recatching Beryl's attention. "And that was not Perry Wilson."

"And I suppose John Windham is the worthy type?" Pastoria chided.

"Maybe," Olympia answered. "But I will tell you one thing, when I do get married it will be the right man and it will be forever. It will be he and I for the rest of our lives."

Beryl wanted so badly to tell Olympia, in all her arrogance, that she would end up married to three different men.

CHAPTER TWENTY-EIGHT

Beryl's Date

Olympia sat on Beryl's bed, resting against the soft feather pillows while advising Beryl on what to wear for her date with Nate. Beryl had already tried on several of Olympia's clothes, but none seemed to work for her. It was a punch to the ego for her to admit, but her grandmother had a slimmer figure than she. Most dresses did not fit, but of the few that did, Beryl only felt she looked good in two of them. Holding them up to Olympia for approval, she commented, "Your clothes are fabulous, Grandmo—sorry, Olympia. I wish more would fit me."

Olympia pointed to the light green dress with the thin shoulder straps and gave a thumbs up. "You know, this isn't a very sustainable situation," Olympia stated. "Tomorrow you and I will go into town and buy you some of clothes of your own. Not that I mind you borrowing mine, but I am bustier than you and weigh less."

Beryl rolled her eyes although it wasn't untrue. "Yes, I have noticed we aren't exactly the same shape. But I cannot have you spending money on me like that. I could disappear tomorrow."

Olympia twirled a long strand of her hair around her finger and replied, "You haven't disappeared yet. There is always the chance you are here to stay. None of us have any way of knowing. And you must have your own clothes. Besides, I don't think my shoes are going to fit you. Pastoria has big feet too; we will look in her closet."

Olympia assisted Beryl while she squeezed into the green dress, it required a little jumping up and down to zip the back, but they managed. "I must say you do look better than I thought you would in this. You are a pretty girl, Beryl. Of course, I'd expect no less from one of my offspring."

Beryl examined herself in the full-length mirror and grimaced. "I don't know. Maybe I'm just nervous."

"Why be nervous?" Olympia chuckled. "He's just a man. One of earth's simplest creatures."

Beryl was beginning to like young Olympia more than she probably should. She sat down on the edge of the bed and placed her hands in her lap. "I am nervous because I am in a strange land. I am afraid I may never get home. And I can't stop worrying I'm going to say something wrong and expose myself or worse, mess up someone's future."

Olympia tossed her hands into the air in exasperation. "And you say I am the one who taught you to worry about all this kind of stuff? Who the hell do I turn into when I get older? Trust me Beryl, life should be lived with a minimum of questioning yourself. Believe what I tell you. It is almost impossible to find yourself in an unhappy place if you don't spend your time worrying about what could go wrong. Don't think so much! Life is way easier drifting where it takes you. This is just a date. One little date. Stop stressing."

"Yeah, but it sounds like you date all the time. I never date."

Unable to believe the statement, Olympia joined her on the bed. "How can a girl as attractive as you not get asked out? Your hips aren't *that wide*. It is because you are a doctor, isn't it? Beryl, you cannot let men know you are smarter than they are. You must play the game. Make them believe you are in awe every time they speak, then manipulate them into whatever you want them to do or be."

Beryl nudged her shoulder into Olympia's. "You are nothing like my grandmother. Actually, you remind me more of my sister. But it isn't that men are insecure around me. They ask me out sometimes, I just decline. I'm too busy with my career and the family."

Olympia jumped to her feet in exasperation. "Well, that is just stupid. There will always be sick people, but men tend to find someone else if ignored too long." Olympia lifted Beryl's hands into her own. "I recognize in your world you are rather accomplished. An accomplished woman is an anomaly here. So, while you are here, for however long that may be, allow yourself to be a woman." Beryl was looking into her eyes as she said this. Olympia was being sincere, trying to give honest advice, not simply lip service. It was the first time she seemed similar to the woman she knew back home. Beryl had always known Olympia Blanchard to impart wisdom where needed. Although this brand of advice conflicted a little with the older version of herself, it was still wisdom. "Do not sacrifice the wonderous feeling of being cherished by a man. I tell you, there is nothing like it."

Nate arrived right on time for his meeting with Olympia. Beryl was nowhere in sight when he came in, just as Olympia advised. "Reveal yourself at the end and dazzle him." While Olympia went over business matters with Nate, Beryl hovered upstairs, nervously awaiting the cue for when she was to elegantly descend the stairs the way Olympia taught her. Hearing the study door "accidentally" shut too hard behind them as they left the room, Beryl recognized the signal and started down. As Nate's eyes caught sight of her descending the stairs, his breath caught in his lungs. She was even more lovely than he remembered from the drug store. "You look like an angel," he said boldly kissing her hand.

As they made their way to the door, Olympia placed her hands on Beryl's shoulders and whispered, "Be a woman," into her ear.

Parked at the edge of the porch was Nate's chrome plated, cream striped, mauve Studebaker. Once again, Beryl found herself marveling at yet another classic car she never dreamed she'd ever see in person. He opened the passenger side door for her, waiting until she was comfortably seated before closing it. No man had ever done that on date with her before. *I like the past. Men are so gallant.*

Nate entered on the other side, placing his briefcase on the seat between them. The lid wasn't secured properly, popping open revealing many papers. "You wouldn't want these to fall out." Beryl said, closing it for him.

"No, I wouldn't. Thank you."

As he cranked the car, she asked a question she probably should not have asked. "So, is Olympia mortgaging the house?"

Her comment took him by surprise. She must have seen something in the briefcase to spark the question. Though he normally did not discuss his clients' personal affairs, he forgave the inappropriateness. She was most likely nervous to be out with a stranger she'd only just met. The question was probably her way of breaking the ice. Since she was family, he didn't feel he would be speaking out of school by answering.

"Not at all. Paying it off, actually."

"I see," Beryl nodded. "So, she has plenty to live on, I hope? I'd hate to think my being here is a burden to her."

Nate sent her a bright smile, "I couldn't imagine you being a burden to anyone." His tone turned more serious though as he added, "However, Olympia and Pastoria only have enough for a little while longer, unless they sell the house or mortgage it again."

With the car accelerating onto the main highway, Beryl realized she was not buckled in. She reached to her right to grab the seatbelt clasp but could not find it. She leaned to see if it was wedged down between the seat and the door, but it was not there. Inspecting above her where the strap should be connected to the wall panel, she found nothing.

"Have you lost something, my dear?" Nate asked.

"The seatbelt," Beryl said. "I can't find it."

"The what?"

Beryl paused. "Seatbelt?" she asked timidly. "Does your car have one?"

"I am not sure what you are referring to," Nate replied. "There's a fan belt under the hood, but I have never heard of anything called a seat belt. Do you need me to move the seat closer to the dashboard, or further back? Is it the seat handle you mean?"

Cars don't have seatbelts yet, dummy! She reminded herself. *Olympia's didn't have one either.*

Nate guided them to the outskirts of town, where a charming log cabin roadhouse named Gracie's stood with a blue neon sign flashing proudly on the rooftop. As they stepped inside, Beryl was delighted by the atmosphere. Tables adorned with blue gingham were complemented by red glass candle holders casting warm glows throughout the dining room, making for a cozy ambiance. A symphony of tantalizing aromas of sizzling steaks, mouthwatering hamburgers, and fresh baked bread greeted them.

Just as she was about to express how much she liked the place, Beryl's attention was drawn to the approaching waitress, whose attire immediately offended her. The waitress wore a long tan skirt, white blouse, and a red checkered headscarf, not unlike that of the old Aunt Jemima pancake boxes. It was at that moment that Beryl became aware every single waitress in the restaurant was African American.

"Are these people for real?" Beryl exclaimed with disgust.

Caught off guard by the reaction, Nate asked, "I beg your pardon?"

Beryl leaned close to whisper in his ear, "They are all dressed like Mammy from Gone with the Wind!"

"Yeah," he nodded. "It really makes you feel like you've stepped back in time."

"I know a little something about stepping back in time," Beryl replied indignantly. "This is not appropriate."

Nate had not expected his dinner companion would be so opposed to the establishment or the women it employed. Hit with a sudden disheartened feeling, he feared he had been wrong about Beryl. He never expected she would be prejudiced. Disappointed now in who she was turning out to be, he was about to drive her back home, when she said something else causing him to now not understand what she was trying to say.

With a touch of outrage reddening her face, she asked, "Don't you find this offensive?"

"In what way do you mean?"

"What other possible way could I mean," she snapped. "These black women dressed this way, serving white people dinner. It's demeaning. They shouldn't be forced to costume themselves like slaves to serve our meals."

As one of the waitresses came forward to guide them to a table, Nate and Beryl eyed one another questioningly until the woman stepped away. Both beginning to speak at once, Nate backed off allowing Beryl to express her thoughts which he was not yet sure he understood. Soon it all became very clear. He felt foolish even suspecting for a moment she might be racist. He laughed out loud, taking her gentle hand in his. "Thank goodness!" Nate smiled. "When we walked in, I thought you were bothered having colored people serve our food."

"I am!" she cried. "These poor women are forced to dress up like slaves!"

Nate nodded his head, "I completely understand your meaning now. What I am saying is I misinterpreted your outrage as being prejudiced. What you are really upset about is the way the staff are dressed, not that they are colored."

A waitress approached the table with two glasses of water and a big smile for Nate. "Mr. Nate, it is so good to see you again. Been too long since you stopped in."

"It is great to see you too, Shirley. How is the family?"

"Fine. Fine. My oldest boy just started Miles College. Gonna be an engineer he says."

They bantered a moment before the waitress left Nate and Beryl alone with the menus. Beryl did not know what to make of anything now, until Nate explained. He opened up about his work in the cause for fair treatment of colored people in the community. Humbly, he shared how he had been instrumental in convincing the owner of Gracie's to employ colored women for their waitstaff. He admitted the costuming might be interpreted as inappropriate by some, but it was a small price to pay for the opportunity. Nate told Beryl how women of color were trapped in a cycle of limited employment outside of being a maid. At Gracie's, colored women were now earning a dignified living in an environment which demanded far less work from them than domestic service would.

"I apologize for misjudging you and this restaurant," Beryl said. "I forget I am in a different place than I am used to."

"Mobile isn't that far away," Nate countered.

Beryl gave her date a playful, mischievous wink and said, "Let's just say I am a woman ahead of her time."

Toying with her fingertips between his own, he gently replied, "I'm glad you are here, wherever you come from."

"I am too actually," she grinned. "I find I am enjoying my visit here."

"And maybe enjoying the company you are keeping a little too I hope?"

Stroking the back of his hand, she smiled. "Definitely."

CHAPTER TWENTY-NINE

Absolution With a Side of Acceptance

Olympia had not heard a peep from John Windham. Days rolled by, one after the other until another weekend was upon her. She could have easily moved on to and resume her courtship with Martin, and she wasn't shunning the idea, but she wasn't yet ready to write John off. She filled her time with one or two minor Association cases which did not require more than a day away. There wasn't much to be done on the Beryl front, because none of them had any answers as to how she arrived there. Strange as the circumstances were, she'd grown accustomed to Beryl's presence in their lives rather quickly. Beryl blended in as if she'd always been one of them. Olympia had to sometimes remind herself Beryl would one day probably go back home. As Friday and Saturday night rolled around, Olympia watched Beryl and Pastoria go out on dates while she remained home. She had no lack of offers for a date, but she still found herself waiting to see if *he* might call.

It was early Sunday morning, well before Beryl or Pastoria had awakened, when Olympia stepped outside to retrieve the morning paper. Instead of finding the paper rolled up in a rubber band at the edge of the porch, her downward staring eyes spied two black leather shoes. John, dressed in his blue suit and paisley tie, held her paper in his hand. He did not wait for her reaction. He immediately made his intentions known.

"I have spent three weeks now considering the things you revealed to me."

"Four," she corrected.

John continued his obviously rehearsed monologue, "I have contemplated all possible outcomes of my life with you and without you." Taking a pause for breath, she noticed him twisting the paper nervously in his grip. "I am the sort of man who values normalcy. I do not like deviations from a future I planned for myself long ago. Having a witch for a wife does not fit into that plan."

"I see."

"No, Olympia you do not." Dropping the rumpled paper to the porch, he took hold of her arms, pulling her closer to him. "I could find someone else to marry. I could have several normal children with her and live a prosperous and simple life. It would all be straight forward and clean. Everything I have always envisioned for myself. The problem I am having is that I don't see how I would ever love her. I do not believe I am any longer capable of becoming interested in another woman. I have tried once or twice these last three weeks."

"Four."

"No one interests me. I've concluded it will be impossible for me to love someone who is not you. You have beguiled me Olympia Blanchard, and I see no future for me without you at my side."

Tears fell from her eyes. She had fervently told herself that whenever she saw him again, no matter what he said, she would not be emotional. He would not see how deeply she missed him or how malignantly her need for him had spread to her heart. Now, whether she liked it or not, she was crying. John pulled her against him, kissing her passionately. "You have ruined my life's plan, woman. This forces us to begin a new plan together. We will both have to make compromises, but we will make it work."

"Of course, we will John."

"Beginning today," he announced. "We are going to church together."

"Church?" she exclaimed.

John looked upon her sternly. "If I can marry a witch. You can attend church with me on Sundays."

Attempting to protest, Olympia barely got a word out before John shook his head and placed his finger to her lips. It was the first time he would put his foot down as her husband. He directed her inside, ordering her up the stairs to get dressed. As she rushed about her room, dressing as quickly as she could, she did not understand why she was behaving like this. *Who am I to allow a man to tell me what to do!* Checking her hair and makeup in her dressing table mirror, she answered her own question. *I am a woman in love.*

Driving into town, neither said very much. She wanted to ask him what he had been doing during their weeks apart and who these women were he had tried to force himself to fall for. He had his own questions. Had she seen any other men during their time apart? Both felt it best to ask nothing. Drawing nearer to his church, John turned to his intended and asked with a grin, "You won't explode or anything if you walk into a church, will you?"

Not appreciating his attempt at bad humor, Olympia pinched his arm with a twist. "We are not demonic, John Windham. God gave us our power. And it might interest you to know I am a great believer in God and the teachings of Jesus. It is not disbelief which keeps me away from places of worship. It is the people who worship there."

"Explain."

"You did not grow up here," Olympia reflected. "I did. And these Christians who position their oversized behinds in the pews every Sunday are the same people who tormented my sister and myself all through school. Even now they whisper behind our backs and cross to the other sidewalk when we pass."

"That will be different now," John proclaimed. "As my wife no one will dare insult you. I am well respected in Daihmler. I have helped many leading citizens with legal matters. You will see. It will be different."

Heads turned as John Windham strolled down the aisle of Daihmler Methodist Church. He was prepared. For every head which turned to stare at the legendary woman on his arm, he paused to greet with a cheery hello, introducing them to his fiancée. Suspicious faces soon turned to smiling hypocrites as John proved his word was true. No man, nor that man's wife, would be anything but welcoming to John Windham's bride. Olympia even found her own disposition changing from one of cold contempt to gracious appreciation as the congratulations poured over them with each pew they passed. Until...

She had not expected it. It never once occurred to her on the drive that Martin Caswell was also a member of this congregation. There he sat alongside Lauralee, three rows from the front. Olympia felt terrible for having him hear the news this way.

"I offer you both my best wishes for your new life together." Martin offered graciously.

Olympia felt compelled to explain, "It only happened this morning. We hadn't seen each other for a while, and he showed up this morning to propose."

"I understand."

Lauralee was a little more excited than she should have been considering her brother's feelings. "Oh, Olympia! How marvelous! You'll be the most beautiful bride."

As the organist began playing the first hymnal, John and Olympia took seats on the left side, second row. As Reverend Talbot ascended the pulpit, he presented an elated smile to John and a wink of approval to Olympia. It was then she knew the good reverend had been privy to John's plan all along. The minister was rather proud of himself. After all these years he'd managed to acquire a Blanchard into his flock.

By the time John drove Olympia home after church, Pastoria had already heard the news from town. Presenting a glaring look of disapproval at them when they entered, she stormed upstairs to her room. Beryl, hearing the commotion, came downstairs, stopping short halfway when she saw the man below. Beryl's eyes stuck to him in a mix of shock and excitement. She had only ever seen a few pictures of her biological grandfather.

"John," Olympia introduced. "This is my cousin Beryl. She is visiting us for a while. Beryl, my fiancé, John Windham."

Knowing how long Olympia had been waiting for a response from John, Beryl was happy to hear the news. Shaking John's hand in congratulations felt surreal. This man was her mother's father. And he had no idea. It also appeared Olympia herself had forgotten or was too giddy to stop and consider the momentous occasion of the introduction. It was obvious John was not going to be told who she really was. Listening to Olympia chatter away recounting his showing up on her doorstep, then whisking her away to church, Beryl only half paid attention. She could not stop looking at him. Thankfully he was too busy staring at his beloved to notice the strange woman studying his features. *Mother and Aunt Artemis get their eyes from him. They are almost purple.* By the time Olympia finished chattering, Nate had shown up to take Beryl to lunch, but he wasn't alone. Pulling up in the driveway right after him, was Lauralee Caswell. Seeing Nate and Beryl to the door, Olympia greeted Lauralee as she walked up to the porch.

Bearing a second rose bush in her arms, Lauralee Caswell had come to pay another visit to Blanchard House that very afternoon following church services. This time the rose was peach colored. Olympia thanked her for the thoughtful gift and sat it on the porch by the railing before she invited her inside. John met her guest in the foyer, greeting her politely, commenting on how lovely she looked in her Sunday finery. Lauralee blushed from the compliment.

Sitting beside her guest on the sofa, Olympia asked, "What brings you out this way on a Sunday afternoon, Lauralee?"

"I just thought I'd call on you after I left church," she replied. "I told Martin I was coming this time and he said I could. He asked me to offer his congratulations again."

A little embarrassed by the situation, Olympia changed the subject. "I suppose you were very surprised to see me this morning in church?"

"Not especially," Lauralee answered. "Church is for everybody. But now that you will be coming regularly, we can sit together, and I'll fill you in on everybody."

John couldn't help but smile at the grown woman's childlike quality. "What will you tell her Miss Lauralee?"

"You know, Mr. John." Lauralee giggled. "You know how everybody is." She tugged at Olympia's elbow and continued. "Surely, Olympia you noticed how Bertha Koontz just mouths the words to the songs. If you don't believe me just watch her next time we sing "On the Solid Rock, I Stand. She only knows the first stanza." Olympia giggled, spurring Lauralee to continue her many observations. "And Reverend Talbot always comes out with a breath mint in his cheek. Sometimes he forgets it is there. Listen for him to cough real fast when he accidentally swallows it. Then there's Phyllis Decker, she's the woman who wore the big yellow hat. She's real nice, but if she doesn't ever speak to you, it is only because her dentures came loose, and she can't open her mouth."

Lauralee's visit was brief, although longer than her first one had been. After she said her goodbyes and drove away, Olympia asked John to stay for dinner to celebrate the engagement. While she went into the kitchen to prepare the pot roast, John excused himself out on a quick errand, swearing he'd be back before dinner was served. Begrudgingly, Pastoria agreed to help Olympia in the kitchen but refused to speak to her. Olympia was glad of it. The last thing she wanted to hear was anymore talk of how much her sister disliked her fiancé. Of course, what she did not convey with words, Pastoria Blanchard expressed with banging pots and clanging pans and the occasional utensil thrown hard into the sink. Beryl, back from her date by early afternoon, popped into the kitchen to referee if needed. With the silence keeping the sisters from feuding, Beryl made herself useful and steamed the vegetables. The little kitchen was much too small for three cooks, so Pastoria excused herself to wait in the living room until the others arrived. Beryl had asked Nate to join them and of course Zelda would be coming over, typically just in time to miss having to help cook.

Someone should have thought the plan out further before allowing Pastoria to answer the door, because once John returned, he was not greeted with the most generous of spirits. Pastoria delivered him an eye roll, deep sigh, and abandoned the doorway, leaving him standing there. Nate arrived shortly after which helped keep John entertained while dinner was finishing. Once Zelda made it, everything was ready. The kitchen being too small to accommodate everyone, the men dragged the table into the living room and placed a folding card table beside it, allowing ample seating.

Before the meal began, John made an announcement. "As you all know today was the glorious day in which this lovely creature agreed to become my wife. Alas, it cannot be made official until there is a ring." Pulling a box from his coat pocket, he watched Olympia's excitement grow she pulled it from him to open. It was a beautiful, moderately sized diamond. John placed it on her finger to raucous applause from the table, except Pastoria. Olympia looked as if she might cry. Ironically, it was not Olympia brought to tears, but Beryl. Nate and John each handed her a napkin.

"Sorry," she said. "It is just so beautiful to see."

The men accepted her outburst as feminine hormones and thought nothing more of it. But Olympia understood. She sent a sweet smile Beryl's way. It isn't often when a woman gets to witness to the day her grandparents got engaged.

CHAPTER THIRTY

Don't Be Love

The days since Beryl Blanchard had seen her mother and the rest of her family back home had grown into weeks. Though not a day passed when she didn't think about them, she was becoming a little uncomfortable with how comfortable she felt living in the past. Though her hope of returning home remained, she found herself loving the people here just as much. She felt quite at home with Olympia, Pastoria and Zelda, so much in fact, she often had to remind herself they were the same three people she knew later in life. Everything about them was so different in their youth. Beryl no longer thought of Olympia as her grandmother. Olympia was just Olympia. Her friend. Almost a sister now. And of course, there was Nate.

She fully understood now why she should not have accepted that first initial date with him. Beryl now worried that whatever spell sent her there would eventually be broken and she would disappear, losing him from her life forever. She was in love for the first time and with a man she stood practically no chance of remaining with.

It was a struggle within her whenever she was with him—which was growing more frequent. He had no idea who she really was or from where she truly came. It wasn't possible to tell him even when she so desperately yearned to. Keeping such a powerful secret from a man who was falling for her as deeply as she was for him was agony. It was wrong to continue moving forward with the relationship. She owed him better than that. She owed herself better. Yet her connection to Nate was too strong for her to refuse his invitations. And truth be told, Beryl Blanchard had never been in love before now and as anyone who has ever truly loved someone else knows, you want to spend every moment with them...even when you know it cannot last. So, she did her best to keep things as harmless as possible; never asking him too many questions about himself and evading his questions about her. Normally that approach worked when they were at movies, or dinners, or playing cards with

Olympia and Pastoria, but today was more difficult.

Sitting in the little rowboat they'd taken out on the pond; Beryl did her best to evade his glances because she could tell they carried a desire to speak those words she'd been doing her best to avoid either of them saying. The yellow boat glided gently across the tranquil water; the blue sky mirrored upon its surface. The unspoken thing between them weighted the air. As he steered the rowboat toward the little island, he watched Beryl shining under the sunlight. "You are extraordinarily beautiful, Beryl Blanchard."

She blushed. Her heart doubled its pace, more from the words he left unspoken than his tender compliment. The nose of the boat touched the bank of the small island causing the drifting current accompanying it to splash against the side making tiny trickling sounds. Nate stepped from the boat to shore, extending his hand for her. Above them, obscuring the sun, soft rustling leaves fluttered with a breeze carrying the scent of wild honeysuckle. Nate laid out a blanket while she unpacked a basket of cold fried chicken and potato salad. They still were not talking much, both sharing the unvoiced emotions of whatever was happening between them.

Breaking the quiet, he asked the question he had been dreading the answer to. "Do you know how much longer your visit here will last?"

"Trying to get rid of me?" she teased. She made a clumsy attempt at a flirtatious hair toss, but it didn't land well. Her hair was shoulder length and curly and didn't have quite the same toss effect as if Olympia did it.

"On the contrary," he said. "I'm hoping it'll be a while before you go back to Mobile."

"I really have no idea how long my visit will be," Beryl said. "I'm taking things day by day."

Nate opened a bottle of wine, pouring them each a glass, and said the thing she had tried to keep unsaid. "I'm falling for you Beryl."

"Don't say that Nate," she whispered. "I cannot stay here. I shouldn't even be seeing you because I know I cannot stay." Tears swelled in her eyes. "I have never felt like this about anyone. Why did it have to be you? Here? When I must go back."

"Why do you have to go back? You could stay here with me."

"I can't explain," Beryl said. "But trust me. It isn't possible."

"Is there another man at home?"

Beryl laughed. "No. Definitely not. There have never really been any other men.

You are the first I have ever cared for. I mean that."

"Then stay with me, Beryl. Let us see where this could go. I can see a beautiful life with you." Their kiss brought them down atop the blanket, clutched in one another's arms as the discarded glasses of wine spilled out onto the wildflower laden grass.

CHAPTER THIRTY-ONE

The Monster of the Furnace

When the assignment came from the council for Olympia and her team to investigate reports of a rogue vampire spotted in Birmingham, Pastoria was thrilled. Not only was the city merely an hour away and would not require lengthy travel, but she was also eager to wage another fight against a bloodsucker.

"I should go with you," Beryl suggested.

"No," Olympia cautioned as she continued to pack the duffle bag with items they may need. "This is very dangerous. We work for the Consort, not you. I can't put your life at risk on our case."

Beryl laughed out loud. "Olympia, you don't know this, but I have successfully helped slaughter a pack of werewolves and an insanely evil witch who had the power to jump into other people's bodies. I think I can handle a vampire. Besides, if one of you gets hurt, I'll be there to heal you."

"Well, Beryl's got my vote!" Zelda shouted, passing Beryl a cannister sprayer and starting towards the door.

Olympia and Pastoria, each carrying bags in their hands, made their way outside as well. Beryl, carrying the cannister, followed. "At least tell her how to use that thing, Zelda!" Pastoria chastised.

Beryl grinned again, examining the familiar metal can. "Believe it or not. If this is what I think it is, I know exactly how to use this. This thing is full of acid. I've seen it used in combat before. Let's roll!"

On the drive to Birmingham, Olympia read from the file the Witches Association sent over detailing the case. Reports of unexplained deaths were increasing at an alarming rate at the Sloss Furnace Iron and Steel Company. At first, the deaths were deemed to be workplace accidents—after all it was a steel mill. What more dangerous environment could there be for workers? Steam engine combustion blowers, scorching hot boilers, and liquid melted iron from inferno fires. Men died regularly during a good month, but now the number was suspiciously rising. Not only that, but multiple workers had begun reporting having seen the presence of a frightening stranger as well. However, once the agency heard the details involved, they felt assured these killings were less likely the work of a ghost and far more likely the carnage of a vampire. Several of those who died were drained of blood, although authorities paid little attention to it. The accident rate in such an environment squelched any effort of real detective work when someone died on the job. It was a known fact the conditions at Sloss put workers at slim odds of escaping injury free. Investigations were also most likely skipped because two-thirds of the workmen were African Americans. Local police didn't consider them an important enough demographic to waste time looking into anything.

The traffic on Highway 59 was thinning out by this time of night. For this reason, Olympia permitted Zelda to drive her new car the 60 miles to Birmingham. This gave her more time to immerse herself in the details outlined from the report the Witches Association sent. Rereading the file shed a little light on the perplexing case at the Sloss Furnace. It was easy to see why the first reports of unexplained deaths were disregarded as mishaps, considering the hazardous conditions accompanying any job inside of a steel mill. It was not a crazy assumption to make...in the beginning. However, lately, the death numbers had risen to alarming proportion. With rumors now spreading of the menacing stranger lurking at night, the men were becoming jittery and the mill could not afford more losses of manpower.

The legend of Sloss Furnace had been circulating for some time and was well known to the area. Beryl even heard of it in her time. It was claimed to be haunted by the ghost of a deranged former foreman. This very legend is what led the plant manager to seek the assistance of secret paranormal investigators. As Olympia read over the reports again, she tended to agree with the Association's determination that the killings were not spirit related but held consistencies hinting to a vampire. Several deceased workers had been found drained of blood and with suspicious lacerations, both key facts dismissed by lackadaisical police as being the result of a fall or other work-related injury. But The Witches Association knew general cuts and scrapes do not account for that much blood loss. And even if it had, where was the blood? None of the reports described a bloody accident scene. It seemed amateurish to Olympia for investigators to have missed that detail. Of course, Beryl knew from her history books, white cops didn't work excessively hard to solve cases involving black victims, especially in 1960's Birmingham. The witches were in full agreement they needed to solve the case quickly, because no one wanted a nest of vampires endangering the city.

"Isn't an ironworks plant an odd place for a vampire?" Pastoria commented. "I would expect an old, abandoned mansion."

"You've seen too many old movies," Olympia answered. "Sounds like a perfect hideout to me. He could be sheltering in one of the many abandoned boilers or furnaces. The entire place, according to this report, was updated and modernized a few years ago. There are some parts no longer in use. He simply had to settle into some neglected area of the plant no one ever goes into, and he has a fully stocked buffet of victims working through the dead of night."

Night Supervisor Cyrus Dougan was there to meet the investigation team at the front gate of Sloss when they arrived. As the four women strolled towards him from the parking lot, he met them with a look of dissatisfaction.

"You ain't the people I'm supposed to be letting in here are ya?" He spat a bit of tobacco juice to his right, probably considering himself well-mannered for not directing it where the ladies were walking.

"We are." Olympia informed the disappointed man.

"Well, how ya'll gone do this job? You just a bunch a gals. This place ain't any kind of place for ladies to be going through. It's hot and its sweaty and its more dangerous than you think."

Beryl was not unfamiliar with this type of man, even in the future. "I assure you, Mr. Dougan. We are not as delicate as we appear."

"Ya'll do know something in there is killing folks?"

"What other possible reason would we be here?" Olympia replied, pushing past him to enter the factory.

It did not take long during their cursory tour of the factory to figure out the harsh reality of the hierarchy at Sloss. In the far more comfortable offices worked the managers, chemists, and engineers—all white men. When moving through the hellish temperatures of the boilers, stoves, and furnaces there wasn't a white man in sight. At each of the locations where a corpse was found, Zelda honed her senses to see what she could gather psychically. Unfortunately, the first two spots yielded no impressions being that the bodies had been retrieved, almost burned to a crisp from having fallen (or been tossed) into pits of molten steel. However, by the fourth site, Zelda knew instantly a vampire was indeed responsible for some of the killings. Looking down at the still-stained spot on the ground where the poor man's blood had been devoured, she not only felt his death, but could see the monster who caused it.

Wanting an overhead look at the facility, Zelda coerced Mr. Dougan into unlocking the gate blocking a tall winding metal staircase. It encircled an unused furnace and they followed it all the way to the very top of a smokestack where she could look out across the entire factory. "What's that big thang over there?" she asked Mr. Dougan pointing at a remote darkened building.

"That's the old dehumidification plant. Ain't nobody working there. They shut that down after WWII."

Zelda exchanged telling glances with Olympia and the others, "He's in there."

The women ditched Mr. Dougan as they made their way towards the distant structure. The night air was loud with the hum of machinery. The atmosphere was unbearably hot and sticky from the escaping exhaust of melting steel and the hellish temperatures needed to liquify it. Every enclosed structure put off a massive dose of heat as they traversed the passages between. Those structures which were open on one or more sides were even more unbearable as waves of searing air cast out into the night, funneling through the maze of twists and turns between the buildings. The witches endured the crippling heat towards the decommissioned dehumidification plant. Unused now, the building was shrouded in darkness except for what illumination the low hanging moon provided. Even its light did little to ease the tension, casting unsettling shadows on the rusted metal structure. Anticipation was heavy, as within every shadow and behind every obstructed view, could have been the blood-thirsty monster.

With senses attuned and eyes sharp, Olympia took the lead entering the plant. Her hands were ready to send out her magnificent power with every footstep. Pastoria was behind her, braced for whatever might rush them and prepared to fire her telekinesis at any second. Zelda, with her psychic abilities, scanned the surroundings for any signs of the vampire's presence while Beryl trailed behind, ready to heal any injuries the others might receive. The further into the plant they went, the temperature dropped sending a chilling, but welcoming, breeze to greet them. Zelda and Beryl clicked on the powerful flashlights they'd brought, revealing a labyrinth of tunnels and chambers. Saying nothing, Zelda motioned to a doorway on the right. The witches continued, following her cue through the damp factory. The scent of decay clung to the air as their footfalls seemed to sync to the drip, drip, drip sounds from overhead moisture falling to the rusted metal floor.

Suddenly, Zelda stopped in her tracks, grabbing Pastoria by the shoulder. "*He's close*," she said, speaking to the others with only her mind. "*I can feel him.*"

Beryl's flashlight hit a spot on the floor that aroused her attention. She lifted the light to widen the range of sight. "*Look at the dust and rust on the floor. Drag marks. Two of them side by side.*"

"*Like shoe heels.*" Olympia replied.

Continuing forward, Beryl kept her light trained on the long marks. It was not long after they observed drops of blood along the trail. Then suddenly, a large pool of it! Beryl's light moved up, flashing onto the demonic face of the grisly beast. In the vampire's clutches lay a limp, seemingly unconscious African American male. When the flashlight beam struck the monster's eyes, he flung the body to the ground, charging forward at warp speed. Olympia screamed! Beryl saw her whip sideways, grabbing her face with her hands as if struck by the creature. He raced past Olympia, grabbing Pastoria by the arm, disappearing into the darkness with his captive.

"Where is she?" Zelda bellowed as Beryl rushed to Olympia's aid.

"My face!" Olympia shrieked. Four deep gashes crossed her cheek all the way to her mouth. Though the stream of blood covered most of it, Beryl could see the tissue and bone between. Near her lips, the inside of her mouth was visible through the sliced sections like slits in a window blind.

Pastoria screamed from some darkened place nearby. Zelda flashed her light around, finding the vampire still clutching Pastoria on top of a diagonal pipe leading up to a higher section of tunnel. Beryl yelled to Olympia to immobilize him, but she was too consumed with what had been done to her face to hear anything. The vampire grinned wickedly down to them; his blazoned eyes still illuminated by the flashlight. He dragged his razor talons across Pastoria's neck then tossed her off the pipe. Running forward to attempt to catch her, both Beryl and Zelda stopped suddenly as they saw Pastoria's body hover in place midair a few feet above their heads. Olympia was standing behind them, her hands outreached, she'd halted her sister's fall.

Never having seen anything before as powerful as these women, the vampire knew instinctively he was not dealing with mere humans. His expression of surprise melted away, replaced by a sinister grin across his pale face. "So, you've come to challenge me, witches?" he hissed, his voice crackling as if it hadn't been used in years.

"We've come to kill you." Olympia announced, swiping her hand to release her sister from the spell. Pastoria dropped into Beryl and Zelda's awaiting arms. Her throat was pouring blood even as she was trying to stop the flow with her hands. Beryl was about to do something, but there was no time.

With a sudden burst of momentum, the vampire lunged at them. The witches managed to roll out of his range when he landed sure-footed to the ground. With an amazing display of strength, he tore a large cylindrical pipe from the wall and swept it wide towards them like a deadly jump rope none of them would be able to evade. And then everyone's eyes, including the vampire's, stared onward in utter shock and fascination at the hand gripping the other end of the steel pipe. Beryl's hand. She stood boldly and confidently clutching the blunt end of the probably 200lb. pole. It had happened so quickly; Beryl was only now realizing what she'd done. As the pipe had come sailing towards them, she raised her hand to it—out of some kind of instinct—and grabbed it mid-air. It had not even required much effort. She hadn't even swayed or stumbled from the impact. Beryl simply grabbed it and was still clutching the unwieldy and crushing projectile in her hand as if it were nothing more than a baton.

The vampire shook himself from his astonishment and was just about to wage another strike when Olympia froze him in place. Zelda ran forward with the cannister of acid and unloaded it on the monster. His skin sizzled and fried, dropping in sections like shaved roast beef to the floor. However, he was still alive. Grotesque looking, but alive. The agony of the acid revived him from his unanimated state. He howled in unbearable pain, writhing to the floor as more of his flesh and clothing disintegrated under the boiling acid. Olympia stepped closer to him and sent out a blast of her exploding power. The vampire burst into thousands of pieces across the rusted metal floor.

"Well, that's a mess!" Zelda cried, gagging at the horrific stench.

"My face!" Olympia shrieked once more, remembering her disfigurement.

Beryl was already busy, her hands firmly pressed to Pastoria's throat. Zelda and Olympia looked on in complete awe of the sight they were seeing. Beryl's eyes were closed, her hands were trembling over Pastoria's mortal wound as Pastoria was gasping for her last attempts at air. A golden light began to grow within Beryl's hands. The orb appeared to reside under her very skin, growing larger and lighter until a burst of white light spilled from her hands and blanketed Pastoria's neck. When it dimmed, Pastoria was healed. Her neck, fully intact, showed not a sign of having been sliced.

"Oh, my Lord!" Zelda shouted. "The girl said she had the power to heal! She sure whaddant' lyin'!"

Olympia pushed Pastoria aside, pleading to Beryl, "Do me next! Do me next!"

Beryl did. She healed Olympia's lovely face in record time, restoring it as beautiful as it had been before the vampire tore it open. She was also able to save the poor unfortunate man the vampire had been draining when they first discovered him. The man, still woozy from his experience, did not know what to make of these women or what they had done to save his life. But he thanked them profusely.

The witches stood together, catching their breath, enjoying the satisfaction of having succeeded in their mission. Sloss Furnace was saved from the malevolent creature. Night Supervisor Cyrus Dougan, pretended to not believe the witches' story about the vampire, even with his employee recounting the same tale. Dougan simply thanked the ladies for what they claimed to have done and said time would tell if they had really solved the problem. Of course, they knew they had and their report to the Association would confirm that, but like with so many cases, man would never admit, or even be able to comprehend, what they had to do to keep the world safe.

CHAPTER THIRTY-TWO

Olympia's Very Extended Family

The front porch steps creaked under the weight of several approaching footsteps. It was the sheer amount which alerted Olympia, usually accustomed to having only one visitor at a time. Pulling open the door, she was momentarily stunned by what she found on the other side.

Standing before her was a slim woman with long, flowing blonde hair, not unlike Olympia's. In fact, almost exactly like it. Two others stood with her, but neither fascinated Olympia as the blonde woman did. She couldn't help but feel an inexplicable connection to her. Though the other woman seemed a bit other-worldly, not to mention at least a decade or more older, Olympia almost felt as if she were looking at her own reflection, or a close facsimile of.

"You look like me."

The woman said nothing at first, returning the same dazed look Olympia held. It didn't require much deduction for Olympia to figure things out. The woman resembled her far too much to be anything other than another Blanchard descendant from the future. The woman was even staring at Olympia much the way Beryl did when she first showed up at this same door.

"Hello, Olympia," the woman announced. "I am Nacaria."

"Well, I'll be damned," Olympia sighed. "You look so much like me, except old."

"I am not old!" an indignant Nacaria exclaimed.

"Uh, yeah you kind of are," Olympia smiled. "What are you, like 60?"

"I am in my late 40s!" Nacaria snapped.

"Same thing," Olympia replied as she allowed the woman and her companions into the house.

Behind the woman calling herself Nacaria, followed a man and another woman. The man was muscular with sandy blonde hair and the shapely woman with him had short cropped dark brown wispy hair. She was glancing around the living room with a look of amazement, also not unlike Beryl's first impression of the place. Olympia understood the reaction. Blanchard House was quite different in appearance than in their time. She watched the brunette walk over to the coffee table and lift the lid of a carved box.

"Hey! Don't touch that." Olympia scolded the nosey lady. That box contained Pastoria's marijuana and she would have a fit if she knew anyone had messed with it. Returning her attention to Nacaria, Olympia asked, "So you are my daughter?" Nacaria was impressed by the astute guess. It would spare a lot of wasted time convincing her. Olympia gave a knowing nod, "Beryl told me about you guys."

"Do you know who we are?" the man asked, gesturing to himself and the brunette woman.

Olympia twirled a strand of her hair around her index finger and replied, "You're the boy so you must be Seth. Which one are you ma'am?"

The brunette did not appreciate the question. "Ma'am?" she sneered at Seth. "Hecate just ma'amed me."

Smiling condescendingly, Olympia stated, "I was taught to have respect for my elders."

"I am your granddaughter! My name is Fable."

"Mother," Nacaria began. "We are here to rescue Beryl."

"Please do not call me Mother," Olympia sneered. "It's a little crazy. I am not even sure I ever plan to have any children. I really dislike them."

"Dear Lord," Fable sighed, nudging the man. "I don't think I am ever going to be the same again after this."

Explaining that Beryl was not at home at the present time, Olympia served them some sweet tea and settled them into the living room to wait. "Her date will bring her home shortly."

"Wait a minute! Beryl is dating?" Fable shouted. "Beryl never dates."

Seth grinned, "Maybe the men in our time aren't her style."

"He's a great guy," Olympia replied. "He used to be a beau of mine, but that was never very serious. I'm happy he and Beryl sparked because they are really very cute together."

Pastoria came in from wherever she had been and displayed little interest in meeting the new arrivals. There seemed to be tension between she and Olympia which the others did not understand. It only took a few minutes of witnessing the sisters arguing before it became clear. The moment Pastoria spouted off about Olympia's relationship with John Windham, Nacaria knew they were fighting over her father. As the fight intensified, Nacaria tried to place them in neutral corners, which was received poorly by both.

"Who are you people anyway?" Pastoria squawked.

"Apparently they are more relatives from the future," Olympia answered. "They are Beryl's family, and they've come to get her. Meet my daughter and more of my grandchildren."

"I'll meet them when they're born," Pastoria said dismissively.

"You're as funny as a rattlesnake in a sleeping bag," Olympia scoffed at her sister.

"You know a little something about rattlesnakes," Pastoria retorted. "You are dating one after all. Traitor."

"At least there is someone who wants to date me," Olympia quipped. "I don't see any men lining up on the porch for you much these days."

"There aren't any left," Pastoria smiled viciously. "You dated them all!"

"Bitch."

"Slut!"

"Traitor!"

"You already said traitor," Olympia sneered imperiously. "But you have the intelligence of a dead skunk so I shouldn't expect a deeper vocabulary."

Olympia's future offspring did not know what to make of this extreme behavior. It was so unlike them. Then again, they never knew Olympia or Pastoria when they were young. As the bickering continued, a familiar voice rang out from the front door.

"Are you two at it again?" Beryl cried coming into the room. "I swear I am going to have to stay home around the clock to referee." Her eyes locked on her sister, her aunt, and her cousin. A shriek of joy erupted from her lungs as she ran to embrace the Blanchards of her time.

Behind Beryl, Nate stood in confusion. "Beryl? Who are these people?"

"Oh, I'm so sorry Nate!" she exclaimed, dragging him forward by the arm. "Nate this is my family. My sister Fable; my cousin Seth, and my aunt Nacaria."

"Nice to meet you," he replied. "Are you going to be visiting for a while as well?"

Fable looked at him with suspicion. Something was not normal about the way Beryl held him by the wrist. And the way she'd spoken to him. It was affectionate.

Something was unquestionably going on between them, but no matter what it was, it was going to end because Beryl belonged to another age. "Actually," Fable said. "We've come to take Beryl home."

Nate was shaken by the announcement. "No, you can't do that. Beryl and I—well we, we've been making plans."

"Plans?" Seth repeated.

"Nate wants me to stay in Daihmler and not go back to *Mobile*. But I have told him I don't think that is possible."

"Don't think?" Fable cried. "It is not remotely possible! You are going back, and you are going back right now."

"No, you can't!" Nate pleaded. Grabbing her hands, he waged a plea to her. "Beryl, I am begging you to stay. I know we have only known each other a short time, but there is something special between us. I know this is crazy, but if it'll get you to stay, I'll marry you."

"What?" Beryl gasped. No one had ever asked her to marry them before. Despite the circumstances of her reality, most notably that she was living in the wrong timeline, she could not help but feel immense joy as someone was genuinely proposing marriage to her.

"Yes!" Nate cried. "I want to marry you. Marry me, Beryl Blanchard. Stay with me here in Daihmler. We'll have a fantastic life together."

Exchanging glances with Pastoria, Olympia found herself saying out loud, "Well, this is just weird."

"This is insanity!" Fable exclaimed. "Beryl, you just met this guy! You haven't been here long enough to develop feelings. You two know nothing about each other. He certainly doesn't know about you."

"I know all I need to know about this spectacular lady." Nate smiled.

Beryl patted his cheek gently. "And I know Nate is the kindest, most decent man I've ever known. Not only is he a successful banker, but he is also an advocate for civil rights. Here in Alabama, at this time in history, that's so courageous."

Nate made a peculiar face, "Honey, I'm not a banker."

"You aren't? But I the loan papers—"

"Yes, but I don't represent the bank," Nate explained. "I represent the Blanchard family."

Beryl did not say anything as she looked on towards her new boyfriend. She didn't suppose it mattered much if she had misunderstood his occupation—that changed nothing in the way they felt about one another. But she did feel slightly embarrassed she had not known what line of work he was in.

"It doesn't make a damn whether you know what he does for a living or not," Fable argued. "This relationship is over. You have to come home now, and you know why Beryl."

"Beryl is staying here." Nate announced.

As Beryl gazed her honey brown eyes into Nate's blue, she knew her sister Fable was right. She did have to go. Even if it was going to break her heart. "Oh Nate," she wept. "There is nothing more I would love than to stay here and build a life with you. But I can't. We are from different worlds. Different in ways I am not able to explain. I do have to go back with them."

Nate was about to offer another plea for her to stay, but Nacaria interrupted. She understood the full danger of the situation now and in ways it appeared no one else did. She knew exactly who Nate was and why it was vital she pull Beryl back to her own time before she wrecked the future forever. "We must go, Beryl. Now."

Taking Beryl by the arm and dragging her away from Nate, Nacaria led her into the privacy of the kitchen. Seth and Fable followed on her heels. Linking hands with her son Seth and with Beryl, Nacaria gave Fable a nod to clasp Beryl's other hand and Seth's, forging a circle.

"We must return home. This very second."

Withdrawing a small glass vial from her pocket, its contents shimmering with some kind of magical serum she had concocted herself, Nacaria smashed it to the floor in the center of their circle. Beryl closed her eyes in sorrow. She would never see Nate again. She braced herself for the quickening sensation of being catapulted through time.

Nothing happened.

Looking around at the tiny kitchen which should have now been decades in the past, and realizing they'd gone nowhere, Seth stammered, "Uh, aren't we now supposed to zap away?"

Equally taken by surprise her potion didn't work, Nacaria replied, "Yes, we are."

"Why didn't we?" Fable asked. "Why aren't we back home in our own house?"

"I have no idea," Nacaria answered. "This same potion worked before when I rescued the two of you from the timelines you were both trapped in. It should work here as well."

"Try again," Seth urged. "I can hear Nate and the others coming."

As Nate's hurried voice was calling to Beryl and his hand was pushing open the kitchen door, Nacaria withdrew another vial and tried her spell again with the same disappointing result.

"Mom, why is this not working?' Seth asked.

"I'm glad it isn't!" Beryl exclaimed as Nate rushed into the kitchen with Olympia and Pastoria following behind.

Beryl broke free of the hold on her, rushing into Nate's arms. Extending her hand out to clasp Olympia's, she said, "I have been living with Olympia and Pastoria for weeks, and I care a great deal about Nate. I am not going anywhere without a proper farewell to them."

Scolding Nacaria for such rudeness, Olympia shrilled, "Just like that, you were going to leave?" Beryl is like family to us. That was pretty low-down, ma'am."

Nacaria rolled her eyes, "Would you please stop calling me ma'am when I am your very own daughter?"

"Daughter?" Nate exclaimed. "Olympia doesn't have a daughter. And you are older than she is anyway!" He turned Beryl's chin to face him, "Honey, what in the world is going on here?

Beryl began to cry. Kissing Nate's cheek and pressing her head into his chest she confessed, "There is a great deal you don't know about the Blanchard family. I am so sorry I didn't tell you about us, but that's really up to Olympia and Pastoria."

Nothing made sense for Nate. He had no idea what anyone was talking about, but he also didn't care. As Beryl clung to him with his arms around her, the only thing that mattered was the woman he loved and the distress she was in. He kissed the top of her head, her fuzzy blonde curls tickling his nose.

Seeing the way he held Beryl; Fable knew whatever they felt for one another had already progressed too far. She needed to take control of this situation. "Look, I don't care if you two think you're in love, or if grandmother here thinks we are rude in trying to whisk Beryl out of here. All I care to know right now is why Aunt Nacaria's spell did not take the four of us home?"

Nate was just about to question this strange hostile woman who claimed to be Beryl's sister as to what she meant by the word *spell* and why was she referring to Olympia as her grandmother—but he did not get the opportunity. The kitchen door swung open again, cramming yet another person into the drama.

"I can tell you," Zelda announced.

Everyone looked to the doorway where Zelda stood, hands pressing the frame, huffing to catch her breath.

"Oh my God, that's Zelda!" Seth cried. "I'd know her anywhere!"

Zelda nodded briefly, though confusingly at the boy, but her eyes were focused on the woman with the long blonde hair. The one who looked so much like Olympia. "I have seen you," Zelda said to Nacaria. "I saw you years ago in one'a my visions. You met him, didn't you?"

"Him?" Nacaria repeated.

"Your granddaddy. Constantinople. You knew him."

Olympia glanced incredulously at Zelda, then to Nacaria as she was nodding to Zelda. "My father?" Olympia gasped. "But how could they..."

Zelda waved off her question as she investigated Nacaria's eyes. "He was a great man, your granddaddy. You should feel rightly honored to have met him."

Olympia took hold of her best friend's hand and pulled her forward, "We will unpack that later. Right now, Zelda, tell us about Beryl." Olympia turned to the strangers and added, "Zelda is the most powerful psychic I've ever known. If she says she knows what is wrong with your spell, then she does."

"Spell?" Nate gasped. "Psychic? What is happening around this house Olympia?"

Never one for beating around the bush, Pastoria decided to spill the truth once and for all. She was tired of keeping their secret from a lifelong friend like Nate, and all this back and forth with these future Blanchards was giving her a headache. "Nate, we are witches. You used to know that when you were a kid, but our father wiped your memory. These people are our relatives from the future. That is where Beryl comes from. The future. She's a witch too. There. Now you're all caught up."

Olympia jabbed her sister in the shoulder, furious at her callous bluntness. But when Nate looked to Olympia for the truth, all she could do was nod. "Pastoria isn't joking." Olympia said solemnly to her friend.

"Please Nate," Beryl whispered. "Let me have a chance to explain everything to you."

Nacaria was losing patience with the superfluous drama. She'd come here to retrieve her niece. She'd promised her sister Demitra she would rescue Beryl, just the same way she had earlier rescued Seth and Fable from the similar pasts they had been trapped in. There was also still one remaining loved one left to locate in the chasm of Blanchard family history. Seth's wife Yasmine was not yet rescued from the past she had been flung to. Beryl's romance was complicating matters. They still had to find Yasmine, not to mention Nacaria knew she had to get Beryl out of there before it sent a ripple through time upending something important. "Zelda, can you tell me why my spell isn't working? What am I doing wrong?"

"You ain't done nuthin' wrong," Zelda said with a pained look on her face. "If y'all had all let go of Beryl's hand your spell woulda worked. The three a' you would be back in the future by now. Holdin' onto Beryl is what's stopping it."

Angrily, Fable shouted, "Because Beryl thinks she's in love and wants to stay! Her unwillingness to go is interfering with the potion."

"Nope," Zelda said. "Cause there ain't just four of y'all trying to leave. There's five."

"What?" Olympia gasped. "What are you talking about, Zel?"

Folding her plump arms over her chest, Zelda lowered her eyes to Beryl's stomach, "Beryl's got his baby in her."

A silence fell over the tiny Blanchard kitchen. Eyes widened, looking into everyone else's equally dumbstruck faces. Just as she had in all her life's unexpected circumstances, Beryl looked to Fable for support. Her younger sister, no wiser than she, stared back at Beryl as tears began to glisten in both of their eyes. Nacaria dropped her shoulders in defeat, for the very thing she feared from the start was proving true. From the first moment Olympia revealed Beryl was seeing a man named Nate, Nacaria understood the possible ramifications.

Finally finding words to break everyone's silence, Nate stuttered, "Say that again. Beryl is pregnant?"

All color drained from Beryl's face and despite being a highly intelligent medical doctor, she heard herself say rather ridiculously, "I haven't been here that long."

"Only takes once to make a baby," Zelda announced. "And you are as pregnant as it gets. You got two auras."

Seth recognized the gravity of the situation for Beryl, but he didn't understand why it should prevent his cousin from returning home. "Fine. She's pregnant. Retool the spell to bring both she and her baby home."

Shaking her head to the male stranger before her, Zelda explained, "That baby is from this time, not yours. It ain't goin' nowhere 'till it's born. I'm afraid Beryl's gonna be here for the next nine months."

Nate was shaken by the intensity of it all. Witches. Spells. Visitors from the future. A baby. His baby. Yet as he looked again into his beloved's eyes, he did not care how crazy it all sounded. "I don't know what to believe here, Beryl. But I do know I love you. Stay with me. Become Mrs. Nate Caldwell."

A sudden gasp rang out from Fable's throat. "Oh. My. God." Nacaria clasped Fable's wrist cutting her a sharp look. Fable instantly knew that her aunt had already long figured out who Nate was. This was why Nacaria was so urgently trying to get Beryl out of there.

Zelda suggested everyone go into the living room to sit down while she explained the reason the blonde stranger's spell had not worked. The baby was a natural part of their current timeline. Beryl belonged to another era. As long as the child was inside Beryl, neither of them could jump to another timeline.

Beryl's watery eyes met her aunt Nacaria's in a desperate plea for guidance, "But what does that even mean? I stay here until I give birth, then I return home with the baby?"

Nate sat down on the arm of the sofa and took Beryl's hand. "I really don't know what all is going on here," he told her. "But Beryl, don't you see what this means. We are going to have a child. We will be married. We will have a wonderful life together. All this other insane stuff about you being from the future...I don't understand what game your friends are playing, but if you are truly having my baby—that is wonderful news."

Nacaria scooted off the couch to kneel in front of her niece. She wanted to face her squarely as she imparted the difficult reality. Placing her gentle, loving hands on Beryl's frightened face, she said "I need for you to hear what I have to say, Beryl. This is a jolt. A huge jolt to absorb. Yes, you are pregnant. Zelda is right and that is why I can't propel you back to where you belong. But there is something else. Something which complicates everything."

Beryl trembled. Seeing her fear, Olympia swiped the magazines from the coffee table to sat down before Beryl, placing her hands on her knee for support. Olympia addressed Nacaria, "I think there is more going on here than I understand. But if it helps, Pastoria and I have come to love Beryl. She is more than welcome to remain here however long she wants. Whether it is only for the duration of her pregnancy or even if she wants to marry Nate and live here from now on. She's welcome at Blanchard House however long she wants."

"Thank you, Mother—I mean Olympia," Nacaria smiled. "However, things are a bit more problematic than I think anyone but Fable and I understand."

"Explain it to me then," Beryl asked. "Once my baby is born, I can take it home with me—right?" Looking again to her sister for reassurance, Beryl was heart heavy when she saw Fable shaking her head.

Nacaria took a deep breath and caressed her niece's face. "The baby inside you is Howard."

CHAPTER THIRTY-THREE

Beryl's Shocking Truth

Howard Caldwell was not a name anyone living in 1963 Daihmler, Alabama would have recognized. However, he was a figure the future Blanchards knew well. Like his father Nate had once been, Howard Caldwell was a dear Blanchard family friend and their financial manager. Howard grew up with Olympia's children and had been there to celebrate when Olympia's grandchildren were born. Howard Caldwell was an honorary Blanchard in every way, and now it looked like there was nothing *honorary* about it at all.

"Howard?" Beryl repeated. "Our Howard? Howard who comes to dinner every Friday night?"

Never the first to completely comprehend things, Seth voiced disbelief, "Howard is older than Aunt Artemis! How can he be Beryl's baby?"

"You ain't real bright, are you man?" Zelda snorted Seth's way.

"What I don't understand, is how you couldn't have known you were seeing Howard's father?" Fable asked. "Nate Caldwell. Howard Caldwell."

Frantic to understand herself, all Beryl could say was, "I never knew Howard's father. I didn't even know his name was Nate. And Nate and I, well, we've just been enjoying our time together. I didn't ask questions because I didn't want him to ask questions. I didn't even know his last name, or if it came up, I wasn't thinking about Howard."

Fable was not letting it go so easily. "How could you not think of Howard? You are in the past when our grandmother was young. Did it never occur to you that people you would run into could be directly connected to people we know at home?"

Clutching the side of her head in frustration, Beryl shouted back, "Olympia told me there was no harm in going out and enjoying myself as long as I didn't say anything about who I really am."

Nacaria and Fable turned to give a disapproving look to Olympia. Olympia shrugged, "What do I know? You are all older than I am."

"It doesn't matter now," Nacaria said, retaking control of the situation. "Beryl, I am afraid that the shocking truth is you are Howard's mother."

Unable to accept the idea, Beryl stood to her feet and began pacing the room. "Howard is old enough to be my father. Not my son. His mother died in childbirth! That wasn't me. You are wrong. I'll get back to my time and Nate will marry the woman he was supposed to marry before I came here. It'll all go back to how it was meant to be."

"Who is Howard?" Olympia softly asked Nacaria.

"Howard Caldwell is Nate Caldwell's son. We all believed his mother died in childbirth. Ironically, you serve as a bit of a mother figure to him. You even paid for his college."

Beryl was standing now at the window, looking out into the yard, or perhaps looking into the future, 50 years in the future. "Howard," she murmured pressing her hands to her stomach. Nate got up and joined her at the window. He placed his hand on her shoulder and tried to comfort her with a smile.

"I think you have been his mother all along, honey." Nacaria proclaimed. "We've never known much about her other than she died in childbirth. Mother didn't speak of her often. All I ever knew was she died when Howard was born and that Mother loved her very much."

"Are you saying Beryl is going to die?" Pastoria exclaimed.

Shaking her head, Nacaria explained, "I don't believe now that Howard's mother ever did die. She only went back to her proper time."

The newfound realization clung to the air as Beryl processed it as best she could. Nate understood very little of what anyone was talking about, but he now believed they must be speaking the truth. Everyone was too upset for it to be faked. His only concern now was Beryl.

"Why can't she take him back with her after he's born?" Seth asked his mother.

Irate from the callousness everyone was displaying, Nate shouted, "Could everyone stop suggesting the woman I love leave me and also take my child with her?"

Seth ignored Nate's remark, adding to his question to Nacaria, "What's stopping her from going home with a newborn and just name it something else? Howard never has to know."

Nacaria sighed, closing her eyes briefly. She wished the younger generation understood more about how the Natural Order of things worked. When she opened them, she saw Olympia staring back, sharing her frustration. She was perhaps the only person grasping the gravity of the situation. "Because the same person cannot exist in their own timeline. One of them would simply cease to be."

Olympia moved to the window, placing one of her hands on Beryl's arm and the other on Nate's shoulder. "I am beginning to understand what is going on here," Olympia announced. "This baby already exists in Beryl's natural timeline as a grown man."

"Yes," Nacaria said. "This baby she is carrying is a dear friend of ours."

"But he's a grown man in his 50s!" Seth cried. "It won't be the same Howard."

"It is the same soul," Olympia clarified, confirming her shared understanding with Nacaria. "A soul cannot share the same space with itself. One of them would disappear."

With a heaviness in her voice, Nacaria nodded in agreement. "Howard must stay here and grow up just the way he did. Otherwise, he will die."

Listening to this confusing conversation, the only thing poor Nate could think to contribute was, "Howard was my grandfather's name," as he rubbed Beryl's shoulders.

Pastoria rolled her eyes, "That's nice Nate. Doesn't really seem the time to bring it up though."

"Beryl, this is all really crazy to me," Nate said, wrapping his arms around her waist. "All I know is you and I love each other. You will stay here. You will marry me, and we will raise our child together."

Overcome with far too much emotion, Beryl bolted from the room to escape upstairs. Fable tried to go after her, but Nacaria blocked the way. Olympia was of the same mind when Nate also tried to follow. Waving him back, Olympia said what needed to be said, "That girl has been crushed with some devastating revelations. She needs time to adjust to her startling new reality."

A few hours later, Beryl came back downstairs. Nate was gone now, waiting for Pastoria to keep her promise to call him once Beryl was ready to talk. Beryl's relatives from the future were still waiting, but not to try to take her with them anymore, just to say goodbye for a while.

"We know Howard's birthdate," Nacaria told Beryl, trying to make light of the awkward situation as they said their farewells. "I will return to get you the day he is born. Until then you will remain here."

Beryl understood the plan even if she was still processing the meaning. She said goodbye to her sister, her aunt, and her cousin and watched as Nacaria cast another potion to the ground. This time it worked. As the Blanchards from the future swirled into mist out of sight, Beryl stood arm in arm with Olympia, Pastoria and Zelda. In an odd and unexpected way, Beryl felt relieved to be staying. She did like it here. And these three women linking arms with her, had ceased being reminders of the women of her past and had become the sisters of her present.

CHAPTER THIRTY-FOUR

Mrs. Beryl Caldwell

The heaviness over the house brought by the revelation of Beryl's pregnancy felt a little lighter when morning came. With Beryl's relatives from the future now back where they came from, Olympia hoped Beryl could return to the tranquility she felt before they'd shown up. She tapped at Beryl's door mid-morning and asked if she could come in. Beryl was still on the bed, still dressed in yesterday's clothes, when Olympia lay down beside her.

"I guess we would all rather have to take on another vampire than what you are dealing with," Olympia said trying to coax out a smile. "I want you to know Beryl, I meant every word. You are welcome to remain here for the rest of your life if you choose to. We love you, Beryl. If I am being completely honest, it would break my heart if you were no longer here."

Beryl reached over and hugged her, wiping a tear. She gave off a surprising laugh, "It is so ridiculous. But I do feel so at home here. I love you guys. I half wish I was your sister and belonged here."

"You are our sister. And whether you *belong* here or not is for bigger minds than mine. All I can tell you is Pastoria, Zelda, and I never want you to leave. And I know without a doubt, Nate doesn't. He has called three times already."

Nate found Beryl exactly where she'd said she would be when she called him back that morning asking him to meet her. He knew the place well, though it had been years since he had come down to the creek with Olympia and Pastoria when they were all children.

Pushing a few pesky limbs from his face along the path, he spotted the woman he loved sitting on a fallen tree limb looking out into the crisp spring water. Rays of sunlight cast through the leaves spotlighting her curly golden hair. He paused a moment to admire the beauty of it. He loved her so much and she was having his child.

"Feeling better this morning?" he asked approaching her.

Beryl reached her hands out to him, inviting him to sit with her. She was smiling now. He was glad. "Yesterday was a lot. A lot for both of us."

"It was the witch thing that was the hardest for me to believe," he admitted. "And I guess the whole *you being from the future* thing too."

"Have you accepted it now?"

"Well," he grinned. "I didn't until both Pastoria and Olympia demonstrated their powers for me before I went home yesterday. I guess if you can all be witches, it makes you also being from the future more believable."

"I am a doctor, actually." Beryl confessed with pride. "And I can heal people with my power. I used to think that life was fulfilling enough. But now, since meeting you...I see I have been missing something even more rewarding. Love."

Nate straddled the tree limb and pulled something from his pocket. A ring. "John Windham helped me pick it out. He has experience now with picking out rings."

Beryl laughed at his little joke. "You didn't tell him I am his granddaughter, did you?"

Nate's face grew puzzled. "You know I never even put that together. Wow. That is mind blowing." He didn't say anything for a minute. His facial expression and the way he stared blankly at the bark of a nearby Cypress told Beryl he was now considering the remarkable fact.

"Ahem," she said clearing her throat. "The ring?"

Smacking himself on the forehead for his loss of concentration, he grinned. "Sorry. Yes, this ring! Please marry me, Beryl. I love you. I truly love you." She held it between her fingers, gazing at its shine in the sunlight. "It's real," he insisted. "Not as fancy as what John gave Olympia, but then again, I'm just an accountant. But it is yours if you will have me."

Beryl blushed and touched her forehead to his. "I wasn't examining it for flaws," she laughed. "I want to put this on my finger. I truly do want to be your wife."

"But..."

Again, she couldn't help but smile at his anticipating face. "But if I put this on, we both know it can't last. In nine months, I must go back to where I came from."

"Who says?"

She changed to serious now. "I do. Nate, if I were to stay here it would change too much where I come from. Believe me, I spent hours and hours last night thinking about it. I worked out every possible scenario in my mind, and none of them allowed me to stay."

He looked out to the little stream, "You would miss your family too much."

She cupped the back of his neck with her hand and squeezed, then placed her chin on his shoulder, kissing it twice. "I would. But that isn't my reason. I wish all it would be is me missing my mother, and sister, and cousins. It's bigger than them. Bigger than me. I have saved lives back there. A lot of terminal people were spared because I used my gift to heal them. Not to mention I have fought a few supernatural battles which may not have turned out successfully had I never been there to assist. If I chose to stay here, a great many people will surely die."

He squinted his eyes as if doubting a little of what she was saying. "Sounds to me like there are a lot of you people back home. Witches, I mean. Are you sure they can't survive just fine on their own without you?"

"If I marry you, our life together will only be for a short time. It can be no other way, Nate."

He conceded her argument. With a begrudged smile and weary heart, he told Beryl, "If we only have a short time together, we will make sure the memories from it are powerful enough to sustain us both for the rest of our lives when we are parted."

He kissed her, slipping the ring onto her finger.

Olympia and Pastoria were completely caught by surprise as the happy couple burst into the house proclaiming, "Come to town with us! We are getting married today!"

Barely having time to grab her purse before being yanked out of the door by Beryl, Olympia asked, "What is the mad rush for?"

Beryl stopped on the bottom step of the porch to answer. With bright shiny eyes and the biggest smile, Beryl said, "There is an expiration date stamped on our life together. Might as well start it right now!"

"And you are sure?"

Smiling at her beautiful friend, Beryl clutched Olympia's hand and laughed, "Aren't you the person who told me to just be a woman."

Hugging Beryl tight, Olympia whispered, "Let's go get you married then."

CHAPTER THIRTY-FIVE

Tornado Watch

The unspoken but well imbedded knowledge of living in Alabama is that one must always be ready to take shelter during tornado season. Newspaper weather predictions and the local weatherman reports were as reliable as a sundial at midnight. No one in Daihmler needed to be told the sky looked menacing as the Fourth of July picnic began in Yerby Park. Behind the charcoal clouds lurked a greenish atmosphere which usually meant only one thing.

Disobeying the heavens warning, families continued with their yearly tradition of spreading blankets along the grassy lawns and setting up their wicker basket feasts while their children found companions to play with on the nearby slides and swings. It was the same for lovers too as couples out to enjoy a romantic summer holiday cozied together alongside others or chose more seclusion under the canopy of a tree.

Olympia and John stepped cautiously around the lounging townspeople until they found a free patch of lawn to lay their quilt. Olympia began unpacking the basket, delighting her fiancé with the smells of her roasted chicken, potato salad, and blueberry cobbler.

"I don't know if this sky will hold up long enough for the fireworks tonight." John observed. "But hopefully we will be rain free till at least the concert after lunch."

Olympia wasn't the least bit interested in the makeshift town band serenading the park. The concert was two hours away and she suspected the rain would call that particular brand of ear-torture off. Truth be told, she wasn't even interested in the picnic either. Eating lunch outside in a natural setting was something she did quite often at home. But there were John's wishes to consider now, and she had to get used to thinking of him. He was a leading figure in Daihmler, with many business connections to maintain. His career necessitated being social in the community—a community Olympia had shunned all her life. However, she had to admit that since their engagement, the citizens of Daihmler were treating her differently. Now when someone passed her on the sidewalk, they bid her a good morning and smiled. She was beginning to like that.

The sound of feet shuffling behind she and John, accompanied by the occasional "excuse me," told Olympia that Beryl and Nate had arrived. "We made it!" Beryl cried as Nate attached their blanket to Olympia's. "Sorry we are late. We stopped by Zelda's to pick her up, but she said a tornado is coming and she was not leaving her house."

"I think it'll be all right," John said, gazing up to the sky again. "Those clouds are moving fast; it may pass us by."

Beryl and Olympia exchanged a wink before Beryl remarked, "John, if Zelda says a tornado is coming...it is."

"I know I am new to all this...*witch stuff*..." John said lowering his voice accordingly. "But if you are so sure she's never wrong, why did we come here?" Beryl left the remark unanswered while she and Olympia shared a secret exchange, *because when it does, we will be needed here.*

The overcast sky slowly began darkening little by little while the foursome chatted idly together over their delicious lunch. Beryl raved to Olympia about how much she loved married life, suggesting she and John set their own date as soon as possible. No one made mention of Pastoria's absence. Still nursing her spite over John marrying her sister, Pastoria opted out of the town picnic, and no one felt like even talking about her.

In the distance, a couple of vans could be seen parking in the lot a few hundred yards away. The optimistic band had arrived, challenging the likelihood of rain. They began setting up on the stage located in the center of the park. Olympia was about to say something negative when droplets began falling from the sky. It was only a few specks of rain, not enough to cause the citizens of Daihmler to make a mad dash for cover. People around the park continued their holiday picnics and meandered around the lawns speaking to neighbors and friends. Several people stopped by John and Olympia's blanket to bid hello to the prominent lawyer and his fiancée. Likewise, several citizens of Daihmler who had heard the news paused to wish congratulations to Nate Caldwell and his lovely new wife. Olympia leaned over to Beryl and whispered, "All these women are thinking the same thing, *why are Blanchard girls suddenly stealing all the eligible men.*"

The drops from the sky were now beginning to fall more reliably, picking up frequency and volume. The people in Yerby Park knew the sky had given them all it was going to for the day. Everyone began packing up their belongings, hoping to make it to their cars before the sky fell.

The wind kicked up, displacing the carefully styled hairdos of woman who spent the morning trying to make themselves outshine their neighbor. Air swept beneath the unweighted sections of picnic blankets, flapping them around like flags affixed to the ground. The occasional empty blanket took flight through the air sailing overhead onlookers now growing nervous.

John advised his group to leave but it was a little too late for that as nearby trees began to bend to the wind's whim, whipping their branches dangerously amuck. Olympia and Beryl scanned the landscape for signs of danger, soon finding one. Across the park near the baseball field the invisible current showed itself as particles of dirt from the pitcher's mound rose into the outer edge of swirling wind. It only took seconds for everyone in the park to now see the powerful twister coming their way as grass, stray paper, aluminum cans, and a couple of airborne trash receptacles spun high into the air.

Someone screamed "Tornado!" instigating a panic which swept the park. John grabbed Olympia's arm, pulling her to him as Nate did the same to Beryl. Yerby Park was now under full attack from Mother Nature. Shrieking citizens ran in all directions, unsure where to even go. Olympia shook free of John and walked towards the direction of the funnel. John screamed her name into the wind but by now the roar of the storm was upon them. Beryl joined Olympia, both watching the trees around the park bending now to breaking point.

The storm's fury intensified as the swirling wall swept across Yerby Park absorbing everything in its path. A loud rumble caught their attention as a lone car tumbled across the playground, smashing through the jungle gym, sending rods of iron blasting across the park like missiles. Most of the deadly rods sailed high overhead through the trees, avoiding injury to anyone. However, one rocketed forward, shoulder level with the fleeing masses. It managed to miss the first two people scrambling out of its way but was headed directly towards a cluster of men, women, and children still searching for a place to take cover. As it whirled by Beryl, she reached out and caught it just as she had the pipe the night with the vampire. Once again, she was amazed because super strength and agility were not normally abilities she possessed. She was a healer only, until recently. There was no time to think about the newfound power for a second iron rod was shooting straight towards more people. Beryl ran forth across the lawn and, as if she were a star hitter for the Atlanta Braves, swung the bar she was holding and hit the one flying by. She released her grip on the rod in her hand and watched both deadly objects catapult safely away into the trees.

The moment the near miss was over, the brick-and-mortar walls of the baseball field concession stand ripped apart, disintegrating into projectile sandstone missiles tumbling across the park. Several bricks took flight, whizzing by. John ducked, barely missing an encounter with one. Beryl wasn't as agile. Trying to dodge a bulleting brick, she wasn't quick enough. The brick planted directly into the side of her head. Nate screamed, running towards her. Beryl was still standing, completely unphased. Looking to her shoulder Nate saw brick dust sprinkled along her blouse before the sweeping wind blew it away. Beryl looked at him in as much confusion as he felt. It would have been a mortal blow to anyone else, but she hadn't even felt the impact. With no time to contemplate, she jumped back into action as a massive tree branch took flight from parts unknown and winged directly towards a little family huddled tightly together on their blanket. Olympia was already on it, sweeping her hand towards the branch, stopping it in place while Beryl rushed to the family, dragging them out of its path before Olympia set it back into motion.

John and Nate stood locked in fascination at their women in action. The rumbling storm was growing louder as the fierce tornado widened broader and broader from everything it ate. A decimated path lay behind it where the once standing park buildings, baseball field, playground, trees, shrubs, and parking lot now swirled around inside it, fueling the monstrous storm. A man stumbled by with a long bolt, perhaps from the dismantled bleachers, stabbed into his shoulder. Blood spewed from the injury as he frantically spun in a circle unsure what to do. Beryl reached him, settling him onto the ground. As John and Nate rushed to her side, they witnessed firsthand her amazing power. She yanked the bolt from his body. His scream drowned out now from the howl of the tornado and sound of distant horns, the town's tornado warning signal. Beryl placed her hands upon the man's almost severed shoulder. He was frantic, struggling to crawl free. "Hold him," Beryl shouted to Nate and John. They did as she asked, keeping the man prostrate as she lowered her hands to his gushing shoulder. Closing her eyes, summoning the great power within her, Beryl was unaware how mesmerized the men were at what they were witnessing. A glowing golden light began to emit from her hands, a power she did not actually possess but was lent in times of need. The shoulder wound began to close as the veins, tendons, and sinew reattached to normal condition.

While Beryl applied her healing power, Olympia was busy, halting all debris headed towards them until Beryl could complete her miracle. John glanced up to the air a few times to see the random bicycles, tree limbs, picnic baskets, and a metal playground slide frozen mid-air. A rustling jangly sound swept by. Nate whipped his head around to identify the hazard only to see Olympia, yet again, thrust a hand forth to stop the deadly slinging chains torn from an unseen swing set, from decapitating them all.

The man, now fully restored to health, jumped to his feet, stared briefly in disbelief at his healer, mouthed a fast "thank you" and ran away to safety. Beryl grabbed John and Nate by the arms, directing them several yards behind Olympia whereupon Olympia released the hold she had on the deadly debris, allowing them to return to their tumble. Beryl was heading towards the parking lot, still clutching Nate's hand when he pulled her back, shouting over the roar, "It's too late to drive! We have got to take cover!"

"The baseball field!" John yelled, tugging Olympia behind him.

As the foursome ran towards what was left of the baseball field, the high-powered air made it feel like they were running through molasses. Here and there Olympia stopped flying shrapnel or a random broken treetop from smashing into them. The fence around the baseball diamond was already air born, torn from its posts giving them clear passage onto the field. John led them to the dugout where some people had already taken shelter. Everyone moved down the pit to allow them entry. As Beryl ducked under the header stepping down the brick stairs, she immediately noticed a little boy crying in his mother's lap. His leg was severely gashed longways down the thigh. His mother was trying her best to press the wound to stop the bleeding, but the cut was too long.

"What happened to him?" Beryl asked his mother, the physician within her taking hold as she lifted the boy from his mother's arms into her lap.

"He was cut by something flying by." Desperation filled the mother's voice. Beryl could see right away his femoral artery had been severed. He was pale and losing far too much blood.

"I can save him," Beryl announced. The boy's mother looked grateful while the others shivering in the dugout appeared skeptical. Beryl looked at Nate and John, then to Olympia for a nod of approval. "I'm sorry," she told Nate. "I can't let him die. I must do this with witnesses."

"Save him." Nate said.

Closing her eyes and pressing her healing hands against the panicked boy's thigh, she summoned the power again. His mother, father, and the few others huddled together in the dugout strained against the gust of wind and dirt assaulting their faces. The tornado howled overhead, but all attention was on Beryl's gentle hands. The golden glow emitting from her palms offered some light to the darkness of the pit. Most of what they could see was obscured by swirling sand and clay bouncing around the tiny, confined space, but all saw it happen. When Beryl removed her hands from the child's leg. His injury was gone. Only the stains of lost blood still soaked to his clothes hinted he had ever been hurt.

The boy's mother dropped her mouth in disbelief. "What are you?"

Beryl did not answer. She felt almost accused of something until the mother regained her senses. She pulled her son back into her arms, covering his forehead with her kisses. She looked at Beryl again, "You must be an angel! An actual angel. You saved my boy's life."

Olympia stepped closer, placing a gentle but firm hand onto the woman's shoulder. "You will keep our secret, won't you?"

The father, shaken from his crippling helplessness, reached forward, shaking Olympia's hand with both of his. "To our dying day, Miss Blanchard. To our dying day. Thank you so much."

The only remaining fencing left to the baseball field was the short piece lining the front of the dugout. John's hands gripped the wire as he stared out into the park. "I think its passing."

"Where does it look like its headed?" Nate shouted back.

"I can't tell. But not towards town."

Olympia joined him to look for herself. He was right, the town was in the other direction, as was Blanchard House. But that did not mean people were out of danger. She looked at Beryl, "If the car is still intact, I think we should follow the path. There might be others who are hurt."

Except for a few dings and a broken back window, John found the car unharmed. It cranked without hesitation. The urgency of the situation relieved John Windham, temporarily, of his desire to remain oblivious to Olympia's witchy world. He drove them along the path of destruction the storm left in its wake. Once or twice, he stopped alongside a few toppled cars to see if anyone needed help. Luckily, the cars were uninhabited.

Passing over a hill, Olympia spotted a house crushed midway from an uprooted pine tree. Next to it was another house with the entire right side torn away. Dangling timbers and a sagging roof told the story that this house was not going to stand much longer. Quickly Olympia rushed from the car to check the house. No one answered her call as she shouted into the creaking structure. She abandoned the empty shell to check the house crushed with the pine tree. From the front porch she could hear the panicked cries for help. She motioned for Beryl to join her.

They stooped under an arch of broken timbers where the front door was folding into itself. Two elderly women were wedged against the far wall. Furniture was in disarray and shattered frames of wall photographs scattered across the floor. Seeing the younger ladies coming into the house, one of the older women reached her free arm towards them, as she clutched her friend in her lap with the other. "Can you get us to the hospital?" she begged. "Her roof fell in on her. I think her lungs are collapsed."

Beryl stepped over the fallen debris towards the women. She did not need to utilize her internal scanning abilities to know this woman was correct in her assumption. The labored breathing and concave way her chest rose and fell said it all. One more time, Beryl administered her miraculous power and returned the old woman to health.

"Young lady? How?"

Beryl smiled. "It is not me. It's from above."

"You are Blanchards, aren't you?" the woman asked, tearfully. "We've always heard things."

Olympia placed her finger to her lips and requested, "We must ask you to protect our secret."

"Of course," the lady promised. "You just saved my life. I will not reveal you."

Beryl presented a thankful smile, adding, "Your lungs are fine now...and I also healed your heart. You were about two weeks from a coronary episode. You'll be fine now for several years."

Overhead a timber moaned, followed by a cracking sound. "Olympia! Freeze the ceiling!" Beryl shouted.

Olympia reacted with lightning speed, halting the collapse long enough to usher the elderly ladies outside. When Olympia released the house from her hold, the ceiling crashed to the floor, taking with it the outer front wall which fell onto Beryl. The older women shrieked in terror and Olympia nearly joined them until she saw Beryl's hands pushing the wall off her, flipping it back into the hollow house.

"Beryl, what are you made from? Steel?" Olympia gasped. "First that pole, then the brick, and now this."

Beryl stared back with confusion. "I have no idea what is going on, Olympia. I've never had the power of invulnerability. This is all new."

CHAPTER THIRTY-SIX

Mending Fences

The very last thing Pastoria Blanchard ever thought she would be doing was having dinner with John Windham. In truth, it was foisted upon her by her two scheming friends. It all began when Beryl phoned her one afternoon asking if she wanted to drive into Tuscaloosa to meet for dinner. According to Beryl, Nate was working late on some financial statements for a new client. Claiming she did not want to stay home alone for the evening, Beryl asked Pastoria to join her and Zelda at the new restaurant everyone was talking about, The Lamplighter. Zelda picked Pastoria up at Blanchard House, giving a mysterious wink to Olympia as they strolled out the door. Pastoria wondered why her sister was not being included in this girl's night out, but figured she probably had plans with John.

The Lamplighter restaurant recently opened next door to the Moon Winx Lodge Motel. The Moon Winx, though not very old, was already a Tuscaloosa landmark because of its sign. The bright red and yellow neon crescent moon with a flashing eye that winked on every other flash. The motel even had a pool, which was not customary with other Tuscaloosa motels, making Moon Winx the popular place to stay for passersby or those in town for Alabama football games.

The Lamplighter sat adjacent to the lodge, tucked back a bit under the trees. Its long porch and low roofline presented the appearance of a small mountain lodge–ironic considering the Moon Winx which had *Lodge* in its name looked nothing like one at all. Pastoria was excited to dine at the hip new bistro so many people were talking about. It was only when she and Zelda walked in and she saw John Windham seated with Beryl at the table, that Pastoria knew she'd been tricked.

"Oh no," she said backing away.

Without any patience for Pastoria's animosity, Zelda gave her several sharp pushes forward to the table, forcing her to sit down. "Me and Beryl's leaving and unless you feel like walkin' back to Daihmler I suggest you sit here and eat with him. Ya'll got some stuff to straighten out."

Pastoria shot Beryl a furious look. Beryl rose from the table, giving Pastoria a disapproving look and a mandate. "You must find a way to be all right with this marriage. John loves Olympia, and I know you do as well. Surely two people who love the same person as much as you both do can find common ground."

"I hate this man."

"No," Beryl corrected. "You have unresolved anger over a job he did. Yes, it affected you in a roundabout way, but is that a good enough reason to estrange yourself from a sister who has been your best friend all your life? Just talk to him, Pastoria. John will drive you home after dinner."

"I won't forget this, Beryl. You either Zelda."

Zelda gave one of her signature guffaws and said, "Girl if this is the worst thing happening in your life then you got it pretty golden."

With that, Beryl and Zelda linked arms, turned to leave, and did not look back. As they left, Pastoria could faintly hear Zelda say, "Now let's me and you go get some Kentucky Fried Chicken!"

John sat patiently across the table, waiting for Pastoria to make eye contact. After a few uncomfortable seconds, she gave into the situation and exclaimed, "Well? Do you want to say something to me?"

"As a matter of fact, I do," John answered, very lawyerly. "I have examined the evidence and frankly I have arrived at a conclusion. Though I was the lawyer representing the plaintiff in the case against your former boyfriend's father, I do not believe you are as enraged over my involvement as you pretend to be."

"Oh, you don't, do you?" Pastoria snorted. "You know John Windham, you aren't as smart as you think yourself to be."

"Perhaps," he grinned. "But that case was long ago. You and I both know your feelings for that boy, whatever his name was, are not strong enough to carry this much hostility for this long."

"Is that so?" Pastoria smirked. "It must be wonderful to be so sure of yourself."

"It is, actually," John answered. His unblinking eyes focused upon her, challenging her to look at him. Pastoria steered her gaze in every direction but his. John had no experience with exasperating sisters, but he did have a great deal of experience with hostile witnesses. He remained undaunted, continuing to stare at her until the silence between them swelled to such an uncomfortably long level she was forced to break it. Finally giving in and meeting his stare, her body language made it clear she was acquiescing. "Pastoria, you are afraid by my marrying your sister, life as you know it will be upended. I want to assure you that is not going to be the case."

He'd said nothing urging her to reply, opting to see what else he might say. "All of your lives, you and Olympia only had one another," he went on. "She has told me what school was like for you both. The two of you and Zelda were all you had, besides maybe Nate Caldwell. Now, I have come along, and it appears I am about to steal Olympia away from you. You have lost your father, and it isn't inconceivable for you to fear you may lose the only other family member you've ever felt close to."

"I have Beryl and Zelda, traitors though they may be."

John suppressed a grin. Embittered or not, she was funny. He kind of liked her sour honesty. "No one compares to your sister. I promise you, Pastoria, I respect that relationship. I will never try to come between it. When I marry your sister, we will live at Blanchard House with you. The three of us will be a family, not just Olympia and myself. When she becomes my wife, you become my sister. Family means as much to me as it does to you. I also have been alone. When I am your brother, I will look out for you just as I will her. You are not going be alone. You will never be alone while I am alive."

"My brother, huh?" she said, possibly beginning to soften. "Brothers and sisters often don't get along."

"Doesn't matter if they do," John replied. "They are still brother and sister. Till the end. I will be your brother. Whatever you need, I'll do my best for you. If anyone ever hurts you, they will answer to me. In a way, I am marrying all of you. Olympia, you, Zelda, even Beryl and Nate. I am becoming a Blanchard—not in name, but in sentiment. I have no family of my own. I am asking you to allow me entry to yours."

Picking up the menu from the table, Pastoria began to look it over. "I hear they have good steaks here...if my brother is buying." Though she said it sarcastically, John Windham knew he'd said just enough of the right thing to win a chance from her. And a chance was all he really needed.

CHAPTER THIRTY-SEVEN

Closer to God

There were times when it proved more difficult for Beryl to draw distinctions between her own time and this moment in history, she found herself living in. It seemed to Beryl the longer she was away from her true timeline, the less real that place felt. Of course, habits can be hard to break. She sometimes still reached into her pocket for a phantom cell phone that wasn't there. And once or twice she found herself spreading her thumb and forefinger across the page of a magazine as if trying to enlarge the picture. She also yearned to see an action movie with special effects that would keep her on the edge of her seat. But for the most part she had acclimated to the year she was living in. For all the technology it lacked, it also had its share of perks. The slower pace gave her time to appreciate things in newer ways—sunrises and sunsets, chief among these. Sometimes now when she looked up at a blue and pink horizon she felt as if she were standing inside of a painting. Somehow the sky had become nature's canvas, presenting an ever-changing work of art whenever she glanced up. Automobiles were certainly far more impressive. The style and excess of design made her feel like a movie star when she drove along country roads. Back home almost all sedans looked the same. Differentiating between models could be hard to do when most on the market were the same shape and same boring colors. She also found herself with more time on her hands than most of her peers, especially at night. While most of the people she knew consumed their evenings with the golden age of television, Beryl had seen practically every show on the air a dozen times in modern day syndication. Without any big urge to join the TV craze, she had her nights free to enjoy the undiluted attention of her husband.

Music was the one area she felt torn. Admittedly, there was nothing like unsheathing a vinyl record, holding it in her hand, then placing it on a turntable to lower a needle into the groove to start the music. The ceremony of it was far more satisfying than flipping through a playlist on her phone and pressing a song. Then again, music in this age was starkly different than what she preferred. A person could only hear Doria Day or Frank Sinatra so much before they lamented the lost luxury of summoning up Sia, Beyonce, or Lady Gaga with the touch of a finger. Nate often could overhear his wife singing an unrecognizable tune he liked, only to be told it wouldn't be written for 50 years. And though she would never do it because it would be wrong to steal someone else's future literary achievements, occasionally Beryl imagined writing a bestseller or even a sitcom script based on a hit from her own time. It was all playful fantasy, but who hasn't thought of going back in time and recording all the number one hits a few years before they came out? All in all, Beryl liked this place and this time in history.

She did miss the prestige of being Dr. Beryl Blanchard, however she forced herself to admit she enjoyed being a housewife. The very admission made her cringe as if she was personally setting women back 100 years. Gloria Steinem, if Beryl ever encountered her, would slap her face. Still, Beryl found something fulfilling in just being Nate's wife for a little while. Maybe it was because she knew one day she'd be going back home. She would return to her patients. She would once again, live as a modern successful woman with rights and a voice. But for now, she was enjoying all the things from this age gone by which the women before her fought so hard to break free from. Little things like making her husband breakfast. Ironing his shirts with plenty of starch in the collar. She even enjoyed vacuuming with a good old fashioned cannister and hose. It was fun because it was temporary.

Even her little light blue house with the bright white shutters and literal white picket fence gave her pleasure. She felt as if she were a little girl living in her very own life size doll house. Her days were filled with some housework, but also a good deal of activities. Being Nate Caldwell's wife came with a bevy of luncheon invitations and organizations run by other housewives looking to fill their time. Beryl joined as many as she could, but always she kept lunchtime free to spend at Blanchard House with her sisters.

Sisters. She'd been here so long she sometimes forgot they were not her sisters. Yet their relationships had become so close—their lives so intertwined—that Olympia, Pastoria, and Zelda felt like her sisters. She loved them just as much as she had loved Salem, Fable, and Yasmine back in the old life. It was not unlike Dorothy from The Wizard of Oz movie. When Dorothy was in Oz, all her farm friends were there, just in different roles. Beryl felt similarly. Like she had not lost relationships, they just now wore new faces. And here she had Nate. Nate Caldwell, her husband. *Husband.* She loved him so much. He meant everything to her. And inside her womb their baby was growing. It was always this thought which brought reality crashing back into her daydream. Every time she thought of the baby her heart sank. Beryl loved this baby growing inside her. Yet she knew she would not be there as it grew up. It was still hard to reconcile her maternal feelings for her child with the much older man she knew and cared for back home. Howard Caldwell...was her son. How would she react when she returned home and saw him for the first time? Would she feel that same mother's love within her? Would she be so overcome by the sight of him that she would sweep him up in her arms? Would doing so throw his back out? How often had she healed that thing in the past? Not just his chronic back, but his sinus infections, his tooth ache, and the cholesterol he refused to change his diet for. Never once had she ever sensed when she healed him that he was her son. *When I see Howard again, will I ever feel what I feel right now for this baby?* It was too much to think about, so most of the time she chose not to.

She switched her mind away from the baby and all the difficult thoughts which came with it. Instead, her mind focused back to the tornado. That brick. Then that wall. Why were her powers changing? Was it a byproduct of being here in this time? Would she keep these powers once she went back home? She then remembered something. She had these powers even before she came here. It was nearly two years ago; on the night she and her family stopped the evil witch Atheidrelle. During the battle, which ultimately left two people dead, including Beryl's elderly version of Olympia, the vile Atheidrelle sent a heavy iron chandelier at high speed towards Beryl...and Beryl caught it in one hand. The feat shocked everyone at the time. Beryl only possessed the power to heal. Never had she had super strength. And never would a brick flying at her head not cause severe damage.

What is happening to me? For a moment her mind went back to the baby. It was not uncommon for a mother witch to manifest the powers her baby would one day have while in utero. However, Beryl had not been pregnant when that chandelier was tossed at her. Whatever was happening couldn't be due to her pregnancy. Her thoughts were interrupted before she could arrive at any plausible explanation when a pounding sound came at the door. It was Zelda. In her normal bombastic way, Zelda barged inside already halfway through whatever sentence she'd begun screeching at the door.

"Zelda, I have no idea what you just said." Beryl laughed. "You do realize nobody hears you when you start your conversation before you even get to us."

Zelda plopped down on the couch and gathered herself, taking a deep breath. "Sorry. Just caught up in the drama. What I was shoutin' out there is I just had a terrible reading I did for a woman. I saw her life in shambles. Deep depression. She's gonna start drinking. Gonna ruin her marriage and mess the rest of her kids up for life, if you don't do somethin.'"

Beryl joined her on the couch, "What can I do about that?"

"It's her youngest, see?" Zelda began. "She's got this little girl that's got meningitis. It's real bad Beryl. And when she loses that kid, its gone ruin her whole family forever. But you can stop all that. If you heal that youngen, then that sweet lady won't have her life ruined."

Beryl said nothing in reply. She simply hopped up from the couch, grabbed her purse from the kitchen and said, "Let's go."

The ease with which Beryl and Zelda were able to sneak inside the children's ward at Druid City Hospital was astonishing. In the future when Beryl worked at Daihmler Hospital, one needed clear authorization to get anywhere near the nurse's station, much less into a child's room. Things were far more lax in the past. It took zero effort for Beryl to find the child of Zelda's client. It was written plainly in chalk on a large board behind the nurse's desk. What really amazed Beryl was the uncomfortable style of dress required of the nursing staff. They all looked like period actors in an old hospital drama. Clean, crisp, white uniforms adorned by a starched cap with pointy ends. And there wasn't a male nurse anywhere to be seen—nor a female doctor. The men passing by, all physicians, were similarly uniformed in slacks, white shirts, neckties, and long white overcoats. Dr. Beryl Blanchard, and the rest of modern medical staff, always dressed in colorful scrubs. Seeing these professionally attired people now, she felt slightly embarrassed to have spent her entire career in the equivalent of pajamas.

Beryl and Zelda made their way to the little girl's room. The child was alone when they crept in, closing the door behind them. Beryl approached the bed carefully to not wake her. Gently placing her hands upon the resting child's body, she closed her eyes, allowing the radiant power to surge beneath her fingers. Yet it was different this time.

Something began to happen she'd not experienced before. She could sense another child nearby, perhaps the neighboring room. It was a boy, and he was very sick as well. *I think I can heal them both. And at the same time.* And she found she could. As the power emanated from her hands, she saw a bright glowing strand leave one of her fingers, stretching out and through the wall. She could feel their bodies growing stronger, pushing out their illnesses. And then, she felt it again, the suspicion she could reach even further with her power. It was as if a voice within her was telling her what to do. Before she even realized what she was doing, Beryl was vibrating with force, as glowing tendrils rushed from her hands spreading out across the entire corridor of the Children's Ward.

Zelda jumped back in surprise. "What are you doing?"

"I think I am healing all of them," Beryl whispered with amazement. "I am healing every child on this hall."

Once the last drop of healing power left her hands, Beryl was exhausted. Zelda placed an arm around her to steady Beryl. As they departed the Children's Ward, they could faintly hear the voices of children, once too weak or sickly to speak, now calling out loudly for their mothers. The vigor of childhood and health of body fully restored.

Getting on the elevator, Zelda propped her friend against the wall and observed her carefully. "Beryl, girl you're changing. Your whole aura is way brighter than it used to be."

Beryl was almost afraid to ask. "Zelda, you've always been straight with me. Here and back where I come from. Tell me...what is happening to me?"

Zelda stared at her for a while, not exactly understanding what she was seeing or feeling. Finally, she said, "Beryl. You got God in you."

"Well...thanks," Beryl snickered. "I try to be a good person."

"Naw, girl. I mean seriously. You got God inside you. Like you are glowing with somethin' Divine. I ain't never seen nothing like this."

CHAPTER THIRTY-EIGHT

The Perfect Dress

If there was anything in life more frustrating than helping Olympia Blanchard choose a wedding dress, her companions did not know what it could possibly be. Pastoria was now laying on the soft pink sofa of the only bridal shop in Daihmler reading the latest edition of Look magazine as her sister was in the dressing room trying on the eighth gown. Although an hour's drive north to Birmingham would probably offer a greater selection of shops, Bridal Elegance was owned by Marla Phillips who had been very welcoming to Olympia when she joined John's church.

Beryl kicked at the sofa, pulling Pastoria back to attention. "Would you sit up and at least act interested? It is your sister's wedding dress."

"I have given my opinion on the last seven," Pastoria sighed. "Every one of them was fine except the third one. I'm over this already. Its way past lunchtime."

Zelda yanked the side of Pastoria's hair. "Get on board with this."

"I am on board!" Pastoria shouted. "Hell, I had dinner with John Windham for Pete's sake! I'm fine."

Olympia emerged from the dressing room wearing a knee-high white lace gown with a tiny, belted waistline and off the shoulder sleeve. Stepping up onto a riser platform surrounded by mirrors on three sides, she surveyed the dress. With the mirrors now acting as criticizing eyes, she reconsidered the choice. Though she looked great in it she couldn't be sure if it were she or the dress making it so. After all she looked great in practically everything, but this felt disconnected. "I don't think this is me."

"Oh, it isn't you," Beryl said. Seeing the look of disappointment on Olympia's face, Beryl considered something she had not thought about until just now. "Would you like me to show you the dress you married my grandfather in? I've seen the pictures before."

Olympia exchanged surprising looks with Pastoria then Zelda. She raised her eyebrow in ponderance. "Well, it would save time." Pastoria quipped.

"But would Lympy be picking it or Beryl?"

"Well," Olympia said mulling the thought over. "I mean, obviously I would have picked it myself before. If she has seen a photograph of it. I must have picked it out and been happy with it."

Zelda plopped down on the riser platform, hands on her knees. "Or is Time a cycle and it was always really Beryl who picked it because she was always here when you decided?"

Olympia's eyes widened as the confusing idea raced into her mind. She turned to Beryl and asked, "How does it all work anyway? I have never really given it much thought." She sat down beside Pastoria who seemed equally bewildered. "Were you always here at this time and you just didn't know it?"

"Were you in the wedding pictures?" Pastoria asked.

"Not that I am aware of," Beryl said.

"This hurts my head." Zelda remarked. "Just show her what dress she wears so we can get outta here."

Beryl walked to the long rack of white and off-white dresses where she began sliding hangers aside eliminating dresses she did not recognize. "None of the ones you've tried on were right as far I recall." She perused the entire rack and found nothing resembling Olympia's dress she remembered seeing in the old photo albums. "It is not here. I don't think."

"Could it be at another store?" Olympia asked. "There are some bridal boutiques in Tuscaloosa. Maybe I didn't buy it in Daihmler."

"Maybe she don't remember it that well," Zelda suggested. "I doubt you ever thought you'd have to pick it out of a line up whenever you happened to look at those old pictures."

Beryl couldn't be sure. It was then Marla Phillips excitedly rushed into the showroom from the back. "Ladies, these three dresses just arrived off the truck. Olympia! I think this one would be darling on you! The moment I opened the box it made me think of you."

And there it was. The moment Marla laid the gown across the sofa, Olympia's eyes lit up and Beryl began nodding in satisfaction. "This is it, Olympia! This is what you wear when you marry Grandfather Windham!"

Marla presented a confused look, to which Zelda simply replied, "Nickname."

Olympia's fingers delicately touched the sleek, contoured ivory silk dress. She lifted it against her. As it caught the light, the fabric seemed to have movement of its own, a dance of luminosity as she turned with it pressed against her. It was unlike any of the other dresses she'd seen before. This was a creation from an era gone by, conjuring a timeless glamour from the 1940's. Jean Harlow might have worn this dress to some Hollywood gala back in the day.

The faintest smile tugged at the corners of Olympia's lips as she realized with all certainty, this was the one. "This is it! Without a doubt." Facing her friends, Olympia was beaming. I absolutely adore this dress!"

"Sold!" Pastoria called out to the clerk, happy her sister found it and even happier they could go have lunch now. "We will take it."

CHAPTER THIRTY-NINE

Roses Are Forever

A growing line of rose bushes still in their plastic containers were beginning to stack up along the side of Blanchard House. With every visit to see Olympia, Lauralee Caswell brought another plant in a different shade. There were now nine bushes sitting up against the side of the porch outside the house. Olympia made sure to keep them well watered although she had not yet planted them.

She was reclining lazily in the porch swing against the backing of comfy pillows when Lauralee approached with number ten. Olympia laughed and told her friend, "Soon I will have an even dozen."

Lauralee's delicate face attempted a smile, but it didn't come off well. Empathically knowing something was wrong with her friend, Olympia righted herself in the swing, patting the cushion beside her. "Sit with me." Her friend walked slowly across the porch, taking a seat beside her. Olympia looked into Lauralee's evasive eyes and asked, "What is wrong?"

Lauralee frowned, "My illness is worse. My doctor says I soon will be unable to get around much."

Olympia was shocked. "Lauralee, no!" Olympia had always known Lauralee Caswell to be a dandelion in the wind. It would not require much effort to strip her cottony dander bare. Yet she always possessed a sweetness about her distracting from her frailty.

Lauralee folded her fingers together in her lap, bending them back and forth as if she were a child about to recite the poem about *the church, the steeple, and inside there are the people.* "I have always known my time was limited, Olympia. It is okay. I have made good friends like you. It has been a good life."

Suddenly sitting forward, Olympia exclaimed, "It can be a longer life, Lauralee! And I know someone who can help you. Someone who can fix you."

"A witch, such as you are?" Lauralee asked timidly. Olympia never had any inclination Lauralee knew about her. The surprise must have read on her face, causing Lauralee to giggle. "Olympia it is not a very well-kept secret. Many people saw you stop that tornado."

Blushing from her friend's overestimation of her abilities, Olympia clarified, "I didn't exactly stop the tornado."

"Still."

"Okay," Olympia admitted. "Yes, I am a witch. And so is my family. This is wonderful for you, Lauralee. My cousin Beryl can heal you. She has the power."

Lauralee smiled and shook her head. "I'm fine with death, Olympia. Doesn't seem right to have someone heal me when so many other people are sick too. Besides, I miss my Momma and Daddy. I'm looking forward to seeing them again when I get to Heaven."

"You will see them again," Olympia reassured. "Just do it a little later in life. Live a while longer."

Lauralee thanked her for the offer but still declined. "I'm pretty happy to see Heaven now. Don't feel like waiting for it. I want to know if Jesus really does have long hair. Is He white like it shows in The Bible? I find that confusing. I don't see how He could have been white. But maybe in Heaven we are all the same color. Maybe it is possibly a color we've never seen before. A special Holy color." The innocence behind her eyes caused tears to swell in Olympia's. She had never known a purer soul or more contented heart.

The two friends lapsed into a comfortable silence for a while. Olympia's mind was a canvas of unspoken thoughts. There was so much more she could say yet nothing else really needing to be said. Her gaze drifted, capturing a small sparrow winging by. This chance sighting led her attention to an inconspicuous hummingbird she otherwise would not have noticed fluttering up and down one of the rose bushes. A freshly opened bloom offered a rare chance for nectar to the iridescent bird who had mistakenly come to a yard with few flowers. She thought of Lauralee while she watched the tiny bird perform its aerial ballet. Both were small and vulnerable. Both were creatures the hurried world was too busy to notice. But both were perfect in their own way. Each had their own unique authenticity which most people looked past instead of finding the time to appreciate them.

Suddenly Olympia jumped to her feet with an idea. Leaning over the porch railing she looked down at the treasure of roses still housed in little plastic pots. She whirled around to her friend, exclaiming, "Okay Lauralee, I think it's high time you and I made a rose garden!"

"Really?" her delicate friend squealed with delight, rushing to the rail to join her. "You really want me to help you?"

Olympia wrapped her arm around Lauralee's shoulders, "I would not have anyone else assist me but you. And every time I sit out here and see my roses, I will think of my dear sweet friend who gave them to me and helped me plant them."

Lauralee's face radiated with joy she could not contain. It made Olympia feel she'd given her the gift rather than it being the other way around. The women explored the grounds around the house until they found the perfect location on the right-hand side of the front yard. Olympia noted their choice, "I think this will get the right amount of sunlight, and the oak trees will help keep the petals from scorching during summer."

"What about the back yard?" Lauralee suggested. "The house blocks some of the light and wouldn't they look great up against the side of the house back there? The white wood will make the blooms stand out."

"Yes," Olympia admitted, "But John wants to build a new kitchen back there before he moves in. I wouldn't want to settle these into the soil only to traumatize them with uprooting. I think the side yard is lovely. Your roses will always be the first thing people see when they drive up."

Gathering shovels from the back shed, Olympia and Lauralee began tilling the soil and digging holes deep enough for the root balls. It meant so much to Lauralee to play a part in the garden's creation. She'd given these offerings in friendship over time, and it comforted her to know she would be remembered long after she was gone whenever Olympia looked out at it.

"Let's spread them out far enough so that I can lay a gravel path between them." Olympia proposed. "I'll collect large rocks from the stream for a border and spread pea gravel for the paths."

"Like an English garden," Lauralee sighed dreamily.

Olympia patted her hand and added, "It will be my pride and joy, Lauralee."

The next couple of hours passed unnoticed as they immersed themselves in their labor of love. With every turn of the soil and every tender placement of a bush Olympia felt as if they were etching her feelings for Lauralee into the earth. She allowed Lauralee to make the decisions on where each color rose should sit. Most of the choices were correct, complimenting the neighboring plant. When the choice did not seem wise, Olympia said nothing to dissuade it because the outcome was the intended purpose—to always remind her of Lauralee.

After Lauralee left for home, Olympia went to the telephone to call her fiancé at his office. "I want to speed up the wedding, John. My dear friend Lauralee is growing ill. I am afraid she might be dying, John. I cannot get married without her being there. The wedding will be in two weeks."

CHAPTER FORTY

Here Comes the Bride

It was important to John for the marriage to take place at Daihmler Methodist church. It was Olympia's nature to shirk the idea, understanding his adamancy came less from religious devotion and more from social posturing for business purposes; but she acquiesced regardless. John's career was important, and he was marrying a woman of whispered mystery. If a church wedding was all he required to even the rumors out, who was she to refuse. This was rural Alabama after all. Any decent well-bred couple would be married in a house of worship and not the back yard of a home rumored to house witches. Pastoria balked, of course, chastising her sister for conforming to the social norms of "regulars". However, Beryl took the sting out of Pastoria's tail by reminding them both, "Witches have souls too."

Holding the wedding at the church did save quite a bit of time and money for the Blanchards. Except for the wedding dress, there was no real expense. John, being a church member, could have Reverend Talbot officiate for free. Some of the more prominent ladies of the church offered to prepare food for the reception. And Zelda and Beryl scoured the Blanchard property gathering every blooming wildflower they could find, creating a rather large and lovely flower arrangement for the alter. Of course, bringing it inside turned into a more memorable experience than anyone could have imagined.

With an hour left before the wedding was to begin, Nate and Beryl walked the urn carefully from the car up the church steps to the vestry. Zelda went ahead of them, propping one of the double doors open with a doorstop while she held the other out for them to pass. The Caldwells did a masterful job getting up the steps without disarranging the flowers or spilling a drop of water from the urn. Moving into the church, Nate went backwards, with Zelda guiding him verbally, "Step up. Move left. Watch your elbow on the door." Then as Beryl's feet crossed the threshold of the church, her husband's face, as well as the flowers in front of it, illuminated. Not sure of what she was seeing at first, Beryl assumed perhaps a cloud lifted overhead sending a bright sunbeam down like a spotlight. Nate's mouth hung open and he was squinting his eyes from the glare, but as they moved further inside the light faded—but his shocked expression did not. He was staring at Beryl in utter disbelief.

"What?" she asked him.

Zelda, now between them steadying the urn as Nate's hands began to quiver, cried, "Beryl! Girl you just went all technicolor!"

"Huh?" Beryl replied, not understanding the remark at all.

"Honey," Nate stammered. "Your entire body just glowed."

Continuing to move down the aisle towards the front of the church, Beryl asked for more elaboration. "What do you mean, I glowed?"

"Glowed!" he repeated. "You lit up like a flashlight or a lighthouse beacon or something."

Beryl grinned at the tricksters. "You two are very funny. That was only sunlight from outside. The glow of an expecting mother is figurative, not literal."

They eased the urn atop the white column stand on the pulpit before Nate took hold of his wife's hands and gripped them. "We aren't kidding, Honey. You seriously lit up the moment we crossed the church threshold."

The press for time kept the trio from further discussing the matter which Beryl was not even certain really happened. She and Zelda departed for the bride's room while Nate went on to assist the Groom. Pastoria was with Olympia when Beryl and Zelda entered the little Sunday School classroom being used for the bride to get ready. She was already in her dress, Pastoria smoothing out any remaining lines in the silk around her waist. Beryl hung in the doorway, caught completely off guard by the breathtaking vision of Olympia in her gown. *This is my grandmother,* she reminded herself. She felt she needed to remind herself, to draw the clarification because after all this time spent with her these last months, Olympia had become a sister to her. The town naturally assumed the story fed to them, that they were cousins, but Olympia was in fact her grandmother and John was her grandfather and this was their wedding day. *I am going to watch my grandparents get married.*

No one expected much of a showing on the bride's side of the church when the wedding commenced. The groom's side would of course be filled with colleagues, clients, and various citizens of Daihmler who knew and respected the esteemed man.

Olympia and her sisters knew there would be nothing but empty pews behind them during the ceremony. This fact played a large factor in the way Olympia styled her hair. She kept it down, braided to the side as to sweep across the left shoulder, leaving the right one bare where her creamy smooth skin could catch the light. If the only guests were going to be to the left of her, she made sure that side looked its best. As Pastoria, Zelda, and Beryl guided the bride out the back door and around to the front of the church to make her entrance, the four of them were ready to keep their heads turned to the left during the procession. It would be the only place anyone would be sitting. They were in for a bit of a shock when the church doors opened, and they began their stroll to the organ music down front.

Beryl and Zelda went first, side by side, dressed in their finest. Beryl wore a pale blue skirt with matching jacket over a white blouse. The skirt was cutting into her a bit, causing her to realize after today she would have to buy some maternity wear. Her baby bump was becoming prominent. Zelda nearly blinded the congregation in an electric green rayon dress with wide cuffed sleeves at the shoulder, and a hot pink stripe zig zagging up the center. Around her neck she wore the scarf Olympia's father had given her as a child–her little way of bringing his spirit to the occasion. As they began their procession down the aisle, Beryl's eyes were focused forward at John standing at the altar. Her grandfather looked very handsome in his blue suit. Nate stood beside him as Best Man, equally as dapper in gray. She felt a jab in the ribs as Zelda elbowed her, turning her attention to the not-empty bride's side of the church. In comparison to the groom's side, it was still rather sparse, but there were people there. Unexpected people who had come to honor Olympia Blanchard on her wedding day.

Following behind Beryl and Zelda, Pastoria Blanchard came, dressed in pale yellow chiffon, escorting her sister down the aisle. The congregation marveled at the Blanchard sisters. Unorthodox as it was for a bride to be presented down the aisle by another woman, no one would argue there could be a better choice. They had spent their lives together, much of it alone. The sight of Olympia left more than one man breathless and a fair share of women envious. Her gown shimmered under the church lights and her shoulder swept braid glistened like white ice.

Taking her first steps down the aisle, Olympia paused the same as Beryl and Zelda had when she saw her side of the church housing guests. It was something she never considered. After all, except for Nate and Lauralee, she had no friends. And yet she did. Friends she never realized cared enough to be there for her wedding day. Bristow and Brimford Uding sent her encouraging winks as she entered the chapel. Beside them, beaming at the lovely bride, sat Bedwyr and Beryl Kraven. Olympia smiled proudly at these friends who she never dreamed would take time from their busy lives to be there on her special day. She nodded a heartfelt thanks to them all.

A little further down the aisle, two elderly women sat dressed in their Sunday finest. Pastoria asked Olympia who they were through mindspeak, but Olympia didn't answer. She simply gave them a joyous, albeit demure, wave. The women she and Beryl saved from the house on July 4th, waved back happily. In the next row sat the mother and father of the little boy who had been injured in the baseball dugout. The boy was with them, waving excitedly towards her. Olympia felt her eyes tear up as she continued her march. Then on the second row of the church, all dressed in their best, were Julia and Easty Colburn blowing kisses to the bride and her sister. On the final pew, right up front, was Lauralee. Her happy smile filled Olympia with joy. Beside Lauralee sat Martin Caswell. He smiled affably, making sure his presence was not uncomfortable for the bride.

Pastoria led Olympia to the altar, but not before the bride stopped to give Lauralee a kiss on the cheek. She looked pale and drawn. The kiss brightened her smile. Martin mouthed a sincere congratulations to which she mouthed a thank you. Then with a nudge from Pastoria, Olympia stepped forward to John and Reverend Talbot.

The reverend began the ceremony, welcoming guests to celebrate the love and union of the happy couple. Following his introduction, he asked who consented to give the bride away in matrimony. Pastoria locked eyes with John, both sharing a fleeting moment of uncertainty as to what she might say. The moment, more playful than deliberate, broke as they exchanged genuine smiles. With a lighthearted voice, Pastoria Blanchard announced, "I give this bride away in matrimony." She winked at John, then gave her sister a loving hug before taking her place beside Beryl and Zelda.

Reverend Talbot was unaccustomed to officiating such an unorthodox marriage and it was clear he had not been forewarned when preparing his speech. Beginning the reciting of the vows, he faced Olympia and said, "Do you Olympia Blanchard, vow to love, to honor, to obey, and to cherish John Windham all the days of your life?"

With her signature raised brow and a playful smirk, she replied, "I promise to love, cherish, and honor John all the days of my life. However, I obey no man." John lowered his chin, suppressing his amusement or embarrassment or both. The reaction of the congregation was mixed. Some whispered to one another, feigning shock or insult by Olympia's daring. While others, primarily women, drowned the whispers out with clapping and shouts of "Amen" to the alter. Olympia, always ready to take the center of attention, turned toward her audience and gave a little bow to her admirers. Reverend Talbot, a little more flustered than he'd ever been while officiating a marriage, turned to give John his vows. Olympia lightened the moment by tugging at the good reverend's sleeve, requesting, "Can you leave the obey part in for his vows though please?"

Uproarious laughter came over the church as everyone, even those previously affronted, enjoyed her little remark. John recited his vows, leaving out the obey portion as well. With smiles covering everyone's faces, the minister announced, "By the power in me ordained by God the Almighty, I pronounce you both husband and wife. You may now kiss your bride, John."

Everyone was transfixed on the couple as they shared their first married kiss, so no one was looking at anyone else. Yet as Reverend Talbot had uttered the words *God the Almighty*, Beryl began to glow again. Thanks to the quick wits of Pastoria and Zelda, who instantly stepped in front of her, shielding her from view, no one in the audience saw. However, Nate did. His second time seeing the mysterious light. He couldn't help but notice it happened with the mention of God. Reverend Talbot, amid the hoots and howls of the onlookers viewing the marital kiss, did his best to regain the congregations attention, proclaiming, "I now present to you Mr. and Mrs. John Windham."

The applause was abruptly cut short when Olympia waved her hands up in the air, calling for quiet to make a correction. "Thank you all very much," she smiled towards the church. "But Reverend Talbot misspoke. I am Mrs. Olympia Blanchard, and this is my husband, John Windham."

CHAPTER FORTY-ONE

Honeymoon in Niagara

A honeymoon in Niagara Falls was an Americana rite of passage for the newly married of the time. It was something Olympia always wanted to see for herself, never having traveled any further north than Tennessee. Her first impression of Buffalo, New York was not very complimentary, however after checking into the hotel and walking to the National Park lining the Niagara Gorge, the moment her eyes saw the Falls she was mesmerized. Though actually comprised of three separate falls the one which she, and most people ordained to be Niagara Falls proper, was really named Horseshoe Falls. It straddled the border between New York and Ontario. Bridal Veil Falls and American Falls were very impressive on their own, but nothing captured her breath quite like Horseshoe. The enormity of it was difficult to register. She'd seen waterfalls before—well, maybe one small one–but this was wondrous. And the curvature of the surrounding landscape that formed the horseshoe made the visual all the more mesmerizing. John stood back against a row of viewing benches, armed folded, enjoying his new bride's excitement as she peered over the rail at the crushing power of the falls. A mist of white haze rising from below danced in the air behind her as sunlight caused it and she to sparkle.

"It is truly magnificent isn't, my darling?" he smiled, dodging equally captivated tourists to join her at the rail.

"I have never seen anything like it, John." Olympia squeezed his arm and asked, "Have people really rolled over these rapids in a barrel?"

He laughed, "That's what they say."

A man happened by in a green jumpsuit, a park employee with an ID badge clipped to his chest pocket. In his hand he carried a sack and a long metal pole with a tiny point on the end. Grabbing a stray piece of paper from the point and placing in the sack it became clear he was part of the park maintenance crew. "People have gone over it, ma'am," he interjected to Olympia after overhearing. "Some make it out, most don't. You ever heard about the *Miracle at Niagara*?"

The newlyweds told him they had not. He continued to regale them with the tale. "Few years ago, in 1960 a man was going along the river in a boat. Had two kids with him, his niece and nephew. He didn't mean to get as close as he did to Horseshoe Falls, but he passed the safe zone, and the current grabbed the boat and there was no escaping it."

Pressing her hand to her mouth, Olympia gasped. "What happened to them?"

The man lowered his head as he finished the story. "Brave man he was, and smart. He knew he was going over those rapids. He pushed the girl out of the boat right up there by Goat Island, just before the boat went over. He didn't have time for the boy, but he grabbed hold of him and as that boat sailed over the Falls, that brave man saw the Maid of the Mist below." Stopping the story to explain to John and Olympia, in case they were not aware, "The Maid is a tour boat that sails around the bottom of the plunge pool where the Falls land in the river down there. That man threw that boy out of the boat as it was falling, right towards the Maid of the Mist. The captain saw it happen and they were able to toss that little boy a life ring and pull him to safety. The girl was saved too right before the current dragged her over. Some folks out on goat island managed to get to her before the water took her down. But their poor uncle, we went down and under and was never found. Swept away down river. Water can be a powerfully strong force."

As the park employee walked away, Olympia and John marveled once again at the natural wonder before them. She was leaning over the iron rail, gazing up and down at the river and the massive waterfall powering it. He recognized the mischievous look in her eye. "Olympia Windham, what are you pondering?"

She allowed John and John alone to call her by his surname. Her private gift to him. She did not answer his question at first, knowing he would not like the answer. He pressed her again. "You won't like it," she teased.

"Olympia," he said gripping her around the neck in a pretend choke hold. "Are you curious to see if you can freeze those rapids?"

Whirling around, her long hair sweeping back in the misty wind, she beamed. "Please, John, may I try? I know you do not want me to use my powers in your presence unless it is an emergency. But when will I ever have this opportunity again?"

Looking to his left and right, the number of onlookers was too great to risk it.

He shook his head. "Too many witnesses, my dear."

"Oh them!" she exclaimed. "They are easy." Flinging her hands outward Olympia stopped everyone in the vicinity. John was bewildered by the sight. Men with one foot raised to air for their next step, stood as if a statue, perfectly balanced in place, not teetering at all. Women with windblown hair and skirts were paused in place with their attire still mid ruffle from the now stopped air flow. Running children halted mid-sprint, fists clinched, faces expressing excited shouting which had now fallen silent. Every human being looked as if they were in a photograph.

"Olympia!"

"People are easy John," she repeated turning back to face the falls. "But this! This is something else altogether. Let's see what I can do!"

It occurred to her in the moment she raised her hands to try the massive feat, her husband had not actually voiced his permission, but she didn't care. Olympia sent forth her power towards the top of Niagara Falls. Despite strongly disapproving of the experiment, John quietly admitted to himself he was curious if she could do it. As they stood watching to see if she'd been successful, they observed the river above and the top crest of the waterfall stop. The previously flowing current was now a solidified long sheath—resembling ice, but not technically frozen. As the river reached the edge of the falls, the normally tumbling waters were stationary, capping the top of Horseshoe Falls. The air grew significantly quieter as the roaring crash of water was no longer as powerful. Still, Olympia's attempt was not a total success. Underneath the uppermost portion of where the river fell, water was still managing to escape her spell from the underside. It appeared as if she had managed to stop roughly half the fall's capacity. At the bottom of the falls water continued to sneak down beneath her little barrier much like someone turning a faucet halfway off.

"Damn," she winced disappointedly. "I couldn't do it."

John blinked at the waterfall, trying to focus well enough to accurately gauge her success. "Honey, I think you did impressively well. That has to be about 50,000 cubic feet of water Olympia! And you stopped half of it."

"But not all of it," she replied almost ashamed of herself.

"50,000 cubic feet Olympia! You froze 25,000 cubic feet."

"Speak English John!" she snapped as she released the water from her spell. "What is a cubic foot anyway? How do you measure water in feet. What are the gallons?"

He chuckled at her absurdity. Steering her by the shoulders away from the railing, they almost bumped into a couple of people, still frozen in place. "Uh, Darling…"

Blushing, Olympia sighed, "I have a terrible habit of forgetting to release people from the spell." Waving her hand, everyone began moving about again in unison. The couple the newlyweds nearly bumped into, now flinched in surprise and jumped backwards. Both turning their heads in confusion and disorientation, because Olympia and John had not been directly in front of them before. The Windhams continued walking until they reached a nearby restaurant located within the park. Taking a table with a vista view of the Canadian side of the Falls, they began to chat about the future.

"When we return home, I expect the blueprints to be completed for the kitchen addition." John reported. "Complete with a hidden room beneath for all of your special needs."

Elbows on the table, her face planted innocently in her hands, she sent him a smile. "I must say I do not know which I am more excited about, a brand-new modern kitchen or a secret space all for coven business."

"It will be expensive," John groused. "But considering you come with your own rather large house, and we do not have to buy or build something for ourselves, it's a paltry amount in comparison. I plan to give you the most elaborate, state of the art appliances money can buy."

"It sounds grand, John. We will be very happy."

He scowled a moment, as if reminded of something he would rather not know. "Apparently we end up with a rather large family."

Olympia could see from his crestfallen face; he was lamenting the absence of surprise with their future, but she had not revealed anything about it to him. "I have told you nothing, John Windham. The only thing I have shared is who Beryl really is."

His face recovered from its somber mood, and he let out a laugh of acceptance. "Nate told me the rest. He said he met our grandson and another granddaughter. Nate says you and I end up with three daughters and a slew of grandchildren."

"What else has Beryl told him?" Olympia asked like a child attempting to squeeze out information about Christmas presents. "Beryl will not tell me anything else. She says it might upset the future. I don't see how much more she could upset the future than she has now by becoming pregnant in our time period."

"Nate was closed-lipped on anything else. He didn't even theoretically tell me our future. It was more of his unburdening his problems to me, his friend. Most of the things I know were told in the moment of his hashing out his complicated life. I don't even know how long we live! But I tell you, Olympia, I like the idea of a big family. Your father sure knew what he was doing building that three-story house. All those bedrooms will come in handy."

She smiled, remembering fondly her father's wisdom. "Father was clairvoyant. Not like Zelda. He could look into your eyes and see the generations to come. He never gave me any information, but he must have known the Blanchards would grow and grow. Why else would the four of us have needed such a massive house growing up. He was a very sensible man."

John agreed but returned to his current train of thought. "Maybe it is because I am a 'regular' person as you and Pastoria put it. Still, it is difficult for me to consider Beryl a part of me. I suppose once she is born, and I hold my granddaughter in my arms, I will be able to connect to the thought emotionally. Don't misunderstand, I like Beryl. She's a fine upstanding woman. I simply consider her a distant relative of yours."

"Oh, she's pretty distant I'd say." Olympia laughed.

"I suppose it will mean more to me in the future as I age," John admitted. "Knowing the kind of woman she will grow up to become, even after I am long dead and buried." He paused to sip his coffee while he looked out over the view outside. "I never much thought about the concept of time. It is alive. An ever evolving, growing thing. Yet it must be something like a circle. Or it possesses the ability to fold over upon itself. How else do we explain Beryl coming here. And if we—you and I, I mean—are not living in the furthermost period of time, who is? Is Beryl's era the definitive end where time continues to grow? Or is she, like us, living only within some middle part that has already happened for someone else further along? It boggles the mind."

It was the most John Windham had ever lingered upon magical subjects with Olympia. He preferred unknown things to remain unknown. He preferred her world stay hidden. She liked knowing now that these ideas crossed his mind from time to time. And though she planned to honor her promise to keep him in the dark as much as possible during their marriage, she felt closer to him now when he could understand the beauty and the mystery of her complicated existence."

CHAPTER FORTY-TWO

Taking Up the Cause

Coming through the door after an exhausting day in court, John almost thought he was still at work judging by the heated debate taking place inside when he got home. Olympia was in a full rant pacing the living room when he placed his briefcase on the foyer table. Beryl and Nate were seated on the couch receiving an ear full of her tirade. "I cannot believe he did this!" Olympia cried in outrage. "How can a person possibly be that heartless?"

John did not need further explanation. Variations of this argument had taken place all over town that afternoon—although mostly from the other side of the argument. Earlier in the day, Governor George Wallace, in an attempt to prevent two black students from registering for classes, blocked the door to a University of Alabama building. It was all anyone was talking about.

"I see you've been watching the news again." John replied, longing for the good old days when Olympia's mind was consumed with herself and oblivious to the travails of anyone else.

"It is an outrage, John."

"It is over, Olympia. President Johnson sent in the National Guard, and they allowed the students inside."

"That doesn't exactly fix the problem," Nate weighed in. "Did you see the faces of those on Wallace's side? Pure hate brewing for those kids. It's wrong."

John propped himself on the back of a nearby chair and simply said, "It has nothing to do with us."

Beryl was more than surprised at his disinterest. "It has everything to do with us, John. We are all brothers and sisters together. I can tell you from what I know, this goes down in history as a dark day for Alabama."

Her commentary did little to sway John from his assessment. "The University will figure out the best way to solve things."

Nate looked almost as outraged by John's nonchalance as his wife. "John, surely this stirs something in you? You of all people. You are a lawyer. You fight against wrongs every day. Do you not feel some kind of compassion for the way those two kids were treated?'

John shook his head, "I am a lawyer, yes. I argue the point of view of the one who pays me the most. A good lawyer has no real opinion."

"A cavalier attitude, don't you think?" Nate remarked.

"No," John replied. "A sensible one. I am not in the practice of law to right the wrongs of the world. I do my job and I do it well, representing the one who signs the check at the end of the case."

Beside herself with disbelief, Beryl approached him with distress in her eyes. "John, if you don't want to listen to Olympia or Nate, listen to me. I above anyone in this state—hell, this country—knows how history paints these times. What Wallace did was wrong. He even admits it himself later in life and tries to be a better representative for the black community–albeit mostly for political clout by winning over black voters–but he still turns his view around. Everyone who is opposing Civil Rights is fighting for the wrong side."

John patted her arm and said, "I am not fighting against them. I am staying out of it."

The ensuing seconds of Beryl's silence might easily have been misconstrued for disappointment, but it was much more than that. In those seconds, she weighed the risk of succumbing to her compulsion to blurt out all the atrocities which were coming over the next few years...including the murder of Dr. Martin Luther King, Jr. and an American President. But before she did, her wiser instincts muffled her tongue. She could not risk it. Or could she? Should she? What could the world be like if Dr. King had lived? What if she stopped the bombing of the 16th Street Baptist Church and saved those precious little girls? What if she could save Medgar Evers? Although fuzzy on the exact dates, she wasn't certain she'd still be in the past when those crimes occurred. Still, she could warn Pastoria, Olympia, and Zelda to be ready. The urge to lay out the history her friends were yet to live was quelled by an inner voice cautioning her not to change what had already been. Do not upset The Natural Order. She had already done enough damage in her time here by becoming pregnant.

"Well, I am not staying out of it all!" Olympia huffed indignantly. "I feel compelled to do something."

"For instance, what?" John asked.

"When I know, you will know."

Since becoming John Windham's wife, Olympia received a number of invitations to ladies' luncheons, garden clubs, and charity drives. She'd ignored them all until now. A few days after Governor Wallace's stand, an invitation arrived for a gathering at Christine Whittaker's house. Christine was the president of The Daihmler Dames, a self-proclaimed action committee committed to helping the less fortunate in the county. Olympia summoned Beryl, Pastoria, and Zelda to join her for the upcoming meeting. Zelda declined, "I ain't got no interest in sittin' around some fancy lace tableclothed table sipping tea and eatin' coffee cake while a bunch of privileged bored housewives talk about how to raise a hundred dollars to give some orphanage."

It only took Olympia's glaring eye to back her down and coerce her to join. Zelda knew she would not hear the end of it until she agreed to go. The four witches dressed to the nines, including hats, for the occasion. Of course, Zelda's faux berry covered hat was as oversized as Beryl's growing waistline. The women made a fashionably late entrance of fifteen minutes, but their tardiness only added to the mystique as the other ladies proceeded to fawn over them, all feeling extra privileged that Mrs. Windham had graced them with her presence.

Christine Whittaker rushed to the door with more enthusiasm than she had shown the other arrivals. Eager to lead Olympia and her friends around the room where the mingling ladies waited to be introduced to society's newest member. Admittedly, Olympia relished this newfound adoration. Several of these women were the same horrid little schoolgirls who used to tease and ostracize she and her sister. Watching them now fumble over each other to win favor with Mrs. John Windham, tickled her. She forced herself to not judge them too harshly for their shallowness, reminding herself time has the power to change people in unexpected ways. Perhaps these women were genuine in their kindness. When the ladies were not ingratiating themselves to Olympia, they were encompassing Beryl. Patting her baby bump while regaling her with their own tales of childbirth, the women shared their well-meant advice.

Though it was not unusual among middle class households to find colored women serving as maids, especially at parties, Beryl noticed for the first time how unseen these women made themselves. Moving around the room in their crisp black uniforms, they cleared empty plates and refilled tea glasses while garnering no acknowledgment from guests. Not one of the committee members offered a word of thanks to the women keeping their meeting tidy. It was as if it was communally considered these tasks completed themselves instead of by the chapped, calloused hands of fellow human beings. Not acquainted with this bygone practice of having a housemaid, nor accustomed to such blatant rudeness, Beryl was embarrassed by how these women were ignored. When one of the maids brought Beryl a tall glass of iced tea topped with a lemon wedge, Beryl took it from her with a cheery smile and said, "Thank you so much. That is kind of you." The remark flickered an initial surprise in the maid's eye which quickly changed into anxious contrition, as if the maid had behaved in a way forcing a guest to show her appreciation. Clearly the woman was unsure how she was supposed to respond. Murmuring a low, "Yes, ma'am," she darted away rather swiftly.

Mrs. Whittaker's guests chose to ignore the interaction, preferring to pretend it did not happen. They began to settle themselves around the many folding tables to begin their meeting. Priority on the agenda was deciding which worthy causes to take up for the coming Fall and Winter. Coming as no surprise to anyone, the most popular suggestion was supplying Christmas toys for the underprivileged. It was undoubtedly an already well-established program because much mention was made about simply replicating last year's plan.

Raising her hand just high enough to be noticed, Olympia asked a question to Committee Chairwoman Gloria Ray. "How many underprivileged children are there according to your records?"

Seemingly befuddled by a question, but happy someone was showing interest, Gloria replied. "Oh, about 40 or so, I'd say. We contact local churches, and the pastors supply us with a list of names of struggling families in their congregation. Many live paycheck to paycheck. Christmas is rather meager without our help."

"What about poor families not affiliated with a church?" Olympia questioned. "How do we locate those families?"

Gloria seemed puzzled by the question, as did many other women of the club. "We deal mainly with church families."

Pastoria joined in now, "Wouldn't church members be the most likely to look after their own struggling members? What happens to the children who do not go to church? Do they not have gifts to open Christmas morning?" Several ladies shrugged; they had no answer. It was something they'd not considered before.

"Are these churches all white churches?" Beryl chimed. "I would assume black churches have a fair share of underprivileged families. Do we take them into account when we are collecting toy donations?"

The ladies of the club were not prepared for such in-depth discussion about their charity drive. No one had ever asked these kinds of questions before. However, no one wanted to openly shut down the opinions of John Windham's wife or her companions. Olympia had finally graced their society with her participation. Fearing this might be the first and last time she would, the ladies humored the challenges. "You ladies bring up some good points," Christine Whitaker smiled. "I believe we should begin including colored children and children outside of church membership into our reach. After all, they are children too. Every child should have something from Santa Claus Christmas morning."

Another woman spoke up issuing the counterpoint that they would have no possible way of estimating those numbers, let alone know how to get the toys to the families. Her remarks brought a few nods of agreement around the room as if this one extra step should sideline the suggestion.

"Call the local schools," Olympia said. "Surely, school administrators would know which students come from needy homes and how to get toys to them."

"Even if that is possible," an elderly, and rather pinch-faced woman, declared, "We still would no way to find out about colored children." When Beryl pointed out that colored children also go to school, the woman answered by saying no one in their committee could be seen visiting one of those schools.

"I don't see why that should be an issue," Beryl remarked. "But even if it is, why can't we ask right here?" The women did not understand her meaning, until Beryl rose from her table and walked to the doorway of the kitchen, swinging open the door, revealing several maids inside, Beryl asked if they would mind joining them in the living room. Within a few seconds four wide eyed, rather nervous maids came in. Beryl held the door open for the women and noticed the astonished faces of the committee members seated around the room.

Olympia took over now, hoping to spare Beryl of having to be the only one spearheading the idea, and hoping to be an example to the Daihmler uptight brigade, that society does not crumble if you have a conversation with one of the domestic help. "Ladies, thank you for taking time from your work to let us ask you a few questions." The maids appeared petrified, while the committee members seemed shocked to hear their maids addressed as *ladies*.

One of the maids spoke, her voice shaking a little as she asked, "Was something wrong with the sandwiches or cakes, Miss Whitaker?"

With a quick laugh, Olympia waved her hand and said, "Oh nothing like that. Everything was delicious and we thank you for making it for us." Again, the rest of the room was not exactly pleased with the graciousness pouring from Mrs. Windham. Undetered, Olympia continued. "We have been discussing our hope to provide Christmas presents for some of the children in Daihmler whose parents may not have the means to give them anything Christmas morning. Do any of you ladies attend churches, or have children in schools, where you might know specific families who would be interested in our help?"

None of the maids responded for a few moments, then one, a slightly built younger girl—probably the daughter of one of the other maids—bravely answered Olympia's question. "We can find out. We know lots of folks that ain't got any money at all to even pay they rents. Sure don't have nothing left for Christmas presents."

Olympia stood from her chair as though she'd forged some sort of major accomplishment. Pulling a small card from her purse, she went to the young girl dressed in a maid's uniform—who could not have been older than 15—and handed her the card. "Splendid," Olympia smiled at her. "May I ask your name?"

"Uh, Brenda."

"Nice to make your acquaintance Brenda. I am Olympia Blanchard. This card has my telephone number on it. Would you be willing to collect some names of people who might need our help for Christmas?"

"Yes, ma'am."

Bristling, Olympia quickly chided, "Please, don't call me ma'am. I am not that much older than you." Behind her, Pastoria feigned choking sounds, which Olympia ignored. "Brenda, please call me whenever you have a list together. I am sure you can do a much better job finding the information than we can."

Beryl cringed against the doorframe. Without a doubt she knew Olympia was trying to be friendly and grateful, even if she had just implied Brenda must know everyone of color in need in Daihmler because she herself was colored. However,

Brenda did not appear offended, on the contrary she seemed to be bolstered by the task as if for once in her life being treated as though she had value by a white woman. Beryl chose not to mention Olympia's faux paus later, mainly because she wasn't sure it had been one or not. In Beryl's time the assumption would be offensive. Here in Olympia's days of youth, it was probable the cliché connotation hadn't even become a point yet.

As the committee meeting winded down and the maids returned to their work of cleaning up, the ladies of Daihmler began filing out, returning to their own homes. Just before the first batch of women made their way for the front door, Zelda shouted a loud, "And don't none of ya'll stick the colored kids with the crappy toys," over their departing heads, adding, "A lot of you ladies come to me for psychic advice. And whether you know it or not, so do some of your husbands. You really don't want me to tell what all I know about your own households."

No one from the committee knew exactly what to make of Olympia's little group and their audacious questions and inclusion. Many phone lines were tied up most of the afternoon over it. Though some found their behavior boorish, most were still marveling at the fact John Windham's wife showed at all. Humoring her and her friends in their impromptu devotion to all needy children in town caused something to change none of them would yet notice. Call it a spark. Call it a seed firmly planted in the ground. Whatever it was, in subsequent weeks, and subsequent meetings, club members slowly began to view things with slightly more open eyes. The simple acknowledgment of the maids, as if they were people, remained with the women of Daihmler, even if they were unaware of it themselves. Women who once paid little attention to stories in the news, began to speak openly over time about the disparities around them. Maybe it was mostly to each other and not their husbands, but they were talking now—and not merely about recipes or town gossip.

CHAPTER FORTY-THREE

The Ascension of Beryl

She thought it strange how the things she never knew she was lacking now superseded every success she'd ever had. Cuddled together with Nate on the couch, watching the airing of a first run Beverly Hillbillies episode she already knew by heart, Beryl was blissfully happy. Her life felt complete in so many ways. Her former life as a physician and a healer served to fulfill her sense of purpose; for a long time, she believed that was enough. This new life was fulfilling something within her now she had not known was empty. Love. Home. Stability. She was a wife, which meant she had someone to love who loved her back. This new existence may not save lives or come with the accolades her medical degree supplied, but it somehow meant more to her. And though her role as a mother would be little more than a gestation period, she felt maternal with every kick. As her husband snored against her chest, his cheek pressed against her belly, Beryl couldn't think of a happier time in her life.

She longed to share her bliss with her sister and mother. She wanted them to understand how this seemingly tragic episode of her life was in truth, her paradise. Fable would never believe her big sister would find enjoyment in vacuuming the carpet, frying pork chops for her husband's dinner, or laying on a sofa with a man's snores ringing in her ears. She wanted so desperately to talk to them. An idea came to her. Carefully, she eased herself off the couch, supplementing a round arm pillow in exchange for her body to not wake him. She went over to the desk in the corner of the living room and began to write. Something inside her was compelled to write a letter to her mother–her mother who was not even born yet—still, she wanted to talk to her, and a letter was the only way she had.

At first the letter began rather normally, recounting what her life was now like. She let her mother know how deeply she was missed, yet she also confessed how much she liked her present situation. Beryl began explaining how much she would miss Olympia, Pastoria, and Zelda, whom she referred to quite naturally now as her sisters. In glowing detail, Beryl told her mother about Nate and how sincerely she loved him. It pained Beryl to know she would soon be leaving him once the baby was born. Yet, the more she wrote, the more the tone of the letter changed. Whatever force which had spent months growing within her was a part of her now. With it came an awareness, a knowledge, which once she had not been attuned to. She was now. And she knew things now, unknown to her before. For example, she knew she was not going to return home. Beryl found herself being aware of answers to questions she never asked. All her life, she recognized the power within her to heal was from God, but now that infinitesimal part of Him inside her spoke. Continuing her letter, she explained how she knew she would never be coming back home, yet she would not be staying in the past. There was something more, something bigger coming for her, although she did not know what it might be. The voice inside her only revealed there was a plan laid out for her.

The following day, Beryl drove out to Zelda's house. Zelda was with a client, but Beryl waited on the porch until the psychic reading was over. As the client drove away, Beryl went inside, handing her letter to Zelda. "I have things I need to say to my family back home, things I will never get the opportunity to tell them. I've written this." Placing the sealed envelope on the coffee table, she beseeched her friend, "I need you to keep this safe always. When the time comes, many, many years from now, give it to my mother."

Zelda was unsettled by the request, for a multitude of reasons. "Beryl, what makes you think you ain't goin' back?"

Searching her brain for a way to explain, Beryl walked her fingers across the back of Zelda's couch as she moved into the room. "I cannot explain it," she answered, picking a few stray fuzzies of the crocheted Afghan draped over the back. "I just know. I know the same way you can see things that happen to people. I *know*."

Zelda sat, knees down, on the couch facing Beryl behind it. She took hold of her friend's hands, closing her eyes, trying with all her might to read into her future. Zelda could see nothing. "I can't read you now. It's like that gold aura you got has me walled off."

"It's not for either of us to know," Beryl smiled. "I think there is a larger will at work we are not meant to understand. I feel it."

Zelda raised an eyebrow, releasing Beryl's hands so she could lift the envelope from the table. Tapping the thick letter in her palm, she said, "Which leads me to my next question. Why you givin' this to me? Why not Lympy? Or Pastoria? You afraid they'll open it?"

Beryl did not answer. The silence hung heavy in the air between them, speaking volumes. Zelda now understood, dropping the letter to the floor. "I'm the only one left alive when this happens."

Beryl nodded.

"So, I'm the last one standing." Zelda halfheartedly joked wiping a stray tear. The thought of being left behind in life without Olympia or Pastoria seemed like a dismal future. "I'm alone."

Beryl came around the couch and sat beside her, grabbing Zelda's hands once more excitedly, "Oh Zelda, you are never alone. You have us. All of us. Olympia's children and grandchildren. We all love you, Zelda. You are our family. You are never going to be alone."

Gulping down an emotion she didn't enjoy feeling very much, Zelda remarked, "Well, I guess that's kind of nice then." She lifted the letter from the carpet. "So, I just hold onto this all my life, till the time when you disappear? Then I give it to your momma?"

"Not until today's date, but in the future. Don't give it to her until I am already pregnant and married. We don't want to have them save me before my baby is conceived. Apparently, I was always supposed to come here and be his mother."

"Got it." Zelda winked.

The workings of time would probably be something Beryl would never fully understand. She'd only delivered her letter to Zelda's protection two days ago, but whatever kind of track the future ran upon must have completed its cycle because as she opened the door to Blanchard House to meet Olympia for lunch, she heard familiar voices. Rushing to the kitchen, Beryl nearly fainted as she saw the beautiful face of her mother staring from the table with Olympia.

No words were spoken as Beryl and her mother Demitra ran into each other's arms. Demitra Blanchard pressed her long-lost daughter's head to her shoulder and wept with the joy of holding her once more. When she finally released her, Demitra pulled back to take a long look at her daughter's attire. Beryl's normally trim waistline was replaced with a very round belly poking out over lemon yellow capri pants and a swirly pink and orange maternity blouse. With a questioning eye, Demitra lifted the tail of the psychedelic scarf tied around Beryl's head. "You have changed." Beryl shrugged innocently. Behind her mother, Beryl saw her aunt Nacaria once again, seated at the little kitchen table.

"Touching to see them like this isn't it?" Nacaria said to Olympia.

Overcome by the moment, Olympia wiped unexpected tears from her cheek and replied, "It really is. I couldn't stand my mother! Seeing them like this...are *we* like that when you are all my daughters?"

Nacaria laughed as she wrapped loving arms around Olympia. Demitra joined them, stretching her arms around them both. "Yes," Demitra smiled. "We are exactly like this. You and your daughters are the best of friends, all our lives."

Removing herself from the double embrace, Olympia snatched a dish towel from the counter to dap her eyes before her makeup ran. "That's so sweet." She threw the towel back to the sink and gripped Demitra and Nacaria's hands. "I'm glad we will be close. My mother was such a bitch."

"I've met your mother," Nacaria laughed. "She really was."

Olympia laughed again, more tears falling. "I promise I will not treat you the way she did me. I want you to feel loved, always."

Demitra smiled, giving Olympia a kiss on the hand still clutched with her own. "It is something we never doubt for an instant, Mother. Even when nothing else is assured in our lives, we always know you love us."

"That's wonderful." Olympia nodded, coming back to her composure. "Please don't call me Mother, though. Not until it is necessary."

With the sentimentality out of the way, Beryl expressed her shock at having come home to find these two futuristic women from her lifetime sitting in the Blanchard House kitchen. Demitra explained the reason for the visit. Zelda—the elderly one—had presented Demitra with Beryl's decades old letter that very morning. "That's why I'm here! There is no way I can just never see my little girl again. I had to come back and see you one last time."

Olympia went back to cooking the lunch, now making enough for their unexpected guests, as she talked over her shoulder. "We can't figure out for the life of us what is going on with Beryl. This invincibility thing is nothing like we've ever seen. And now that she's certain she is moving off to some other plane of existence after the baby comes—we are flummoxed. My sister is at the library right now trying to figure it all out. Doubt she'll find any books with this kind of thing in them, but she went to look up India and Zen Buddhist teachings. We figure Beryl is in some state of enlightenment we have never heard of."

Demitra whispered to her daughter, "I know what's happening to you. Take a walk with me after lunch."

The Blanchard women enjoyed the most unique meal any of them had ever experienced. Olympia, dining with her two grown middle-aged daughters from the future; Demitra and Nacaria dining with their long-deceased mother who was now half their own age; and Beryl, sitting with all of them, each from a different point in time. It was nothing to be believed had they not been a part of it.

After lunch, Demitra and Beryl excused themselves for a walk while Nacaria remained with Olympia to clean up the dishes. As mother and daughter walked around the Blanchard land, Demitra marveled at how different things appeared in contrast to her own time.

"Mother's rose garden," she said pointing at the young bushes newly planted. "Was that just put in recently?"

Beryl smiled and gripped her mother's arm, "Did you know what started that garden?"

"No," Demitra replied. "I just assumed Mother liked roses."

Beryl chuckled, "I know so much about our history now. Little things which I suppose seemed too trivial or too personal for grandmother to share. Olympia has a dear friend, an innocent hearted soul named Lauralee. She was the sister of your stepfather Martin Caswell. Lauralee gave Olympia a rose bush every time she visited. She's very sick now so this garden is special to Olympia."

"I never knew that."

"Did you know it was your grandfather who was responsible for the way Zelda dresses?" Beryl gossiped.

"What?"

"Zelda told me that when she was little, your grandfather gave her a scarf which belonged to his mother. It was very colorful. She thought it was so beautiful. She still dresses in the same vivid colors from that scarf."

Demitra was amazed. Beryl indeed knew things she had never even heard about. But more amazing to Demitra was the sheer joy in her daughter's face when she spoke of her time here and their adventures. The happiness she'd written about in her letter was evidenced now in her presence. Demitra had never known her daughter to be this animated or this joyful.

Beryl had questions for her mother as well. She wanted to know everything that had been happening to the family back home in the future. Demitra caught her up to speed, not all of it was happy. The family was going through a great deal of tragedy, and change, back home and now it seemed they would have to face it without Beryl for support.

Pausing their walk by the chicken house, Beryl took hold of an overhead rafter from the eave and hung her head low. "I am sorry I won't be there for you," she said. "I feel such guilt over that. It sounds like the family is hurting. My absence can only add to that."

Demitra took her daughter's face in her hands and pulled it close to her own. This isn't your fault, my love. You are fated for greater things. It is your destiny." Demitra twisted Beryl around to direct her gaze skyward. "Beryl, more and more I am realizing it has been destiny all along for all of this to come to pass. There is a greater reason we are not meant to understand, but I trust God understands. It is the only way I can accept losing you. You, Beryl, will also soon understand. Stitches in time have been sewn, largely by you. What fabric it will create none of us know for sure, but I have accepted there is a reason."

"You are strangely calm, Mother." Beryl wasn't sure if she should be grateful her mother was taking her disappearance from their lives so well, or if she should be greatly offended by it.

Demitra smiled, "While you have been here living a brand-new life, I have been at home learning all about what has been happening. I've known the answer for a long time. I will share it with you now."

"Do you know what is happening to me, Mother?" she asked bravely. "I am not afraid. Not afraid at all. I trust everything I feel. But my curiosity does get the better of me sometimes. What is happening to me?"

Inhaling a deep breath of the waning summer air, Demitra readied herself to explain the unfathomable. "Beryl, you are becoming God. Literally."

As Beryl Blanchard Caldwell stood listening beneath the blowing wind, the rustling leaves of late summer, and the scratching and squawking of three dozen chickens, her mother did her best to help her understand. "They call it The God Strain. There have been others like you throughout time. And now your time has come. It's the only reason I can give you up without my heart ripping to shreds."

At first Beryl could not comprehend any of the meaning behind her mother's words. Surely, she had not told her she was becoming God. How could that even be possible? There was only one God. And even if there were more, Beryl was in no way worthy of such a title. Yet, as her mother went on, the little beacon now shining within Beryl's soul was telling her this tale was true. Demitra explained how much it made sense. Beryl's lifelong dedication to helping others. Her fastidious devotion to the truth. Even the magnificent power she wielded was not a witch's power, it was a healing power. A direct gift from The Almighty. God had chosen her to walk this life in a constant evolution of learning until the day when He deemed her ready to join His ranks. The God Strain. A special bloodline of unique souls who would transcend to act as God's hands on Earth. Angels among the living. Beryl was not God, proper. She was a vein of His greater body, among many others like her walking the earth unseen, acting in His stead.

"Every day for the rest of my life I will mourn the loss of you." Demitra wept as she held her daughter in her arms. "But when I look up at the universe, I will take comfort knowing you are somewhere out there making it all go round in whatever special ways you will. You'll be in everything I see every day. A bloom. A raindrop. An ant crawling. A newborn crying. My daughter. One of God's chosen. A God herself."

CHAPTER FORTY-FOUR

Goodbye My Sisters

Demitra Blanchard and her sister Nacaria did not depart for their own time after Beryl's reunion with her mother. There was not a lot of time remaining before Beryl's due date and Demitra insisted on being there when her daughter gave birth. Olympia was gracious and welcomed them to stay at Blanchard House. It was all a little too much for John, who decided to take a case out of town for a couple of weeks. He knew his life would never be normal married to a witch, but all these yet-unborn offspring was more than his normal mind could handle. Olympia had, so far, done a very poor job at keeping him ignorant of all her witching matters.

It was only three days into their stay when Beryl was overcome with contractions. Of course, Demitra knew it would happen. She knew all too well the date of her dearest friend Howard's birthday. She'd celebrated it every year with him, never knowing until a few months ago he had always been her grandson. It had long been decided by Olympia, Beryl, and Nate that the child's birth would take place at Blanchard House. No hospital was going to allow a husband to be present during childbirth—at least not in the 1960's. And if Beryl were to leave this earth immediately after giving birth, that was not something anyone was willing to explain to a hospital staff.

As Beryl lay in her old bedroom clinging to Nate, the air in the room turned somber as this was as equally a sad occasion as it was a blessed one. Demitra gave them their space, agreeing to come in only at the end. She understood though Beryl belonged to her once, Beryl belonged to Nate now...and Olympia and Pastoria and Zelda. Nate Caldwell would live the rest of his life raising his son alone, loving the one woman he would lose this very night. His and Beryl's was a true love. Unfortunately, like most storybook loves, it was coming with a tragic ending.

Nate Caldwell was not prepared for the loss coming his way although he had always known it was. But knowing something and feeling something can be quite different animals. A quiet panic was setting in as he faced the truth of his situation. For months this was simply some far-away date he did not have to think about. There were far too many wonderful days between to be spent with his amazing wife. He cherished every hour of those now behind-him days. The dreaded date was upon them and not many minutes remaining before his heart would be forever broken. Beryl shared his feelings. Though she trusted whatever was set in motion for her, Nate was the only man she had ever or would ever love. The pain of leaving him was crushing. They spent the hours of her labor, holding one another, remembering their all too brief life together. Once the contractions increased and her dilation reached birthing time, the Caldwells knew it was time for goodbyes if they were ever going to say them.

"I will always love you Beryl, my sweet," Nate sobbed, staring into her beautiful sweaty face as she breathed through a powerful contraction. "I will mourn you; I know. But I will never regret our choices. You are the best gift life ever gave me."

Beryl stared into her husband's tender eyes. "I have no idea what happens next for me, Nate. But my darling husband, I need you to know nothing that has ever happened in my life measures up to a single moment I have spent with you." Taking another inhalation of breath and squeezing it out in successions through the next contraction, she waited for it to subside, then added, "Please let our son know his mother loved him. He can never know until he's grown who I was, but he should know how deeply I loved him."

"He will know, Beryl," Nate vowed. "I promise you."

"I may be missing out on his childhood," Beryl added. "But I have the privilege of having known him as a man. Oh, Nate what a good man our son turns out to be."

Demitra entered the room. She took her place beside Nate, her son-in-law, and lovingly patted his arm. A sudden irony swept her as she realized she had given birth to Beryl in this same bed, in this same room, thirty years from now. "My sweet angel girl," Demitra smiled, stroking Beryl's forehead. "It has been my esteemed privilege to be your mother. I have never loved anything as much as I have loved you, my first born."

"You'll watch over Howard?"

"You know I will."

"I love you, Momma. Thank you for everything you ever did for me. Thank you for being the kind of mother I wish I had the opportunity to be. I became everything

I am because of you..." she paused and looked past them. "And you three fools," she laughed. Demitra glanced behind her to see Olympia, Pastoria, and Zelda crowding the doorway. Beryl motioned them closer so she could place her hands in theirs. "You have been my sisters these last months. My very best friends. Thank you." And to Olympia alone she said, "And later, you're about the most wonderful thing any of us ever knows. Thank you for who you will become in my life." She motioned for her mother to place her hands atop theirs. "We are the Blanchard Witches of Daihmler County, and I love you all."

As the words escaped her lips, the final contraction hit. The air grew electric with anticipation as Beryl's body tightened with the intensity of the moment. Zelda scooted everyone out of the way to get in position to take the baby. Beryl screamed in pain. Nate moved closer, holding her hands as she pushed. Her reddened face shook, and her breath caught as she gave one final push to set baby Howard free in the world. Zelda pulled the baby out and held its mucus covered body up for Beryl to see, the umbilical cord still dangling. Gasping for breath, Beryl's face beamed in joy. Droplets of sweat glistened on her brow and cheeks, a testament to the physical and emotional journey that had brought her here. A broad, radiant smile covered her face as her eyes locked onto the beautiful sight of her son. Beryl felt something within her beginning to shift. She began feeling slightly out of body. Whatever was going to happen to her, was about to happen now. She motioned for Zelda to come closer, she needed to touch her son. She could not leave this world without feeling the soft skin of her son's face. Zelda bent forward as if she were going to hand him off to his mother to hold. Beryl, knowing there was no time for that, did not reach to take him. But instead, found the strength to reach her shaking hand out, her fingertips gently caressing his face. Though she would not be able to raise him, to guide him, or even to really ever know Howard Caldwell as her son...Beryl Caldwell made sure she felt the face of her beautiful boy for one brief moment, and that would have to be enough.

Zelda stepped back, with Howard still in her arms, as Beryl's teary eyes froze his image into her mind. Her shining eyes brightened. And brightened. Then they brightened even again, as if becoming a beacon shining into darkness. Her family stood motionless, speechless as her eyes turned a kind of yellow, then golden, then to almost a piercing blinding white. Involuntarily the others in the room shielded their faces from the expanding rays pouring now from Beryl's being. It was more than the mortal eye could behold. A sudden burst of power exploded from her illuminated form, filling the room like the birth of a sun. Nate and the women turned their heads instinctively– the moment far too Holy for them to witness. The light swelled until there was nothing but light itself in the room. Then, as quickly as it manifested, it was gone. And so was Beryl. The bed was empty. Beryl Blanchard Caldwell had moved on.

Nate fell to the bed grasping the sheets, sobbing for his wife. Demitra stood shell shocked at what she had just witnessed. Olympia intuitively knew what to do. She took hold of the baby from Zelda's trembling hands, handing him to Demitra. Demitra broke from her shock, looking down at her crying grandson. A smile returned to her face as she looked into the eyes of that tiny being, knowing he was a small piece of herself. Lifting him close to her face she gave his forehead its first earthly kiss. "I love you, Howard Caldwell. Welcome to the world. I will be seeing you again in a few years."

She handed the baby to Nate. Unsteady from the shock, he seemed unsure. Olympia steadied his hands, cupping them in place to hold the baby. "Take your son, Nate. Beryl's son. All the love we hold for her, we now give to him."

Nate took the baby, cradling him gently. He grinned at his son. Beryl's son. He knew he would love him always, because he'd loved his mother so very much. But he was afraid. He did not know how to do this. How could he be a father all alone? How would he know what to do?

Understanding her friend's fear, because perhaps she felt some of it herself, Olympia reassuringly professed to Nate, "We will do this together, Nate. I will always be there for him. I will help you along the way in every way I can. Though the world will know him as a Caldwell, this child is a Blanchard. My great grandson. I will always look out for him."

CHAPTER FORTY-FIVE

The Big Easy on a Long Night

It had been a week since baby Howard was born. Demitra and Nacaria returned to their own time and as far as anyone in Daihmler knew, Beryl died tragically in childbirth–her body sent back to her relatives in Mobile. It was all explained away very neatly, so much so that the town came together to lend support to Nate in any way he needed. Nate's clients showed sympathetic understanding, allowing him time to grieve and showing a willingness to come to his home for meetings until a proper nanny could be hired. Women offered their time to help with the laundry and meal preparation until the widower learned to manage for himself. Olympia and Pastoria did their part as well, watching the baby whenever Nate needed them to and organizing schedules for all those volunteering to help.

Olympia did her best to push Beryl from her mind and regard the baby as her lifelong friend Nate's son. Though her heart stirred whenever she held baby Howard, *this is my great grandson*, she knew the longer she held Beryl in her heart the more difficult it would make moving on. She knew one day she would bear children herself and when those children had children, she needed to be able to meet her future Beryl without tethering their past. Howard had to become merely her friend's son. How could she be expected to become a proper mother to her future daughters if her heart's focus was her granddaughter's son?

Of course, there were other distractions to help, but not all pleasant ones. While she had been preoccupied with Beryl's departure and the baby's birth, Lauralee passed away peacefully in her sleep one night. Olympia attended the funeral days after to say goodbye to her dear kind friend. Not having many acquaintances in town, Lauralee Caswell's funeral was sparsely attended. However, Olympia spared no expense ensuring the chapel and her grave were covered in sprays of roses. Martin and Olympia stood together at the burial, holding one another's hand in comfort as the young woman they both held dear was laid to rest.

As if somehow knowing she needed a case to consume her, The Consort sent an assignment her way that very afternoon. John was not pleased to hear it required his wife to travel to New Orleans to flush out and destroy a pack of werewolves. But what could he reasonably say against it? Someone had to save the innocent people being murdered by monsters, and his wife and her coven were the best equipped to do it. Being the gallant, or chauvinistic, male that he was, John wanted to accompany her. His offer did not receive the gushing gratitude he expected. She was more amused by the gesture than anything else.

"John, my darling," she said caressing his cheek with her hand hoping her touch might also caress his wounded pride. "I adore you for wanting to go and wanting to keep me safe, but truly John, what can you do in such a situation? You asked to be left in the dark with these matters. Accompanying me on a mission is not the way to do that. Your participation would only distract me from the job. I do not need the added pressure of keeping you safe. I have Pastoria and Zelda. We can handle it, I assure you."

There was nothing he could offer in evidence to contradict her point. A good lawyer knows when to switch the line of questioning to a more winnable lane. He attempted that now. "Answer me this, Olympia. Why are you even still working for this strange organization? You are a nice normal housewife...practically. I can understand when you were unmarried and needed to provide an income, but now."

"Now I have a man to provide for me. Is that what you mean?" Olympia let him dangle there on her loaded sentence a moment before cutting him loose. "Honestly, John I would love nothing more. Unfortunately, we still live in a dangerous world where my kind must continue protecting mankind from what goes bump in the night. A day will come when these evils have all been wiped out. Until then, people like me are needed. Besides, you do provide a comfortable income, I'll admit. But I have Pastoria to think about. And Howard's future. And of course, Zelda doesn't make enough with her psychic readings to stay afloat. You aren't wealthy enough to provide for us all."

The lawyer knew he had lost the case. She was right. Choosing to salvage some benefit from her absence, John decided it was the perfect time to have the construction crew begin the kitchen addition. He could eat in town at the diner and at the end of the two weeks, Olympia could come home to a new kitchen. Or at least one nearing completion.

Not being familiar with Louisiana, or the city of New Orleans, Olympia relied on Pastoria to be on the watch for signs while Zelda navigated the large folding map. She had only gone through once with her father to a Consort meeting, but he had driven. The beauty of the city she remembered clearly. Its decadence was something Constantinople had shielded from his impressionable daughter. Now as she drove the narrow lanes through the French Quarter, Olympia saw qualities of human behavior she never imagined. A drunken man vomiting around the corner of an elaborately wrought ironed building. A woman standing outside of a tavern, clearly selling herself to the man groping her breasts in plain view. And two men beating each other to a pulp down an alley. She maneuvered out of the French Quarter, following the handwritten directions from her contact at the Witches Association. Following Canal Street to its very end, she heard the gasps from the backseat as her companions glimpsed the destination up ahead.

"Well, they ain't got no shortage of graveyards around here." Zelda remarked as the tops of ornately sculpted stone arches and domes came into view over the gentle fall of the road. "Does ever'body here get their own mausoleum?"

"It certainly appears so, doesn't it?" Pastoria replied.

"The land is below sea level," Olympia explained. "Graves must be above ground, not under like at home. Otherwise, the coffins float up during floods."

"Well, look who read their encyclopedia this morning!" Zelda chuckled.

Stretching for what seemed to be miles, the landscape of graves drifted into the horizon. Multiple cemeteries were housed here, clustered together, separated only by an occasional wall. It was a city of the dead. Moving through these gardens of stone, the car slowed before a great white square mansion. It was adorned by four tall columns on all four sides, topped with capitals, reminding them of crumbling grandeur from another era.

"Looks like a plantation house." Pastoria commented. "Is this considered Neo-classic or Greek revival? I never know the difference."

"Aren't they the same thing?" Olympia asked, caring very little.

"I don't think so," Pastoria answered, leaning over the front seat to stare out of the windshield. "I don't really know. I believe they are considered different styles."

"Does it even make a damn?" Zelda snorted. "We're here to kill a pack of werewolves. Does it matter that much what design this house was built in?"

Pastoria shifted back into the backseat again folding her arms in exacerbation.

"I just like to know things. You can never have too much knowledge, Zelda."

"Well, you sure as hell can have too many graves in one place. This area looks like they are growing up from the ground like weeds."

Olympia parked the car in front of the house, more accurately the mortuary. The mansion, once built as a family home for a wealthy family named Slattery, was now a funeral parlor with a crematorium in the basement. As the women exited the car a ghoulish looking man appeared in the doorway. The girls were not sure if he appeared ghoulish because in fact, he looked that way, or if he looked that way merely because his being a mortician implied such. "Are you the witches?" the man said timidly.

Olympia extended her hand to shake, wishing as she did, she hadn't. She did not relish the idea of her skin touching his. When he did not reciprocate the gesture, she thankfully put her hand down.

"I don't coddle much to witches," he explained. "Not meanin' no insult, mind you. Just try and steer clear of that stuff. But I ain't got no other recourse with this mess. I'll help you what way I can, but I don't want to know more than I got to."

Olympia was on the verge of dressing the crude man down for the insult when another man stepped outside with an explanation eliminating the need. He was dressed rather dapperly in a suit and tie with a matching hat. "Greetings ladies, I am Mayor Broussard. I am the one who summoned you. And if he did not introduce himself to you, this is Elvin. He works the nightshift, embalming and cremation."

Bypassing the creepy mortician altogether, Olympia practically swept Elvin aside as she stepped up to the porch to shake hands with the refined mayor. "Good afternoon, Mayor Broussard. I am Olympia Blanchard. My team and I have come to help you."

The mayor led the ladies into the front parlor, unmistakably the parlor of a funeral home. Maroon cushioned Victorian chairs with matching settees sat in clusters around the room. This was obviously the receiving room for mourning families. Directing them to have a seat and be comfortable, Mayor Broussard went into greater detail of the problem while the mortician hung back near the door. Broussard spoke matter-of-factly regarding the situation. His candor was a refreshing change from other cases where clients maintained a reluctance to admit the supernatural truth which urged them to hire witches in the first place. "We have what I believe to be a werewolf outbreak in the city." The mayor paused as if waiting for his own reaction of disbelief from them. The trio of witches remained expressionless waiting for him to continue. Slightly grinning, he noted, "I see this announcement does not sound outlandish to you."

"Not at all, Sir." Pastoria replied. "Please go on."

Tugging his ear in a bit of nervousness, the mayor elaborated. "There have been, at last count, 16 murders in the last two months. There was one eyewitness, a woman. She reported her husband tried to kill both she and their son. Interesting thing about this is when he was supposed to have attempted this crime, he had been dead for two weeks. Normally, I would have dismissed her account for the reason I mentioned. However, she also claimed in her statement to have seen him turn into a large dog directly in her presence before he attacked."

"I see." Olympia replied.

Mayor Broussard leaned back in his chair while his fingers taped the wooden arm. He shot a look towards Elvin, as if checking to see his reaction to their reaction. Shaking his head with astonishment, Broussard asked, "None of what I said shocks you?"

"Not remotely." Olympia smiled. "As I am sure you have as well, living in New Orleans...we have seen our fair share of things." The mayor grinned in agreement. Olympia asked if it were possible for them to talk to the woman.

Broussard lowered his head somberly, "A few days after she reported her tale to police, she disappeared. Neighbors heard screams from her home and broke through the front door. The woman was gone. Not a trace of her. The boy, however, was another story. It was gruesome."

Olympia placed her chin into the palm of her hand as she leaned forward on her crossed knee. "Was he partially devoured?" Still somewhat amazed by the nonchalance of these women, the mayor did not speak his reply, however, the nod of his head let Olympia understand it must have been horrific.

Pastoria took over the questioning from there. "The woman...had she been injured during her husband's attack? Cuts? Bruises? Bites?" The mayor explained she had suffered some lacerations to her arms, probably when fighting off her deranged husband. Pastoria nodded in understanding, "The woman was infected during her husband's attack,"

Olympia elaborated when she saw confusion in Broussard's expression, "When the moon became full again later in the month, she transformed. Then she ate her son. I am assuming the neighbors who rushed to the scene found the door open or broken?" The mayor nodded. "Based on what you've told us, we have 8 or 9 werewolves at large here."

The mayor sat upright in surprise at this assertion. "How can you—"

"Math." Olympia answered. "There are two nights a month in a full moon cycle. You've had 16 deaths. It is rare for a wolf to feed twice in one evening. You are looking at probably 8 werewolves. Of course, now there is the woman, making 9 for next month."

"That's not possible," Elvin, the creepy mortician scoffed as he wiped his runny nose on his sleeve.

I am so glad I did not shake his hand; Olympia told her partners with her mind.

"I got a question," Zelda chimed in. "Why are we here at this funeral parlor?"

The mayor, seeming to have forgotten to explain that portion of his story, answered robustly. "Elvin here," he said gesturing for the grim man to come closer. "He was just starting the embalming process on a body a few weeks ago when it suddenly jumped up from the table and bolted from the cellar. The man was one of the murder victims. Elvin tried to chase him, believing the man was hysterical. Waking up on an embalming table after a vicious attack when everyone believed you to be dead—well that would be enough to send anyone running off into the night." The mayor waited for a small laugh at his sarcasm. When it never came, he went on. "Elvin saw him run into the first cemetery."

Turning around to address Elvin from over her shoulder, Pastoria asked, "Were you able to see exactly where he went?"

The mortician shook his head no, but added, "My two boys were out there locking up the gates. That graveyard belongs to this place. We close the cemetery at night and lock it up tight. The boys saw him duck into a mausoleum. Figuring something wasn't right, my eldest boy took one of the gate chains and chained the mausoleum door shut so the feller couldn't get out till we could get the police out here. We come back up here to the office to call. By the time they got here, and we went out to the cemetery, the door had been busted right through from the other side. There was claw marks all over the place in there."

"Okay," Olympia sighed. "We need to clarify some things." She directed her comments to the mayor. "You said there were 16 people killed. But this man was one of them?"

"Yes. I know it sounds insane."

"It's not insane at all," Olympia replied. "But it skews the total. Mayor Broussard, how many of the 16 dead, were truly dead—eaten, I mean—or otherwise rendered impossible to rise back up again?"

It was clear he did not quite understand the question at first, but slowly it dawned upon him. "Oh, I see," he replied. "Of the 16, I'd say 14 of them were torn to pieces—and missing pieces too, I might add."

"That is important," Olympia nodded. "From this we can safely ascertain there are 14 victims we no longer have to worry about becoming wolves themselves. This leaves 8-10 werewolves to find before the moon becomes full again. I will need a list of every person in New Orleans who has gone missing within the last 90 days."

Broussard appeared shaken by the enormity of the task. "I'll see what I can do, Miss. New Orleans has people disappear more often than you would imagine."

"Oh, I bet I could!" Zelda chuckled. "Mister, I am a psychic, and I can just walk into a place and know stuff. You ain't just got a werewolf problem. You got vampires here. Voodoo shit out there. You even got a couple of Cat People roaming around. I'm surprised you still got enough citizens living to fill Jackson Square."

"Are you serious?" the mayor gasped. "You are pulling my leg? Not all those things exist?"

"Man!" Zelda cried. "You believe you got some werewolves, but you can't admit you got other monsters too? Lord have mercy. Don't worry none, Mayor. We will scrounge up all the evil we can and get rid of it for you."

Proving himself a fiscal politician, Mayor Broussard adjusted his tie before nervously asking, "Will that cost more? I paid your organization for the wolf problem. I don't think I can finagle any more money out of the budget for that other stuff. It was hard enough to disguise what I was using the already substantial funds for."

"Just go home," Olympia advised, almost laughing. "We have everything under control."

The mayor was only too happy to make his swift departure, not wanting to linger any longer in the dismal setting or be seen too long in the company of the witches he clandestinely hired to save his town. Olympia, Pastoria, and Zelda stood at the open gate of the cemetery, staring ahead at the endless pitches and rooflines of carved stone graves. Clutched in Pastoria's grip was a long duffle bag, full of things they might require.

"We are starting here?" Pastoria asked. "Not in town?"

"Oh yeah," Zelda chuckled. "They're here. I can feel 'em."

Olympia wrapped her fingers around the iron bars of the fence, looking deep down at the narrow lanes between the ghostly houses of resting places. "Werewolves typically stay in their packs. If the dead man rose and transformed, his imbued wolf instinct would have directed him where to find his pack. Basically, he could smell them. And this is where he ran to first."

"But he was only trying to escape being seen or caught," Pastoria replied. "Not necessarily looking for friends."

Olympia gave off a little sarcastic laugh as she gestured behind the fence. "Pastoria, if you were attempting to get away from someone would you run directly into a maze such as this? Too little room to run and maneuver?" Staring back through the iron bars, examining the ornate mausoleums, Olympia added softly, "Somewhere in this chasm of stone a pack of wolves are hiding."

The witches spent the better part of two hours searching the never- ending twists and turns of stone structures. None appeared to be damaged in any unreasonable way outside of natural erosion. Most of the mausoleums contained heavy steel doors, if they even had a point of entry at all. These weren't the types of structures people generally tried to get out of. Exactly what they hoped this search would turn up was something they assumed they'd see once they ran across it—such as a loose door or a hole in a mausoleum wall. As the sky darkened above the weary explorers, Olympia felt a little silly when she saw, without much effort, the obvious exit neither of them had considered.

"Well." Zelda stated rather plainly as her eyes spotted a half dozen wolves climbing out from the top of a rather large mausoleum, six rows away. "There they are."

Like ants evacuating a stirred- up anthill, the great beasts clawed out of a broken hole in the roofline and scattered in all directions. Some pounced onto the roofs of nearby structures, using them as a roadway to the cemetery wall where they could leap over. Some darted between the other gravesites, becoming lost amid the hedge of stone and crosses. Olympia threw her hands forward attempting to freeze the great animals in their place. She managed to stop two, but the others were too far from her magic radius.

Pastoria took care of the two immobilized wolves with a flick of her wrists, sending her power of telekinesis bounding towards them, snapping their necks and severing their spinal cords. Of course, being supernatural creatures, she couldn't trust this was enough, so she tossed Zelda her father's sword from the duffle bag. Zelda sprinted towards the fallen beasts with Constantinople's sword raised high over her shoulder. Giving each monster one clean swipe, she decapitated them as an additional precaution.

"Man, I never get tired of slicing heads off!" Zelda exclaimed, wiping the blade with a towel from the bag.

"Those others who escaped are probably halfway into The French Quarter by now." Olympia estimated. "You two drive back and try to track them."

With a raised eyebrow Pastoria asked her sister, "And what will you be doing while we hunt a pack of werewolves?"

Olympia pointed to the mausoleum where the pack had fled. "I'll be investigating their nest. There could be more in there."

Pastoria thought for a moment she should caution her sister not to face such a danger single-handed until she remembered Olympia never listened to anyone. Besides, Olympia could freeze them all rather easily which was more than Pastoria or Zelda would be able to do.

As her teammates headed towards the Quarter, Olympia looked around for something to use as a ladder to get on top of the stone structure. It only took her about three seconds to remember she knew how to levitate. It wasn't a power she ever needed much, therefore she often forgot she could do it. It was one of those little minor powers she had developed with her mother in the Magic Room as a child. She concentrated on condensing and solidifying the air under her feet until she began rising towards the roofline. She jumped into the hole the wolves had made and landed safely on the stone floor inside. The interior of the mausoleum was dark, much too dark to see very much except the stone casket in the center, highlighted by a thin stream of moonlight casting down from the hole in the roof. Enough light filled the tomb for her to see a second hole, this time in the floor. A faint flickering reddish light seeped up from what appeared to be stairs leading down. Olympia tread carefully down into the hole, noticing along her way it was more of a raised trap door than a hole the creatures had tunneled. Reaching the bottom did not take long, only about eight feet beneath the tomb above. She was now in a somewhat larger chamber strewn with old mattresses, pillows, and makeshift bedding. Two lighted kerosene lanterns hung on opposite walls. The place was empty otherwise. Or almost empty. Something caught her eye beside one of the dirty mattresses. A small, scattered assortment of photographs—each pinned to a particular article of clothing. One hat, one scarf, one shirt, and a sock. Each picture depicted a different person; a person who obviously belonged to the corresponding item of clothing. It became undeniably clear what was going on now.

If Pastoria and Zelda were worried about how to track the loose wolves roaming the streets of New Orleans, they needn't have been. A panic-stricken man streaked across the road, disappearing into an alley. "Well," Zelda snorted. "If he ran that way…I guess we should go the other way." They exited the car, immediately hearing the horrified screams coming from around the corner. Bounding towards the cries, Pastoria led the way with Zelda hard on her heels brandishing the sword again. Rounding the corner to the next street the witches found themselves outside of Lafitte's Blacksmith Shop, now a popular bar, where Zelda almost ran smack into one of the ferocious beasts. Startled by their near collision, Zelda jumped backwards in perfect time to evade the wolf's powerful jaws snapping at her. The surprise attack caused her to drop the sword just as the ravenous monster made another attempt on her. Already synchronized for defense, Pastoria foiled the strike by sending a green wired trash can sailing into him. Zelda scrambled to recover the sword. Grasping the handle from the ground, she brought it up in a diagonal swing, landing the blade right into the side of the giant wolf's throat. As the wolf's head flew several yards back, landing in front of Lafitte's. Instantly, the shriek of a man's cry rang out.

Standing with the toe of his oxford shoes directly inserted mid-step into the gushing opening of the animal's neck, stood a slender and meek looking man. His eyes met Zelda's as his mouth dropped open.

"Well, you sure turned the corner at the wrong time!" Zelda laughed. "You okay?"

The man, shaken and dazed, nodded his head slightly. His terrified eyes looked down at the animal head his foot was now thoroughly lodged in. His beleaguered attempt to speak was unsuccessful, too preoccupied by the head of a canine stuck to his foot. He began stomping his foot which only resulted in wedging the head further up his ankle. His widening eyes pleaded towards Zelda for assistance.

"Well, don't smash it in deeper!" she cried, kneeling to jerk the animal's head from his now gooey and bloody foot. The shoe came with the head, now implanted tightly into the wolf's neck.

When the man managed to break through his incapacitation enough to utter words, all he could get out was, "My shoe."

Zelda tossed the head, and the shoe, down the sidewalk. "Oh, I don't think you'll be wantin' that thing anymore."

Pastoria tapped her on the shoulder, exclaiming, "In case you've forgotten we have about four more of those things to hunt down!"

Offering the shellshocked fellow a playful wink, Zelda told him, "I tell you what. You go in this bar right here and have yourself a stiff one. I'll wrap this up and come back to check on you. You gonna be okay?"

The man nodded nervously again. Zelda gave him another wink and asked, "What's your name feller?"

"Fred."

"Alrighty, Fred. You go inside where you'll be safe. My name is Zelda. I'll come back and check on you in a bit."

As Fred stumbled cautiously, single shoed, into Lafitte's, Zelda smiled at Pastoria and said, "You know he's kinda cute."

The two witches tracked down the next wolf relatively easily as he had run directly in front of and collided with, a taxicab. As he attempted to limp away, Pastoria impaled him with the sword. The taxi driver, much to their surprise, simply rolled down his window and asked, "Werewolf?"

"Yep." Zelda answered.

"Thought so."

She and Pastoria chuckled to themselves as the driver casually drove away. Olympia caught up with them shortly after, explaining she had the answers to the mystery now. Tracking the others down was probably unnecessary as heavy cloud cover was moving in from the Gulf, obscuring the moon and its power over the wolves. "We'll get back to their nest and wipe them all out at once."

"Mind if you two take care of that alone?" Zelda asked her friends.

Pastoria let out a chuckle while Olympia looked at Zelda suspiciously, "Have something better to do tonight, Zel?"

Moving her hands through her hair, primping it as best she could without a mirror handy, Zelda replied. "Matter of fact, I think I do. I'll see ya'll back at the hotel."

As Zelda rushed off down an avenue headed back towards Lafitte, Olympia gave her sister a puzzled look. Pastoria clasped Olympia's hand and laughed, "I think

Zelda fell in love tonight."

Back at the cemetery things went much as Olympia expected they would. The remaining wolves indeed fled back to the safety of their underground shelter where Olympia was waiting. With a simple burst of her magic, she immobilized all of them. When Olympia came back up the little staircase in the floor of the tomb, Pastoria was waiting with a lighted torch.

"Did you empty those kerosene lanterns on them?" she asked.

"As a matter of fact, I did." Olympia smiled.

Pastoria waved her hand towards the opening in the floor and sang out, "Nighty night." She tossed the torch into the hole as Olympia slammed the trap door shut. With the gruesome beasts still rendered motionless by Olympia's spell, no cries of agony rang out from below, however the smell was rather rank. The Blanchard sisters crawled back out of the roof of the mausoleum and marched towards the mortuary.

Mayor Broussard was waiting for them on the porch just as they'd asked him to when they telephoned half an hour earlier. As requested, the mayor had two armed patrolmen with him. Elvin, the creepy mortician was taken by complete surprise when the armed policeman placed him in handcuffs. Broussard flipped through the photographs Olympia recovered from the crypt and shook his head.

"Yessiree, every one of these folks has some kind of ongoing feud with our Elvin here." The mayor informed the Blanchard sisters. "Dawson Bowles foreclosed on his house. Mary Peters, well, she wasn't interested in his advances—if you know what I mean. This guy in this picture, I believe that's Nelson Carter. Elvin, didn't he sell you that pickup truck that fell apart a month later?"

Pastoria smirked, "A mortician with a grudge making deals with werewolves. Trading a place to hide in exchange for revenge on his enemies. Now that takes the cake."

"Yeah, I guess old Elvin here has a lot of explaining to do and a lot of time in jail to do it." Broussard sneered. "You ladies sure you got all the monsters? Not any others left behind we gotta watch out for?"

Olympia smiled and reached her hand out to shake, "We got all the monsters we were hired to get Mr. Mayor. But this is New Orleans. I am afraid you have no shortage of creatures here. Call us again if any get too far out of hand."

CHAPTER FORTY-SIX

The Family We Choose

As the months passed, things around Blanchard House seemed about as typical and commonplace as any other household in Alabama. With the new kitchen addition completed, Olympia and Pastoria had their own hidden secret room to house all their paraphernalia, weapons, spell books, potions, and charms. John never had to encounter anything which wasn't absolutely normal in the house. Another benefit to the addition he had not predicted was its effect on Olympia. Having a big new kitchen, complete with all the latest modern appliances, awakened some new wifely enthusiasm in her. It had become her favorite room in the house. If ever John suggested they dine in town, Olympia was quick to shoot down the idea, detailing another elaborate meal she planned to make. She became an excellent cook. John's waistline was testimony to that. Moreover, she was becoming quite the socialite. At least twice a month a gaggle of committee ladies descended upon the house where Olympia dazzled them with her hosting abilities. Of course, John insisted on redecorating the living room to a more suitable style. *Suitable* to John meant understated...conservative. *Suitable* to Olympia and Pastoria meant boring. However, Olympia put up no fight to keep her loud décor. If truth was told, she was a little sick of all the psychedelic patterns herself. With Olympia's committee meetings came an influx of visitors to Blanchard House, something which had never happened before. Olympia was making connections to the more elite wives of Daihmler offering the Windhams entrance into branches of society reaching further than their own little town. John was learning Olympia was quite an asset to him at parties and business functions. She knew how to charm any man in her radius while never arousing too much jealousy from their wives. It was this brand of wifely expertise which propelled John Windham up the ranks in the law firm, making Partner with little effort. Every man of means seemed to want John Windham representing them.

Once or twice, John questioned her on whether she was using magic to build his career. He was always half-kidding when he asked, but only half. Each time she would shine her bright smile and say, "I do not require magic to charm a man, Husband. Men will do virtually anything if a stunning woman is involved."

For all his wife's personal growth, her arrogance never faded. It was one of the traits he loved most. "You, being the woman in question?" he teased.

"Who else?" she answered. "Face it, John, your associates are usually in their 50's, overweight, astonishingly unintelligent considering the positions they hold. Their wives aren't much better. When given the opportunity to spend an evening across a table from me—hanging on their every tiresome word as if they are Socrates—is all it takes."

The Windhams were the "it" couple in Alabama these days. Dashing John and gorgeous Olympia found themselves with full calendars year-round. However, no matter what invitations came, how prestigious the client, or how much trouble it was to maintain, Olympia always kept one night perpetually open, and fiercely protected it. Friday night supper at home was a non-negotiable factor. Friday nights were spent at Blanchard House with family and nothing was important enough to change it. John was not always pleased with the arrangement, suggesting the dinners could be moved to other nights when needed, but she always refused. Friday was in stone and would be until the day after she died. John gave up the fight.

Every Friday Nate Caldwell came to dinner, bringing with him baby Howard. Pastoria made certain to never have a date on Friday, or if she did it was understood the date would be a dinner guest at the family table. Zelda was no longer coming alone to Friday dinners. Fred Henry was a frequent companion and a welcome addition to Olympia's little clan. Since that unforgettable night in New Orleans, Fred was devoted to Zelda. A district manager for a chain of shoe stores, he had been in The Big Easy for a wholesale convention on the latest in European styles. It would be his first and last trip to New Orleans. He traded his old regional territory to be assigned to the Birmingham, Tuscaloosa, Huntsville, Montgomery area. He was now always within a two-hour drive from his sweetheart. Changes were in the air for practically everyone. Even Pastoria had taken a job in town at a dress shop while going to college three days a week. It was Olympia, however, who was changing the most. It was not only her power to beguile business acquaintances, or her transformation into the perfect housewife, a mothering instinct was creeping in.

Whenever baby Howard was in the house, John could see a side of his wife he hadn't before thought existed. She doted on the baby, barely allowing anyone else to hold him, feed him, or change him while she was around. She often kept Howard for Nate whenever his normal nanny—which she paid for—was sick or taking a day off. When John watched his wife with Howard, he longed for a child of their own. One night after Friday Supper, when everyone had gone, he broached the subject.

They were upstairs in their bedroom, readying themselves for sleep. John stepped from the bathroom, teeth freshly brushed, to find his wife removing some of Howard's blankets and stuffed toys from the bed where he'd been napping earlier. Absorbed in her thoughts, she was unaware John was there as she placed Howard's things in the chair by the window, all except the stuffed bear. John watched her holding it to her chest as she gazed dreamily out the window. He quietly admired her beauty as she stood at the window, bathed in moonlight. Her hip-length silk lavender nightgown complimented her soft alabaster skin. Feeling slightly intrusive watching her this way, he was about to say something when she began to hold the bear in her arms as she always held Howard, cradling the bear like a baby. John suddenly felt a pang of resentment he was not proud to be feeling. He cleared his throat, registering his presence. Olympia turned around, appearing a little embarrassed to be caught with the bear. Tossing it to the chair, she forced a smile.

"I'd like a child of our own, Olympia." He did not mean to be so blunt. The words erupted from some place of longing he had been managing to hold at bay. It was out now, his truth unmasked and laying bare in the open.

Glancing at him strangely, she replied with a touch of humor in her reminder, "Darling John, we are going to have three. You already know that."

"Yes, Olympia but when? I am ready to be a father now. Don't you want a baby of your own?"

Repositioning her hair behind her shoulders, she gave off an unwarranted laugh. He did not understand what was so amusing about his question. He watched her stroll to the bed where she lifted a small square decorative pillow. Playfully, she tucked the pillow underneath her gown. "Are you saying you won't mind it when my stomach pokes out this way?"

John grinned and said, "I don't think you could be more beautiful if it did."

Removing the pillow, tossing it aside, she huffed, "Remember you said that." He wasn't sure he understood what she was implying until her lips parted into a broad smile. "I am already pregnant John. Two months I believe. You will have that child before the year is out."

Sweeping her into his arms, John Windham smeared her neck with kisses. "It'll be a boy!" he exclaimed. "The first one will be a boy. Then we will have a girl next. Then a tie breaker!"

She nudged his chin from her throat, so his eyes aligned with hers. "I know you like to pretend we are ignorant about the future, John. This baby is a girl. So is the next one. And the one after that."

A flicker of disappointment crossed his face, but it was as fleeting as a blink. Quickly, he righted himself, replacing any regret with genuine joy. Lifting his wife into the air he shouted, "Who cares! Three girls, ten girls, it doesn't matter! We are having a baby!"

Her laughter rang out as he twirled her in his arms. This was to be a new chapter for them, and although it was not totally unknown—not exactly a mystery—she could feel he was making his peace with it. Most couples begin with a blank canvas which they paint together as the years go by. Olympia and John did not get that experience, seeing the canvas fully painted well before even beginning to lift a brush. Not everyone gets the opportunity to see the canvas blank before the artist begins painting. Because of Beryl's appearance in their lives, they already knew what the finished work would look like, but that didn't mean they could not enjoy the process.

CHAPTER FORTY-SEVEN

Bloody Sunday

The world seemed to be changing month by month and in ways which kept everyone on an uneasy footing. Gone were the innocent days when it felt like nothing earth shattering ever happened, or perhaps Olympia had been too young or too self-involved to notice. She found herself noticing a great deal now. Over the last few months, the newspapers consumed her with reports of the goings on of the world. Nelson Mandela had been sentenced to life in prison in South Africa. Olympia wasn't exactly sure who he was, but the news made it sound as if he was important. In Singapore, the Chinese and the Malays were rioting against each other. Vietnam was in full swing, sparking protests all over America. Hundreds of students were arrested at Berkeley, while Martin Luther King, Jr. was awarded the Nobel Peace Prize. But the things happening in Alabama were the primary concern to Olympia. Suddenly Alabama was awash in controversy over Civil Rights. Marches, boycotts, and much too common police retaliation saturated the news.

Olympia heard of plans being made to organize a march from the city of Selma to Alabama's capital Montgomery to register black voters. Though the right to vote was granted to black people the prior year, the south was entrenched in schemes, loopholes, and acts of downright intimidation to keep colored people from voting. Many lived in abject fear if they tried.

"I want to go with them," Olympia told her husband.

"Absolutely not!"

"I am not asking," she replied sternly.

Grasping his petulant wife by the arms, John pled for her not to get involved. "This has nothing to do with us, Olympia. It's for coloreds to figure out. It is their fight, leave them to fight it."

"That is like asking David to go up against Goliath!" she bellowed. "Wait, bad example. But you know what I mean."

"No, it is a perfect example," John declared. "Sometimes the Davids win. Let them try. But you, Olympia, are a privileged white woman with nothing at stake here. You are pregnant with our child. Are you willing to risk our baby for this?"

"It is a peaceful march, John. I'm not walking into war."

John rolled his eyes at her innocence. "Peaceful, huh?" he sighed. "Like that peaceful sit-in in Marion a few weeks ago. The police came in on those peaceful protestors and beat the living hell out of them, Olympia. One colored man died!"

"John, I am fully capable of protecting myself. If I can stop a horde of vampires or werewolves, a few angry racists have no chance against me."

As was usually the case, Olympia refused to back down from her beliefs. She wanted to be part of the march, to show her support for a group of people she, regrettably, never considered until recently. Whenever she thought about what these people had to go through just to exercise their very right to participate in the American experience, saddened her. Over the last months she'd read as much as could on the history of blacks in America, slavery, emancipation, Jim Crow, everything she could find at the library. Colored people had already endured more suffering than humanly imaginable just to win their rights to be citizens, and even now those rights were being treated as if they meant nothing at all. It was something Olympia felt deeply passionate about. She knew what it was like to live on the fringe of society, never fully accepted. And as awful as her childhood had been regarding society, it could not begin to compare. John continued to argue of the potential danger involved with the march to Montgomery, but he only strengthened her adamancy, citing if she were there, she could stop any violence if things grew out of hand. Knowing he could not stop her; he decided to go with her. She argued it was not necessary but he was absolute in his insistence.

John drove to Selma with Fred at his side and their three stubborn women in the backseat. A palpable mix of anticipation and exhilaration rode along with them. Once they rolled into Selma, there was no confusion as to whether they were in the right place or not. The roads were clogged with an impressive number of parked vehicles. Cars and trucks filled every available lot, every inch of streetside parking, and the rest lined the roadside shoulders of Highway 80. It was a testament to the solidarity of the cause. John left the car in a makeshift parking lot in a field where dozens of others had parked. John and Fred led the way with their women on foot to the asphalt highway where a sea of people was congealing together. John and Fred admitted to their wives they were impressed by the turnout. It was a sight to behold, an overwhelming wave of unity converging together from all walks of life. John was surprised to see many whites had come to march as well. He had not expected that. Men and woman, of all ages and backgrounds stood shoulder to shoulder, forming a collective front in the fight for what they passionately believed to be right.

"Hell, we are way at the back of this line." Zelda commented as they neared the army of protesters. "I told you men we should'a left an hour earlier."

Fred sent his wife a snide glare and reminded her, "Zelda, you are the one who wanted to stop at Stuckey's for pecans." Unable to argue his point, Zelda shrugged it off.

"Look, there are more people moving in behind us," Pastoria noted. "I don't think we are too late, and the line is moving, so I guess that means we are marching now." She was excited at first, then asked her brother-in-law, "John, how far is it to Montgomery anyway?"

Almost in an *I told you so* way, John answered, "Roughly 50 miles."

"50 miles!"

"It'll take days," Fred chimed in. "But you gals wanted to come. So, we are here."

Olympia pretended the distance was not unknown to her even though her mind was screaming at herself for choosing fashionable shoes over comfortable ones. The five of them continued walking, merging with others along the way. The numbers swelled greater and greater as they proceeded. At first it seemed like a rather joyous occasion. Marchers linked arms and sang songs in unison. Men and women, black and white, held onto one another in brotherhood and sisterhood, all one family of human beings. People made conversation with their neighbors walking beside them, everyone learning a little about everyone else's story. An air of hope was arising as if a new and equal world was dawning before them, or because of them. But that lofty dream was abruptly ended.

As the throngs of marchers approached the edge of The Edmund Pettus Bridge, none of them expected the ruthless opposition ready to confront them. Unbeknownst to the joyful and peaceful demonstrators, the county sheriff had prepared to stop them. Issuing an order, the day before, to all white men in the county over the age of 21 to join his unit as deputies, Alabama law enforcement charged forward. State troopers, horse mounted forces, and county officers began their push back on the marchers over the bridge.

It took a few minutes for the Blanchards to understand what was going on. Tucked near the back of the procession, blocked by a sea of bodies before them, their view of what was happening was obscured. The wail of screams coming from the head of the line, as well as the firing of gunshots, and cracks of whips soon told them this was indeed a battleground after all. Ignited cannisters of tear gas sent toxic gray smoke drifting overhead. In the distance, the sound of horse hooves, from not yet visible riders, stampeded through the crowd, trampling anyone in its way.

"What is happening?" Pastoria shrieked as John snatched her by the arm, dragging her backwards to safety. He had his wife by the other hand and was retreating as fast as his legs could move through the chaos of frightened people in retreat. Fred was right behind them ushering Zelda back.

Olympia could feel herself being dragged from the scene by her husband, but her mind fled her immediate circumstance for a moment, as her father's words flooded her mind. "Battle, my daughters, comes to pass when two sides feel so strongly for their cause that both are willing to die for it. Your adversaries will be as motivated and as assured in their rightness as you." Her father saw many battles in his lifetime. European villages plagued by ravenous wolves on the hunt, townships locked down in terror of hording vampires stalking the night roads, Rain People draining dry the lands and flesh of southern France. The teachings of Olympia's father rang through her head as if he were there with them now, seeing this injustice for himself. "When both sides have absolute faith in their cause, the victory is never fully won. Your adversary may be stopped, but if there are others of a like mind, the war continues."

Snapping back to her present situation, Olympia broke free of her husband's grip. Her feet turn direction dashing to a nearby car parked on the road's shoulder. She scrambled up the hood to the top of the cab for a better vantage point where she could see the tumultuous interactions at the front of the bridge. Heart thumping in her chest, she witnessed the brutality taking place up ahead. "We must do something!" she exclaimed. "They are beating them with batons and spraying them with gas!"

Pastoria crawled onto the car, with an assist from her sister's hand, so that she could see the spectacle playing out. The acrid stench of gas assailed the senses while screams reached peak levels. As the chaos intensified, three mounted officers came charging at the panicked crowd, their powerful horses bulldozing through the masses. While some people were knocked to the ground, others were hit with such brute force they were sent airborne before smashing down onto unforgiving pavement. The ground beneath the stampede of horses and frightened demonstrators was marred by blood from ripped wounds and trampled bodies. Amid the pandemonium, one of the officers on horseback galloped towards the sisters, his raised baton poised to sweep their legs, toppling them to the ground.

Pastoria swept her hand out towards the attacking patrol man. Both he and the horse started to tumble backwards into a merciless roll. Thinking fast, Olympia blasted her freezing power at the horse, saving it from a crippling fall. She let momentum take its toll on the cop, allowing him to crash shoulder-first into a concrete barrier. While Pastoria straightened the horse's legs telekinetically, Olympia raised her arms emitting a force greater than any she manifested before, except perhaps on her honeymoon when she tried to stop Niagara Falls. A tidal wave of the witch's power cast over the crowd like Neptune's fury, freezing everything in place as far as the eye could see. Silence settled over the scene. A solitary horse hung in the air, mid gallop, as if held in place by invisible wires. Gunshots, freshly fired, lingered in the air inches from the guns firing them. Tear gas, dropped like war bombs, no longer sprayed their hostile vapor while the toxin already unleashed now hovered unmoving in the air. The running masses of terrorized people, mouths still open mid scream, were paused in place along with their egregious tormentors. Olympia scanned the demonstrators' traumatized faces as well as those of the hate twisted bigots. It all now seemed more like a grotesque art installation conveying the horrors of war.

Hopping from the car, Olympia quickly unfroze her family. John and Fred both stood flabbergasted at the amazing sight before them. "I told you I could stop danger if it broke out," Olympia smiled proudly to her husband. "Now let's get these poor people out of harm's way."

Pastoria looked at Zelda, unsure how to do it. There were hundreds of people. How were they supposed to save the day? Should they start with the ones in immediate danger of bullets? Would Olympia's magic hold long enough to help everybody? It was John who settled the matter. Breaking from his awe of what his wife had done, he cupped his hands around her delicate face. "My Darling, we must leave here now. You cannot do anything to help these people."

Her cheeks reddening with outrage, she pulled from his grasp. "I cannot believe you are saying this, John! You see what these maniacs are doing to these poor people. They were doing no harm. They were committing no crimes."

"I know." John said softly. "But I am afraid witchly heroics cannot help here today. It is time to go home Olympia."

Shaking her head furiously as she gestured to the bloodshed encompassing them, she cried, "Some of these people may die today, John!"

John sighed, looking again at the already tragic sight and knowing more was to come. The figurative powder keg had only just exploded, it had yet to reach its pinnacle. "Some of them may, Olympia. "Yet we are leaving nonetheless."

Fred approached them. As he began to speak, Zelda was behind his shoulder, nodding in agreement with what he had to say. "Olympia," Fred began. "It was a noble idea. But don't you see, this isn't a fight you belong in. It's their victory or their defeat. A human one, either way."

Olympia paced frantically back and forth, "You three just don't understand. This is what we witches are here for. To protect those who can't protect themselves. If you don't want to help me, I will do it alone. I will help these defenseless people."

With a sterner approach to his wife, John raised his voice almost as if he were the one outraged. "By robbing them of their great battle? No, Olympia. It is not your place. You cannot just cast a spell and make things better for the disadvantaged. Real change comes with sacrifice and dedication. Do not steal this moment from those who have bravely devoted their lives to its cause."

The words stung. *Those who have devoted their lives.* She knew he was right as much as she wished it weren't true. It might very well have been her father saying it. John's words were not unlike what her father once explained about battles and the causes behind them. When both sides feel they are right...even if one side wins, it doesn't change the enemy's resolve. Olympia understood what John meant now. The real heroes are the ones willing to take the mortal risks with everything to lose. Win or fail, nothing truly can change until the world witnesses them try. Only then can those who were wrong understand the passion of those they stood against.

Placing her empathetic hand onto Olympia's shoulder, Zelda pointed down the road in the distance. "There are news cameras here. All this is gonna be seen by ever'body in the country. Maybe the world. If we fix it...if we move all these people to safety, ain't nothing gonna change for them. Folks gotta see what they are doing to people down here. The fellas are right. We ain't got no business here trying to fix it for them."

They hurried back to the car and sped away into the distance as Olympia released her hold over the riot. She could hear the cries resume behind them, along with the gunfire, as John raced down the empty highway towards home. Painful as it was to witness the events that day, Olympia realized how wrong she was to try to interfere. She had no right to meddle in the birth of a revolution.

CHAPTER FORTY-EIGHT

Olympia Integrates the Consort

After the events which unfolded in Selma back in March, Olympia gave up on entering any real protests within the black community, resigning herself to making whatever small strides she could within a community she could persuade. Olympia planned to integrate The Witches Association.

Coming up with her plan was the easy part. Finding African American witches within surrounding communities proved a little more daunting. For white skinned witches, Consort events were all one needed to meet their own kind. The formation of Witches Association a generation ago was for that very purpose. For years, witches had easy access to their brethren in times of need. However, the founding witches—her father included—never considered the witch line could extend to other races. It had been a short-sighted prejudice, although she could fault them for following the morays of their era. Discovering witches of black descent was like trying to cook a meal without any groceries. Luckily for Olympia, she had Zelda. Though Zelda's power of second sight was often considered a lesser gift in the witching community when compared with more active abilities such as Olympia and Pastoria's powers, without Zelda's abilities, Olympia could have never implemented her plan.

Zelda expelled a considerable amount of psychic channeling over the coming weeks to zone in on nearby witches' energy fields. Once she circled the locations on a map, it was up to Olympia and Pastoria to weed out who they knew to be white. That part wasn't too stressful. The addresses often told the story for them. Whites lived in certain areas and blacks lived in others. And most of the white witches were Association members already, so identifying names helped cross them off the list. As for the witches of color, Olympia searched through various town phone books until she uncovered who she was seeking out. She then made a drive out to the various townships hoping to persuade them to join her for the next Consort meeting. Most did not even know there was such a gathering where witches came together quarterly to commune. Of the twenty-six witches of color, she discovered residing in Alabama, only eleven agreed. John was not too pleased about having to buy eleven bus tickets departing from eight different cities to get everyone to Mount Dora, Florida for the next meeting—but he gave in eventually.

The site chosen for the season's Consort was a spectacular Queen Anne house owned by the Archer witches. The Archer family was well respected in the Association; newer money than others, but these days who wasn't? Daryl Archer was a highly sought after architect with a heart to match his sizeable talent. The Archer house was the crown jewel of the county. Painted a crisp white, much like Blanchard House, the Archer home boasted a multitude of stained-glass casement windows and dormers, several balconies on all three levels, and a wraparound veranda. Tongues were wagging throughout the Association when the location for the meeting was announced. People had longed to see the house.

Olympia knew of course, she could not very well show up to someone's home, let alone a community meeting, with eleven strange black people. Witches were still people, and segregation was still as much a part of the south as it had ever been. For her plan to work it would require the Archer's to be gracious enough, and open-minded enough, to welcome the eleven strangers to their home. Olympia wrote Mr. Archer a five-page letter explaining her endeavor and the convictions behind it, then she waited a week for his response. Tearing open the envelope when his note arrived, Olympia was elated to discover the Archer family to be as liberally minded as she. Archer applauded her daringness, pledging his full support. Out of courtesy, she decided she should forewarn the King, to preempt any initial outrage and allow him time to let the idea settle in. Not knowing King Meade personally, she wished Bedwyr were still in charge. The new king of witches was not so open-minded as Mr. Archer, but he agreed to let Consort members make the ultimate decision of membership by vote.

Olympia and Zelda arrived at the Consort purposely late to ensure the socialization part of the evening would be concluded and the business portion commencing. Every curious head turned from their seat to stare upon Olympia Blanchard as she entered the illustrious mansion with eleven colored men and women following behind her.

Rising rather animatedly from his seat at the Council table, Marvin Copeland exclaimed tersely, "What is the meaning of this Miss Blanchard?"

She noticed right away how Bristow Uding hung his head, pressing his palms to his bristly cheeks. His reaction was one of disapproval tinged with a bit of *leave it to Olympia to do this.* From the third row of the congregation, Olympia saw his son Brimford staring at her, trying not to smile. Brimford, one of her Generation, enjoyed her tenacious spirit. Hugh D'Angelo was grimacing from the eighth row with searing condemnation. The way he covered his mouth with his handkerchief made her wonder if he was becoming physically ill from his revulsion.

"Ain't you ever seen black people before?" Zelda shouted out at him over the crowd.

Patting her arm, in appreciation and to shush her up, Olympia called out over the Consort members, "I would like to introduce some new friends to you."

A woman Olympia had seen at Consorts before, but wasn't familiar with, stood up clutching her arms to her chest. She appeared to even be shaking. In a quivery voice, she declared, "I demand this woman be removed from this meeting and exiled from our society! She has put us all in mortal danger here tonight."

Unable to stifle a laugh at the unreasonably petrified woman, Olympia replied, "How have I endangered anyone? Do you believe black Americans are out to harm you?"

"We are witches!" the woman cried. "It is against our laws to reveal our community to non-witches."

Strolling the aisle to be closer to her accuser, Olympia said, "What gives you cause to assume my friends are not witches?"

"Well, for one thing," Marvin Copeland started to say until his chronic cough stopped him.

"There are no negro witches." Hugh asserted haughtily.

"Is that so?" Olympia smiled. "What on earth has led any of us to believe such nonsense? I'll admit, I was just as guilty of the assumption once. It never occurred to me there could be witches of other races. But of course, there are. And I have found a few of them."

Hugh D'Angelo slammed his hand down onto the back of his chair with brutish weight. "Voodoo worshiping animals. That is what you have found Olympia. Voodoo priests and priestesses."

Fired up by the inference, Zelda spat at the floor and cried, "You think I ain't smart enough to know the difference between a witch's aura and a practice of voodoo!"

She then realized in her indignation, she had just spit on the Archer's lovely floor.

Hugh narrowed his eyes menacingly at Zelda before directing his response more to the congregation than she herself. "I come from the swamplands and marshes of South Carolina. Voodoo is as common as She-Crab soup. I know one when I see one. Or eleven in this case. They are not the same as us."

"I agree," Olympia smirked. "My new friends are a good deal nicer than you are Mr. D'Angelo."

"When it comes to a witch's energy and aura," Zelda shouted for all to hear. "You don't know half as much as I've forgotten, Hugh. These people are witches. They are southerners. They are powerful. I don't see no reason why they shouldn't be able to join this Association."

Seizing the moment Zelda presented her, Olympia addressed the congregated members again. "I would like for you to meet our potential new brothers and sisters: Minnie Richardson, Minerva Carpenter, Garrison March, Henry Cuspins, Lola Cuspins, Ora Danner—"

Once again, Hugh D'Angelo displayed his refusal to consider the situation. "You are disrupting this meeting, Olympia! You are also casting grave insult upon all gathered here tonight. As a lifelong member of this Consort, I demand all of you leave at once."

From somewhere along the second row of seats, a voice perked up, "Um, last I checked, this is my house," Daryl Archer reminded Hugh. "Miss Blanchard sought my permission days ago to bring her guests tonight. Furthermore, she confided her wishes to nominate them for Consort membership. I fully extended my support on both."

It did not take long before the assembly of witches reached a full-fledged verbal war with one another. Some saw no harm in hearing Olympia out while others allowed their bias to keep their minds fully sealed shut. It was only when the King called everyone to silence that the house fell quiet. He was about to make a statement of his own when stalwartly Bristow Uding stood up from the Council table. "I admit this is all highly unusual for these proceedings. However, nothing will be solved by turning against our fellow witches. I say we allow Olympia to plead her case. Afterward, I invite any dissident opinions to be heard. No harm has ever come from simple consideration." After Uding's statement the King knew he could not justify refusing the request now without looking like a total ass, so he allowed the discussion, declaring an immediate vote to follow after.

Olympia began her recitation, walking the aisles between the chairs of Consort members to be heard, *and felt*, while making her case. She described an array of cruel injustices she had seen committed against human beings simply because their skin was not white. She resurrected European witch history of how their own kind was once persecuted in much the same manner. She reminded everyone in attendance of a witch's vow to help the least of their fellow man throughout the world. With passion, unlike her friends had ever seen her display before, she referenced a witch's duty to stand against evil and spread light into the dark places. Olympia made parallels between those who stand against Civil Rights with the evils of the world witches have long fought to eradicate. When she was finished, several opposing voices addressed the room, yet their numbers appeared to be fewer than before she spoke. Those unwilling to confront their own prejudices but emboldened enough to argue their case, did so far less eloquently than Olympia. With little else but a flimsy pretense of upholding tradition, nothing they put forth was credible. Their argument being so weak, in fact, that some who had been among the opposition switched sides upon hearing the ignorance aloud.

Bristow Uding surprised Olympia, his son Brimford, and himself as he stood to give his two cents worth on the matter. Echoing America's forefathers in the affirmation of every person's right to life, liberty, and equality he advocated for change...evolvement as he put it.

The final voice to speak came from one of the very people the debate was about. The elderly Minerva Carpenter, stood at the back of the room where she and her fellow blacks had remained through the entire ruckus, and she addressed the whole of the Consort. "I have huddled inside the cabinet under my kitchen sink while white men have ransacked my house." Her opening words silenced the room and garnered everyone's attention. "Do you all know what it is like to have bricks come through your window while somebody shouts *nigger* from the very front yard you own? I ain't talkin' about some yard some landlord owns I pay rent to. I mean my own yard. The yard of the house I brought my children up in. The yard me and my husband worked day and night to pay for. Land I pay my taxes on, same as you, every single year. Those men stood in *my yard* and called me nigger."

A hush had covered the room from the moment Minerva began to speak. If it was broken now, it was only by a gasp or a sigh or an overly amplified heart beat stirred by the emotion in her words. "I didn't know what they wanted," she went on. "I hid away under the sink, hoping they'd go away, thinking me not home. They broke down my door and stormed my house, screaming out for my grandson. He wasn't there. Hadn't come home yet." She looked directly into the eyes of those closest to her. "My daughter was a witch. Got cancer. Died two years after she had her boy. Her husband was not one of us, but he was a good man. Worked as a porter. Died in Korea. Fighting for his country. Fighting for all of you."

Minerva stopped for a moment; perhaps overcome by painful memories she had long shut out. Her aged black face was shining from a mixture of perspiration and tear stains. The man beside her, another colored person, pulled a handkerchief from his coat pocket for her to wipe her tears.

"Please continue, Mrs. Carpenter." Daryl Archer asked from his seat.

Minerva realized now she had the undivided attention of the room. All eyes fell on her as they waited to hear the rest of her tale. "I stayed under that sink. I just prayed they'd leave. Prayed my grandson wouldn't come home while they was there. I held my breath, scared they'd hear it. Only time I breathed was when I heard them break something of mine, hoping the noise would cover my gasp for air. Those men smashed up my belongings. Broke up my bed, my table, and the only two chairs I owned. They took my money from the jar I keep under my mattress. They even threw my Bible in the coal burner. I got just three rooms to my little house. It was real clear wasn't nobody home. 'Cept me, hiding under the sink."

Zelda stepped closer to Minerva and placed her arm around the shivering woman's waist. "Tell 'em the rest Miss Minerva."

Nodding in compliance, the old woman finished her sad story. "They finally left. I crawled out of the cupboard and saw what they did to my house. Clothes tore up. Money gone. Food from the stove all over the floor." She swallowed hard, pushing down the saline drainage from her nostrils. It tasted bitter. With her head raised a little higher than it was before, she finished her difficult tale. "Ya'll know why they were looking for my grandson? Want to know why I ain't never seen him again since he left for work that morning? Cause he didn't tip his hat to those men when he walked by the store step they were sitting on. Ain't nobody ever found his body, but I know they killed him."

The empathy for the poor woman's tragedy was drenching the room. No eye was saved from tears as this fragile and haunted woman poured her pain out for them to witness. Perhaps one man was dried eyed. Hugh D'Angelo had listened respectfully but unmoved by anything he heard. However, he was still a well-brought-up enough man to disguise his ambivalence in gentle fashion. "I am certain I am not alone in my profound sympathy for your harsh circumstances, Mrs. Carpenter. However, I do not see how your rather long, albeit touching story has any bearing on why we should admit your kind into our venerable Association."

As if considering his statement a challenge, Minerva answered Hugh, and shut down his arrogance. "Because I got the power in me to cause anybody I want to go blind, or get sick, or just die if I want them to. Right now, I could cast a sickness on you and ain't nobody else's magic gonna rid you of it. But ya'll know what? I ain't never used that gift a single day in my life except to give the animals we raised for food, a peaceful end. Never used my power on a human being. And I didn't use it on those men neither. Those men who tore my house apart and killed my only living relation. I did not use it to avenge him." She glanced around the room at the shocked faces looking back at her. "And you folks sit here *scared of me*. Scared cause I don't look like you. None of you have ever had to walk in my footsteps or feel the kind of hate and fear anybody who looks like me feels every day of their lives. Thought if ya'll knew me and these other black folks with me were like you, we might finally know what it feels like to feel safe. To have some white folks look at us like there ain't nothing wrong with us. We are you. Just darker. I ain't never seen anybody build another stable for a black horse just cause he don't look like the white one that was there already."

Zelda was crying her eyes out after Minerva's speech. Olympia faced the Consort, asking for a vote. Eleven black witches became members of the Southeastern Witches Association that night in a vote of 96-24. It was also the last time Hugh D'Angelo was ever in attendance at a Consort meeting.

CHAPTER FORTY-NINE

Daddy's Little Witch

Artemis Blanchard was born at home, upstairs in Olympia and John's bedroom, delivered by Zelda and Pastoria. All through the labor, John paced back and forth down the path from the house, past the chicken coops, past the grapevines, all the way through the apple grove. It was only when he heard Zelda yelling from the second-floor window that his daughter was born, did he bolt back to the house. Tired and mildly cranky after such a lengthy delivery, Olympia was in no mood for his outpour of sentiment when he rushed to her bedside. It didn't matter much because the moment Pastoria placed the baby in his arms, he forgot about his wife, all-consumed by his daughter.

Olympia observed his face looking at the perfect baby in his arms. Never once since she'd known John Windham had she ever heard from his lips the silly, baby-talk he was now speaking to their little girl. He ushered the child around presenting her to Pastoria and Zelda, as if she were the next monarch born into the line of succession. "You know we have seen her," Pastoria teased. "We are the ladies who brought her into the world."

"I know, I know," John grinned, "But have you ever seen a more perfect baby in your life!"

"Don't worry about me, John." Olympia cajoled from the bed. "I am doing just fine. No need to ask."

Her husband frowned, immediately moving to her bedside. "I'm sorry, my darling. I am glad you are all right. Truly. It is just that our daughter—she's perfect! What should we name her?"

Pastoria let out a giggle from the chair she was resting in. "She's already named, John. Remember? Her name is Artemis."

"I don't like that name," he replied to his sister-in-law. His eyes seemed to be urging her to back him up. "Let's call her Patricia."

With a sudden forward rocking motion to propel her up from her seat, Pastoria waved a military salute on her way out of the door, suggesting, "You try to explain that to your wife."

John did not win the two-day argument over the baby's name. Olympia was against the name change, arguing she had been calling the baby Artemis, since she discovered she was pregnant. She was accustomed to it now. Zelda made the case that it would be toying with Fate to alter the course of history since they knew what the girl's name is supposed to be. Pastoria didn't care one way or the other and said so. She was happy to have a niece no matter what her name became. John let the matter go although he did wonder from time to time, who actually named their baby? Was it Olympia or was it Beryl? The answer was too muddied by the all-too-established future for his average mind to reason. John resigned himself to the name. There might be confusion as to how it was come by, but there was no question in his mind Artemis Blanchard Windham was his pride and joy.

While most of his male contemporaries shirked baby duties, relegating responsibility to their wives or maids, John Windham jumped into fatherhood at full steam. Other men may have drawn the line of their parenting responsibility at being the breadwinner, but John was an engaged and involved dad. He spent weeks impatiently awaiting when Olympia declared it was alright for him to take the baby into town. It soon became a normal sight along the sidewalks of Daihmler to see John Windham pushing his daughter's carriage up and down Main Street on Saturday mornings. People found his devotion to his daughter endearing. He was known to stop for anyone who desired marveling at her. In the beginning most conversations revolved around the oddity of her name. However, John's reply, "My wife loves mythology," was received well. The length of time he spent in town varied week to week depending upon who else was there that morning. It was well known around town that John could while away the better part of an hour chatting with others about teething habits, diaper rashes, or what store brand baby food was better than homemade.

Olympia seldom joined him on Saturdays, claiming she was happy to have a couple of hours to herself. The truth of the matter was she did not want to intrude on her husband's treasured father/daughter time. She knew the value of knowing a father's love. Olympia credited her strength and self-assurance solely to that same love. She could see shades of her own father in John now. She would not have interloped on his time with Artemis for anything.

Week after week, John and Artemis became regulars in town on Saturday. They forged a routine friends and neighbors came to expect. They would pop into the barber's shop to bid good morning to Mr. Fricker the barber, and Mayor Corley, who had his weekly shave every Saturday at 9am. Sometimes John would play a fast checker game with one of the men waiting for a haircut, if Artemis was sleeping. By 9:30, they would roll into Dough Re Mi, the bakery run by Dodie Thompson for John's weekly blueberry muffin. She never failed to have one freshly baked, in the bag, ready for John's midmorning snack. He'd confided in her once, "Muffins are the one thing Olympia doesn't make well." Once the muffin was eaten and much of the local gossip had been poured into his ears from Dodie, John liked to steer Artemis into the sporting goods store to check out any interesting new fishing lures Mr. Shirley may have gotten in that week. John Windham wheeled his daughter through every amenable doorway on the street to say a cheery hello to people. Some men thought him crazy for carrying on so much over his daughter, while many women wished their own husbands cared half as much about their children.

One Saturday morning when Artemis was nearly a year old, she and John met Fred Henry coming out of the Barber shop. "How is our little Arty today?" Fred cooed at the happy little girl sitting up in her carriage. Artemis smiled and giggled at him. She adored her Uncle Fred.

"She is just fine," beamed John. "You know I think she'll be saying Daddy soon. Olympia keeps trying to get her to say Mama first, but I think it'll be me who wins."

Fred chuckled and slapped his pal on the back. "Nothing like a little competition between husbands and wives." Fred patted his stomach and went on, "That sure was a fine meal last night. Olympia knows how to make a pot roast. Wish Zelda could cook. Getting' tired of franks and beans and TV dinners."

"I expect she'll learn." John assured. "You two have only been married a couple of months. She's new to being a wife."

"We will see."

Fred went on his way as John continued his stroll down Main Street. He stopped in front of Braxton's Department store window. There was a display of various toys gearing up for the upcoming Christmas holidays. Lifting Artemis from her carriage, he pointed to the pink stuffed reindeer in the display. "Would you like Santa Claus to bring you that lovely deer, my precious? Wouldn't he make a good friend?"

Placing her back in the carriage, John pushed along towards the butcher's shop. Surprising Olympia with a couple of steaks for dinner wouldn't be a terrible idea. For a few weeks, he had been bringing home little things to show his love. Sometimes it was flowers. Sometimes jewelry. And sometimes he would simply bring meals he could cook himself on the grill, saving her the chore of dinner preparation. It was romantic and it was thoughtful, but it was also part of his agenda. John wanted another child before Artemis was too old to be its playmate. He figured the two years difference between children was far enough. Grilling steaks tonight while his wife rested, might lay the groundwork for getting started on that new baby.

Just as John was about to wheel Artemis into the butcher's shop, he heard his name shouted down the sidewalk. Whirling around to see who had summoned him, he saw Fred rushing forward, his hand stretched out to grab an object midair. It happened so quickly all John saw at first was a pink blur and Fred's hand coming forward. Fred pulled the pink reindeer down to his side. Huffing for breath when he reached John and Artemis, he said, "I don't think anybody saw."

"Saw what?" John cried. "How did that stuffed animal—"

Fred looked down at little Artemis sitting up with her arms raised, reaching for the toy. Her blue-violet eyes shining with delight. Fred rubbed the top of her head where her black hair was beginning to thicken up. "Man, I think that girl of yours has her momma's ways in her. You better watch that. Won't do you no good if folks see your baby floating toys towards her."

Fred left them there, taking the reindeer with him. He ducked quickly into Braxton's, tossing the toy back in the window without anyone seeing him. John lifted his daughter into his arms, looking at her sternly. She touched his face with her soft, delicate fingers and laughed. His disapproval evaporated into a chuckle of his own. He kissed her cheek and said, "Well, well, well. I guess you're gonna be a witch too."

John placed his daughter back in the stroller and turned around, deciding it was best to get her home before she pulled another stunt someone would see. Retracing his steps back past the storefronts on his way to the car, he noticed something. It was something he'd seen time and time again yet never quite registered until now. Little rectangle signs posted in the corners of shop doors bearing the stark message, WHITES ONLY.

For a few seconds the only tangible thing regarding the signs which bothered him were the sheer number of them. How many times had he been inside Braxton's, or

Wheelers Appliances, or Duffy Hardware and never paid any attention to the fact *some people* were not allowed inside. He began to wonder why this bothered him at all. Surely colored people had their own stores where they felt more comfortable with their own kind. Perhaps the segregation was mutual. Yet something about his rationale gnawed at him, making him feel disgusted with himself. He looked down at Artemis in the carriage. *She is different. She isn't like the other babies. What if someone arbitrarily decided she shouldn't enter their store?* The thought of his daughter being treated differently than her peers made him angry. She could not help what she was any more than colored people could control the shade of their skin. Who was it who decided white people deserved deference over other races? What if the world learned witches were real? What would Artemis' life be like? It was then he calmed himself from his fear by realizing, b*ut she can blend. No one would suspect she was different.* The relief his thought provided him was double edged. It came with a bit of shame. Whether she could blend in or not, did not negate the injustice. His wife's words echoed in his memory now. This was exactly what Olympia was talking about when Governor Wallace pulled his stunt at the university. John told her then it was none of their concern. Now, looking down at his innocent daughter, he felt otherwise. Social injustice was no longer an abstract concept. It was tangible, it was real, and it was personal...because eventually it could be applied to anyone.

John Windham did not expect to come to an epiphany over racial equality when he ventured out that morning with his daughter. But it was exactly what happened.

CHAPTER FIFTY

Kindergarten Witch

The house was much too chaotic for John to handle the morning school began. Twice he had done his best to calm Artemis and convince her it was a great day in a little girl's life. He didn't believe it himself and was desperate to avoid any more of her tears. In cowardly husband fashion he dressed quickly for work, rushed down the kitchen stairs, pecked his wife on the cheek at the kitchen table, and left for the office without breakfast. He did offer a meaningless, "Good luck," however, as the door shut behind him.

Olympia rolled her eyes while continuing to feed two-month-old Nacaria in her arms. Her attention was divided between feeding the baby, and urging two-year-old Demitra, seated beside Zelda's eldest, to eat her waffle. All Demitra had done so far was play fork-duel with Sarah.

"Ain't that just like a man!" Zelda scoffed from the table after a sip of coffee. She gestured over to a nearby playpen where her youngest daughter clutched a bottle. "Fred ain't much help with Melinda, though he's getting' better with Sarah now she's older. Says Melinda is too breakable."

"Eat, Demitra," Olympia pleaded. "Don't you want to grow up to be a big girl like your sister so you can go to school too?" Olympia twisted around in her chair, searching the kitchen stairs to see if any little feet were coming down. "Speaking of which," she murmured half to herself before shouting in the general direction of the stairs, "Artemis! Are you dressed yet? It's almost time to go."

"You letting that child dress herself for the first day of school?" Zelda asked.

Olympia shook her head, "No, I laid out her dress on the bed."

Sensing her friend's mood, Zelda commented, "You are as anxious as a red dressed whore walking into a Baptism."

Olympia cracked a smile. "You remember how it was for us. We were so alone and frightened back then. It was only once you and I found each other that school became bearable."

Zelda nodded. "I remember very well." She looked down at her baby in the playpen. "Too bad my girls are younger. But at least Demmy and Sarah will have each other when their time comes. And Nikki and Melinda will be in the same grade."

Olympia smiled, "That will be helpful for our younger daughters, but I'm afraid it won't do much good for Artemis. Then we also have her powers to worry about. She has no control over them. Any time she thinks about something, it happens."

A little girl with long raven hair and deep violet eyes stepped meekly down the kitchen stairs wearing a light blue dress. "Momma, don't make me go."

Olympia stood, handing Nacaria off to Zelda as she crossed the room to her daughter. Placing her gentle, reassuring hands upon Artemis' shoulders, Olympia said, "Oh my darling, it will be fun. You will make friends. You will learn new exciting things. Kindergarten will be great."

"You promise?"

"I promise."

Zelda cleared her throat, "Don't lie to that child, Lympy! Arty, come over here."

Timidly Artemis crossed the room to Zelda, a person who made her nervous on a good day. Zelda looked into the child's eyes and gave her best shot of advice. "Artemis, it ain't gone be easy. You ain't nothing like those other kids. And boy, howdy they will figure that out fast. But all you gotta focus on is doing what the teacher says and try to get through the day. Do everything you can to keep your mind focused on what you are supposed to do. Don't let your thoughts stray cause that's where you get in trouble. But if by chance a thought gets by you and something weird happens in front of everybody...act like you are just as surprised as everybody else. Don't let anybody know it was you."

Olympia picked up a metal Holly Hobby lunchbox from the counter placing it in her child's shaky hand. With a kiss on the top of the head she told her eldest it was time to go. From behind Artemis' back Olympia exchanged nervous glances with Zelda. Zelda gave her a nod of encouragement and tossed the car keys from the table to her. "Go," she told Olympia. "I got these girls and I ain't got any readings to do till after lunch, so you stay as long as it feels right." Olympia picked up a bright orange oversized hat from the counter and started directing her child from the room. "Skip the hat," Zelda advised, but it was too late.

Daihmler Elementary was a small red brick, rectangular schoolhouse, much larger than the one Olympia and Zelda went to when they were girls. Mother and child walked to the school doors converging with several other first-timers clinging hesitantly to their own mother's hands. Older children, accustomed to the rigor of school, stalked inside like a funeral procession, mourning the summer freedom now behind them.

"Olympia!"

She whirled around to see Nate Caldwell rushing into the school towing little Howard behind him by the arm. Howard appeared to be just as terrified as Artemis.

"It's a big day in their lives, isn't it?" Nate smiled. "The first day of school."

The two friends exchanged brief morning banter on their way to the children's classroom. Walking in with Nate helped ease some of Olympia's worry. The teacher, Miss Bremer greeted her new students with a fresh morning smile at the door. The moment Olympia stepped inside the classroom, her dread intensified as the eyes of every parent and child stared at them.

Olympia hadn't given much consideration to the stigma the name Blanchard still carried. In adult circles, Olympia enjoyed protection from the ostracization of her childhood by being the wife of John Windham. However, it did not appear their daughter would be afforded the same deference. From the stares of parents and children alike, it was clear to Olympia that though she was publicly accepted at parties, behind the private doors at home, society still gossiped about her family. It probably did not help matters that Olympia overdressed for the occasion. While other moms wore more casual attire of capri pants, jeans, and basic blouses, Olympia was wearing a flowy white sundress cinched at the waist by an oversized orange buckle belt. Looking around now at the other mothers, Olympia told herself, *and why did I put on this hat?*

Nate and Olympia stood with the other parents against the wall, listening to Miss Bremer's orientation speech with the children. Olympia could feel the other women staring daggers at her. She had always been hated by other women. Whenever she entered a room no one saw anything else but her. *It isn't my fault I am beautiful.* Still, she wished she'd skipped the oversized orange hat. It was a little too precious now.

The children were shown their specific cubbies where they could place their belongings. Artemis put her Holly Hobby lunchbox on her shelf and went back to stand by Howard. Miss Bremer began placing the children at tables in alphabetical order. It puzzled Olympia for a moment when her daughter seemed to be skipped. Howard was already seated, and the teacher had moved on to assigning Kelly Carter a seat. Olympia stepped forward to ask.

"I am so sorry to interrupt," she told Miss Bremer. "Did you overlook my daughter's seat? Artemis?"

Miss Bremer fumbled through her list, checking the order. "No, she's here. Artemis Windham. She comes at the end."

Let it go. The voice in Olympia's head told her. *Let this go. Do not make a fuss. It isn't important and it would make John so happy.* But of course, Olympia disregarded the voice of reason in her head. There was another one even more authoritative. *We are the descendants of Constantinople Blanchard. The Blanchard name must live on. You promised him.*

"Again, I am so sorry to make problems." Olympia said to the teacher. "My daughter's last name is Blanchard. Not Windham."

Miss Bremer looked very confused. "Oh, my form says her father, Mr. John Windham, signed the enrollment forms."

Hoping a warm smile might pave over the embarrassment, Olympia replied. "Yes, John Windham is my husband. But the women in my family hold onto the Blanchard name." Every adult looked on as if judging her. Only Nate gave his friend a supportive wink.

"So, her last name isn't Windham?"

Again, Olympia held the smile. "No. She and I share my last name, Blanchard."

And there it was. She did not need psychic powers to know what the others were thinking…illegitimate. Olympia did her best to clarify. "When I married my husband, I kept my surname in respect to my father. He never had sons. So, I continue my father's name through my daughters."

"I see," the teacher said, almost disapprovingly. She then disarranged the last few children she'd seated to make room for Artemis with the B's. Miss Bremer then asked Olympia, "Should I refer to you as Mrs. Blanchard or are you a Ms.?"

It was a fair question. Women's liberation was taking hold, and many women were rejecting the label attaching them to their husbands. Once all the children were seated at their assigned tables, the mothers were dismissed, saying their final goodbyes for the morning to their terrified children. As one by one, the moms filed out of the room, Olympia approached the door. Call it instinct, or agile reflex, but the moment Olympia faced the door she saw it twitch. Flinging her hands up, she froze the room completely still…except for her daughter.

"Artemis," Olympia sighed, walking over to her little girl. "You must control your thoughts and your powers. That door was just about to slam shut all by itself in front of everyone. Now, how would that look to your new friends if the door suddenly closed in front of your mother to keep her from leaving?"

"Not good."

"Right." Olympia kneeled and patted her little girl's hand. "We must blend in with other people Artemis. We cannot risk exposure. It is our job in this world to do what?"

Artemis looked up with innocent eyes and answered, "To protect The Natural Order of Things."

"Correct. There are things in this world normals are not equipped to fight. That's why we are here. But we can't protect the world if the world fears us. Please, do your best to keep your powers under control. I do not want to have to bind them. I want you to be able to use your abilities when you need them. But you must control your thoughts."

Before she released the class from her spell, Olympia approached little Howard, who was frozen in place like everyone else. She stroked his brown hair lovingly. With Artemis listening, Olympia was not able to say what she wanted to say to the special boy. But she felt glad she was at least able to have a mental moment regarding him on what was also his first day of school.

When Olympia released the room from her spell, she exited the class with the remaining mothers. What Artemis did not know was Olympia spent the next two hours standing in the outer hall, listening to everything going on inside until she trusted her daughter would be okay.

CHAPTER FIFTY-ONE

A Widowed Witch

It was Fred who came with the news, a sober messenger weighted with a heavy heart. After spending the morning in the field picking peas, Olympia and Zelda had returned to the house with six buckets brimming over. There were more to be picked, but it was time for Zelda's favorite soap opera, *All My Children.* They only just sat down in front of the television with bowls in their laps for the peas and paper bags at their ankles for discarded shells, when Fred came in.

Looking up from her program, Zelda was on the verge of reprimanding her husband for not being at work. The black aura covering his spirit silenced her interrogation. Unshed tears brimmed in his eyes. She looked over next to her, to Olympia's terror-stricken face. Placing the bowl from her lap aside, Olympia rose from the couch. Her feet moved as if trudging through heavy syrup as she crossed the room. It was as if they knew she might slow the devastation if it took longer to hear it. When she reached Fred, he didn't say anything at first, the unspoken understanding between them released the need. Olympia lifted her index finger to touch the side of Fred's cheek, collecting a fleck of blood. She examined his freshly washed hands but the stains on his shirt cuffs told the story. Calmly, she asked, "What happened?"

Fred took her hands in his, both gripping the other tightly as he told her the story. By the time he'd finished, Zelda was at Olympia's side, bracing her in her arms. A blown tire. Something as simple as a blown tire sent her husband careening from the bridge on Watermelon Road, altering her life forever. John's car hit the rocks below where the creek was low.

"How did you—" Zelda asked.

"Sheriff Dayce came and got me from work. He knows we're good friends." Fred turned back to Olympia. "I was with John while the medics were working on him. He didn't want you to see him like that. Told me to tell you he loves you. Said, you made his life full and beautiful. Said to tell you to take care of those girls." Fred looked back to Zelda, "He told me to tell you to take care of her."

Zelda led Olympia upstairs, laying her down on the bed. Stilled by numbness, perhaps shock, Olympia did not cry. She did not speak. Zelda lay beside her, cradled Olympia against her chest in silence. It wasn't easy for Zelda to remain silent, but she knew Olympia's mind was probably far too noisy to understand anyone else's words yet.

While Zelda looked after Olympia, Fred took care of everything else. He called Pastoria in Mobile. She told him she would drive to Daihmler the second her husband could come home from work to watch their son Seneca. Fred called John's office, requesting if they had anything they needed from Olympia, to contact him. He next phoned the school to tell the principal what happened and asked if they could keep it quiet from Artemis, who would be picked up after school by Nate Caldwell. Once Demitra and Sarah woke from their naps, he made them a couple of peanut butter and banana sandwiches to eat while they watched Sesame Street on the TV. He heated bottles for Nacaria and Melinda, feeding and burping them, then changed their diapers.

Upstairs, Olympia eventually drifted off to sleep in Zelda's arms. Zelda did not sleep. She sat for two hours stroking her friend's arms and sorting things out in her own mind while there was time. Olympia would have questions. She would want to know what happens next. She would wonder how to tell the children. She would ask what she is supposed to do now without her husband. Zelda needed to form answers before the questions came, so that when she told them to Olympia, she could say it with resolute certainty. If Olympia glimpsed the slightest fear in Zelda, she would fall apart.

Olympia's body began to shiver under Zelda's arms, signaling she had awakened, remembered, and begun to grieve. Zelda continued holding her, promising everything would be okay in time.

"How do I tell those little girls they will never see their father again, Zelda? How do I tell myself that?"

"Them girls are little, Lympy. We really only got to worry about Artemis. She's tough, like you. She will be okay."

"Nacaria and Demitra won't even remember him," Olympia realized. "Their own father and they won't even remember him."

"We will remember him. They'll learn about their daddy from us."

The following days were difficult in countless ways. Fred, Zelda, and their girls stayed at Blanchard House with Olympia and her girls. Pastoria was there as well, doing her best to be supportive for her sister while helping take care of her nieces. Nate accompanied Olympia to make the arrangements, while almost everyone in town dropped off food at Blanchard House. John's funeral took place at the church, the way he would have wanted it. But his burial took place in the Blanchard family cemetery, the way Olympia wanted it.

A great many papers had to be signed and Pastoria went through them all with Nate before presenting them to her sister. John's law partnership had to be dissolved and there was a modest amount of money coming due to Olympia. There was an insurance policy which would help as well, and John thankfully had the foresight to provide modest trust funds for his girls. However, Olympia would have to consider how to support her family eventually. John wasn't rich and however generous his finances were, they would not last more than a few years.

Olympia couldn't worry about that. She had to figure out how to be everything her daughters needed in a mother and a father while also figuring out how to live the remainder of her life without the only man she'd ever loved. Processing her grief while reshaping her life into an unfamiliar new mold, was not a straightforward journey. There were times when she wanted to break. Times she felt like giving in to the weight of pressure pushing down onto her soul. She sometimes wondered where that other Olympia went. Her younger, selfish self. The girl nothing phased. What happened to her? Olympia knew very well what happened to that girl. She became a mother, transformed by unshirkable responsibilities. Three little lives were solely dependent upon her, not only for physical support but emotional strength. She could not allow herself to break. Had she been alone, she might have. But she could not afford to break now because to do so would take other people down with her. Often, she had to remind herself, *I am Constantinople Blanchard's daughter. No one is stronger than me.* And it was almost true. Yet sometimes, late in the night when the girls were all in bed and Olympia was alone in her room, she held John's picture until she cried herself to sleep.

As weeks passed into months, months converged into a new year, then another one, Olympia found she didn't feel like crying anymore. There was no specific date which could be marked on a calendar as to when she didn't cry anymore, it had been more of a slow progression into someone new. Somehow when her daughter's laughed, she found herself laughing with them. When Artemis and Demitra played outside, Olympia watched them from the window feeling a sense of happiness by the sight. Nacaria's urge to join them over time was welcomed by her sisters rather than fought against due to her age. Olympia observed her daughters building a triangle of love and support with one another that reminded her of her own in youth. Now when Olympia thought of John, it brought less anguish and more sympathy. He did not know these girls now. All three were so different from when he'd been their father. They were *her girls* now, only hers. A certain guilt arrives with such conclusions, no matter how accurate. Her memories with her husband would always be golden, but they would also only ever be her memories. The girls were too young to be a keeper of those times. The fact of this divided Olympia's life into sections. Now she was living in the realm of her girls. She had three witches to raise. There was no time to linger in the past.

CHAPTER FIFTY-TWO

Second Time Around

No one would have been able to tell from the looks of the Blanchard House living room that money was running out. Olympia's growing financial challenges were something she kept private from everyone but Nate—and he only knew because he managed her money. Nothing of her money woes was reflected in her merriment of this holiday season. The Christmas tree aglow in the window was packed with presents underneath. Since their father's death a few years ago Olympia had unknowingly used Christmas as a time of abundance to compensate her daughters for the irreplaceable loss in their lives. Perhaps it was because Christmastime was supposed to be when families all come together, and the best memories are made. An overindulgence of presents was one way she tried to distract them from what was really missing in their family. More would be missing this year than in years past because Pastoria and her husband were not coming home for the holidays. His thriving hardware store could not be closed for the week as it had been in the past. Not to mention, their boys were older and reluctant to leave their own home on Christmas. Zelda, Fred, and the girls would be there of course, along with Nate and Howard, but without Pastoria's branch of the family it would not be the same. Hopefully the gifts would suffice. And there were a lot of them. Olympia spared no expense for her daughters, or Howard. She also always made sure Zelda's daughters had plenty to open, especially since Zelda proved herself rather stingy when it came to Sarah and Melinda.

There would be another guest this year as well, one which would change everything from now on. Martin Caswell, Olympia's old beau, had come back into her life earlier in the year. Having never gotten over his affection for her, despite the number of years since they'd dated, Martin was proving himself quite devoted to Olympia these days. In the years after John's death, Martin reestablished himself in her life as nothing more than a friend. She held no interest in seeing men romantically during those years, instead devoting her life to her daughters. However, the girls were older now, with friends and lives of their own. Olympia found herself craving a little companionship—safe companionship. None came any safer than Martin Caswell. In the past few months, the two of them saw quite a lot of each other. Olympia was fond of Martin. Fond enough to stand with him on the precipice of a new chapter, a testament to becoming open to second chances.

At fourteen years old, Artemis believed herself to be quite grown up. She'd even placed herself in charge of a good portion of the Christmas meal preparation. She was busy in the kitchen when Nate and Howard arrived. Howard quickly disappeared to the kitchen under the excuse of helping Artemis, but Olympia and Nate shared concerned glances, worried the friendship may be budding into something else now hormones were starting to rage. They both vowed to keep their eyes open for anything crossing the line of friendship between their children. There was no possible way to tell either of the teenagers they were related by blood.

Zelda's entrance announced itself as always when she bounded through the front door shouting "I think I just barely missed running over Rudolph on my way over!"

Olympia moved forward to hug her friend, stopping short a moment as she took in Zelda's appearance. Her hair was freshly dyed red, contrasted by a small green hat with a bird perched on the side. The hat matched her homemade green dress trimmed in red faux fur. She looked like a berserk cast member ousted from a Bing Crosby Christmas Special. Sarah and Melinda filed in and ran upstairs to see Demitra and Nacaria. Fred, as usual, was left to haul in the presents and food by himself. Nate went outside to offer help.

"What did you do to your hair?" Olympia accidentally asked, not meaning to say it out loud.

Zelda tossed her hands up in frustration, "Don't you start too. Fred hates it. I dyed it myself. Looks like it too. But it's starting to grow on me." She saw Olympia was about to say something, but Zelda swiftly shut her down by adding, "Last year when you cut your hair up to your shoulders and stopped coloring those gray streaks, I didn't say a word. You can just keep your big trap shut too." Olympia nodded in compliance and helped her friend out of her coat. Zelda moved on to another subject. "Ain't gone be right with Pastoria missing this year," she remarked. "But I 'spose it's a chore to get her whole brood this far up for two days."

When Fred returned holding a stack of pies, Olympia and Zelda lifted them from him and started for the dining room where desserts would be placed, like always, on the sideboard. Sitting the pies in place, Zelda's attention was drawn to the table. Calculating the math at lightning speed in her head, she asked, "Lympy? Who's the other place setting for?"

Sighing, Olympia readied herself for the argument, "Martin is joining us for Christmas lunch."

Smacking her hand onto the swinging door back to the living room, Zelda stomped through before whirling around to challenge her friend. "Dammit, Lympy!" she said shaking a finger in her face. "I told you not to do that! Please don't tie up with that boring old man again. There are a million fellers out there who'd cut off their ear to be with you."

"Martin is a wonderful man, and a good friend. We share friends and history together. If I choose to see him, it is my affair."

"Naw, that's where you are wrong!" Zelda opposed. "Ain't no affair at all! That's the problem. You need yourself an affair. A real one. With a man that sends you to the moon. You are only dating Caswell because you don't feel no spark for him. Since John's been gone, you are scared to death to let yourself feel something for another man—really feel something."

Olympia did not appreciate the lecture and the sharp look across her face expressed it. Zelda threw her hands up in defeat and agreed to mind her own business, which no one in the room believed she could do.

"Just keep out of Olympia's private life," Fred urged his wife quietly out of everyone else's earshot. "Just be her friend and allow her to make her own choices."

Zelda bellowed loudly, "If I let ever'body make their own choices you'd still be a traveling salesman probably dead from a werewolf in New Orleans! Olympia don't know what's best for her like I do. She'd be wise to listen to me."

Before any real animosity could swell, the energy shifted as the children ran down the stairs excitedly to examine the presents under the tree. Zelda transferred her scolding tongue to her daughters, finding fault in almost everything they were doing from the pitch of their voices to how many footsteps they took to cross a room. To Demitra and Nacaria, she sweetened her tone and complimented their appearance.

"You just get prettier and prettier Nikki. Look like an expensive China doll. And Dee, you're getting to be as tall and beautiful as your sister."

Olympia placed loving hands on the shoulders of Sarah and Melinda and said,

"And you two darlings look so lovely in your Christmas dresses. So sweet and pretty."

"They look like that gal who swole up into a ball in that Willy Wonka movie!" Zelda replied. "If they don't stop eating the way they do we're gonna have to widen the front door next year."

Fred looked angry, "Zelda please don't berate the children in front of people. They do have feelings, you know."

"Oh, calm down, Fred! The girls know I'm just kidding around, mostly."

It did not take long for the room to become flooded by shreds of wrapping paper and tissue after Nate gave the children permission to open their presents. They tore into their gifts with gusto. Toys, clothes, record albums, games, books, and a new 8 track tape player for both Artemis and Howard. Within the span of an hour, most of the presents around the tree were gone, providing more room on the floor for everyone to gather as lunch finished cooking. Fred and Nate worked in tandem disposing of the debris and discarded boxes into the fireplace. With every scrap fed to the flames the fire swelled higher and hotter before shrinking back to less intense burning logs.

Punctual as always, Martin arrived promptly at noon. Over his shoulder was a sack of presents with a Santa hat donning his head. He handed gifts out to the children, who all replied with a courteous thank you. Demonstrating his attention to detail, his gifts were tailored to each child's interests, a consideration appreciated by Olympia. Demitra received a paint set and easel, reflecting her newfound interest in her art class at school. Artemis received several cookbooks along with a set of shiny new pots and pans. Nacaria got a carved wooden box housing a set of beautiful combs, brushes, and a pearl handled mirror. Howard received an archery set. Melinda a box of colorful ribbons and clips to fashion her own hair bows. And Sarah got a miniature loom with several spools of yarn as she had taken up weaving. One final present lay in the bottom of Martin's bag which he fished out excitedly. It was a thin, rectangular box, tied with a silver ribbon. He presented it to Olympia.

"My dear Olympia," he began. "We have known one another more years than we probably care to recall. However, my affection for you has never waned."

"Oh, dear God!" Zelda exclaimed, unable to suppress the comment. She knew what was coming.

Undeterred, Martin went on. "Once long ago, I hoped to become your husband, but destiny had other plans for you. Perhaps fate needed more time. And since you have already been given an engagement ring by the very good man you married first, I will not insult his memory by giving you another." He opened the box revealing a lovely necklace of pearls. "Instead, I offer you this in the hopes you will honor me by becoming my wife."

Olympia suspected he might ask, although she hadn't expected it to be that day. Many times, she had rehearsed her response for whenever this time came. Practicing her answer both ways as she was never sure if she would say yes or if she would say no. Now on the spot in front of her loved ones on Christmas Day, she could not remember any of them. All eyes were pressing into her, waiting for her answer. As discreetly as she could manage, Olympia flicked her hands, casting everyone in the room under her spell as she stopped time.

She had to think. There was no way to avoid answering. She couldn't comprehend why this was so difficult now, she'd weighed all the pros and cons for weeks since she began to suspect he would propose. Of course, she thought he would do it New Year's. That would have been way more symbolic. Who proposes at Christmas? She paced around the floor, not an easy task with ten other people crowded around. Her thoughts raced to Zelda's earlier comments about Martin being a safe choice. How he awakened no passion in her. But passion did not work out too well for her last time. And so what if he were a safe choice? Perhaps it was time for making sensible decisions. She looked at the frozen faces of her shell-shocked daughters, awaiting her response with the same curiosity as everyone else. The girls needed to be provided for and Olympia's money was running out. In fact, it was already gone. The only way to keep afloat would be mortgaging the house again or going back to work for the Witches Association. She did not want to have to do that. She could not risk leaving her girls orphaned if something were to happen to her. Martin was a decent and wonderful man. He was also a very successful man. She could do much worse.

Olympia retook her original position on the floor where she had been standing before rendering everyone still. She released her spell, once again feeling the peering eyes of everyone upon her. "I accept," she answered, turning her back to Martin so he could clasp the necklace around her delicate neck. "I will marry you, Martin Caswell."

Zelda thrust her hand out towards her husband. "Go on! Give it to me."

Blushing in embarrassment at his wife's crudeness or maybe his own tastelessness in participating, Fred reached into his pocket and removed a five-dollar bill, slapping it into Zelda's hand

CHAPTER FIFTY-THREE

The Stepfather

As neither Olympia nor Martin was any longer in the spring of their youth, it seemed absurd to delay the marriage. It seemed even sillier to turn it into an elaborate event. Olympia had experienced the grandeur of a traditional wedding long ago and had little appetite to try and replicate it. Likewise, Martin was a sensible man who cared very little for pomp and circumstance. He only wanted to make Olympia his wife and the sooner the better. Only one stipulation came with the event, Olympia insisted it take place in her rose garden. Martin found her request to be heartfelt. It was his late sister Lauralee, after all, who'd helped Olympia plant that very garden many years ago. It touched him to know Lauralee still resonated in Olympia's heart. Olympia married Martin Caswell in a brief, albeit shivery ceremony in mid-January. The only guests were the children, Zelda, Fred, and Nate.

Martin Caswell's move into Blanchard House marked a significant shift. For the first time in their lives Olympia's daughters had to adapt to her belonging to someone other than them. Perhaps if they had known their father better it might have been a more problematic adjustment, but Martin's genteel personality and devotion to all four of them made genuine acceptance rather easy for Artemis, Demitra, and Nacaria. The girls quickly warmed to Martin and soon discovered his presence brought unexpected benefits far outweighing any reservations.

With Martin came Martin's modest wealth. The girls found their closets fuller now with fashionable clothes and shoes now that Olympia was given a generous household allowance. Though the girls had long learned to let the natural trails, stream, and meadows of Blanchard land entertain them, now the family ventured out more often. Weekly visits to the movie house to see the latest releases, dinners at nicer restaurants, even the occasional tickets to a play at the Alabama Theater in Tuscaloosa. Out of all her daughters, only Artemis understood the real reason her mother remarried. She did it for them so that their teenage years would not be spent in fear of poverty. Artemis kept this knowledge to herself, never wanting her mother to feel embarrassed or ashamed of the practical choice she had made.

Apart from the financial improvements, the girls found having a man in the house offered an occasional ally when going up against their mother. Martin turned out to be a great mediator between Olympia and the girls. "It is only a C- my dear," Martin argued when Olympia waved Demitra's report card in his face.

"She is not a C student, Martin," Olympia snapped as she whirled back around to her terrified daughter. "This is because of that telephone we installed upstairs in the den. You stay on it all the time, Demitra, talking to your friends instead of finishing your homework."

"Now, now, Olympia," Martin said trying to sooth his wife fury. "The world isn't ending over Demitra's grade falling a little." He motioned for the child to come closer. "Demitra, do you promise to study harder and to not call friends until all of your work is completed?"

Demitra nodded, trying desperately to look contrite when really, she had taken the report card to Martin well before her mother saw it, knowing she would need his supportive intervention. "I think she will do better now," Martin announced, allowing Demitra to flee to the safety of her room. Although Olympia did not appreciate his contradicting her parenting, she had to admit it was nice not having to parent alone anymore. She knew she was hard on the girls sometimes and was glad they thought of Martin as a friend, even though he was not always the best influence.

Once while Olympia and Zelda were away at an out-of-town Consort meeting, Martin declared it to be a holiday for himself and the girls. He kept them out of school and drove them to Chattanooga for two days to go to Rock City. They had a marvelous time together, despite the scolding they all received once Olympia returned home. Artemis especially appreciated the way Martin never treated her like a child. He spoke to her like the young woman she was. And once, he even placed himself between she and her mother when they were deeply at odds.

"I don't see the big deal, Mother!" Artemis shouted. "It's a school dance. Why should I not go with Howard if he has asked me?"

Olympia was rarely one to be unreasonable with her girls and this severe resistance to Artemis dating Howard was puzzling to both Artemis and Martin. Olympia was not backing down. "I said you will not be Howard's date to that dance, Artemis.

There will be no further discussion on the matter."

"Why?" Artemis shrieked. "I should at least be told why. I thought you liked Howard."

"I love Howard," Olympia declared. "That's precisely the point. Howard is like family. It is too messy for the two of you to become involved."

Martin cleared his throat, as he tugged the side of his mustache with his thumb and forefinger. "I wouldn't exactly call one single school dance, involved."

"She isn't going with him Martin." Olympia's tone made it clear she was unmovable on the subject. Her husband had never known her to be so obstinate.

Pleading for a reasonable explanation, Artemis cried, "Are you afraid we will start some big love affair and break up?" Artemis asked. "Do you think we would ruin your friendship with his dad?"

"Howard has grown up with you and is very close to this family. I do not want those lines blurred. There are plenty of other boys out there. Date them. But you are not to go out with Howard Caldwell."

Artemis stormed off up the stairs to her bedroom, leaving a bewildered Martin in the kitchen with his wife. "Would you care to explain to me why this has you so upset, my sweetheart?"

Olympia made her best attempt at softening her beleaguered face. She knew she was coming off as angry when in fact she was not angry at all, only terrified. There was no safe way to let he or Artemis know the truth. Keeping the secret and keeping the amorous teenagers apart was her cross to bear. She patted Martin's cheek as lovingly as she could muster and said, "It is not something I can explain. I simply need you to trust me on this."

"The way I trust you in the supernatural department?" he replied. "Things I am best kept unaware of?"

"Precisely," Olympia nodded. "Exactly like that. It's best if I do not burden you with things I know. Just trust I am doing what is right for everyone."

"Then that is all need be said. I will support your decision."

Nate Caldwell was as confused on what to do as Olympia. Chatting about the situation over coffee one morning after the children were all at school and Martin was at the bank, they tossed out ideas.

"If we told them the truth," Nate suggested. "They would understand and not be so hurt by our refusal to let them date."

Olympia waved away his statement, "And then we put the future at risk. One day Demitra is going to give birth to Howard's mother. How can we logically expect your son to handle that? What if somehow Beryl was to find out the truth while she is growing up. She might never go back in time. She might choose to avoid that future picnic when that ridiculous spell gets accidentally cast."

"But Howard is already here," Nate argued. "He has already been born. Would it make a difference?"

Olympia pushed her bangs out of her eyes, wishing she'd never cut her hair. "Nate, listen to me," she urged. "I have no idea how time works. If it takes a divergent path without changing what comes behind it, then yes, apart from a great deal of awkwardness, nothing terrible would happen if we told the children. But Nate, I don't know how the universe works. No one does. This hasn't ever happened before to my knowledge or the knowledge of any witch I know. If time is a circle, repeating back upon itself like a record playing over and over again, our telling them the truth could very well undo Howard's birth. Do you want that?"

Nate sat forward in the rocking chair with a touch of anger in his eyes, "Of course not, Olympia! You know that I don't. He is my son!"

Calming his outrage, she patted his hand. "And he is my great grandson, I love him too. I will never risk his existence, even if that requires he and Artemis hating us for a while."

Nate hung his head low to his lap, griping his fingers together. "I wish Beryl were here. Beryl would know what to do."

Olympia looked out over the tops of the oak trees in the yard where the noonday sun was shining through, casting dancing shadows of leaves across the greening grass of early summer. "Beryl knew what to do, Nate." Olympia reminded him. "She left him with us, and she transcended into a greater being. Our Beryl was destined for huge things. Chosen by the Almighty. Dare we ever risk tampering with the journey Fate set forth for her? Howard's mother will remain a secret."

CHAPTER FIFTY-FOUR

When a Door Closes, A Window Opens

By the time the diagnosis of cancer came, the cruel reality that it was already too late to treat left nothing to do other than keep Martin as comfortable as possible. For weeks Olympia did what she could for him even though the unseen adversary growing inside him had the upper hand. While the disease progressed, even the girls tried to eradicate its horrible effects on his body. Nacaria, showing a keen propensity for creating spells, labored night and day trying her best to concoct a magical cure. None of them worked. Artemis, with her power of manifesting things into happening, did her utmost to envision Martin's cancer shrinking. But it didn't. It was finally when Demitra, with her clairvoyance, told her sisters she had already seen Martin's death in her visions, that everyone stopped fighting the inevitable.

Artemis, now 18, took over the care of the house. She did all the cooking, cleaning, and laundry while also looking after her sisters. This allowed Olympia to play nurse around the clock in those final days of Martin's life. Martin Caswell died in his sleep two months after their third anniversary, closing a brief chapter in Olympia's life. Once again, she found herself a widow. It was different this time, less impactful. Perhaps she was simply accustomed to the station now, or maybe it was because her fondness for Martin never compared to her all-encompassing love she had felt for John. Martin was buried in the Blanchard family graveyard next to John. There was something ironic about the symmetry of their resting places. A man she loved, and a man she didn't, side by side through eternity. They somehow canceled each other out in her mind. Two eras of life wrapped up behind her. Seeing them both laid to rest there gave Olympia an inappropriate and inexplicable sense of freedom from her past. Their deaths untethering her from being anything other than the mature indominable witch she was.

A few days after the funeral, Nate Caldwell, with his son Howard as his office clerk, drove out to Blanchard House to go over Olympia's financial situation. She received them in the study where she'd prepared coffee and tea cakes for the meeting. Nate complimented his old friend on how well she appeared to be doing under the circumstances. Olympia felt uncomfortable with the praise because she knew she ought to not be holding up so well. She hadn't even cried. Though she did mourn the passing of a kind and dear man, her heart was just as intact as it had been before. If a scar lay on her heart, it was from losing John, and even it was faded.

"It seems this time, Olympia, you are left much better off than you were when John passed away." Nate informed her.

"Is that so?"

"Martin was a little wealthier than most people knew. His investments were sizeable. He even owned majority stock in the bank."

News of this caliber perked her up a bit. "Are you saying I own the bank?"

Nate chuckled without meaning to. "Not really. The terms of the bank's bylaws require the surviving partners to purchase the deceased's shares at current market value. If they are unable or unwilling to do so, the stock reverts to you. However, the partners are going to purchase the stock. This will give you a sizeable amount of money."

Howard chimed in. "I also discovered among the things in Mr. Caswell's safety deposit box that he owns some prime real estate across the southeast. Some land is undeveloped, while some have buildings and tenants. You can either sells these or keep the rents as additional yearly income."

"My," Olympia said, trying not to appear pleased. "Are you boys saying I am rich now?"

Nate raised both brows, sending her a look to subtly indicate her greed was showing and to dial it down, especially in front of Howard. "In comparison to most people we know, yes. I'd say you have a couple of million when we combine stocks, cash, and property values. And if you keep the properties, the rents will be substantial income. You are going to be fine Olympia. You and the girls do not have to worry about money ever again."

The sense of security this news gave her meant more than even she could have known. After so many years struggling following her father's death, then again after John's, to know she never had to worry again was quite a relief. She signed the necessary papers Nate presented and asked Howard to go upstairs to the den to see the girls, so she could have a moment alone with his father.

Once Howard's unmistakable footfalls could be heard trudging up the third-floor stairs to the den, Olympia explained her wishes. "My girls have trust funds set up by their father. You have been the agent of those funds for many years. How well are they fixed for adulthood?"

"Well fixed. Each of your daughters will have a nice nest egg once they reach middle age."

"Fine," Olympia said. "John took good care of them. Now with my girls provided for, it is time for me to see that Howard is."

Not expecting this, Nate began to shake his head in refusal. "No, no, Olympia. He is my son. My responsibility. You have done a lot for him over the years. I will not ask anything more from you."

Olympia stood up from her chair to appear more imposing. "You are not asking me. I am telling you. Howard is a Blanchard, Nate." It had been years since either of them had said it out loud. Both having fallen into the routine of the lie they'd created at his birth. "I cannot provide for him in the open," Olympia continued. "But I can provide for him privately with you. I know he has applied to several colleges and been accepted to three."

"He is going to stay here and go to the University of Alabama. They have a fine business school, and he will be able to live at home."

"I want him to go to the college of his choice, Nate. Be it here or out of state. I want you to pay for his entire education from my account."

Nate would not consider it. His male pride superseding his reality that he was not a wealthy man. She argued him down, using every bit of her wit, charm, and Olympia-style manipulation. When he finally had no counterargument, she ended the conversation. "Wherever Howard goes to college, I am paying for it. I am also buying him a car which you should probably say is from you. I have stood in the background of that boy's life never able to claim him as part of me. You will give me this chance to help him now when I can fully afford to. Both our blood runs through his veins, Nate. Both of us."

Time moved forward, bringing many changes to the landscape of Olympia's life and family. Howard did indeed go away to college. Though his father advocated the benefits of The University of Alabama, secretly Olympia encouraged him to branch out further than home. "You should leave Daihmler for a few years, Howard," she urged. "See how other people in other places live. Discover new ideas. Explore new ways of thinking. Live on your own for the first time in your life."

"It sounds wonderful, Olympia," he admitted. "But I can't leave Dad. Ever since mom died, I am all he has."

"Untrue," Olympia snipped. "He has me. Your father and I have been great friends since we were children. Zelda and I will never let him feel alone. Do not sacrifice what you want from life for anyone else."

Howard decided on Penn State University for their prestigious business school. Olympia was thrilled with the decision. Penn State was the college she most hoped he would choose. The moment he shared the news with her and went home to break it to Nate, Olympia jumped on the phone to her old friend Brimford Uding. Brimford's wife Urma was from Pennsylvania, and it so happened her brother was the Dean of Students for Penn State. With two phone calls Olympia now had someone looking out for her godson without his ever being aware. Another benefit of his choice of school was the distance now placed between he and Artemis, as she suspected their little romance never really dwindled away.

Other changes were taking place as well. Artemis, now graduated herself, was off to culinary school in Birmingham. Demitra was now a senior in high school and had a boyfriend for the first time. Olympia had not yet met him, but there was no denying her daughter seemed happy. Nacaria was entering her sophomore year as the belle of the ball. She could have been a living replica of Olympia at that age, and the boys were buzzing around her like crazy.

Olympia was becoming rather popular herself these days. During her first marriage, she developed a few lasting friendships of substance sprinkled among the shallow women who used to faun over her simply because she was Mrs. John Windham. It was the same during her brief stint as Mrs. Martin Caswell. Olympia now embraced these friendships. Her daughters were grown now with lives of their own. Time and boredom weighed heavily on Olympia, causing her to rejoin society. Now that she was an independent woman of means, Olympia Blanchard decided to become active in the community again filling her calendar with dinner parties and committee meetings.

One of the friendships fostered over the years was with Eleanor Daihmler, the widow of one of the descendants the town was named after. Coincidentally, Eleanor's daughter Rosamund had become a rather close chum of Demitra. Olympia and Eleanor shared similar paths in their life. Besides both having lost their husbands early in life, Eleanor also only became a woman of means through marriage, the same as Olympia had. Because of their mutual modest upbringing, both felt a great need to give back. The two friends formed their own organization to help make a difference where they could. Their community work further bonded them in friendship. It also helped that Eleanor thought Zelda was the funniest and most loyal person she'd ever met. Above anything else, this sentiment endeared Eleanor to Olympia. She could have no friends who couldn't accept or "get" Zelda.

Once the prominent women of Daihmler learned Olympia Blanchard and Eleanor Daihmler were forming a club, membership exploded. Of course, the excitement waned slightly when the silly housewives of Daihmler realized it was more of an environmental committee than a social-set charity one. However, no one dared back out for fear of Eleanor Daihmler striking them from her annual party list. Olympia took the lead role in deciding which causes were the most pressing, although she did sadly have to educate most of the club members on the realities facing the planet.

"We are steadily approaching a dangerous time for our dear planet Earth," Olympia declared, shocking the frivolous ladies to attention. "Do you know that the aerosol we use in our hairspray cans every day is dissolving the ozone layer of earth's atmosphere?"

"What is an ozone layer?" Bittie Simmons squeaked from the third row of the chairs set out on the Blanchard lawn.

"Factories have so desecrated our skies that a constant fog of pollution covers the Birmingham skyline. New York City is plagued with smog. And our very automobiles emit toxic fumes into our air." Olympia continued.

"Well, goodness Olympia," Hester Sulligent replied. "What can we possibly do about those things?"

Eleanor stood to back up her friend, "Anything we can do is better than doing nothing. We can appeal to our state senators or congressmen. We could form a movement to educate people on these situations. We could start with our own City Council."

"I think that kind of stuff should be left to the men to handle," another woman remarked. "We should stick to charity work."

"The men are doing nothing to save our planet," Olympia stated angrily. "You know as well as me, it takes a woman to truly get a job done."

"What do you expect us to do?" Bittie asked. "How could we even start to change anything?"

Olympia smiled as she lifted a cloth from the large map board sitting on the easel in front of them. "I am so glad you asked. We can begin here, in our own state. This is a map of the Talladega National Forest. Right now, there is a section of land, roughly 25,000 acres, adjoining the protected forest. A company is attempting to purchase this land, in order to deforest the trees and develop the area. They intend to build a couple of neighborhoods, a mall, and office buildings. I believe this land should become part of the protected area of the State Park. I want us to stop this company."

"Who is the developer?"

"The company is called Sinclair Industries. They are apparently a huge conglomerate from the North. The CEO is a man named Randolph Sinclair."

"And just how can we possibly go up against a massive corporation?" Bittie asked. "Our little penny ante organization is no match for them."

Olympia smiled to her friends with a twinkle in her eye as if inspired by the challenge. "I believe Mr. Randolph Sinclair will find we can be just as formidable as he."

Zelda let out a huge telling laugh, "I ain't gone say a word. But I already know this Sinclair feller is gone find he's met his match with Lympy!"

Madam Zelda was never wrong. Mr. Sinclair did meet his match in Olympia Blanchard. They battled mightily over the issue and fell in love through the process. Over the years, Randolph Sinclair became Olympia's frequent opponent in environmental issues while maintaining his status as the absolute love of her life. And their story would live on indefinitely in the hearts of their grandchildren and great grandchildren. They were quite the match indeed.

Micah House is the author of *The Blanchard Witches* series which has won several awards since its debut, including the NYC Big Book Award, The Indie Excellence Award, and The BookFest Award. His southern style of storytelling weaves drama, humor, emotional connection to characters, and plenty of page-turning suspense. He currently resides in Birmingham, Alabama with his husband and son and their five dogs.